JN

DEVOTED

Woody Bookman hasn't spoken a word in his eleven years of life. Not when his father died in a freak accident. Not when his mother Megan tells him she loves him.

For Megan, keeping her boy safe and happy is what matters. But Woody believes a monstrous evil is behind his father's death and now threatens him and his mother. And he's not the only one who thinks so. An ally unknown to him is listening.

Woody's fearful suspicions are taking shape. A malicious man driven by evil has set a depraved plan into motion. And he's coming after Woody and his mother. The reasons are primal. His powers are growing. And he's not alone . . .

DEAN KOONTZ

DEVOTED

Complete and Unabridged

CHARNWOOD
Leicester

First published in Great Britain in 2020 by
HarperCollins*Publishers*
London

First Charnwood Edition
published 2020
by arrangement with
HarperCollins*Publishers*
London

The Author has asserted his right to be identified as
the author of this work.

This novel is entirely a work of fiction. The names,
characters and incidents portrayed in it are the work
of the author's imagination. Any resemblance to
actual persons, living or dead, events or localities
is entirely coincidental.

A catalogue record for this book is available
from the British Library.

ISBN 978–1–4448–4611–9

Published by
Ulverscroft Limited
Anstey, Leicestershire

Set by Words & Graphics Ltd.
Anstey, Leicestershire
Printed and bound in Great Britain by
T. J. International Ltd., Padstow, Cornwall

This book is printed on acid-free paper

To Joe McNeely.
Among his many virtues
is the ability to laugh at himself —
along with the rest of us.
The world is better with him in it.

All knowledge, the totality of all questions and all answers, is contained in the dog.

— *Franz Kafka*

We are alone, absolutely alone on this chance planet; and amid all the forms of life that surround us, not one, excepting the dog, has made an alliance with us.

— *Maurice Maeterlinck*

If you pick up a starving dog and make him prosperous, he will not bite you. This is the principal difference between a dog and a man.

— *Mark Twain*

A dog is the only thing on earth that loves you more than he loves himself.

— *Josh Billings*

DARKER THAN DARKNESS

TUESDAY 4:00 P.M. – WEDNESDAY 5:00 P.M.

1

Three years after the accident, Megan Bookman's heart and mind were in a good place, although occasionally anxiety afflicted her, a feeling that time was running out, that a sinkhole might at any moment open under her. This wasn't intuition at work, but just the consequence of being widowed at thirty. A love that she'd thought would endure, a man she had believed would grow old with her: All was taken away without warning. This current sense that somewhere bells were tolling toward her final hour would pass; it always did.

She stood in the doorway of her only child's bedroom, watching him at his computer with its array of associated equipment, as he researched whatever currently fascinated him.

Woodrow Bookman, Woody to everyone, had never spoken a word in his eleven years of life. At birth and for a few years thereafter, he cried, but not once since he'd turned four years old. He laughed, although seldom at anything that was said to him or at any comical sight. The cause of his amusement was often internal and a mystery to his mother. He had been diagnosed with a rare form of autism, although in truth the doctors didn't know what to make of him.

Fortunately, he had none of the most challenging behavior associated with autism. He wasn't prone to emotional meltdowns, wasn't

3

inflexible. As long as he was in the company of those he knew, he never recoiled when touched or suffered mentally from physical contact, though he found strangers suspect and often frightening. He listened intently to everything that was said to him, and he was at least as obedient as Megan had been in childhood.

He didn't go to school, but neither was he homeschooled. Woody was the ultimate autodidact. He taught himself to read only a few months after his fourth birthday, and he was reading at a college level three years later.

Megan loved Woody. How could she not? He had been conceived in love. His heart began beating as he formed within her. As far as she was concerned, it beat in sync with hers all these years later.

Besides, he was as cute as any kid in a cookie commercial and, in his own way, affectionate. Although he allowed himself to be hugged and kissed, he neither hugged nor kissed in return. At the most unexpected moments, however, he reached out and put a hand on hers, or he touched her jet-black hair and then his own, as though to say that he knew he had received it from her.

He seldom made eye contact, but when he did, his eyes sometimes glimmered with unshed tears. Lest she think that he might be sad on these occasions, he always favored her with a smile, almost a grin. When she asked if his tears were happy tears, he nodded yes. But he could not — or would not — explain what made him happy.

4

The difficulties of communication meant they couldn't share their lives to the fullest extent that Megan desired, which was a persistent sadness. This kid had broken her heart a thousand times, but with his sweetness, he had also healed it a thousand times.

She never wished that he were normal and not afflicted, for then he would have been a different boy. She loved him in spite of — in part *because of* — the challenging journey that they were taking together.

Now, watching him from the doorway of his room, she said, 'Is everything okay, Woody? Are you all right?'

Although intently focused on his computer, his back to her, he raised his right arm full length, pointing at the ceiling with his index finger, a gesture that she had long ago learned was positive and more or less meant *I'm on the moon, Mom.*

'All right, then. It's eight o'clock. Bed at ten.'

He made a whirling gesture with the raised index finger, and then his hand dropped back to the keyboard.

2

After saving the document that he'd titled 'The Son's Revenge: Faithfully Compiled Evidence of Monstrous Evil,' on which he'd been working for a long time, Woody Bookman, eleven, switched off his computer and went into his en suite bathroom and brushed his teeth with a battery-powered Sonicare toothbrush. He wasn't allowed to own a manually powered brush because he was an obsessive brusher who, left to his own devices, would scrub his teeth hard for twenty minutes. Over time, this habit would wear away his gums and require transplants. At ten, he had needed oral surgery to save three teeth on the lower-left side.

These days, periodontists used sterilized, irradiated tissue from cadavers for such repairs. Woody already had some dead guy's gum tissue around three teeth, and he didn't want more. Not that anything weird had happened because of the dead-guy tissue. Woody didn't experience memory flashes of the donor's life or have the urge to eat someone, like on *The Walking Dead*. The transplant hadn't turned him into a zombie. Such an idea was stupid science.

Woody was embarrassed for people who believed stupid science, which a lot of them did. He was also embarrassed for people who got angry over petty things, for people who called other people names, for people who were mean to animals. For a lot of reasons, a great many people made him embarrassed for them.

He was embarrassed *for himself*, that he was a danger to his own teeth. The Sonicare had a two-minute timer; you were never supposed to scrub with the bristles, but instead let the sound waves remove the plaque. Without the timer, Woody's mouth would be a graveyard's worth of gum tissue.

He was also embarrassed because sometimes

he thought about kissing a girl, an act that never crossed his mind until recently. Kissing seemed gross — *yuck* — swapping spit. Something must be going wrong with him that he would yearn for it. He was *also* — yet again, it never stopped — embarrassed because if he ever did ask some girl's permission to kiss her, he would never tell her about his dead-guy gums, for fear she would vomit and run away. He'd lie by omission, which was mortifying to contemplate, because lying was a prime source of all human suffering. The word *mortification* could be defined as a painful sense of humiliation, worse than embarrassment.

As long as he could remember, Woody had been embarrassed for himself and for other people. That was one reason he never talked. If he dared to talk, he'd tell people what they did that embarrassed him, and he'd tell them what he found embarrassing about himself, which was a long list. He was a mess. He really was. People didn't want to hear about what a mess he was or what a mess they were. But not to tell would be to lie by omission, and the thought of lying so mortified him that he became nauseous. Better to stay silent, say nothing, and maybe people would like you. And if you didn't tell them what an embarrassing mess you were, maybe they wouldn't notice.

One of the most embarrassing things about people was how unobservant they were.

After he brushed his teeth, he went to bed and turned out the night-stand lamp. He wasn't afraid of the dark. There weren't ghosts or vampires or werewolves or anything like that, and there was zero chance that a dead guy might creep into the bedroom to take his gum tissue back.

The only monsters were people. Not all people. Just some of them. Like those who had killed his father. Dad had been dead for three years, and no one had been put in prison for murder. Everyone still thought his death had been an accident. Woody knew better. Now that he had at last finished 'The Son's Revenge: Faithfully Compiled Evidence of Monstrous Evil,' those individuals responsible would be brought to justice.

Woody was very smart. He'd been reading at a college level since he was seven years old, which maybe didn't mean a whole lot, considering that many college graduates didn't seem to know anything. He was an accomplished computer hacker. During the past two years, he'd penetrated highly protected computer systems, in which he had planted rootkits that allowed him to swim through their networks without their security becoming aware that a secret fish explored the data depths. His explorations had also led him into strange places on the Dark Web.

Now, waiting for sleep, Woody encouraged himself to think of something pleasant. He was embarrassed when he imagined himself kissing a girl whom he had seen in a magazine photo. He tried to turn his mind to another subject, but he couldn't. He wondered if one day, a few years from now, he might meet a girl who'd had gum transplants, which would give them something in common. He had been kissed on the cheek and on the forehead, though not on the mouth, but had never kissed anyone in turn. If he met such a girl, maybe that would be a nice place to start.

3

Dorothy smelled of death.

She was seventy-six. She would be gone shortly after dawn.

This was a hard truth. The world was a beautiful place, but it was full of hard truths.

The live-in hospice-care nurse, Rosa Leon, attended to her in the bedroom where Dorothy had slept most nights of her long life.

Rosa smelled of life and strawberry-scented shampoo and the peppermint hard candies that she enjoyed.

In this room, Dorothy and her late husband, Arthur, had made love and conceived one child, Jack.

Arthur had been an accountant. He died at sixty-seven.

Jack had died in a war at the age of twenty-eight. His parents outlived him by decades.

Losing a child was the central tragedy of Dorothy's life.

But she was proud of Jack, and resilient, and she carried on, living a life that mattered.

Kipp had never met Jack or Arthur. He knew them only because Dorothy had so often spoken of them.

9

Rosa sat in an armchair, reading a paperback, unaware that Death was en route.

At the moment, Dorothy slept, sedated and without pain.

Kipp suffered when Dorothy was in serious pain. He had lived with her only three years. But he loved her desperately.

It was his nature to love beyond reason.

Before the moment of her passing might come, he needed to steel himself, prepare to deal with the loss.

He went downstairs and out through his door and onto the deep back deck to get some fresh air.

The house stood about twenty feet above Lake Tahoe. A minimal tide lapped softly on the beach, and sharp-edged reflections of a scimitar moon shimmered across the rippled water.

A mild breeze brought a rich mélange of odors: pine trees, cedars, woodsmoke from a fireplace, forest mast, wild mushrooms, squirrels, raccoons, and much more.

Kipp was also aware of a strange continuous murmur. He'd only recently begun to hear it.

He'd first thought it might be tinnitus, with which he knew some people suffered, but it was not that.

He could almost hear words in that strange unremitting flow, which came from somewhere to the west. West by northwest.

After Dorothy died, Kipp would need to investigate, find the source of the sound. He was grateful to have an immediate purpose.

He descended from the deck to the yard to

stare for a while at the stars, wondering.

Although he was exceedingly smart — only Dorothy knew how smart — he had no idea what it all meant.

Join the club. All the philosophers of history, much wiser than he, had failed to conceive a theory that satisfied everyone.

Shortly after he returned to Dorothy's bedroom, she woke.

Seeing Rosa reading a novel, Dorothy spoke in a frail voice. 'Rosie, dear, you should read aloud to Kipp.'

Humoring her patient, the nurse said, 'Don't you think Dickens is beyond his grade level?'

'Oh, not at all, not at all. He enjoyed *Great Expectations* when I read it to him, and he adored *A Christmas Carol*.'

Kipp stood bedside, gazing up at her, wagging his tail.

Dorothy patted the mattress, an invitation.

Kipp sprang onto the bed. Lying at her side, he rested his chin on her hip.

She put one hand on his burly head and gently stroked his pendant ears, his coat of golden fur.

Even with hateful Death on the doorstep, sweet bliss found an equal home with grief in Kipp's heart.

4

The two-lane blacktop is a dark snake slithering through the moon-washed paleness of the Utah wastelands. In the nearly empty vastness, small clusters of lights glimmer here and there in the distance, like extra-terrestrial pod craft that have descended from the mother ship on some nefarious mission.

Traveling south out of the Provo suburbs into ever-greater isolation, Lee Shacket dares not take Interstate 15. He uses less-busy state highways, undivided federal highways when he must, anxious to put as much distance as possible between himself and the events at the Springville facility.

If he has committed as much evil as any man in history, he has done it with the best intentions. He believes that those intentions matter more than the consequences of his actions. How could humanity have advanced from caves to orbiting space stations if all men and women were risk averse? Some seek knowledge and rise to challenges at whatever cost, and because of them, progress is made.

Anyway, all may be well in the end. The final result of the project is not yet known, only that it's gone wrong in mid stage. Every scientific endeavor is marked by setbacks. Ultimately, failure can be the father of success if one learns from the errors made.

Initially, however, he is treating this failure as absolute.

He is driving neither his Tesla nor his Mercedes SL 550, because eventually the authorities will be looking for him. He is tooling along in a fully loaded bloodred Dodge Demon that he purchased for $146,000 through an LLC based in the Cayman Islands, to which his name can't be linked even by the most determined investigator. The vehicle bears a Montana license plate. In the unlikely event that a connection between him and the car might be made by law enforcement, the GPS has been removed from the Dodge to prevent its location from being discovered by satellite.

One of two suitcases in the trunk contains $100,000. Another $300,000 in hundred-dollar bills can be accessed by disengaging two pressure latches on the back of the front passenger seat, revealing a secret compartment. Sewn into the lining of his supple black leather jacket, which is cut like a sport coat, are thirty-six high-quality diamonds worth half a million to any gem wholesaler.

These assets are not intended to support him for the rest of his life. They are to be used to allow him to go to ground for a few months, until the furor over the Springville fiasco subsides, make his way out of the United States, and get safely to Costa Rica by an indirect route involving five countries and three identity changes. In Costa Rica, he owns a retreat under the name Ian Stonebridge, and he possesses a valid Swiss passport in that identity.

He is the CEO of Refine, a multibillion-dollar division of a mega-valued conglomerate. Few CEOs of multibillion-dollar companies have the foresight to imagine a corporate crisis dire enough to require the preparation of a new identity and the hiding away of sufficient capital overseas to sustain a high standard of living for decades to come. Shacket takes pride in the fact that he has been wise and discreet for a man so much younger than most other CEOs.

He is thirty-four, which isn't all that young for a guy in his position in an economic sector where companies have been founded by technology wizards who became billionaires in their twenties. He answers to Dorian Purcell, the chairman of the board of the parent company, who was a billionaire at twenty-seven and is now thirty-eight, but Shacket himself is worth only a hundred million.

Dorian wanted the research at Springville to proceed at a breakneck pace. Shacket obliged because, were they to succeed in their primary project, stock options would make him a billionaire, too, although probably not a multibillionaire, while Dorian's fifty-billion-dollar fortune would most likely double.

The injustice of this unequal compensation causes Shacket to grind his teeth in his sleep; he often wakes with aching jaws. A mere billionaire is a nobody among the princes of high tech. In spite of their pretensions to social equality, many of this crowd are among the most class-conscious elite bigots the world has ever known. Lee Shacket despises them almost as much as he wants to be one of them.

If he has to go into hiding for the rest of his life with only a measly hundred million to sustain himself, he will have a lot of free time in which to plot the ruination of Purcell and little or no inclination to do anything else.

From the start, Lee Shacket has understood

that, should something go very wrong, he will have to take the fall. Dorian Purcell will forever remain untouchable, an icon of the high-tech revolution. Nevertheless, now that Shacket is having to pay that price, he feels deceived, tricked, bamboozled.

Driving through the early night, he is racked by anger and by self-pity and anxiety, but also by what he believes to be grief, an emotion that is new to him. Ninety-two Refine employees are in the locked-down high-security facility near Springville, prevented from communicating with the outside world, in their final hours of life. He's as pissed off at them as at Dorian. One of those geniuses — or several — has done something careless that sealed their fate and put him in this untenable position. Yet some are his friends, to the extent that a CEO can allow himself friends among those he must supervise, and their suffering, as it should, distresses him.

During the building of that complex, he'd taken pains to ensure that the module containing his office and those of his immediate support staff — five others — would go into airtight lockdown ninety seconds *after* all of the labs were hermetically sealed in a crisis. When the alarm sounded, he assured his staff that they were safe, that they should stay at their posts — and he quietly departed.

He had no choice but to lie to them. The alarm didn't announce impending disaster, but an immediate one. They are as contaminated as the researchers in the labs. Shacket is likewise contaminated, but in mortal circumstances like these, he isn't capable of lying to himself as easily as he lied to them.

Anyway, he's always been clever about eluding the consequences of his mistakes. Maybe his luck will hold through one last escape.

He'll soon be hunted, the quarry of legitimate authorities but also of Dorian's ruthless cleanup crew. He hopes, in what he believes is a spirit of mercy and sorrow, that all employees at Springville will perish before any can bear witness against him.

5

When Rosa Leon went downstairs to make a sandwich for herself, Kipp was alone with Dorothy.

The lamplight was low, the shadows as smooth as still water, the stately pine beyond the window silvered with moonlight.

She said, 'I have arranged with Rosa that you will be with her when I've gone. She'll take good care of you.'

By way of acknowledgment, Kipp thumped his tail three times on the mattress. Three meant *Yes, all right*. One thump meant *No* or *That feels wrong*.

In truth, his destiny would take him elsewhere than with Rosa.

No need, however, to distress Dorothy.

'Short stuff, you have been a gift of no less value to me than my son, Jack, or dear sweet Arthur.'

Kipp raised his head from his mistress's hip to lick her pale hand, with which she so often smoothed his coat and fed him treats.

'I wish together we might have found a way to solve the mystery of your origins.'

With a long sigh, Kipp expressed agreement.

'But in the end, our origins are all the same, born in the heart that shaped all that is.'

Kipp yearned to say so much to her while time remained.

Although his intelligence had somehow been enhanced to a human level, he lacked the vocal apparatus for speech. He could make many sounds, but none were words.

She had devised a clever method of communication, but it was in a ground-floor room, and she lacked the strength to go downstairs.

It didn't matter. Everything he wanted to say to her had been said before. *I love you. I will miss you terribly. I will never forget you.*

'Dear child,' she said, 'let me look into your eyes.'

He adjusted himself, laid his head upon her breast, and met her loving gaze.

'Your eyes and heart are as golden as your breed, dear Kipp.'

Her eyes were blue and clear and deep.

6

Lee Shacket parks his Dodge Demon in a far corner of the lot at the Best Western motel in the small town of Delta, Utah. Sitting in the car, he shaves off his immaculately trimmed beard, which he's had since he was twenty-four. He washes his hands with a sanitizer and inserts nonprescription contact lenses to change his eyes from tungsten-gray to brown.

After pulling on a baseball cap to conceal most of his blond hair, he heads south on State Route 257, transitions to Route 21, then to Route 130. After 125 miles, he arrives in Cedar City, where he registers at the Holiday Inn, using a driver's license and credit card in the name of Nathan Palmer.

In his room, before dyeing his hair, he needs to know if the situation in the Springville facility has made it to cable news. Standing in front of the television, the first thing he sees is video taken near the end of the workday, before nightfall. When he'd fled, the lab complex hadn't been ablaze. The fire broke out minutes after his frantic departure. The ferocious flames tower sixty or seventy feet above the lab complex, from one end to the other.

The blaze must have been triggered to obliterate the truth of what happened in that place. Without his knowledge, fuel of some kind and an ignition system must have been incorporated into the structure to ensure that all proof of the nature of the work being done there would never be discovered in the aftermath of a crisis.

He has no doubt that the researchers were intentionally burned alive — incinerated, nothing but bones left, if even that — to deny the

18

coroner evidence. Although they might have died anyway, in days or weeks, the profound cruelty of the incineration of the staff shocks Lee and leaves him so weak in the legs that he needs to sit on the edge of the bed.

He had abandoned those people to their fate, yes, but Dorian had decided their fate for them. There are degrees of evil, and Lee Shacket takes refuge in the thought that what he's done pales when compared to what his boss has done.

Surely Dorian Purcell has secretly authorized this extreme measure, his idea of a fail-safe. Dorian fancies himself a visionary, as does nearly everyone in the press who writes about him, and a true visionary knows that progress requires sacrifices, that what matters is not the short-term cost in lives and treasure, but the great benefit to humanity that will be achieved in the long term. To justify murdering tens of millions, Stalin is reputed to have said, 'A single death is a tragedy; a million deaths is a statistic.' By comparison, ninety-two deaths might be, to Dorian, nothing more than a mere footnote to the great enterprise that has been undertaken at Refine's Springville laboratories and will be relaunched elsewhere a year from now.

On the TV, a news anchor solemnly reports that the research being conducted at the facility involved seeking a revolutionary cure for cancer. This is a ridiculous lie, but the newsreader no doubt believes it. Cancer research isn't so dangerous as to require that it be conducted in a walled, isolated compound a mile from the last residences on the outskirts of a Provo, Utah, suburb. However, in an age when news departments operate on tight budgets, many in the media tend to believe whatever they're told by any source they trust, reserving investigative journalism solely for those they find dishonorable or suspicious. In public, at least, Dorian Purcell holds all the right positions on issues that matter to the opinion makers and is all but universally seen as one of the good guys.

The preliminary official explanation for the fire is that the facility maintains its own dedicated power plant to minimize outages that would affect research projects, that the plant is fueled by natural gas, and that perhaps a leak under the foundation went undetected until the building was basically perched on a bomb.

'Yeah, right,' says Lee, switching off the TV.

Later, having become a new brown-haired brown-eyed clean-shaven man, he goes out to dinner. Never a snob about food, he has happily eaten his share of Holiday Inn fare and the equivalent over the years, although on this occasion, nothing tastes appealing. The salad greens are bitter. The vegetables are vaguely metallic. The potatoes have no flavor. He is able to eat the chicken, but it isn't as savory as it ought to be.

He craves something else but doesn't know what might satisfy. Nothing on the menu holds any appeal for him.

In his room again, he mixes spiced rum with Coca-Cola and drinks until he can sleep.

At three thirty in the morning, screaming, slick with cold sweat, he wakes from a nightmare of which he can remember not a single detail.

The disorientation that is characteristic of dreams remains with him. At the windows, an otherworldly cobalt-blue light leaks around the edges of the draperies, as though in the world beyond these walls, a silent catastrophe is emitting lethal radiation. He is sober, but the small room feels vast, the bed adrift on a sea of undulant shadows. When Lee throws back the covers and sits on the edge of the mattress, the floor crawls under his bare feet, as though carpeted by an insect horde. He fumbles with the nightstand lamp and finds the switch. Sudden low light beaches the floating bed and reveals no insects. Yet the place is almost as shadowy as — and no less eerie than — it had been in the dark.

After rising from the bed, he stands in indecision, certain that coiled within the nightmare had been an urgent presentiment of an onrushing evil that isn't merely a sleeper's fantasy, that is instead a truth on which he needs to act to save himself. But still he has no memory of the dream.

He settles in a chair, gripping the upholstered arms with both hands, rocking back and forth even though the chair isn't a rocker and doesn't move in sympathy with him. He can't seem to be still. He needs to move, as if to prove to himself that he's alive.

In the nightmare . . . He recalls something now. He'd been trapped, paralyzed, wrapped tightly, as though cocooned, a white translucent material across his eyes; formless shadows

21

swelling and receding; sounds rising and fading around him.

With a shudder, he wonders if the spectrum of genetic material with which his cells have been contaminated might include that of some worm that dies only to be born anew from a cocoon.

He was helpless in the dream, and lonely. He rocks ceaselessly in the unmoving armchair. He has immediate getaway money and an elegant residence in Costa Rica and $100 million where no authorities can find it, but a profound loneliness makes him vulnerable, with no meaningful purpose.

He feels powerless, as when he'd been a child under the iron rule of a violent alcoholic father and a mentally disturbed mother.

He can't endure being powerless. *He cannot tolerate it.*

In addition to the scientists at Springville, twenty-two hundred Refine employees had answered to him. Now he has authority over no one. He had power, position, respect, twenty Tom Ford suits that he wore with colorful sneakers. All that is gone. He is alone.

Only now does he realize that the worst of all miseries to afflict the human heart is loneliness.

Lee Shacket has never been good at relationships. He's had girlfriends. Hot ones. He's not a troll. Women like the way he looks. They admire his ambition. He has a sense of humor. He can dance. He has style. He's good in bed. He *listens*. But he's never been able to *sustain* a love affair. Sooner than later, each woman starts to seem inadequate, inauthentic in one way or another.

The relationship begins to feel shallow, lacking worthwhile emotional nourishment, a mere teaspoon of romantic essence; nevertheless, he always eventually feels as if he's drowning in that teaspoonful, suffocating, and he needs to escape.

He has gone still in the armchair. His stillness alarms him, as if staying alive depends on remaining in motion. He thrusts to his feet and paces the room, increasingly anxious.

Something strange is happening to him.

In the low lamplight, his restless reflection in the mirror is spectral, as if it's the spirit of some former guest who died here and is wanted neither upstairs nor down, who has nowhere to go.

As he circles the room, he tries to recall when and where his life went wrong, not regarding the events at the labs, but prior to that. When had he last been truly happy? It seems important that he remember. When had his future been most promising?

Although Lee has achieved great success with Dorian Purcell, each promotion comes with such a significant increase in stress that, in spite of making a fortune, he can't honestly say he has been happier during these years than before.

Even prior to Purcell, Lee hadn't always been in high spirits, but his *prospects* for happiness had been greater then. He'd had hope in those days. The options open to him had seemed infinite; whereas now he has few, perhaps only one.

And he is alone. No one to listen. No one to understand. No one to care. No one who must answer to him.

23

The turning point, the motive force that changed Lee's life, is Jason Bookman, a friend since college. Initially, Jason's career soared, while Lee's labored along. Then Jason brought him into Dorian Purcell's inner circle.

As he paces, his reflection in the closet-door mirror disturbs him. His face. Something strange is happening to his face; something is wrong with it.

He hurries into the bathroom, where the light is better. His eyes are brown, hair brown, beard gone. Maybe others won't recognize him, but he knows himself. His mud-brown glower is unimpressive when compared to the piercing tungsten-gray stare with which he had cowed so many junior executives. Otherwise, he looks all right.

But he doesn't *feel* all right. His face is as stiff as a mask. He works his facial muscles — yawning, puckering, grimacing. With his fingertips, he massages his chin and cheeks and brow, pinches his nose, pulls on his lips, searching for . . . some wrongness. Finally he decides that the stiffness is merely a consequence of anxiety. His body, too, is tight with apprehension.

Jason Bookman changed Lee's life, which led to his current disastrous circumstances. However, the worst thing Jason did wasn't bringing him into Purcell's orbit. Worse, Jason married Megan.

Gazing at himself in the bathroom mirror, Lee has an epiphany. Jason was so farseeing, so aware of the long-term risks of working for a power-mad narcissist like Dorian Purcell, that he brought Lee into the company to serve as a fall guy, a role that otherwise might have gone to Jason. Why hasn't this been clear till now? Is he being unfair, paranoid? No, no. What once seemed like an act of friendship is abruptly, belatedly revealed as a Machiavellian maneuver. It wasn't enough that Jason stole Megan from Lee; he also schemed to set up Lee to take the blame if things went wrong at Refine.

Lee remembers the warmth of Megan's kiss. Megan Grassley. Now Megan Bookman. Almost fourteen years ago, they dated for two or three months. He'd never gotten more than a kiss from her. He was used to easy girls, and she insisted on commitment before sex. He'd decided to teach her a lesson by taking a break from her and going out with a hottie named Clarissa, so Megan would understand that servicing a man's needs was the best way to gain his commitment. But after a month, Jason began dating Megan; eventually they married. At the time, Lee hadn't blamed Jason for poaching. He was magnanimous. He wished the couple well and counseled himself that his friend would regret hooking up with such a frigid bitch.

Evidently, however, Megan had no problem giving it up for Jason. They flourished together, and year by year she looked hotter, much hotter than Clarissa. Okay. No problem. Lee hadn't wanted her; she wasn't fast enough for him. She was a Honda, and he needed a Ferrari girl. He had better options than her. The world is full of good-looking women, especially when you're making seven figures a year and piling up stock options.

But now he is jobless, alone. Soon to be an outlaw on the run.

If he'd been more patient with Megan, she might have given herself to him. They might have married, and everything after that surely would have been far different from the current calamity.

He suddenly knows when he had been happiest, when his future had been most promising: when he was dating Megan.

Meeting his eyes in the mirror, he realizes that nothing is wrong with his face. The problem, if it is a problem, exists *behind his face*. Something is happening to his mind. There is a fever in his brain. If he purchased a thermometer, his temperature would prove to be normal; he has no doubt that it would be 98.6 precisely. However, there is a *fever of excitement* in his brain: agitation, fermentation, effervescence. This isn't necessarily a bad thing. He is exhilarated, electrified, galvanized.

He knows what he must do. He can't travel back in time fourteen years and marry Megan, but he can go to her in California, where she lives now. She is a widow. Three years a widow. She will be easier now than she was when they were younger, ready for a new life, for the *right* life, the one that they would have had together if Jason Bookman hadn't come along. Lee will take her with him to Costa Rica. The boy, too, if she really wants to bother with a mentally disabled mute. Hot Megan and steamy Costa Rica: This prospect stimulates Lee, inflames him. He can be happy again, with a fine future that holds great promise.

In the bathroom mirror, the reflection speaks to him, though it's not his image any longer, but somehow that of Jason Bookman, the poaching Machiavellian betrayer of friends. *'You're infected,'* Jason declares. 'They're swarming inside you. *Something's going wrong with your mind.'*

'Liar,' Lee replies. 'You just don't want me to get in her pants.' He snatches up the pint of spiced rum and throws it.

The shattering bottle fractures the mirror, instantly beheading and dismembering Jason Bookman, daggers and dirks and stilettos and scimitars of glass spilling out of the frame, slashing down upon the sink and the faux marble encircling it, ringing like the silvery bells of some demonic fairy church. The aroma of spiced rum — orange peel, cinnamon, coconut, vanilla bean — spurts across Lee Shacket, splashes off the wall behind him.

In a state of high excitement, two hours before dawn, he returns to the bedroom and quickly dresses for the long drive.

7

For a few hours, Dorothy phased in and out of sleep, her hand always on Kipp, either still or caressing.

He remained awake, alert to her condition, asking only for another minute of her company, another and another.

Then she passed away.

Kipp smelled his mistress leaving first her flesh and then the room.

He cried the only way that his kind could cry, spilling not a tear, but issuing a series of thin, miserable whimpers.

In tears, for she had loved Dorothy, Rosa said, 'Oh, sweet Kipp, please stop, please don't, you sound so pathetic, you're breaking my heart twice.'

But for the longest while, he could not stop, because Dorothy had gone where he couldn't follow.

He was not merely alone now. He was reduced to half of who he had been.

8

Woody never needed more than five hours of sleep. Perhaps he'd slept more when he'd been a fat-cheeked baby, but though he had an exceptional memory, he could recall nothing of his infancy other than a mobile that hung over his crib: colorful Lucite birds — coral pink, yellow, sapphire blue — circling around and around, casting cheerful prismatic patterns on the walls. Maybe the mobile was why, all these years later, he sometimes dreamed that he could fly.

Medical authorities unanimously agreed that everyone needed eight hours of sleep every night. Less sack time supposedly led to difficulty focusing the mind, disordered thought processes.

Most people who wound up as vagrants or embezzlers or serial killers had perhaps been shaped by sleep deprivation. That was a theory, anyway. In Woody's case, however, if he languished in bed too long, *that* left him fuzzy-headed, with a lingering attention deficit. At 3:50 a.m., his eyelids flipped up with an almost audible click, and he became *awake*, with no chance whatsoever of falling back into sleep.

This embarrassed him. He was different from other people in half a gajillion ways. If only he had needed eight hours in the sheets, he would have been a little less *alien*.

On this Wednesday morning, Woody did what he always did on arising. He had his routines. Routines were his salvation. The world was vast and complex, part of a larger and even more complex solar system, an enormous galaxy, an infinite universe — *trillions of stars!* — and he didn't want to think too much about that. There were uncountable choices that were yours to make, innumerable things that could *happen* to you. The options could paralyze you with indecision, and all the threats could petrify you with fear. Routines made the infinite finite and manageable. So he took his usual four-minute shower and dressed and went quietly downstairs.

He was allowed to prepare his own breakfast cereal and toast, but it was too early to eat.

Anyway, he liked to have breakfast with his mother when she got up for the day. He never spoke a word as they ate, but he enjoyed listening to her. Sometimes she didn't say much, either, and that was okay, too, as long as she wasn't quiet because she was sad.

He always knew when she was sad. Her sadness passed through him like windblown sleet, and he became chilled into sadness, too, which he otherwise never was.

From a kitchen drawer, he retrieved a Bell and Howell Tac Light and his trusty Attwood signal horn. The latter was a small aerosol can with a red plastic Klaxon on top, which could produce an earsplitting WAAAAAHHHHH that reliably scared off potentially dangerous animals, though he had rarely seen any of those and had only used the horn twice.

Thus equipped, he stepped to the security alarm keypad next to the back door. He entered the four numbers, and the recorded voice said, '*System is disarmed.*' The volume was turned low so that his mother wouldn't be awakened by anything but the alarm itself.

The back porch offered a pair of teak chairs with thick blue cushions, a little table between them, a bench swing hanging from stainless-steel chains, and darkness all around.

Woody wasn't afraid of the night.

The night could be magical. Cool things had happened to him in the dark morning hours while his mother still slept. Once he'd seen a fat opossum waddling across the lawn, trailed by her babies, all their tiny lantern eyes shining with curiosity when they saw him. He had seen foxes and countless rabbits and families of deer. The only thing he'd needed to scare away with a long blast of the horn had been raccoons that approached him hissing and baring their teeth.

30

His faithful obedience had earned him the right to sit on the porch at night as long as he was careful to leave the door unlocked to facilitate a quick retreat. He wasn't permitted to venture into the yard alone. It was a deep yard, almost three acres, and at the farther end waited the forest.

Animals more dangerous than mean raccoons lived in the forest. Mother Nature wasn't really motherly. Mom said nature was more like a bipolar aunt who treated you kindly most of the time but, now and then, could be a real witch, conjuring killer storms and vicious animals, like big toothy mountain lions that, if given a menu, would always order tender children.

He sat on the porch steps. His mother expected that he would sit in one of the chairs or on the swing, or stand at the railing. But the steps put him closer to the action, if there should be any action, and he was still living by the rules, the primary one of which was that he should not go into the yard. The Tac Light lay beside him, unused, and he kept the air horn in his right hand.

The moon floated in the west, not yet behind those mountains, as radiant as some exotic jellyfish in the sea of space, and the sky twinkled with more stars than Woody could count in a lifetime. After his father's death — *murder!* — they moved from a busy town in Silicon Valley, which his mother said was more of a concept than it was a real place, and they came here to the outskirts of the community of Pinehaven, in Pinehaven County, where no city-light pollution dimmed the stars.

Woody was on the steps not more than ten minutes when the three deer materialized out of the darkness: a buck bearing a magnificent rack of antlers, a doe, and a fawn that was maybe five months old and still wore a spotted coat. He'd lose his spots in winter, as he finished growing into an adult.

Deer didn't always travel in families, often in small herds and equally often alone, but the previous year, a family like this had visited almost nightly for three months, drawn by the sweet grass of the lawn. Woody had come to know them, quartered apples for them, and put the fruit on the porch steps and retreated to a chair. Gradually they had become confident enough to eat the apples off the bottom step while he had sat on the top one, and eventually, with their soft lips, they had taken the apples from his hands.

These three visitors were not those from the prior year. Woody remembered the markings of those adults, and these were different. The deer were aware of him, and they were cautious, remaining at a distance as they grazed, their shadowy forms vaguely patinaed with moonlight.

Sometimes he wondered what had happened to that other family, if one or more had been killed by hunters, if perhaps a mountain lion had gotten the doe or her fawn. Keeping a family together and safe was really, really hard.

He didn't dare go into the kitchen and quarter a few apples and try to lure these new deer to the steps. Just by getting up he might scare them

32

away. If they returned a few times and became accustomed to his presence, he could begin to try to make friends with them.

For the time being, watching them was pleasure enough. They enchanted him. They were beautiful and graceful, though neither their beauty nor grace was what most moved him. What fascinated, enthralled, *spellbound* him was that they were three, together and safe and grazing under the stars, unafraid in this world of fear, looking as though they would be together forever.

The night lay so quiet that Woody imagined he could hear the stars burning light-years away, though of course what he heard was the circulation of his blood through the capillaries in his ears.

He whispered, 'Hello.'

Although the boy's voice had been soft, the buck raised its antlered head to stare at him.

They regarded each other for a long moment, and then Woody whispered, 'I love you,' because the deer couldn't spoil the moment with the wrong words and because the gulf between their species ensured that neither of them could embarrass himself or the other.

9

Megan Bookman was awakened by the voice of the security system when Woody entered the disarming code. The volume was low through most of the house, so that he would not worry about waking her, but louder here in the master suite, to ensure that she would always know when he had gone to the back porch.

She got out of bed and eased through the gloom to the Crestron unit embedded in the wall. The screen brightened when she touched it, and she selected the word CAMERAS from the menu. Fourteen two-camera modules were installed at points around the exterior of the house, one camera that could record either by daylight or outdoor lamps and the other gathering infrared images when, as now, there was neither sun nor landscape lighting.

The system translated the red images into wavelengths that were nearest 555 nanometers, the green part of the spectrum to which the human eye was most sensitive. Nevertheless, the video offered little detail. Although she could see Woody sitting on the top step, gazing out at the backyard and the forest beyond, he was a pale-green form among shadows of various shades of green, as if he might be a forest spirit drawn by curiosity to this human habitat.

He would have his Attwood signal horn and Tac Light. He never forgot those things.

At the first suggestion of a threat, he would use the horn and bolt into the house. Megan had no concern that Woody might fail to recognize a threat. He feared strangers and anything with which his routine had not familiarized him.

Pinehaven wasn't a hotbed of crime. Even the national drug epidemic had thus far not seriously sickened this quiet backwater. Their property was just beyond the limits of the town in which she had been born and raised, and she had come to feel safe here.

Leaving Woody alone on the back porch wasn't ideal. But he was eleven, and he cherished what independence his condition allowed him. She couldn't be at his side around the clock, and it wouldn't be good for either of them if she kept him close with a tether of fear as inhibiting as a leash.

She returned to bed, where she would most likely need half an hour to go back to sleep.

A small gun safe was attached to the bed rail. On retiring each night, she opened it for access to the weapon. On rising for the day, she'd lock it again. The pistol was a 9 mm Heckler & Koch USP with a ten-round magazine.

She had bought the gun a week after Jason died. She had taken shooting lessons from a former police officer who ran a self-defense school. Three years later, she continued to practice regularly.

Lying awake in the dark, she wondered if she really felt as safe as she claimed to be.

10

As far as Lee Shacket is concerned, southwest Utah sucks, sixty miles of austere moonlit 'scenery' on State Route 56 from Cedar City to the state line, as far from a Starbucks or a good sushi restaurant as anywhere on the planet. But he still believes it's necessary to travel by tertiary routes that are less policed than the interstates.

Compared to southeast Nevada, however, Utah is a lush paradise. Toured via a series of two-lane back roads, Lincoln and Nye Counties prove to be a hellish wasteland over which a fierce sun now rises like an omen of an impending thermonuclear holocaust. From the sleepy whistle-stop called Caliente to the nowhere burg of Rachel, he races through eighty-seven miles of Nevada nothing. The next town lies beyond another fifty-four miles of desolate land and lonely blacktop, a stretch of hara-kiri pavement on which rattlesnakes, bored and despairing, slither and lie waiting for the wheels of fate that will release them from the tedium of desert life.

Miles in the distance, to either side of the highway, fester settlements with names like Hiko and Ash Springs, served by state and county roads, and others like Tempiute and Adaven that can be reached only on unpaved tracks. At 6:50 a.m., he stops to fill the fuel tank at a combination service station and convenience store that, with a house behind it, stands alone at a crossroads a few miles short of Warm Springs. The gasoline at the two pumps is an overpriced brand he's never heard of, and the building housing the store is fissured pale-yellow stucco with a blue ceramic-tile roof.

With his old life in ruins behind him and his new life with Megan still far away in California, Shacket has been in a foul mood since leaving Cedar City. Mile by mile, the arid Mojave leaches out of him what little human kindness has not been drained away by the endless injustices he has suffered.

The gas pumps aren't as old as the fossil fuel they provide, but they aren't of a generation that reads credit cards. He goes into the store to provide the cashier with his Nathan Palmer Visa, to activate the pump.

The man is evidently the owner, and Shacket despises him on sight. He is old and fat. He wears khaki pants with suspenders, a white T-shirt, and a narrow-brimmed straw hat, which seems like a costume, as if he is *playing* at being a desert bumpkin.

After Shacket fills the tank, when he returns to the store to sign the Visa form and get his card, the old guy says, 'Beautiful mornin', isn't it?'

'Hot as a furnace,' Shacket says.

'Well, you're not from here. To us, it's a mellow mornin'.'

'How do you know I'm not from here?'

'Seen your plates when you pulled in. They're not Nevada. Looks like maybe Montana.'

As Shacket signs the form, he says nothing. He concentrates on the signature, because for a moment he forgets the name that's on the credit card. He almost signs *Lee Shacket*. Something is wrong with his mind.

'Only eighty-two degrees,' the cashier says. 'That's cool for these parts, this time of year.'

Shacket gets the Nathan Palmer right. He meets the old guy's rheumy eyes. 'What parts are you talking about? Your private parts?'

'Excuse me?'

'Excuse you from what?'

The cashier frowns and slides the Visa card across the counter. 'Well, you have a nice day.'

37

Shacket doesn't understand the anger and contempt he feels for this stranger. It scares him a little. And is irresistible.

'Excuse you from what?' Shacket asks again. This geezer pisses him off with his phony howdy-neighbor style. 'Did you fart? Excuse you from what?'

The cashier breaks eye contact. 'I didn't mean no offense.'

'Did you offend me?'

'Sir, I truly don't believe I did.'

A buzzing arises in Shacket's head, as if a hive of wasps has taken residence in his cerebellum. 'That's what you believe, is it?'

The cashier looks at the window, toward the pumps, maybe hoping another customer will drive in. Nothing is moving out there except a cloud shadow that slides a measure of darkness along the highway.

The old guy's tension, his unexpressed fear, excites Shacket. 'Do you have a *core* belief?' he asks as he takes a candy bar from a display on the counter.

Shacket himself once had core beliefs, a sense of limits. He's sure of it. He just can't remember what those limits were.

'What do you mean?' the old man asks.

'Well, like, do you believe in God?'

'Yes, sir. I do.'

'You do?'

'Yes, sir.'

'Where is God?' Shacket asks, stripping the wrapper off the candy bar and letting it fall to the floor.

The old guy meets his eyes again. 'Where is God?'

'I'm just wondering where you think He is.'

'God is everywhere.'

'Is He over there by the cooler with the beer and soda pop?'

The cashier says nothing.

Shacket takes a bite of the candy bar, chews it twice, and then spits the sticky lump on the counter. 'This thing tastes like shit. It's a decade past the expiration date. What's your God think of you selling shit like this? Doesn't He notice? Where is He? Is God maybe back there by the potato chips and Doritos?'

The cashier looks down at the credit card processor. 'I run your card, it's electronic, over the phone is how it works. The number and name, they're out there at Visa already, the purchase.'

He's telling Shacket that if something mortal happens here, there's proof that Nathan Palmer stopped for gas around the time that it all went down.

But of course Shacket is not Nathan Palmer.

The angry buzzing in his head grows angrier. He needs to do something to stop the buzzing. He knows what he needs to do.

He takes another bite of the candy bar and chews once and spits it on the counter. 'Is God over there by the magazines? You have some dirty magazines over there, don't you? Some skin magazines?'

A tremor has arisen at one corner of the fat old guy's mouth, which further excites Shacket.

Yet the trembling reminds him of his grand-father, a kind man, who had a tremor. Something that might be pity for the cashier overcomes him. It passes quickly.

'You're not much of a conversationalist, are you? You say it's a beautiful morning, then you have nowhere to go after that.'

Shacket throws the remainder of the candy bar at the old man, and it sticks to the white T-shirt.

Shacket isn't Nathan Palmer, but he needs to use the Palmer driver's license and credit card for a while yet. If he'd paid cash, he could do what he needs to do to stop the buzzing.

'You're a lucky sonofabitch, aren't you?'

The old man does not reply.

'I said, you're a lucky sonofabitch, aren't you?'

'Not that I've noticed.'

'Not that you've noticed? Well, then, you're as stupid as you are lucky. You're a lucky sonofa-bitch. It's your lucky day, gramps. I'm going to walk out of here and let you go on breathing. You call the sheriff about this, you know what's going to happen?'

'I'm not callin' nobody.'

'Some cop pulls me over, he better kill me quick. 'Cause if he doesn't, I'll kill him, then come back here and shove a pistol up your fat ass.'

'I'm not callin' nobody,' the old man repeats.

Shacket walks out to the Dodge Demon. Under the driver's seat, snugged in a belt holster, is a Heckler & Koch Compact .38. He needs all of his willpower not to retrieve it, return to the store, and empty the magazine into the old man.

On the road again, past the jerkwater called Warm Springs, heading toward Tonopah on federal highway 6, Shacket accelerates to 120 miles per hour, then 130, the Dodge roaring, gobbling blacktop. He's agitated, excited, electrified, and he needs the speed to work off his agitation, to calm himself.

Ever since Springville, Utah, something has been happening to his mind. For his entire life, there's been a Dorian Purcell to whom he has had to answer, a Purcell by one name or another, from whom he has taken shit when it is shoveled at him. Well, no longer. He is free at last. He's in control of his life. No one is the boss of him anymore. Something is happening to his mind, and he *loves* it.

Thirty-five miles from Warm Springs, about ten miles short of Tonopah, the buzzing in his head stops, and he is able to slow down.

The state line is maybe ninety miles away. He will soon be in California. On his way to lovely Megan.

He is hungry. Nothing had tasted good at dinner the previous evening. He had skipped breakfast. The candy bar really had tasted like shit. He is exceedingly hungry. Ravenous. He'll stop to eat as soon as he's in California. He doesn't know what he wants to eat; nothing he can think of makes his mouth water; he'll figure it out when he gets there.

The highway rises into the White Mountains and Inyo National Forest, the wastelands falling away behind him, the past falling away with them, the past and all restraints.

41

11

When the mortician came to collect the body, Kipp at last got off Dorothy's bed.

While others were too busy to notice him, he made his way down through the house, through his special door, and into the backyard.

The September morning had come. The day was warm and bright and like unto other mornings, as if nothing terrible had happened.

He howled silently, mentally howled to others in the Mysterium, that they might know his grief and share it, wherever they were and on whatever task they might be engaged.

There were only eighty-six, all golden retrievers or Labradors.

Now and then a new, young member found his or her way to others of their kind, for they could speak to one another on the Wire, a mental communication medium unique to them.

Their origin and history remained a deep mystery to them, but they sought to plumb it.

They were dogs unlike all other dogs, changed as only humankind had the power to reshape other species.

But who had done it? Where had it been done? Why?

And how had they come to be roaming a few counties in north and central California, in search of their meaning?

On the Wire, the peculiar murmur that wasn't tinnitus increased slightly in volume.

Kipp began to suspect that the insistent sound

was not coming from some new member of the Mysterium, not from another canine.

A human being. He thought it might be a young boy.

This was a new thing. Kipp had never heard such a call from a human being before.

Then again, it wasn't really a call. The boy, if it was a boy, very likely didn't know he was transmitting.

Kipp stood for a while, looking at the house to which he'd been brought as a puppy.

He expected to regret leaving it. But with Dorothy gone, it was just a house, no place special.

She'd been seventy-three and in good health when she brought him home. She'd expected to outlive him. Then the cancer.

He avoided leaving by the side of the house where the hearse was in the driveway. He didn't want to see her being taken away.

The murmuring boy, if it was a boy, lived somewhere west by northwest of Lake Tahoe.

As if it were a radio, he could turn off the Wire. But then what would he do? He needed something to do.

This might be a perilous journey for a stray dog, but Kipp felt compelled to undertake it.

He wasn't afraid of dogcatchers. He was quicker and smarter than they were.

However, the world was full of worse things than dogcatchers.

He set out at a trot, staying as best he could to backstreets and forest-service roads, to woods and meadows.

From time to time he heard himself whimpering in grief. Love was the best thing when you had it, and the most terrible thing when it was taken from you.

12

Wednesday afternoon, Megan Bookman was in her ground-floor studio, listening to a Beethoven sonata, *Pathétique*, while working on a painting. The big windows provided good northern light. The room smelled of turpentine and stand oil and paint, a fragrance as lovely to her as was that of roses.

She'd been painting most of her life and had been selling her work since the year she graduated college. The glorious decade with Jason and the special needs of Woody had slowed her production, but she never stopped refining her intentions and techniques.

When she lost Jason and faced the prospect of raising Woody alone, painting became the slow but sure curative for grief, as well as the means by which she gained the confidence to face the future unafraid. After a year of widowhood and long exhilarating hours in her studio, she had landed representation by a major gallery with outlets in New York, Boston, Seattle, and Los Angeles.

Her approach was a rejection of fashion art from Picasso to Kandinsky to Warhol, and an embrace of realism. Her subjects were from the

44

world around her, rendered with meticulous fidelity, yet with a quirky sense of composition and a regard for the complexities of light that suggested something magical — even supernatural — about even the most mundane scenes.

This wasn't an approach likely to win her critical acclaim in the blinkered world of critics steeped in postmodernism and all that sprang from it. Yet during the past eighteen months, there had been positive — growing — buzz about her work in the right places.

She didn't care whether critical acclaim waxed or waned. She painted to satisfy herself. Her first life had ended with the death of Jason, and she was profoundly grateful to have discovered that there was life after life. Her art and her child were graces enough for her. Whatever else the future might bring would be a lagniappe.

Because she closely guarded her smartphone number, she also had a landline for the house. The studio extension stood on a table near her easel. When it rang, the caller's number meant nothing to her, but she put down her brush, swiveled on the stool, and answered it.

'Hello?'

'Megan? Megan Bookman?'

'Speaking.'

'This is Lee Shacket.'

She didn't know quite what to say, though her high spirits sank slightly. 'Lee, how have you been?'

'Terrific. I've been terrific.' He sounded a little manic. 'No complaints. None at all. How've you been?'

She'd dated him briefly, before she met Jason;

but there was no chemistry between them, no intimacy. He was cute, earnest. He was amusing at times, in the hyperbolic style of the late comedian Robin Williams. He was hardworking, with big dreams that were charmingly naive rather than pretentious. But essentially he'd been a young man on the make, too into himself to care much about anyone else. Eventually Jason recognized enough intelligence and self-discipline in Lee's hustle to recommend him to Dorian Purcell, and indeed Lee climbed the corporate ladder faster and far higher than Jason.

'I've been well,' she said. 'I've been painting, being a mom, you know.'

'How's the kid? The boy. How's the boy doing?'

'Woody? He's fine. He's busy being Woody.'

Megan hadn't had occasion to speak with Lee Shacket since a corporate event eight or nine years earlier. He had not called with condolences when Jason died.

'You moved back to Pinehaven. That's where you were born, isn't it? Weren't you born in Pinehaven?'

'Yes. It's quiet here. It's a good environment for Woody.'

'Not much happening in Pinehaven. Not a lot of glamour.'

'Just how I like it,' she said, wondering what motivated him to call, what he might want.

'Are you financially okay, Megan?'

The question struck her as bizarre. 'Excuse me?'

'I know Dorian didn't treat you properly after Jason died.'

Jason had stock options that would have made

46

her and Woody rich if not wealthy. However, the employment contract had included an unusual vesting clause allowing more than one interpretation, and Dorian had not been inclined to be generous to a widow.

'We're okay,' she assured Shacket.

'It wasn't right. Dorian can be a hard-nosed sonofabitch. You should have sued him.'

'He had way deeper pockets. It would've taken years and years, with no guarantee I'd win.'

'It's just so wrong. Jason would have wanted you to sue. He'd *earned* what Dorian took from you.'

'I was grieving, and there was Woody to worry about. We had enough. I didn't want to mess with the whole court thing.'

'Dorian screwed me, too. He set me up, put me out on the ledge to take a fall for him, screwed me bad, but I still came out of it rich. I came out of it with *a hundred million.*'

She didn't know what to say to that. Shacket's voice had at first withered with acidic anger, but then had swelled with pride.

Seemingly unaware of her moment of speechlessness, he hurried on. 'If you need anything, anything at all, you can count on me. I have resources. Whatever you need. Anything.'

She'd dated Lee Shacket maybe six times. She had seen in him a better boy than the man he'd become, one who adapted a cocky self-assurance to repress the humility and self-doubt of his youth. She might have liked him better if he'd let that boy become a different man. Lee had been out of her personal life for thirteen years, a business associate of Jason's whom she'd seldom encountered. There was nothing substantive between them; there never had been. She couldn't fathom the purpose of this weird conversation.

'That's kind of you, Lee. That's very thoughtful,' she said, though in fact she found his offer not just inexplicable but also somewhat creepy. 'However, Jason left us well set, with insurance and all, and my paintings have been selling. We're fine, we really are.'

'When you make a hundred million,' he said, 'you start thinking about giving back. I'm all the time thinking about giving back. I just want you to know that you and the kid, the boy, I just want you to know that I'm here for you. I care. I'm here.'

Again, he left her speechless.

He remained so oblivious of the effect he was having that he rambled on before Megan's uneasy silence became apparent to him. 'Have you ever been to Costa Rica? It's quite a place, a fabulous place. The blue Caribbean. Nothing like the sea along California. Tranquil, like a jewel. San José, the capital, is a sophisticated city. Friendly people, great night-life. A hundred million in Costa Rica is like a billion here, hell, like two or three billion. I'm going down to Costa Rica, Megan. I'm getting out of the rat race. I'm going to lay back, enjoy life, really *live* while I'm young. But nothing is as good as it ought to be when you're alone. What I need is someone to share it with. You and me, we had something special once. Really special. I was too

48

callow, too frantic for success, too much of a jerk, to realize what we had. But I've always regretted that we drifted apart. If you'll give me a second chance, you'll never regret it. I'll take good care of you, Megan, you and the boy, no one would ever take better care of you.'

She wondered if he was drunk. Or high on something. He talked fast, but he didn't slur his words. Whether intoxicated or not, this out-of-the-blue proposal was irrational and profoundly awkward.

She might once have been less than polite in this circumstance, but sweet Woody had taught her patience. She carefully considered her response. 'I'm flattered that you've thought so well of me all these years, Lee. Though I'm sure I don't deserve it. Not only young men can be callow. Young women make a good job of it, too. But I've got Woody. He relies on me. Woody is all I want for now, all I need. I couldn't possibly take him to Costa Rica. A trip to the barbershop emotionally exhausts him, and he needs days to recover from going to the dentist. I'm afraid you underestimate how a special-needs child changes your life.'

His rapid speech gave way to a silence of his own, and then he said, 'But it has to be Costa Rica. I've planned it all. The way is prepared. I can't change that now. I could fold you into the plan, you and the boy, but I couldn't come up with a new plan, not now, not after . . . Give me a chance. Just tell me you'll think about it, Megan. Think about it overnight and call me tomorrow. Please call me tomorrow.'

He gave her the number, and she wrote it down with no intention of calling him. 'All right, but I'm afraid our time has passed, Lee. What's best for me is what's best for Woody, and that's not Costa Rica. You've made a life for yourself that anyone would envy, and I've no doubt you'll find someone to share it with. You deserve to be happy, happier than you'd be with me.'

He began to importune her again, and she lied to bring an end to this excruciating conversation. She said that Woody was calling out to her, that he was having one of his tantrums — Woody never had tantrums — and that she had to go to the boy right away.

After hanging up, Megan turned her attention to the canvas on which she had been working. Her own backyard served as the setting. The hour of the scene: perhaps four o'clock in the morning. Only the moon to illuminate the moment. This eerie luminosity was a metaphor for the light at the heart of the world, the unseen light in all things; therefore, though its effects were rendered realistically, they were subtly exaggerated, so that the softest reflections of moonglow seemed to emanate from *within* certain pale elements of the composition: from the slices of apple in the boy's hand, from his face, from the soft coats of the three deer, from the white blossoms on the apple tree. The dark forest loomed over all.

To the best of her knowledge, Woody had never ventured into the yard after dark, alone. He had lured the deer to the porch steps to feed from his hand. Sometimes an artist had to stage events as they might have been, slightly different from how they *had* been, to best convey the truth of them.

And what had been the truth of Lee Shacket's call?

It eluded her.

Unable to get back into the mood of the painting, she put her brush in a jar of turpentine.

She went to the tall French doors and the flanking windows that provided her with ample north light. This was not the lawn in the painting, but the forest embraced this side yard as well, looming somewhat closer than at the back of the house.

When a narcissist like Shacket had a $100 million to fall back on, he didn't fall into melancholy under any circumstance, didn't become sentimental and brood about days gone by and all that might have been. He went out and bought what he wanted, whether it was a Ferrari or a piece of arm candy with long legs and canyonesque cleavage.

The explanation had to be inebriation. Wherever he was calling from, perhaps it was much later in the day than half past three, and maybe he'd gotten an early start on the bottle.

He hadn't been the kind of man who'd spoken of his heart, only of his opinions, which were dogma to him, and of his high ambitions, which he had been certain would be fulfilled. He had never loved her, only wanted her. When the alcohol wore off, he would regret what he'd done. He wouldn't phone her again. And if he did, Megan wouldn't take the call.

51

The quality of the light had changed, not just because the afternoon was waning, but also because the sky had begun to grow pale-gray scales, its fine blue skin molting away in favor of a serpent's dress.

As always, there was magic in the day, though not the kind to inspire in her the enchantment that she needed to do justice to the painting of Woody and the deer.

Every Monday, Wednesday, and Friday, Verna Brickit came to do light housekeeping, which concluded with preparation of a meal that Megan could reheat for dinner. By now, Verna would be at work in the kitchen; she welcomed an assistant cook, and Megan was good company.

Megan cleaned her brushes, put away her paints, and washed her hands in the bathroom that adjoined her studio.

When she looked at herself in the mirror above the sink, she was surprised to see such unmistakable anxiety in her face, in her eyes. Lee Shacket's reentry into her life had disturbed her more than she wanted to admit.

Always he had hummed with a dark energy, the memory of which came back to her now by degrees. He had wanted one thing from her, and like a puppet master, he pulled strings with such finesse that, in her youth and naivete, she had not at first felt him tugging on them. When she began to see through him, he tried using another girl as a weapon. What had her name been? Clarissa? Yes. He'd used the threat of Clarissa's sexual availability to manipulate Megan, and she'd let him manipulate her right out of his life.

Where she intended to remain.

She went to the kitchen, looking for Verna Brickit.

13

When thirst troubled Kipp, finding water to drink required little effort.

Lake Tahoe was among the deepest and purest lakes in the world, and drinking from the streams that fed it involved no serious risks.

The water was cool and clean.

He paused in his drinking to watch torsional fish, their fins wimpling as they swam through the sun-pierced pools in which the descending stream periodically gathered itself.

Hunger proved a greater problem.

As a canine, he was a hunter by nature. But he'd never actually hunted.

Except when Dorothy had played hide the ball and he'd been tasked with finding it. He'd found the ball a thousand times, but he'd never *eaten* it.

The meadows were full of rabbits nibbling grass in the sun. When they spotted Kipp, most of them either tensed and froze and pretended invisibility or raced away in terror.

A few rabbits regarded him warily, then continued eating as though they perceived his weakness.

Kipp was physically strong, seventy pounds of muscle and bone. He was mentally strong, too.

But emotionally . . . compassion remained at odds with instinct.

Nature's way was for the sharp of teeth to feed on those whose teeth were blunt, for the strong to rule the weak.

But he was a dog with the high-order intelligence of a human being, neither canine nor human.

Intelligence gave rise to culture, culture to ethics.

Although he was in the form of a dog, he was in spirit both a dog and a human being. This had been done to him before his birth.

He had been as a child to Dorothy. His culture and ethics were hers, were human.

Some human beings could kill their own kind in anger, for gain, and even just for the thrill of it.

Neither Dorothy nor Kipp were that decadent.

Most human beings could kill in self-defense, and so could Kipp, child of Dorothy.

But rabbits were no threat to him. Neither were squirrels or field mice.

He passed through meadows and woodlets alive with lunch and dinner, and his hunger grew.

It would seem that, starving, he could kill anything blunt of teeth to save himself. After all, rabbits and squirrels were neither canine nor human.

They were not his kind. Nature meant for him to have them as he needed. They were prey.

This was where, in his present circumstances, the blessing of human-level intelligence became almost a curse. He knew compassion.

Mercy. Pity.

Those are burdensome qualities.

Compassion. Mercy. Pity.

At moments like this, smell became a philosophical issue.

The sense of smell was central to a dog's life, as much as twenty thousand times greater than that of a human being. His nose had forty-four muscles, as compared to four in the human nose.

His sense of smell alone brought him more information than all five human senses combined. In this case, too much information.

Among the lower animals, every creature found joy in the fact of living. Kipp could smell their abiding joy as pungently as he could detect the odor of their droppings, musk, breath, and warm blood.

Compassion and mercy and pity versus the survival instinct.

Human beings resolved the problem — sort of — by putting distance between themselves and the source of some of their life-sustaining fare by establishing slaughterhouses and the profession of butcher.

Kipp had no credit card to pay a butcher.

This moment in which he found himself was called a 'crisis of conscience.'

His hunger grew.

Being entirely in the form of a dog, and half a dog in spirit, he didn't drive forward relentlessly toward the boy whom he'd set out to find or toward the satisfaction of his appetite.

He was distracted by a dog's need to frolic.

A small swarm of butterflies captured his imagination. He didn't try to bite them, but capered after those bright wonders, marveling at their effortless air dance.

55

Perhaps a half mile later, a foil balloon, partly deflated but still buoyant with helium, floated over a field he was crossing.

The word HAPPY was clearly printed on it in red.

He gave chase.

The second line of letters, crinkled in and out of the deep creases in the material, seemed to spell BIRTHDAY.

He had seen such balloons before. Nevertheless, this one struck him as irresistibly strange because of its dislocation.

The bright, mirrored Mylar drifting across this isolated meadow enchanted him. It seemed to *mean* something.

Kipp pursued it, leaping to bite at the long red ribbon that trailed from it. His teeth closed on empty air, and in frustration he leaped higher the next time, higher still.

Just as he chastised himself for succumbing too completely to his inner puppy, the balloon proved to have meaning, after all.

He came upon a fluttering bird lying on bare ground. One wing was broken.

In fright, the creature rolled its eyes and worked its beak without making a sound. Terror and pain robbed it of song.

Nothing could be done for the bird. Its fate was to be taken by a hawk or a fox or something else, and eaten alive.

Kipp considered it for a minute.

He thought, *I'm sorry, little one.*

With one forepaw, he stepped on it, bore down with all his weight, and broke its neck.

When humans went to a theater to see a tragedy, it was a play in which some great person fell from a height, destroyed by fate or a character flaw.

Kipp had watched comedies and tragedies on TV with Dorothy.

A bird could have no character flaw. And yet birds, like all the little animals, had their roles in tragedies every day.

In this beautiful but hard world, fate spared no species.

This bird was plump. There was a satisfaction of flesh under the feathers.

Kipp turned away, leaving the bird untouched. He had no taste for tragedy.

Less than a mile later, an aroma came to him that was familiar and delicious. Hamburgers on a grill.

And not just hamburgers. Also frankfurters.

Drawn by the smells, he raced toward a wall of trees, through an evergreen woods, and out into a campground with a mix of tents and small motor homes.

People. Adults and children.

He had a thousand wiles and stratagems by which to charm them. He would be fed.

In his hunger, he forgot for the moment that not all people were good. If even a hundred of them were kind, there would be one whose every intention was wicked.

14

Shacket calls her from a motel parking lot on the outskirts of Truckee, California, north of Lake Tahoe, and he pours his heart out to her, confesses having made a mistake by not romancing her better back in the day, offers her the world, the world in Costa Rica, and at first she seems pleased that he's called. Judging by her tone, he thinks she regrets not letting him bang her, because if he, instead of backstabbing Jason, had knocked her up, there would be no Woody, no mentally disabled mute dragging her down day in and day out. He and Megan would have had a beautiful son, a good-looking and smart-as-hell kid they would have been proud of. So, yes, at first he thinks she wants him, she needs him, he's got her.

But then a superior tone comes into her voice, a snottiness he doesn't like, doesn't deserve, just can't tolerate. *I'm afraid you underestimate how a special-needs child changes your life.* Does she think he's stupid? How can he not know how some idiot mute would screw up her life? *I'm afraid our time has passed, Lee.* As if she has twenty guys worth a hundred million bucks beating on her door. As if she ever gave him the time, which she never did; their time never *passed*, because she never gave him the time, never gave him the chance to pin her down and show her what she was missing. *What's best for me is what's best for Woody, and that's not Costa Rica.* Can she really think he doesn't

58

realize that she's shoveling shit at him? Hell, he can smell it over the phone. What she's *really* saying is that some pinhead kid who can't even talk is more interesting than Lee Shacket, that a dead-end life in a backwater like Pinehaven is preferable to white beaches and the blue Caribbean and the good life *if all of that comes with Lee Shacket.*

The angrier he gets with Megan, the hungrier he becomes. He's hungrier than he's ever been, inhumanly hungry. Five hours earlier, he stopped to eat in Bishop at this dump that some shit-for-brains critic rated three stars, and they couldn't even make a hamburger the way he wanted. He sends it back twice, trying to make them understand what *rare* means. The third time, it's still wrong, and the manager comes to the table, says, *Sir, what you seem to be asking for is steak tartar as a burger, but I'm sorry to say we aren't a restaurant that's prepared to pull that off. There are health considerations with ground beef.* Shacket wants to take his knife and fork, slit open the bastard, show him exactly what *rare* means, but instead he orders two more burgers not one degree more well done than the medium-rare patty they've already served him. He eats all three burgers but only one bun, and none of the fries. He pays, but he doesn't tip.

On the way out, the waitress smiles at him and tells him to have a nice day, and he is reminded of his unbalanced mother, who refused the drugs prescribed for her condition, who could slap him hard enough to split his lip and pull his hair until he cried and then, with apparent sincerity, claim to love him more than life. In this moment, the waitress *is* Mother, and Shacket has a score to settle with her.

'Has anyone ever told you that you look like that actress, Riley Keough?' he asks.

This woman is twentysomething and shy enough to blush. 'Oh, she's gorgeous. I'm not gonna rush to a mirror and be disappointed.'

'Good for you,' he says. 'Because, fact is, that's a lie. You have a face like a shithouse rat, and any guy who ever humps you will want to commit suicide afterward.'

Her pleased expression collapses into hurt, into bewildered anger.

'Have a nice day,' he says as he walks away.

He has long known that cruelty is a kind of power, but until recently he has not embraced it as a weapon in his arsenal.

Now, hours later, he needs to eat again. There's a diner associated with the motor inn at which he's parked, but he doesn't want to go in there and get bad food, as he did at the other place. Besides, he's too angry at Megan, the snarky bitch. She thinks she's too good for him. Furious as he is, if he goes into the diner, he'll take his anger out on a waitress or on someone else, and the food will stink, and there'll be a scene. He's got to remember that in spite of what his driver's license says, he's not really Nathan Palmer; he is Lee Shacket, the former CEO of Refine, and he's on the run from what happened at the facility in Springville, Utah. He has changed his appearance, yes, all right, but it's nonetheless a mistake to call attention to himself.

He can eat something when he gets to Megan's place. She'll cook it the way he wants it. She'll do *everything* the way he wants it. He now sees what his mistake was all those years ago. He was too nice to her, too considerate of her feelings. Niceness and consideration get you nowhere with an ice-queen bitch like Megan Grassley Bookman. He'll give her what she deserves, what she wants but doesn't know she wants, and when she's begging for more, he'll walk the hell out on her, leave her in shitty Pinehaven and go to Costa Rica.

It's maybe ninety miles to her place. He will be there before night-fall. They'll have a reunion, talk about the old days, while he does to her what he didn't have the nerve to do back in the day. *I'm afraid our time has passed, Lee.* She'll learn different. He'll turn back the clock. It'll be their time again, all right. *I'm afraid you underestimate how a special-needs child changes your life.* He will show her what she really ought to be afraid of, the bitch. He'll also show her that her changed life can be changed again, for the better, just by slitting the little mute bastard's throat.

He starts the engine and pilots the Dodge Demon out of the parking lot, onto 1-80, heading west. In twenty-four miles, he will leave the interstate for State Route 20. For his entire life, he has been a target of injustice, used and discarded, set up to take the fall for someone else, set up by everyone from Dorian Purcell, to Jason Bookman, to hot Megan Grassley, but he's not going to take it anymore. He feels a power growing in himself, a new Lee Shacket. He is

becoming someone who cannot be denied, someone who doesn't need to play by any rules,
someone who always gets what he wants, someone unlike the world has ever seen before, something
special, something.

15

Because she had not been merely a hired
caregiver during the eighteen months that
Dorothy had battled cancer, because she had
come to love Dorothy almost as if she'd been her
daughter, Rosa Leon felt obliged to be present
during the cremation. She waited hours at the
mortuary and received the urn while it was still
warm from the ashes that it held.

She took that bronze reliquary back to the
grand old house and placed it on the mantel in
the living room. During the next month, as she'd
been instructed, she would continue to live in
the guest suite and organize a memorial service
to be catered on the premises by Dorothy's
favorite restaurant.

*It must not be a solemn affair, Rosa. I want a
celebration. Old friends gathered to share good
memories. Laughter, not tears. Upbeat music.
An open bar, so they can raise a toast to me in
my new life.*

In the absence of Dorothy, the lovely Victorian
house, always a warm and cozy place in the past,
felt cold and cavernous. Although Rosa had
maintained professional composure throughout

62

this sad day, as she stared at the urn on the mantel, she could not restrain her tears any longer.

Dorothy Hummel had been the first experience of tenderness in Rosa's hard life. Hector Leon, her father, a housepainter, had walked out on her and her mother, Helene, when Rosa was just three. By ten thousand slights and insults, Helene had let her daughter know that she was unwanted, the product of rape and forced marriage, though there was ample evidence that the claim of rape was untrue, that her parents had once loved each other, if only briefly. When she was sixteen, Rosa located her father and paid him a visit, seeking only some small measure of the affection that any father owed his child. Hector had none for her. He said Helene had been the biggest mistake of his life, that Rosa was *the mistake of a mistake*, and he forbade her to return. Judging by the disrepair of the old bungalow in which Hector lived, considering the whiskey with a beer chaser standing on his breakfast table at nine o'clock in the morning, he worked too little and drank too much. Perhaps not having him in Rosa's life might be a blessing, but at the time, the rejection hurt.

Throughout high school, she worked weekends in a restaurant, prepping vegetables for the cook and doing whatever scutwork was assigned to her. She received a scholarship to nursing school, paid what it didn't cover out of her own savings, and found that she took pleasure in caring for those in ill health; she soon specialized in home-care patients. She had friends, though none that were close, because she was always working. She had met no men who respected her and one who so *dis*respected her that she had become wary of dating.

Then at the age of thirty-four, she had taken the job with Dorothy and found herself in the very lap of kindness, a caregiver cared for. Her patient was also her nurse. Dorothy saw Rosa as an injured bird who had fallen from the nest before she learned to fly, and if anyone had ever been born to teach a broken spirit how to soar again, that anyone was Dorothy Hummel. Rosa had never read for pleasure, and Dorothy seemed to have read *everything*. Then Dorothy insisted that Rosa read aloud to her, and month by month she found the truth of life in literature, the truth and hope and a new way of living. After residing in this house a year and a half, Rosa's heart grew stronger, and her sense of herself clarified.

If Dorothy had lived *another* year and a half . . .

But she had not. She was gone.

Whatever healing Rosa still required was up to her to achieve.

Blotting the tears from her eyes with a handkerchief, turning from the urn on the mantel, she thought, *I still have Kipp to care for, and he'll look after me just as he did Dorothy. We'll heal each other, me and Kipp.*

The dog was like a child to Dorothy. The bond between them went deeper than mere pet and owner, terms that Dorothy disliked. *I'm not his owner. I'm Kipp's guardian, and he's my*

64

guardian. There was something mysterious about their relationship; Dorothy often hinted as much. In fact, she said that when she was gone and Kipp became Rosa's to care for, there would be a revelation of some kind. *I might just haunt the place so that I can watch it happen!*

And where was Kipp now? He could come and go by his special door, but he never left the property. He must be somewhere in the house. Ordinarily, he would have come running to greet her, a huge grin on that great golden face, his eyes shining with delight. He must have found a place to curl up and grieve.

Moving from the living room to the hall to the dining room, she called for him, but when he didn't come at once, she stopped seeking him. She remembered how pitiable his whimpering sounded the previous night, when Dorothy passed. He was a keenly sensitive boy. He knew Rosa was here, and when he was ready for company in his mourning, he would come to her.

Now she found herself in front of the study door, across the hall from the library. During the eighteen months that she lived and worked in this splendid house, the study door was always locked. Mrs. Champlain, who came in to clean house three days a week, never set foot in the study. Dorothy dusted and swept that room herself until the last six weeks of her life, when she no longer had the energy for the job.

Of course I trust Mrs. Champlain and you entirely, Rosa dear, but that room is my most private place, where I keep all my deepest, darkest secrets. *You may think I'm a foolish old lady who's lived a pampered life, with no secrets darker than having shoplifted a tube of lipstick when I was sixteen, but I assure you that I once had a wild side. And if you don't believe that's true, at least give me the courtesy of assuming there's a one percent chance I might not always have been as boring as I am now. Treat the study as if we're in a Daphne du Maurier novel, as if this house is an alternate-universe version of Manderley, and I am keeping either the murdered and mummified corpse of Rebecca or Mrs. Danvers — or both! — behind that locked door, to spare myself from a long prison sentence.*

From a pocket of her slacks, Rosa now withdrew the key to the study door. Dorothy had given it to her the previous afternoon, ten hours before the crisis came, and instructed that it be used within a day of her passing. Rosa had not been told what she would find in the room, other than a computer on which were stored video files that she must watch.

Although she knew there would be no dead bodies, mummified or otherwise, she hesitated. If indeed there were secrets in this room, and if they might alter her opinion of Dorothy, Rosa Leon didn't want to know them. In the lonely struggle that had been her life to date, she had met few people she admired, none more so than Dorothy. In the unlikely event there had been a dark side to Arthur Hummel's widow, some ugliness of spirit, that discovery would pierce Rosa hardly less than if an archer put an arrow through her breast.

Yet she had promised to view the files on the computer and do what her heart told her was the right thing. A promise made must be a promise kept.

Rosa unlocked the door and went into the study.

The large room measured perhaps twenty-six feet by thirty, with tall windows offering a view of the fabled lake through descending ranks of pines.

To the right stood an antique Biedermeier desk that was large for furniture of that period. Behind the desk, a wall-length work area had been built to match the desk. On it waited a computer, printer, scanner, and other equipment.

In the center of the room were a Biedermeier sofa and two Art Deco armchairs ordered around a large coffee table fashioned from a Chinese kang bed, on which stood an arrangement of antique Japanese bronze vases. Dorothy and Arthur had eclectic tastes and a talent for making a variety of periods and styles work together.

The most unusual thing was the alphabet painted on the wall to the left, twenty-six one-foot-tall black letters stenciled on a white background, plus a series of punctuation marks. There were also symbols: & and % and + and = among them. On the floor in front of that wall stood a low contraption for which she could not discern a purpose.

Rosa went around behind the desk and sat in the office chair and swiveled to face the computer. She switched it on.

During the weeks that Dorothy lacked the

strength to clean the study, a light dust settled on everything, but the system worked.

Dorothy's password was LOVEARTHUR.

There was a separate file of videos. They were numbered.

Rosa clicked on the first one, and when it began to roll, she was surprised to see a healthier Dorothy than the woman she had more recently been caring for. Dorothy appeared as she had been maybe ten months or a year earlier, sitting behind her desk.

Directly addressing the camera, she said, 'Rosa Rachel Leon, you precious girl, I was fortunate to find you in my hour of need, and not merely because you have been giving me excellent care. I'm fortunate also because you're honest, ethical, and blessed with genuine sympathy, with humility in a world of pride and selfishness. Furthermore, you're far more intelligent than you believe.'

A blush warmed Rosa's face, as if she were receiving this praise in the company of the living woman, and tears formed again. She plucked a Kleenex from a box to blot away her blurred vision.

'Within forty-eight hours of my death, Roger Austin will come to see you. As you know, he's my attorney. He will inform you that I have made you my sole heir.'

This was news to Rosa, and she found herself shaking her head as if this must be a dream, as if she must deny what Dorothy said in order to avoid bitter disappointment when she woke.

'The law forbids a caregiver in a hospice

68

situation to inherit from a patient. That's why, after five months in my employ, when I had come to know your heart, we changed your title to Executive Companion and did so with such ironclad legal process that my will can't be undone. Anyway, I've no relative to contest it.'

Rosa found herself so nervous that she wanted to move, work off a sudden frantic energy. But she was so weak-kneed when she got up from the chair that her legs failed her. At once she sat down again.

'After taxes,' Dorothy continued, 'you'll receive this house and all its contents plus liquid assets in the amount of twelve million dollars.'

'I don't deserve this,' Rosa declared, as if the woman on the screen could hear her and be persuaded. 'I was only with you for eighteen months.'

Dorothy had paused in the video, as if she'd known Rosa would at this point talk back to her benefactor. Her smile was impish.

'How I wish I could be there to see you now, girl. I know you will feel overwhelmed, maybe even afraid at first. Fear not. Roger Austin and my accountant, Shiela Goldman, are good people. They will give you reliable investment advice. And in time, if I know you — and I *do* know you — you'll grow wise enough to handle it all yourself.'

'Never,' Rosa said, with a tremor in her voice.

'Yes, you will,' Dorothy insisted with another smile. 'And now to an even bigger surprise. Much bigger. Excuse a bit of crudity, child, but this one will knock you on your ass. Are you ready?'

'No.'

Her arms on the desk, leaning forward, closer to the camera, Dorothy lowered her voice and spoke with a profound seriousness that mesmerized Rosa. 'You know Kipp is a smart dog. But he's enormously smarter than you realize. He's a mystery, a wonder — and out there in the world are others like him. They call themselves 'the Mysterium.' I can only assume he's the product of genetic engineering. Somewhere in his lineage must be laboratory dogs that were products of radical experimentation and perhaps escaped. Dear Rosa, he is as intelligent as we are, and he is a treasure who must be protected. You must be his guardian now. And after you see the videos that follow, after you watch dear Kipp communicating with me using the alphabet on the study wall, you'll not only believe me, but you will, I'm sure, feel that you've found your life's calling.'

Rosa swiveled in the chair to look at the foot-high black letters on the farther wall.

Behind her, Dorothy said, 'Since I was just a little girl, which was a very long time ago, I've had this strange feeling down in the deepest and most secret place in my heart. I think you've had the same strange feeling and, just like me, you've felt you'd be a fool to speak of it.'

A pleasant chill craped the nape of Rosa's neck. She looked through the big windows at the descending forest, the lake beyond: a mystical scene in the waning light, the water like a mysterious loch in another land, where something lived that spawned a legend.

'All my life, Rosa, I've felt that there's hidden

magic in the world, that life is more than what our five senses can reveal to us. I've believed miracles really happen and that one day a miracle would happen to me.'

Even a girl raised in poverty and without love could entertain such a feeling. Perhaps it was *especially* true of a girl raised in poverty and without love, who had no hope other than what she spun from her imagination.

'Life crushes that secret feeling out of us if we let it,' Dorothy continued. 'But I never allowed it to crush that feeling in me, Rosa, and one day the miracle came to me on four paws.'

16

He was a lucky dog.

Children ran and jumped and capered throughout the campground. Little kids and older kids both enjoyed sneaking food to dogs.

As further proof of his luck, he seemed to be the only dog here for the children to feed. Kids tossed balls and skimmed Frisbees through the air, but nothing on four feet joined in the play.

Not everyone had begun cooking yet. A little early for dinner.

But at least two men stood ready at their portable barbecues. The scent of hot charcoal graced the air.

One of the cooks was marinating steaks in a deep pan. He had just begun to light his charcoal.

He was lean and deeply tanned, with his hair slicked back.

On his T-shirt blazed the words FORK OFF, under an image of a fork with three tines. Two tines were bent down. Only the middle one was straight.

This guy did not appear friendly. He smelled of envy and anger.

The second man had thick hamburger patties sizzling on a gas griddle and frankfurters swelling-sweating-charring on the grill.

Kipp took up a position where the action was, next to the grill master with the lesser meats.

He sat, sweeping the ground with his tail, pendant ears pricked as much as their nature allowed, head cocked. Being cute.

Kipp had few peers at this, even if he did say so himself.

Dogs were incapable of bragging, but they were also incapable of false modesty. Things are what they are, and that's that.

The grill master was a person who talked to animals. He was no Doctor Dolittle. He didn't hold a *dialogue*. But he seemed nice.

He smelled of kindness, and he wasn't wearing a rude T-shirt.

He called Kipp 'buddy.' He said, 'I had one like you when I was a kid.'

Instead of swishing his tail, Kipp thumped it on the ground.

'Are you lost, buddy?'

Kipp stopped thumping his tail.

Being lost made him more sympathetic, more likely to be fed.

In fact, however, he wasn't lost. He knew where he was going. The murmuring boy on the Wire drew him.

If he whined and did movie-dog shtick to suggest he was lost, that would be lying.

Those in the Mysterium did not lie to human beings who smelled of kindness. This wasn't exactly a commandment, but it was a serious protocol.

Deceiving people who smelled of anger or envy — or worse — was justified because they were dangerous. Deceiving them could be a matter of survival.

'Are you hungry, fella?'

Kipp thumped his tail against the ground, harder than before.

Without being deceived by a whine, the man who smelled of kindness evidently decided that before him sat a lost and hungry dog. 'I've got something for you.'

With tongs, he put a big, mostly cooked hamburger patty on a paper plate. He put a fat frankfurter beside it.

'When these cool a bit, you can have them.'

Kipp could whine now, because this was a whine of gratitude.

The man stooped and examined Kipp's collar and said, 'No name. No phone number. Maybe you've been injected with a chip.'

Kipp didn't have a chip, but the clasp of his collar contained a GPS and a small lithium battery to power it.

Dorothy hadn't feared that he would run away. But she worried he might be dognapped.

After flipping a few hamburger patties, the man cut into pieces the burger and frankfurter that he set aside for Kipp, to help the meat cool faster.

A woman herded four children to a nearby picnic table. The two boys and two girls resembled her and the kind man. Their puppies.

On the table were potato salad and potato chips and pasta salad and other things that smelled wonderful.

The woman carried a platter of cooked patties and frankfurters to the table. The kids cheered and started building sandwiches.

This was a happy place.

The kind man put the paper plate on the ground, and the meat was cool enough, and Kipp ate it with pleasure.

He did not whine for more. That would have been ungrateful.

Besides, the children at the table were digging into the feast. All he had to do was hang around. More food would be forthcoming.

Indeed, he had to be careful not to accept too much and make himself sick. All of it was delicious.

The moment was lovely, with the food and all, with everyone in this family smelling right, smelling safe, no anger or envy or other more bitter scents arising from them.

Then the Hater arrived behind Kipp, who smelled him too late.

The Hater clipped a leash to Kipp's collar and pulled it tight and said to the kind man, 'Is this your dog?'

'I suspect he's lost. We thought we'd take him home with us.'

'This is a dog-free campground,' the Hater declared. 'He's not allowed. I'm taking him with me.'

He was wearing khaki pants and a khaki shirt, like a uniform.

'When we leave day after tomorrow,' the kind man said, 'we'd be happy to take him with us.'

'He won't be here then,' the Hater said.

He jerked hard on the leash to make Kipp understand that he was in control, and he headed across the campground toward the office at the entrance.

Kipp went without a struggle. This was not a kind man. He might react to resistance with violence when they were out of sight.

The stink of hatred was more intense and more frightening than any other smell, except for certain scents that identified different kinds of insane people.

Sometimes a person smelled of hatred *and* insanity. This man reeked only of the former.

Depending on what all he hated and how intensely he hated it, this might be a difficult man from whom to escape.

Haters lived to hate, to exercise power over those they hated. They were obsessive about it. Focused. Relentless.

The campground office was in a small log cabin at the end of the entry lane from the highway.

Kipp did not want to go in there.

His collar was too tight for him to slip out of it.

He would not bite except in the most extreme

circumstances. That was a protocol of the Mysterium. And it was only right.

Maybe there would be someone else in the office, someone who was not as wicked as this man.

They climbed the steps and went inside.

No one else was there. Only Kipp and the Hater.

17

The day synchronizes with Lee Shacket's mood, the sun fading behind gray shrouds as smooth as casket satin, the overcast slowly descending like a heavy lid. The late afternoon darkles into a long and sullen twilight.

He leaves I-80 for a two-lane state route that rises and falls over nature's wooded contours, cleaves flowering meadows, and for mile after mile offers isolated human habitats only here and there. Shadows gather among the trees in threatening convocations, and the late-summer wildflowers, once bright, seem now to smolder in the fields like fragments of some meteor superheated and shattered as it plummeted through Earth's atmosphere.

Shacket's unrelenting hunger is not merely for food, but as well for justice, for transformation from the victim he has always been, for an undefined but amazing transcendence that he feels will be his. Pressure is building in him like superheated steam in a boiler, psychological

76

pressure but also what seems to be some kind of powerful escalation of his physical abilities. Hour by hour, he feels stronger; his eyesight grows sharper, his hearing keener.

What he feels has something to do with what happened at the Refine facility in Springville, Utah. Engaged in longevity research, seeking to greatly extend the human life span, the richly financed experiments were, at the insistence of Dorian Purcell, focused intensely on archaea, the third domain of animal life. The first domain is eukaryotes, which includes human beings and all other higher organisms. The second domain is bacteria. Microscopic archaea, which lack a nucleus, were long thought to be a kind of bacteria. But they have unique properties, not least of which is the ability to effectuate horizontal gene transfer. Parents pass their genes vertically to their offspring. Archaea pass genetic material horizontally, from one species to another. Their mysterious role in the development of life on Earth is only beginning to be understood, and perhaps it is madness to seek to harness them for the purpose of improving the human genome and extending the human life span.

On the other hand, although Shacket had first thought of the events at the Springville facility as catastrophic, he is beginning to wonder if the opposite is true. Although he has perhaps breathed in hundreds of billions — even trillions — of programmed archaea that are carrying longevity-fostering genes from many species, perhaps it is a mistake to regard the breach of the organism-isolation labs as an existential

77

crisis. One of the scientists in a position of high authority — or Dorian himself — evidently thought it was exactly that and triggered the security program to lock down the complex and eventually burn it to the ground.

Shacket alone escaped, violating protocols by not staying with the ship. To hell with the protocols. He has done the right thing, *the right thing for himself.* Having fled Utah in a panic, he has had time to recover his composure, to reconsider what the consequences of the Springville meltdown might be.

He feels free for the first time in his life. *Free.* He senses some awesome power growing in him, and a thrilling new confidence. In fact, leaving Utah, crossing Nevada, and now motoring west by northwest through the mountains of California, he feels as if he is leaving mere humanity behind. What if horizontal gene transfer via archaea is in the process of editing mortality out of his genome? What if the catastrophe at Springville was not a catastrophe at all, but a great if accidental success, with him as the only beneficiary? He feels a most satisfying contempt for everyone whom he once wanted to please. He's *becoming*, developing into someone superior, and he is excited by the prospect of proving it, of doing any damn thing he wants with any damn one he wants, *to* anyone he wants, starting with Megan Bookman, the ice-queen bitch who needs to be humbled. He will *rule* her.

Or maybe he doesn't have to wait for Megan. In his becoming, perhaps he has already achieved the power to do what he wants, take what he wants. Ahead, on this lonely state highway, a car is stopped on the wide right-hand shoulder. A man is changing the rear tire on the star-board side. A young woman stands watching him. She's wearing shorts and a halter top. She is a hottie. All of Shacket's life, there have been women he wants and can't have, women who respond to his overtures with disinterest or even scorn. This looks like one of those women. She looks like *all* of them.

He slows and pulls off the pavement and stops his Dodge Demon behind the car. It's a black Shelby Super Snake, the quintessential high-performance car, possibly $125,000 off the showroom floor.

He gets out, smiling, being the Good Samaritan. 'You need some help with that?'

'Just a flat,' says the man who is squatting by the rear tire well, using a lug wrench. 'I've almost got it changed.'

'Is this beauty a Shelby?'

'Super Snake, last year's model,' the asshole proudly confirms.

No traffic is in sight in either direction.

'That's true power, sir. That's an epic vehicle. But you can't open her up proper on this back road.'

'Not if you don't want to end up in the trees,' the Super Snake guy agrees. 'But it's fun the way it handles the curves.'

'You like handling the curves, do you?' Shacket asks.

The asshole hears the sneer in Shacket's voice and at once gets to his feet, the lug wrench in hand.

Indicating the woman, Shacket says, 'That bitch of yours sure isn't last year's model.'

'Something wrong with you?' the Super Snake guy asks.

He's tall, as solid as a linebacker, with the arms of a powerlifter. He's never backed down from anyone. He's the kind who's used to intimidating the hell out of other men with just a frown.

'No, sir, nothing wrong with me,' Shacket says.

Under the low sky, the day is still. No sound of oncoming traffic. He would hear engine noise perhaps half a minute or more before any vehicle came into sight.

He smiles. 'Nothing wrong with me that a fine piece of ass like her wouldn't cure.'

'Get in the car, Justine,' the guy tells the bitch. He starts toward Shacket, his face as hard as a sledgehammer, confident in his size, holding the lug wrench as though he'll crack a skull with it.

The woman doesn't move, as if paralyzed by fear. Or maybe she's excited, thinks nothing bad can happen here, gets off watching her man beat the crap out of people.

Like an omen of perilous events, three ravens pass high above, issuing no flight calls, their wings slicing the air with sharp silence. Everything means something important now.

From under his sport coat, Shacket draws the Heckler & Koch Compact .38, which is loaded with hollow-point rounds, and he strides toward the linebacker, putting four bullets in him.

Justine breaks her paralysis and screams. She's the Jamie Lee Curtis of her time, scream queen of the Sierra Nevada. She turns and runs,

80

scissoring her long, smooth legs.

Her strong man collapses, as dead as anyone ever gets, and he rolls down the embankment, limp as rags, all the muscle gone out of him, into the tall grass below.

This is what it's all about, being in command, being empowered, without fear, untouchable. Shacket is a changed man, a *changing* man, fast becoming, becoming someone new, *something else*.

The woman is running down the middle of the highway, heading west, evidently hoping a car or truck will appear.

Instead of sneakers or anything practical, the bitch is wearing sandals with a medium heel. She stumbles once, and then again. One sandal flies loose. She hobbles forward.

Laughing at her frantic, feckless escape attempt, Shacket goes after her.

A black feather floats in front of Shacket, a raven's shedding from on high. He snatches it out of the air, pockets it, a symbol of death bestowed on him as a sign of his new power, to assure him that he may decide who will live and who will die and with what degree of suffering the condemned will perish. Everything seems like an omen now, means something important.

He holsters the pistol, races after the woman, seizes her by her long hair. He yanks her off her feet. Justine tumbles to the pavement. Shacket punches her once, leaving her dazed and limp.

He feels as strong as her dead boyfriend had looked. He scoops her off the blacktop as if she is weightless and carries her to the shoulder of the highway and drops her, kicks her, sends her

81

rolling to the bottom of the slope.

In a fever of desire and triumph, he descends to the woman where she struggles to get up from the tall grass. He falls upon her, pins her beneath him. Recovering from the punch, she struggles under him. But this contest is settled before it's begun, for she is the gazelle and he the lion, she the fly and he the spider.

The sound of a truck engine arises, approaching on the highway above. No one can see them here in the grass, at least twenty feet below the roadbed. Although it's unlikely that anyone in the truck could hear Justine if she screamed, Shacket slams the heel of one hand under her chin and shoves hard, pushing her mouth shut, forcing her head back, her elegant neck arching, trapping her cry in her throat.

Maybe the two cars, one behind the other on the shoulder of this lonely road, will seem curious to the driver of the truck. But with no one in either car, no one flagging passing traffic for help, there isn't any reason to stop and investigate. In fact, in this often lawless and dangerous age, a wise man would keep moving and avoid the risk of involvement.

Judging by the sound of its engine, the truck seems to slow, and Justine apparently has a moment of renewed hope. She bucks and twists under Shacket, tries to force a scream through clenched teeth as he jams the heel of his right hand harder against the underside of her chin. Her taut and supple body squirming under him, her utter helplessness, his absolute power: Although neither of them is naked, this is the most erotic moment of

Shacket's life, and he is rampant.

Justine's hope is a false hope. The truck accelerates, and the sound recedes. She stops struggling, stops trying to scream. The quiet of the wilderness descends, deeper than before, without insect buzz or birdsong, as if every creature that lives here is aware that among them has come one unique unto the world, one who is changed and changing still, one who lives by no rules either of man or nature, who fears nothing, and who should be feared.

He removes his hand from Justine's chin, hoping that she will scream for him, for him alone, now that there's no one else to hear. She looks up into his face, her blue eyes wide, her nostrils flared, breathing hard, and says only, 'Please.'

Shacket likes the sound of that: the word, the pitiable note of entreaty, the recognition that he is her absolute master.

'Say it again.'

'Please. Please don't hurt me.'

He intends to rape her. Instead, to his surprise and hers, he bites. She screams. He bites again, and the biting is wonderful, exhilarating, the most fulfilling thing that he has ever done.

Her terror is his ecstasy.

18

Woody in his room. At his computer. Seeking justice.

They said Woody's IQ was 186. His reading comprehension rate was 160 words per minute. Deduct 160 from 186, and you had the number of letters in the alphabet.

He was born at 4:00 a.m., July 26. July was the seventh month. Twenty-six multiplied by seven was 182. Add four, representing the hour he was born, and you had his IQ.

This was a Wednesday. Woody's dad died on a Wednesday. Exactly 164 weeks had passed since his dad died. Woody began working on 'The Son's Revenge: Faithfully Compiled Evidence of Monstrous Evil' on the second anniversary of his father's death, sixty weeks earlier, when his hacking skills were refined to the point at which no security system, no digital defense, could stand against him. Deduct sixty from 164, and you had the number of pages that were in the document that would convict his father's killers.

None of these numbers — from his IQ and reading comprehension rate to the amount of pages in the report — meant anything useful. They were mathematical coincidences, or perhaps they were patterns indicating a series of algorithms underlying the operation of the universe; but even in the latter case, they were so deeply woven into the matrix of reality that they were beyond human understanding.

However, the way Woody's mind worked, his recognition of such coincidences or mysterious patterns was constant.

This mental quirk, the recognition of obscure patterns, helped him pilot his way through all levels of the internet, from the World Wide Web that everyone used, to the remote archives in the deep web, to the ominous byways of the Dark Web.

To Woody, the internet was a planet of its own, every site a village or a city with its neighborhoods and streets, a planet across which he traveled as if by magic, typing a brief incantation and, with a click, teleporting from one continent to another.

He had opened back doors in numerous computer systems and had implanted rootkits, which made it possible for him to return often and search their archives on such a deep and subtle level that even the best IT-security types were unlikely to detect his presence.

Just in case someone scoped him out as he was cruising through their data, he never went directly from Pinehaven to any back door, but spoofed his way through numerous domestic telecom exchanges and used other tricks, so anyone backtracking him would be flummoxed.

In more than a year of intense effort, he had taken one known fact and Sherlocked his way to more than a hundred pages of evidence that a special counsel, appointed by the attorney general of the United States and given a platoon of investigators, might not have discovered in a decade. When you were a high-functioning autistic genius, your developmental disorder, coming with a singular ability to *concentrate intensely* for long periods of time on what might seem to be mundane facts, was an advantage of great value.

The one fact he'd begun with was his dad's disillusionment with his boss, Dorian Purcell, the megabillionaire. Woody overheard his mom and dad talking once about Purcell's 'messiah complex' and about Dad's desire to give his notice as soon as certain stock options had vested, before 'I have to support ambitions of Dorian's that are just flat-out crazy.'

Once inside the computer system of Parable, Inc. — the parent company of Purcell's sprawling empire — Woody had found his way into Dorian's email and phone directories. They had provided him with a network of other people to learn about. Many of those hundreds of individuals were on one another's directories, a web of elites, but he had noticed that sixteen of them shared a contact with an odd name that intrigued him — Gordius.

When you're an autodidact who teaches himself to read at the age of four, and when you're reading at a college level three years later, and when you're an inward-turned autistic who doesn't spend hours every day in social interaction or engaged in any of the pursuits that occupy most people, you have a great deal of time to fill. The most pleasant way to fill it is by studying and learning things. One of the things Woody had greatly enjoyed learning was classical mythology.

In Greek mythology, Gordius was a peasant who became king of Phrygia. He tied an extremely complicated knot — the famous Gordian knot — that no one could untie. When Alexander learned that whoever solved the knot was destined to rule all of Asia, he simply sliced it with his sword.

This man on sixteen people's directories was named Alexander Gordius. To anyone lacking Woody's unique mind, the name would have looked like just another in a long list. But, to him, it seemed unlikely that someone would be named for both the creator of the Gordian knot and the man who solved it with a sword.

To him it looked like a potential false identity.

Woody had been curious enough to want to know more about this Mr. Gordius. Through a back door in the telecom company that carried the account, he initiated a search and discovered that the billing address for Alexander Gordius was a general partnership based in California, which was owned by a limited liability corporation in Delaware . . . and from there the chase took numerous turns.

He had needed a few days to discover that a bewildering variety of corporate entities, behind which Gordius hid, were all connected in one way or another with Refine, Inc., whose parent company was Parable, Inc. Eventually he had squirreled through the back door of the Refine computer system. Once in there, he'd found and penetrated Alexander Gordius's email files — and discovered that Gordius was actually Dorian Purcell.

To the very exclusive sixteen elites on his directory, Dorian wrote essays identifying serious problems facing humanity — and then proposing solutions. Often controversial solutions. He covered everything from overpopulation to declining population, global warming to global cooling, nuclear-fusion power to the practicality of million-acre solar farms, likely paths to curing cancer, and the possibility of drastically extending the human life span.

Some of what Purcell wrote was intelligent, thoughtful, maybe even doable. However, much of it was as lame as it was pompous. He knew computers and solid-state technology and much related to those fields, but he imagined himself to be an expert on *everything*. Although Woody had studied and learned a great deal, he was well aware that there were vast areas of knowledge about which he was ignorant and probably always would be. There was only so much *time*. He knew what he didn't know. Dorian Purcell, on the other hand, seemed not to know what he didn't know.

The Alexander Gordius email directory contained the sixteen names Woody already had, but in addition there were three very long email addresses that weren't names, that were nothing but series of random letters, numbers, and symbols. He understood that these must be sites on the Dark Web. The primary way to acquire one of these closely guarded addresses was from a like-minded individual. Maybe these were sources for drugs or for child pornography; maybe they were online weapons dealers selling illegal stuff like machine guns and C-4 explosives and shoulder-launched surface-to-air missiles.

Woody had hesitated to check out these sites. He had thought about it for days.

Eventually he had chosen one with forty-six characters in the address and had spoofed to it through the Alexander Gordius email account.

He had been greeted by a black screen with one word in white block letters: TRAGEDY.

A series of quick clips from various TV news programs, both national and local, followed for three or four minutes. There were photographs of people who had died, video of crashed planes strewn across fields and wrecked cars and burning buildings and racing emergency vehicles with flashing lightbars on their roofs, of hospitals and somber police officials in front of microphones and somber doctors in white coats at other microphones. With the images came snippets of audio, the voices of newsreaders and of the grim-faced officials in the clips: '*Died in the flash fire following a violent gas-leak explosion . . . committed suicide by hanging himself from a barn rafter . . . perished in a freak accident . . . was killed by a hit-and-run driver . . . a senseless drive-by shooting thought to have been committed by a member of one of the gangs that plague the city . . . a murder-suicide that rocked this upscale community . . . of a sudden massive stroke at the young age of thirty-eight . . . one of three dead in what police believe is a terrorist event, though no one is yet taking credit . . . *'

When a photo of Jason Bookman flashed onto the screen, Woody had been so startled that he heard only the last few words of the audio: ' — *in the crash of a helicopter owned by the company.*'

Then his dad's face was gone, and more tragedies were cited until the site greeting came to an end. The screen went black, and then three words appeared in white block letters: ENTER YOUR PASSWORD.

Of course Woody hadn't been a user of whatever services were being offered. Therefore, he didn't have a password.

He had exited the site.

He'd sat staring at his blank computer screen for a long time. Maybe an hour. Maybe two. Thinking.

Eventually, with pen in hand and tablet ready, he had spoofed through the Alexander Gordius account and again entered the forty-six-character email address.

TRAGEDY.

The montage of images and audio began to play once more. As the newsreaders and others spoke of the deaths, Woody jotted down the names of the victims.

He was prepared for the photo of his dad. As before, the still shot was followed by video of the smoldering helicopter. '*Jason Bookman, right hand to Parable founder, Dorian Purcell, and his pilot died today in the crash of a helicopter owned by the company.*'

At the end of this introduction, the screen again instructed ENTER YOUR PASSWORD.

Woody had exited the Dark Web site, backed out of the computer system that included the Alexander Gordius email archives, raveled backward through his spoof chain to quiet Pinehaven, this house, this room, and switched off his computer.

That had been months earlier. Since then, he diligently researched the circumstances of the forty-one deaths that had been referenced in the video introduction to the website.

If any of the accidents seemed suspicious to the authorities, none had been reassessed as anything else.

The suicides were confirmed as suicides by medical examiners in the various cities where they had occurred.

None of the gang shootings and terrorist acts had resulted in the arrest of perpetrators.

Certain subtle patterns in these events were apparent perhaps only to an obsessed high-functioning autistic boy with an IQ of 186, who had thousands of hours to devote to such an investigation. Of the forty-one deaths reported, only two others seemed to have ties to Dorian Purcell.

Which meant nothing more than that Purcell wasn't the exclusive user of this Dark Web service.

The site was not a statement about the fragility of life. It wasn't a memorial, an internet wailing wall against which to lament the role of tragedy in the human experience.

Week by week, month by month, Woody had gathered compelling circumstantial evidence that Tragedy was a murder-for-hire operation.

He had been careful not to return to Tragedy, for fear that they might have a way to detect repeated visits that did not result in the input of a password. He'd prowled through Dorian Purcell's email archives both under the billionaire's name and the Gordius identity, but he had not been able to ferret out any password related to the Dark Web site.

Now it was a fateful Wednesday, exactly 164

weeks after Jason Bookman died, sixty weeks to the day since Woodrow Bookman began his investigation. One hundred sixty-four minus sixty equaled the number of pages in 'The Son's Revenge: Faithfully Compiled Evidence of Monstrous Evil,' though he hadn't crafted it to achieve that length. Mere coincidence. Or a consequence of mysterious algorithms by which the universe functioned.

Woody planned to present the document to his mother in the morning. First, however, he intended to return to the Dark Web to confirm that the wicked site was still in operation and that its introductory video remained as it had been months earlier.

As before, he spoofed through several telecom exchanges before invading the Refine computer by the back door that he had long ago established. He used the Alexander Gordius email account to enter the forty-six characters in the Dark Web address.

Black screen, white letters: TRAGEDY.

His vision blurred with tears when he saw his father's face.

For the most part, he hid his grief from his mother. On those occasions when she caught him in his anguish, Woody smiled or even laughed. She asked if they were happy tears, and he nodded, yes.

When he saw her crying, her tears embarrassed him, because he knew they weren't happy tears, also because he felt he should do something to comfort her. But he was who he was — Woody the Mess — and there wasn't anything he could do, so his embarrassment grew into mortification. He didn't want *his* tears to mortify his mother.

The video ended, and the screen presented him with the command: ENTER YOUR PASS-WORD.

He stared at the three words, wondering how much you had to pay to have someone killed so that it looked like an accident or suicide or a terrorist attack. He didn't have any money. His mom bought him what he needed. He couldn't ask her to pay to have Dorian Purcell killed by a runaway truck or by a fall down a long flight of stairs. She might be sent to prison. She wouldn't like it there.

Woody would be okay with going to prison himself; he didn't mind being alone in a small room, with nothing to do but read and think. But of course they didn't send eleven-year-old kids to the stir. Anyway, the murderers behind Tragedy probably wouldn't kill Purcell even for a gajillion dollars. As far as Woody could tell, this murder-for-hire website catered exclusively to evil people who really, really, really wanted good people to die. If it had been the other way around, if their business model had been to wait for good people to pay for evil people to be killed, they probably wouldn't have a lot of customers for their service. Good people didn't solve their problems that way. Which was one reason why bad people got away with being bad for so long.

He might have continued staring at ENTER YOUR PASSWORD and brooding about good and evil, but a strange and disturbing thing happened. The three words vanished from the screen, and after a few seconds of blackness, two words in white letters appeared before him: YOU AGAIN.

19

In the study of the house above the lake, through a series of videos, the late Dorothy Hummel chronicled her wonder-filled time with Kipp. Rosa Leon, still in a pleasant state of shock occasioned by the news that she had inherited her employer's estate, watched one after the other with fascination.

Speaking to the camera, Dorothy said that she had bought Kipp from a breeder when he was sixteen weeks old, a fast-growing ball of fur, full of spirit and curiosity. She'd had dogs before, all golden retrievers, and she knew how puppies usually were, so in just a few days, she realized that Kipp was different from others of his kind.

She fed him two meals a day, one at seven o'clock in the morning and one at three thirty in the afternoon. By the third day in her company, Kipp fell into the habit of coming to Dorothy five minutes before each feeding. He'd sit before her and gently, politely tap her foot with a fore-paw. Dorothy said she'd previously had dogs with an intuitive sense of time, but little Kipp took it one step further a week into their relationship. Dorothy was curled up in an armchair, engrossed in a novel, and Kipp had no foot to tap. He wasn't a barker, so when she failed to notice his impatient pacing, he went into the kitchen, leaped onto a chair, retrieved her wristwatch, which she'd taken off and left on the table, brought it to her in his mouth, and dropped it on her lap.

When Dorothy realized it was feeding time, Kipp's act stunned her. She got up from the armchair and stood looking at him, and he returned her stare as if to say, *What do you think about* that?

She had always talked to dogs as if they understood her, and she didn't feel the least bit foolish when she asked him if he knew the purpose of a watch. In answer, he went to the archway between the living room and the downstairs hall, and she followed him as he led her to the grandfather clock in the entrance foyer. Wristwatch and clock. He turned and padded along the hallway to the kitchen, with Dorothy close behind; she found him standing past the pantry door, gazing up at the wall clock.

Snatching her iPhone from the table, she had made a video that she later imported to her computer and that now replayed for Rosa. Dorothy asked Kipp to identify the refrigerator, and he went to it. She asked him to go to the sink, and he did. She asked him to go to the cooktop, to the back door, to the trash compactor, to the hall door, to the laundry room door, which he did, did, did, did, did, tail wagging the whole time.

The next day, Dorothy had bought a video camera.

As if he had second thoughts about revealing his extraordinary nature, Kipp refused to repeat his performance. He reacted to her entreaties with yawns and puzzled expressions, wandered away, found his nearest bed, and took a nap.

Over the next couple of weeks, however, Kipp discovered he was a dog who loved stories. He was unable to play dumb dog any longer.

20

YOU AGAIN.

As Woody considered those ominous words, his mouth flooded with saliva, as if maybe he was going to throw up, his heart pounded, and he felt as if the o in You was an eye that stared at him without blinking.

They couldn't be looking at him. For one thing, he had a piece of painters' tape over the camera in his computer. Besides, he had spoofed to them through multiple exchanges; and there was no way that they could track him to source in the short amount of time that he had been on their site today.

The two words blinked off the screen, and letters appeared from left to right, as if someone was texting him: Y-O-U A-R-E N-O-T . . .

Woody watched with growing horror as the message completed: YOU ARE NOT ALEXANDER GORDIUS.

They couldn't know all the exchanges through which he'd jumped to get there, couldn't know his origin, not this fast, but they knew whose account he had hijacked to visit them.

Those words blinked off the screen, and four more appeared letter by letter: WE WILL FIND YOU.

He bailed out of the site, dropped off the internet, switched off his computer. He wheeled his chair backward, crawled into the knee space of his workstation, and pulled the computer plugs, though that precaution seemed both unnecessary and pointless.

The security program at Tragedy evidently monitored the origin of each visitor to the site. And if someone visited but had no password to enter, the program apparently issued an alert to the effect that they might be the target of a fishing expedition by someone not on their client list. He had gone to the site twice before. Although months had passed between those contacts and his third visit today, their security system had been lying in wait for him.

Okay.

All right.

Stay cool. No reason to sweat it. No problemo. Zip, zero, nada. In such a short time, they can't possibly have tracked him to source through a series of nine exchanges. Anyway, he had used a few other deceptions to cover his trail. And he would never, never, never go back there.

Sweat broke out on his brow, and nausea rolled through him. He needed something to settle his stomach. A Coca-Cola. That was all he needed, a Coca-Cola, and then he'd feel all right.

21

Kipp in the kingdom of the Hater.

Stitched on the pocket of the man's khaki uniform shirt was the name FRANK.

He had a black mustache and eyebrows almost thick enough to be two more mustaches. His eyes were hard little green marbles.

Frank smelled not only of hatred but also of garlic, verbena aftershave, coconut-scented hand sanitizer, antiperspirant, and ChapStick, among other things.

His work shoes exuded the odor of fresh human urine, suggesting that when he had most recently peed, he'd not at first aimed well.

In addition to a metal desk and two visitor chairs and an office chair and file cabinets, the front room of the cabin contained a grizzly bear.

The life-size sculpture had been carved out of a log. The seven-foot-tall bear stood on its hind feet, arms reaching, teeth bared.

The bruin looked so fierce that Kipp whimpered even though he knew it wasn't real.

Evidently out of concern that the grizzly would topple over in a quake and crush someone, two steel rods extruded from its back and were bolted to the wall.

Frank the Hater tied Kipp's leash to one of those rods.

Pretending meek submission, Kipp settled at the feet of the bear and sighed as if with resignation.

In fact, he was waiting patiently for an

opportunity to escape.

Dogs were the most patient creatures on the planet. They passed their lives waiting for their humans to walk them, play with them, cuddle them.

No matter how attentive their people were, dogs spent more time waiting than doing.

Which was okay. Humans were busy, with more responsibilities than dogs would ever have. Most dogs.

Frank the Hater went around behind his desk and sat in his chair and plucked the handset from his phone. He keyed in a number.

When someone answered, the Hater said, 'I have us a good one, Fred. He's a golden, maybe from pure stock. Looks like a show dog.'

After a listening pause, Frank continued. 'Didn't have to nab him from anyone. He's a stray.'

I'm not a stray, Kipp thought. *I'm an orphan on a mission.*

'If we breed him to every golden bitch we can find,' Frank said, 'it'll be like printing money.'

Fred said something, and Frank replied. 'He's the docile kind. He'll take to a cage and do what he's told. See you in an hour?'

After he hung up, the Hater looked across his desk at Kipp. Now he also smelled of greed.

'My brother's gonna breed you till you drop, young fella. There's worse ways to spend a life.'

They were puppy-mill operators.

The breeder dogs in those operations lived their entire lives in small cages. Poorly fed. Rarely if ever exercised. No medical care. Never bathed, their coats matted, bodies riddled with ticks.

Puppy-mill dogs lived in despair. They never

knew affection or play, only cruelty.

Kipp gave no indication of alarm. He yawned and sighed and closed his eyes as though to take a nap.

Maybe the time was coming when the protocols of the Mysterium would allow him to bite Frank the Hater.

22

Rosa Leon needed a drink. She didn't use alcohol often, just an ice-cold bottle of Corona now and then. Becoming a millionaire and the caretaker of a superintelligent dog, both in one day, called for something stronger than beer.

Dorothy had liked a cocktail or two in the evening. Her study included an under-the-counter refrigerator and an icemaker. The refrigerator contained, among other things, lemon-flavored vodka.

Rosa found a glass, put some ice in it, and poured a double shot. She returned to the office chair and the computer — and the amazing videos.

After the day of the watch and the clocks, almost two weeks passed while Kipp had played dumb puppy. He was concerned that he should not have revealed his true nature so soon after coming to live with Dorothy — or perhaps ever.

Those in the Mysterium had different views about to whom and when the truth of them should be revealed. Their protocols forbade making such revelations to anyone who smelled of hatred. They were to take into their confidence only those who smelled of kindness and love, who had about them no scent of envy or greed.

Dorothy was certainly a person of righteous qualities, but young Kipp had been impetuous when he did the trick with the watch and all that followed. In the experience of the Mysterium, people needed to be carefully prepared for this revelation. They handled it better if they first had slowly come to *suspect* they were dealing with a dog who was more than a dog.

Kipp's love of stories made it impossible for him to keep his great secret for years or even months. Dorothy had been a lifelong heavy reader, as had been her husband, Arthur. Books were a key decor item in their house, rooms shaped around shelves. When she cooked or worked one of the large jigsaw puzzles she enjoyed, she didn't listen to music, but instead to audiobooks. The dog could not conceal that the narrator's voice enthralled him. Whether he sat or stretched out in one position or another, his eyes remained on the MP3 player. He never napped when a book was playing. Dorothy watched him surreptitiously and saw how reliably startled he was by unexpected twists in the story and how certain emotional scenes caused him to pant or whimper or chuff in ways quite appropriate to the circumstances of the characters.

As Dorothy had spent a December morning and afternoon in the kitchen, baking for the coming holiday, the audiobook they listened to was *A Christmas Carol* by Charles Dickens. In the chapter titled 'The Last of the Spirits,' when the Ghost of Christmas Yet to Come conveyed Scrooge into the Cratchit house on the day of Tiny Tim's death, Kipp retreated to the farther end of the kitchen and sat facing into the corner, his head hung low. Dorothy watched him for a moment and then paused the audio to ask if he was sad. Kipp turned his head to look at her over his shoulder, and he issued a sorrowful whimper.

Now, as Rosa watched the video of Dorothy recounting all this, she realized that she had become as enchanted with her benefactor's story as Kipp had been with *A Christmas Carol*, and she wondered why she had no doubt whatsoever that it was true. Well, for one thing, Dorothy had been neither delusional nor a liar. And in retrospect, Rosa saw that in her own interactions with Kipp, there had been moments when he had charmed her with behavior that seemed unlike that of an average dog; on other occasions, he had been so quick-witted that he briefly disquieted her. Intuitively she had known something about Kipp was wonderfully strange, but the hard life that she had led conditioned her to reject any consideration that there might be magic in the world and instead to resort always to cold reason.

On the computer screen, Dorothy introduced the rest of her story with a wide smile and a shake of her head. 'And so I told him that the Ghost of Christmas Yet to Come was showing Scrooge not what *would* be, but only what *might* be. I put the MP3 player on the floor and told him that Tiny Tim wouldn't die, that I'd play the rest of the book for him only if he stopped this pretense of ordinariness.

'He ran to the player and stood over it, staring down at it, wagging his tail furiously. I turned it on, and he sat listening to the rest without moving. That night, I designed a rather clumsy version of the pedal-operated laser pointer that would eventually be refined, and which Kipp would use to spotlight letters of the alphabet to communicate with me. I must tell you, Rosa, I felt like a bespelled child in a fairy tale or some little girl in a Spielberg movie, and at the same time I wondered if I might be going mad, a doddering old woman who could no longer trust her senses. But if I doddered into anything, I doddered into the fantastic truth of what Kipp is.'

23

The carved grizzly was stupid. Maybe brown bears and black bears roamed the California mountains, but not grizzlies.

What was the point of having it here, anyway?

To terrify the campers and drive their business away?

Although dogs had lived with people for thousands of years, a lot of things people did mystified Kipp — giant wood grizzly bears no more or less than abstract impressionist art and nose rings.

103

Worse than a grizzly bear, Fred, the brother of Frank the Hater and probably a Hater as well, was en route.

Even a dog of greatly enhanced intelligence might find it difficult to escape from a puppy-mill cage and chained servitude.

The leash tethering Kipp to the carving of a bear was eight or ten feet long. He managed to turn and get a mouthful of it.

Although the fabric proved to be tough, his teeth were up to the task. He chewed and tugged vigorously.

From his office chair, Frank the Hater said, 'What the hell are you doing?'

Even if Kipp had been able to talk, he wouldn't have stopped chewing to explain his intention to escape.

If the question wasn't rhetorical, Frank was even dumber than he looked.

'I know your kind, dog. I know how to deal with you.'

Green eyes flashing under his mustache-size eyebrows, the Hater came around the desk.

Kipp growled but continued chewing on the leash.

When the Hater tried to grab the back of the dog collar, Kipp sidled around to face him, growling more ferociously as he chewed.

'Better shut you in the bathroom till Fred gets here.'

Frank the Hater reached up to untie his captive from one of the steel rods between the bear and the wall.

Kipp dropped the leash and snapped at his

captor. He didn't intend to bite, just to scare the man off.

Suddenly reeking of anger as much as he did of hatred, Frank backed away a few steps.

He took off his belt and clenched the tongue of it in his right fist. The buckle dangled at the free end.

'Teach you a lesson,' said Frank the angry Hater.

When he lashed with the belt, the buckle missed Kipp and cracked against the wooden bear.

'*Down!*' the man ordered.

Kipp did not lie down. He growled and bared his teeth.

'Down! *Down*, damn you!' the Hater commanded.

He raised his right hand high, intending to whip harder this time, more accurately, maybe repeatedly.

Just then, the front door opened and a stranger came in. He said, 'Hey, hey, hey! What're you doing?'

'Stay back,' Frank the Hater warned. 'I've got a vicious damn dog here. He's a half-wild stray.'

Wagging his tail, Kipp whined as pathetically as he knew how and cowered before the Hater's raised fist.

'Never hit a dog,' said the newcomer.

The stink of Frank's anger grew more intense. He was enraged now with both Kipp and the stranger.

'Get your ass out of here before you're bitten,'

said the Hater, 'and leave this to me.'

'I'll leave when I've got my dog,' the man declared, stepping between Kipp and the Hater.

'Your dog? He's a damn stray. No license tag on his collar.'

Untying the lead from the steel rod, the newcomer said, 'He's my dog.'

'Like hell he is.'

'If you strike at him again, so help me God, I'll cinch that belt around your neck tight enough to make your face turn blue.'

In addition to the garlic, verbena aftershave, coconut-scented hand sanitizer, antiperspirant, ChapStick, pee on the shoes, anger, and hatred, Frank also smelled of the particular kind of fear that had a sour edge and was called cowardice.

'This here's a dog-free campground,' he blustered. 'Always has been dog-free, and I mean to keep it dog-free. You can't have a dog on my watch.'

Reading the name on the khaki shirt, the stranger said, 'I won't be checking in, Frank. Cancel the reservation for Hawkins.'

'If you haven't checked in yet, he can't be your dog.'

Ignoring the Hater, the newcomer smiled down at Kipp. 'Come on, boy, let's blow this dump.'

As Kipp's rescuer opened the front door, Frank the Hater made one last attempt to assert his authority. 'He can't be your dog.'

'Put your belt on before your pants fall down, Frank. I haven't had dinner yet, so don't ruin my appetite.'

24

Rosa sat for a few minutes in the grip of the strangest web of emotions that she had ever known. Spending this time with Dorothy's recordings had sharpened her grief. Yet the videos of Dorothy and Kipp communicating with the aid of the alphabet wall and the laser pointer had been captivating, exhilarating. Sadness contested with elation in a way that she had never before experienced. Amazement, which was of the intellect, and astonishment, which was of the heart, matured into awe that weighed so heavily on her that she could not get up from the chair. And then she did.

She went to the alphabet wall and stood staring at it for a minute or two before kneeling at the motorized laser pointer. The device, based on Dorothy's design, had been built for her by a local mechanic named John Cobb. Mr. Cobb had wondered for what reason she required such a thing. She'd told him that it had applications in a classroom and that she would say no more because, after a period of testing, she intended to obtain a patent on it. This lie satisfied Cobb as perhaps he would not have been satisfied if she had told him that she needed it to better communicate with her dog.

A flip switch on the center column turned on the laser pointer and the motor that operated it. Mounted on a gimbal, the pointer swiveled at once to fix its red dot on the letter *A*. Four canted pedals controlled the device. From left to right: The first pedal moved the red dot up; the second moved it down; the third to the left; the fourth to the right. They were meant to be pressed by a paw, but Rosa's hand served just as well.

Remembering as best she could what she had seen in one of the videos, to get a sense of how laborious had been this method of communication, Rosa worked the answer to a question that Dorothy had asked Kipp: *You say you can communicate with others of your kind at any distance. But how?*

One by one, with the use of the pedals, the pointer now picked out the letters as Kipp had done, which Dorothy had written down as she watched from her desk, and which Rosa had copied.

TELEPATHY. BIRDS HAVE A FORM OF IT, WHICH IS WHY EVERY MEMBER OF A FLOCK CAN CHANGE DIRECTION IN FLIGHT AT THE SAME INSTANT. ELEPHANTS HAVE IT, THE WAY THEY COME FROM A DISTANCE TO THE SIDE OF ONE WHO IS DYING. BUT THE MYSTERIUM'S TELEPATHY IS MUCH STRONGER. WE CALL IT THE 'WIRE.'

Either the first of their kind learned English in some genetics lab where they had been engineered, or after escaping, maybe they picked it up by listening to the people who cared for them. The how of this was lost in the mists of their creation. Currently, however, the young dogs received the English language and packets of other knowledge from their elders over the Wire, in mere minutes, in what amounted to the installation of a program.

Many high-tech mavens, like the flamboyant Elon Musk and the lesser-known Ray Kurzweil, dreamed of the Singularity, the moment when human and machine intelligence would merge, ushering in the posthuman era. They claimed that augmented human brains, injected with a neural lace, would connect with one another by telepathy and almost instantaneously share vast architectures of knowledge and theory that once would have taken years for one person to teach another.

The Mysterium had achieved at least that one goal of the cult of the Singularity without the need to become partly machines. They didn't know how this might have happened, whether their creators intended it or if the telepathy was an unanticipated consequence of the genetic engineering that had enhanced their intelligence. What was, simply, was; they saw no need to brood excessively about it.

Rosa switched off the motorized laser pointer and got to her feet and stood for a moment, trembling at the prospect of seeking out Kipp, wherever he might be huddled in grief, and trying to begin a life together. He had loved Dorothy with such devotion. No one had ever loved Rosa with such fervor. She doubted that anyone could. She was not as special as Dorothy and could only be a disappointment to Kipp.

She went to the windows that provided a view of the forest in which the overcast had laid down an early twilight. A mist rose off the lake, creeping uphill through the trees, its millions of tiny droplets reflecting what little light the day offered, fluorescing as if it were not a cloud but the ghost light of spirit legions haunting the day's end.

Perhaps because Rosa Leon had been abandoned by a father who called her 'the mistake of a mistake,' and because her mother had not loved her, and because she had grown up without the experience of affection that would have taught her how to make friends more easily, she acutely felt not merely the wonder of sweet Kipp and the Mysterium, but also the essential loneliness with which they surely contended even though telepathy was a powerful bond.

After all, they numbered only eighty-six, such a small community that existential angst must on some level trouble them. For lack of numbers, their kind could go extinct. New members of the Mysterium appeared on the Wire so seldom, the assumption had to be that the gene sequence that made them unique among all other dogs was not easily passed down from generation to generation. As far as Dorothy and Kipp had been able to determine, he alone of his litter was a Mysterian.

Although one like Kipp could show up in the litter produced by two ordinary dogs, that was rare, the expression of Mysterian genes that were recessive either in the male or female. As a consequence, Mysterium protocols that regarded mating had for some time required them to choose a mate only from among their own kind. But as the number of males and females was not

110

always in perfect balance, at times some of them had no immediate hope of a mate. At the moment, there were more males than females.

Two other constraints hampered the growth of their community. First, monogamy. In nature there were many species that mated for life. This was not ordinarily true of dogs, but the Mysterians had decided that it was true for them, and they were faithful to their mates as perhaps most of humanity was not. Also, for whatever reason, they didn't produce large litters, as did ordinary dogs. There was a tendency for some females to be barren and some males to be sterile, and even when litters formed, they were no larger than three; often there was no litter at all, just one pup.

With no prospect of a mate and having lost his beloved human companion, Kipp had only the community of the Wire. Although that was precious, it was not enough for a creature as sociable as he'd always been. In Rosa's estimation, he deserved better than her.

She sighed and said, 'But I'm what you have, dear Kipp.'

As the ascending mist pressed through the pines and reached the yard beyond the flagstone terrace, Rosa turned from the window and went in search of the grieving dog who was more than a dog, who was in fact hers to cherish and protect, like the child she'd never had.

She started in the kitchen, because that and the library were Kipp's favorite rooms. Earlier, before she'd gone to the mortuary to make arrangements and attend the cremation, she had put out a bowl of food for Kipp and another of fresh water. Both were untouched.

In his grief, he might have had no appetite, though goldens were chowhounds. Nevertheless, he would have needed water.

Disquieted but not yet alarmed, Rosa went room to room through the ground floor, calling his name. Her voice echoed off the walls with an eerie hollowness, as if all the furniture had been removed and the windows boarded up and the house abandoned to the merciless progress of time and decay.

As she climbed the stairs and reached the upper floor, Rosa was shouting urgently. 'Kipp! Where are you, Kipp?'

Disquiet swelled into a terrible apprehension, a piercing fear that she'd already failed at fulfilling this greatest responsibility of her life. Chamber by chamber, through closets, along corridors, peering under this and behind that, upstairs twice from end to end, downstairs again, front to back, she searched but wasn't rewarded by the sight, the sound, or any trace of him. Kipp was gone.

25

In the front passenger seat of the Range Rover, safety harness snugged around him, Kipp liked what he smelled of his rescuer.

Kindness, confidence, a hint of soap, the fresh minty scent of chewing gum, the fragrant juice of trodden wild grass on his shoe soles, and very little ear wax, among other things.

No aftershave, no coconut-scented hand sanitizer, no misfired urine anywhere on him.

As they pulled out of the campground toward the state route, the man said, 'Thanks to my mom and dad, my name's Brenaden. If they know what's good for them, people call me Ben.'

In the campground office, he had told Frank the Hater to cancel the reservation for Hawkins. So he was Ben Hawkins.

'What do people call you?' Ben asked.

Kipp grinned at him.

'You're the strong, silent type, huh?'

They turned northwest. That was good. The murmuring thoughts of the young boy on the Wire were coming from that direction.

'I'll think of a name for you. I'm good at names.'

Kipp leaned forward in his harness to sniff the glove box. It contained some kind of cheese crackers.

'But we won't rush the name thing. Names are important. In my line of work, I have to come up with a lot of memorable names.'

Kipp could smell peanut butter between the cheese crackers in the glove box.

'I write novels,' Ben said. 'What line of work are you in?'

To convey certain emotions to Dorothy, Kipp had developed a few special noises. As an expression of amusement, he made a soft rapid panting sound: *Heh-heh-heh-heh-heh*.

'I used to be a Navy SEAL. When I signed up

113

for that, I didn't realize how many people would be shooting at me. So after like eight years, when I was still alive, I decided to change careers.'

Kipp looked away from the glove box, cocked his head, regarded his rescuer with interest.

'Now some book critics snipe at me, but they don't kill anyone. Though there's one I suspect has bodies buried in his basement.'

Nature was full of patterns, and life was full of coincidences, and Kipp believed that something like destiny was always at work.

Dorothy loved books.

Kipp got his love of stories from her.

Now here was a writer of stories.

Who was also a warrior. If destiny was real, the warrior part of Ben Hawkins was probably as important as the writer part.

Which meant maybe serious trouble was coming.

'It's getting late to set up camp.'

On both sides of the highway, the woods filled with gloom.

Ben said, 'We'll find a motel. They might not take dogs, so you'll have to use your invisibility cloak.'

Kipp issued a *heh-heh-heh-heh-heh* and squirmed partly free of the harness, so that he could lie on the seat, below window level.

After driving the better part of a minute in silence, and glancing repeatedly at his passenger, Ben said, 'There's something strange about you, Rin Tin Tin.'

Kipp grumbled rather than growled.

'You don't like that name?'

114

Again Kipp grumbled.

'Okay, all right. We'll find a better one, Scooby-Doo.'

Heh-heh-heh-heh-heh.

26

A meat loaf was finishing in one oven, and a potato-and-cheese casserole appeared nearly ready to come out of the other oven, and on the breakfast table, a platter of muffins glistened under lemon icing. In the refrigerator were a bowl of egg salad, chicken breasts in a marinade, cleaned cauliflower, peeled and sliced carrots.

Verna Brickit, the three-times-a-week housekeeper, who would be perfect casting if Hollywood ever remade the old Ma and Pa Kettle movies, washed dishes, while Megan dried them and put them away.

The two dishwashers were of the generation produced after the latest round of government regulations related to water and energy usage, and very little came out of them clean. The main purpose they served was to fill in what otherwise would have been two gaping holes in the cabinetry.

Verna said, 'What makes people who've never designed a useful piece of machinery in their lives think they know how a dishwasher ought to work?'

'Hubris,' said Megan.

'A pox on all their houses!' Verna declared. 'And don't get me started on toilets. Will there ever be a toilet again that gives you enough water so you only have to flush once, or am I just doomed to carpal tunnel syndrome of the right hand?'

'TMI, Verna.'

Verna refused to vote for any of the current political parties on the ballot. She was waiting for a new party to be formed that she called 'the Common Damn Sense Party.'

'Would you go to Mars with a group of damn fools who think they can colonize it tomorrow?' Verna asked.

Drying a colander, Megan said, 'I wouldn't go to Mars even with the greatest group of geniuses who ever lived. I like having air to breathe.'

'I saw on TV this Chinese billionaire wants to get a colony going on Mars in seven to ten years, so if an asteroid hits the earth or nuclear war wrecks the planet, humankind won't all be destroyed. Hell, there's about enough water on Mars to flush a toilet twice, but he thinks it could be a swell place to live.'

'Some people, if they get enough billions,' Megan said, 'it seems to give them a little too much self-confidence.'

'I'll guard against that when I make my first billion.' Verna set the last dish, a mixing bowl, in the drying rack. 'The meat loaf and potatoes should be ready in a few minutes. I'll put them out to cool and then be off.'

'Give my best to Sam.'

'He threatened to fix the lawn mower himself this afternoon. I want to get home while he still has both hands.'

As Verna snatched up a large plastic bag by its

knotted neck, to take it outside to the trash can, Megan hung the damp dish towel on its rack. 'See you Friday.'

'Tell Woody I made the muffins specially for him. Have a couple yourself, skinny as you are.'

'I bet they don't have good muffins on Mars.'

As she opened the back door, Verna said, 'They don't have shit on Mars.' She paused before stepping outside, turned to Megan, and said, 'I haven't breathed a word to you about the painting you've been working on, Woody and the deer, but now it's almost done . . . ' She hesitated. 'I'm no fancy art critic, so maybe I don't know what I'm talking about.'

'Most fancy art critics don't know what they're talking about, either. You've got eyes. So tell me. I won't be offended.'

'Well, I've got to say it's a damn good thing you came back to Pinehaven. You healed your heart here and came into the fullness of your soul. You couldn't have painted anything that good if you were somewhere else.'

'Thank you, Verna. That's very sweet.'

'I wish your mother had lived to know Woody and to see that painting, how it brings a chill along your spine, a good chill.'

Sarah Grassley had died of leukemia when Megan was fifteen. Her father remarried five years later and lived now in Florida with his new family. She wasn't estranged from him, wished they were closer, but he was a man with a limited supply of affection. He seemed able to deal with her only as if he were an uncle rather than her father.

117

Verna took the trash outside, leaving the door open behind her.

Not having connected with Woody in a while, Megan went upstairs to make sure that everything was all right with him.

27

After the action in the wild grass with Justine, Lee Shacket finds himself following the wet scent and the slithery susurration of a stream that flows through the meadow. He kneels on its bank.

He is satiated. His limbs are heavy, and his thoughts are slow, and he has never felt more complete.

In the fading light, the sliding water doesn't make a good mirror. His reflection is faint and distorted, and his eye sockets appear to be empty.

With one hand, he smooths the water, as though he can still its rippled surface and see himself more clearly, but this doesn't work.

He washes the blood out of his hair, from his face. He cups his hands and scoops from the stream and drinks. At first, the water has the flavor of blood, but then it acquires a lesser taste.

He strips off his black leather sport coat. After shrugging out of the shoulder rig, he puts it aside with the pistol. He discards his spattered shirt.

He's gotten blood on his T-shirt and jeans, though not much. Anyway, the T-shirt and jeans are black, so the stains don't show.

Besides, the scent appeals to him. Semi-metallic. Not like any other smell. It's the exciting odor of power, dominance, triumph.

In his great triumph, he wants to leave the meadow for the woods and find a safe place and curl up there and sleep.

He stands now on the bank of the stream, staring across it and into the trees, into the shadows coiling around the trunks and up into the branches, a serpentorium of shadows.

Darkness is gathering within and without him. He senses that it's different from all other darknesses that have come before it. This will be a generous and welcoming darkness, one in which he will at last feel at home and never again be a victim.

In time there will be Costa Rica and all the money to have anything he wants — anything, anybody — but right now he feels the need to give himself to the arms of darkness and sleep.

Then he sees the pistol in the holster, lying at his feet, and he is reminded of Megan Bookman, remembers how she treated him back in the day and earlier this afternoon on the phone.

He can't tolerate being disrespected like that. If you allow yourself to be disrespected, you're weak. The weak inevitably become prey. Prey dies. Prey dies by tooth and claw.

Leaving the holster behind, pistol in hand, he retrieves his black sport coat and sets out across the meadow.

He thinks he's going to his car, the Dodge, but somehow he finds himself standing over the dead woman, Justine.

A sort of manic glee overcomes him at the sight of her ravaged corpse, a sense of immeasurable superiority. A wet, snickering laugh escapes him.

Who was she, after all?

Just another hot girl.

So easy to take, to break.

All his life, he had allowed such girls to say no to him. He should never have let them say no to him. No isn't a choice for them any longer.

A sudden exhilaration burns away his lethargy. His heavy-lidded eyes open wide to the wonder of what he is becoming.

He spits on her remains and spits again.

Without quite realizing what he is about to do, Shacket finds himself urinating on the corpse. His stream is strong and fragrant.

This kill belongs to him. Nothing else can want it, claim it.

He makes his way through the tall grass to the corpse of the man whose muscles availed him nothing. Shacket urinates again.

He is renewed. He zippers himself away. Like something that might live under bridges in expectation of passing children, he scampers up the long slope to the roadway, where the two vehicles wait.

In his Dodge Demon, powering forward, he leaves one state highway for another, heading north toward the great attractant, toward the woman who should always have been his.

Not much farther. He knows her address. He has seen her home from the air on Google Earth, also on Google Street View.

Ever since Jason died, Shacket has been

keeping track of Megan, the ice-queen bitch. He knows what she needs better than she does, and he will wake her to the need to please him.

In half an hour, he reaches Pinehaven, passes through town, and continues on the state route until her house appears on the left. He almost swings into the driveway, but realizes that too bold an entry will be a mistake.

He continues past the house. In less than a quarter of a mile, he arrives at a lay-by. He pulls off the pavement and parks in the deep shade of ancient pines.

When he gets out of the car, he stands by it, inhaling the pleasantly cool air, the fragrance of pines, the forest mast. He can also detect the scents of small animals cowering in the underbrush; he can't differentiate one from the other by species, although maybe one day he will.

With the highway to one side of him and the wilderness to the other side, he is a creature of two worlds. Perhaps some men, during a profound becoming such as this, would worry that they might soon belong in neither world. Shacket doesn't doubt that he will belong in both, will *dominate* both.

The billions of programmed archaea that he inhaled in the Utah facility have swarmed through his blood, through his flesh and bone and brain, where they remain at work, inserting new genetic material into every cell in his body. What that material might be, he cannot say. But the particular group of researchers at Refine's Springville laboratories had been identifying those useful genes in everything from fungi to insects to lower animals that they believed would enhance the human immune system and increase longevity.

They had the best of intentions, and intentions mattered.

They're all dead now, gone to ashes because some damn fool panicked and pressed the doomsday button, convinced that a release of programmed archaea into the environment would precipitate some genetic plague. But archaea are not bacteria; they can't replicate the particular genetic material they brought with them into Shacket. Whatever it might be, that material was a one-time cargo with which the scientists loaded them. If Shacket is infected with biological catastrophe, he can't pass it on to others, nor can these redesigned archaea, which have been engineered to be short-lived and incapable of reproduction.

Anyway, there is no biological catastrophe. He is stronger than he has ever been. His hearing and sense of smell are growing more sensitive by the hour.

His sight in particular is improving. When he turns to stare into the forest, the details of that woodscape resolve out of the steadily deepening shadows as they might for a cat. Felines have a degree of night vision thanks to the many-layered mirrors behind their retina.

And what secrets of the night can be seen by the multifaceted, metallic-sheen eyes of certain moths that thrive in darkness?

Instead of a biological catastrophe, Shacket is a triumph of science, a man becoming more than a man, the only one like him in the world, ascendant.

Leaving the coat in the car, holding the pistol at his side, he crosses two lanes of blacktop and enters another arm of the forest.

Guided by inerrant senses he didn't previously possess, he makes his way through the trees and onto a lawn at the side of the Bookman residence. The house stands perhaps a hundred feet away.

He surveys the windows, some curtained and some not. No faces at any of them, no movement beyond. A stillness upon the house.

Shacket crosses the yard and moves along the side of the house. He comes to the back porch just as a woman — not Megan, apparently the housekeeper — comes through the back door, carrying what appears to be a bag of trash.

She doesn't look toward him, descends the steps, and bustles around the farther side of the residence. She is older and of little interest to him, except he will have to kill her if she sees him.

He doesn't want to kill her if it can't be done quietly, and it probably can't. He wants Megan to become aware of him only when he slips naked into her bed and wakes her in the night.

The moment the housekeeper is out of sight, he swings over the railing, onto the porch. He crosses to the door that she left open and steps into the kitchen.

The room is bright and clean and warm. The air is redolent of cooking odors.

He hears the lid of a trash can clatter into place outside. The older woman will be returning.

A swinging door leads into the hallway. He eases it shut behind him, stands listening. All is quiet until the housekeeper returns and begins attending to whatever tasks remain at the end of her day.

This house is large, but it's not so grand that live-in help is required. When the housekeeper leaves, there will be just Megan, the mute boy, and Shacket.

Then there will be consequences for the disrespect with which he has been treated.

Before he reaches the front of the house and the main stairs, there is a side hall to the left. The walls here are decorated with Megan's paintings, which tend to be large.

He has studied her art online. Initially, he wanted to like it. But he never could relate to it.

Now it seems even more absurd and childish than previously. He can't comprehend her purpose or why anyone would purchase such art other than to burn it.

She obviously is not woke to the new world that is coming with unrelenting fury.

As technology races onward and with it enlightened thinking, as hidebound society is reshaped and outdated mores are consigned to the dustbin of history, as thrilling new social norms replace the old, as previous virtues come to be seen as mere weaknesses and raw power is rightly understood to be the sole remaining virtue, much will need to be burned. Shredded and burned, torn down and hammered into dust. A shining future cannot be built on a past of ignorance and error. To build a brighter tomorrow, it's necessary to descend into a place darker than darkness, to clean the corrupt world with blood and destruction.

By the time he reaches the end of the hall, he is convinced that Megan's paintings prove she is not woke to the better world that can be, will be.

Shacket will wake her to it.

Bella on the Wire

Bella was six years old. She was a yellow Labrador retriever.

She was always happy.

Even on those occasions when she was a little bit sad, she was at the same time happy on top of the sad. The sadness was secondary.

As far as she could recall, there had been only one period of unadulterated unhappiness in her life, and that had been related to an encounter with a skunk.

There was more intelligence of different degrees and kinds in nature's creatures than human beings knew, but not in skunks.

Skunks were a stupid and dangerous species specifically because they didn't *need* to be smart to survive.

Whenever she looked at herself in a mirror, Bella was always surprised by how big she was. Seventy pounds and not fat.

She'd always thought of herself as small. In a world of humans who stood high on two legs, it proved difficult to maintain a proper sense of her own dimensions.

She lived in Santa Rosa, a small city approximately fifty-five air miles north of San Francisco.

Although she'd never flown in an airplane or otherwise, Bella knew air miles. And a lot more.

She resided with Andrea and Bill Montell. Bill was an attorney. Andrea owned a bookstore where Bella was welcome.

She never annoyed the bookstore customers and never let on that some of them had literary tastes she found unfortunate.

Andrea and Bill had four children between the ages of seven and fourteen. In ascending order: Milly, Dennis, Sam, and Larinda. All were homeschooled.

They were a tightly knit, loving family. They all adored Bella, and she adored them, so it was a typical dog-human family situation.

Kids, bookstore, law office: Bella's days were busy, filled with play and affection, walks with Andrea, runs with Bill, games with the kids, public relations work at the bookstore. Bella was never bored.

In addition, she had a secret life.

The Montells were aware that their dog was quite smart, but they didn't have a clue as to the extent of her intelligence.

They knew nothing of the Mysterium.

They didn't know she retrieved books from their library and read them at night.

When she was much younger, Bella decided that revealing her true nature would be unfair to the children.

To develop a healthy psychology and the right measure of self-esteem, every growing child needed to stand center stage, in the spotlight, from time to time.

Once Bella had revealed the truth of herself, the center stage would always be hers, no matter how she insisted on relinquishing it to each child.

Anyway, what was to be gained by openly being an intelligent dog in a world that had not yet found any use for such a thing?

She loved the Montell children. She wanted them to have normal lives, each with opportunities to be the center of attention.

Some other members of the Mysterium had shaped their lives as Bella had shaped hers.

Sometimes there was sadness in not openly being all that you should be, the person that you really were. But, again, there was happiness on top of the sadness.

Maintaining her secret had certain advantages, not least of all that she knew more about each child than Andrea and Bill knew, more than she would know if the kids realized how smart she really was.

When they were at risk of going astray, she had the canine wiles with which to subtly steer them back on course.

When that didn't work, she had become clever at bringing the problem to the attention of Andrea and Bill without them always realizing who was the agent of revelation.

In addition to being one of five Montell siblings and their clandestine nanny as well, Bella was the editor of the Wire.

The Wire could be turned on and off like a radio. Not all members of the Mysterium were listening at all times.

However, it was possible to send an insistent message that would open even closed neural

128

pathways and ensure that everyone received it.

Bella's job was to gather important news and share it in a timely manner.

She had volunteered to remain open for transmissions during daylight hours.

She didn't have to worry about spreading rumors and untruths. No member of the Mysterium had ever known a dog to lie.

On this Wednesday evening, as the Montell family sat for dinner in the dining room, Bella curled on a bed in the corner, pretending to sleep, when in fact she had big news to impart to her kind.

Bellagram. As reported two weeks ago, Rusty and Mandy, members of the Donald and Georgina Curtis family of Corte Madera, were pleased to announce five pups, by far the largest known Mysterium litter at that time. All remain healthy. Now all five are transmitting telepathically at a limited distance and are able to quick-learn language by the Wire.

They should be able to transmit at a distance soon. Donald and Georgina Curtis are fully aware of Rusty's and Mandy's nature, and are prepared to keep all five pups. Much joy in Corte Madera.

Something exciting is happening out there. Just today, Caesar and Cleo, members of the Robert and Mei-Mei Ishigawa family of San Jose, produced a litter of six, all healthy. Robert and Mei-Mei are likewise aware of the Mysterium, and the offspring will remain in the family.

We have long wondered where we came from, why we are here, and why there are so few of us. If suddenly our numbers are increasing, perhaps answers to our first two questions, the reason for our existence, will soon be revealed to us. Rejoice. Be true. Stay tuned.

THE
UNINVITED
GUEST

WEDNESDAY 5:00 P.M. – THURSDAY 1:00 A.M.

THE

28

Ben Hawkins stopped at a Tahoe City market to buy a case of canned gourmet dog food not unlike what Dorothy had served, as well as deli sandwiches for his own dinner.

Kipp waited in the Range Rover. He didn't mind. He wasn't lonely. A colorful variety of people came and went from the market. Especially when unaware that they were being watched, human beings were always interesting.

When Ben returned, he said, 'I knew you wouldn't steal the Rover and leave me stranded. Maybe a poodle, but not you.'

They traveled a few miles farther to Olympic Valley, which was twenty-five miles or so from Dorothy's house above the lake.

They were still moving toward the boy who murmured all but constantly on the Wire. Before morning, Kipp hoped to determine if Ben expected to continue in that direction.

Olympic Valley offered four-star accommodations at Squaw Valley Lodge and at the Resort at Squaw Creek.

However, anti-dog bigotry required Kipp and Ben to take a room at a two-star operation. Enlightenment was ever ongoing.

The mom-and-pop owners had a dog of their own. He was a Welsh corgi named Llewellyn.

He came out through the gate in the check-in

133

counter to greet Kipp. He had stubby legs and a beautiful coat.

Llewellyn smelled of oatmeal-based shampoo. On his breath were cooked carrots, green beans, and poached chicken, which he evidently had been given for dinner.

If Llewellyn's weight and height were a disadvantage in any contest with a larger dog, they were ideal when it came to being in the best position to sniff Kipp's crotch and butt.

Llewellyn seemed surprised when Kipp failed to return this traditional greeting.

He was a friendly fellow, however, and he took no offense. His short tail was always wagging.

The motel room proved to be simple and clean. Next to a small coffee brewer were complimentary packets of coffee, creamer, and sugar.

Ben put his sandwiches and two cans of beer in the under-the-counter refrigerator.

Like ghosts, the smells of people who had stayed here in the past haunted Kipp's nose. The ugliest thing he found was a little dead pill bug in one corner of the bedroom, which wasn't terribly offensive.

Unexpectedly, Kipp was given an informal grooming.

Ben produced a box of moist pet wipes in foil packets. He also had two different grooming combs.

He hadn't bought those items at the market. For some reason, he'd already had them in the Range Rover.

'This will do till we can find a place to get you a real bath.'

Living with Dorothy, Kipp had been bathed

134

every Thursday and regularly trimmed. Everyone said he looked like a show dog.

During the long day of overland travel, which had brought him to the campground, he'd gotten a bit dirty and bedraggled.

Ben didn't take off Kipp's collar, but otherwise gave him a thorough wipe down.

Of course he had to endure a brief session with a hair dryer. Every life had its ups and down.

Once Kipp was dry, Ben produced a water bowl and a food bowl.

Both were white ceramic and made for dogs. The green-lettered name on each was CLOVER.

These, too, had come from the Range Rover, not from the market in Tahoe City.

Ben filled one bowl with water and emptied an entire can of the gourmet food into the other.

Although he'd had the burger and frankfurter earlier, Kipp ate this offering with pleasure, though not with canine haste.

One of the first things that Dorothy had found peculiar about him, as a puppy, was that he savored his food rather than gobbling it in typical doggy fashion.

With his sandwiches, beer, and a book, Ben settled in a chair at a small table by the window.

After he had licked the bowl clean, Kipp considered the mystery of it. He was exhausted after a busy day without naps, but curiosity wouldn't let him sleep.

With one paw, he tipped the empty bowl on its side. With his nose, he rolled it across the carpet to Ben Hawkins.

The writer looked up from his book and watched this performance without comment.

Kipp stopped the bowl next to Ben's chair, with the name CLOVER clearly visible. He sat and cocked his head and regarded the man.

'You want more food?'

Kipp thumped his tail once, which meant no. But that was code he'd developed with Dorothy. This man couldn't know what it meant.

Kipp shook his head from side to side.

Ben inserted a bookmark in the novel and set it aside. His expression was unreadable. As a former Navy SEAL, he was a man of reason who was cautious about making assumptions.

After a silence, Ben said, 'Did you just shake your head no?'

Without hesitation, Kipp moved his head up and down.

They stared at each other. Kipp had learned that a direct stare could convey considerable information, depending on the intensity and duration of it.

Now he lowered his eyes to the name CLOVER on the dish, then looked again at Ben Hawkins.

The writer picked up his can of beer, hesitated, and put it down without taking a drink.

'You know you're a little spooky?'

Patiently, Kipp watched him, waited.

'Clover was my dog for eight years. A rescue. I got her a few weeks after I was out of the navy, the day before they would have put her down. She was a golden, like you.'

Kipp issued a whimper of sympathy.

136

'Clover was a fine girl. Fearless but with the sweetest heart. Cancer was eating her alive. Five months ago, I held her in my arms while the vet put her to sleep. It was the hardest damn thing I've ever done. Me, a big, tough Navy SEAL. The hardest thing.'

Kipp thought of Dorothy. He was very tired. He had never been so tired before.

He padded to the farther end of the room and stared at the writer across the bed.

'You want to sleep up there? It's all right with me.'

Marshaling what energy he had left, Kipp sprang onto the mattress. He circled and laid down and closed his eyes.

He heard the writer getting up from the chair, moving around.

The seal on the refrigerator made a soft sucking sound as the door opened.

The click-tear of the pull tab on a can. The smell of fresh cold beer.

A moment later, the chair creaked as the writer settled in it once more.

'Spooky,' Ben said again.

Dorothy smiled at Kipp in the dream and put a hand on his head and smoothed his fur and said, *My special boy.*

29

Megan found Woody lying on his bed, atop the spread, fully clothed, in the fetal position, eyes open, which meant that he was distressed about something. He remained as silent as the versions of himself that appeared in some of her paintings, including the one of him in the moonlight with deer, which was currently on her easel.

When she spoke to him and he wouldn't even look at her, she could do nothing for him other than climb on the bed, spoon against his back, and put her arms around him. He had no objection to being held, though he never returned a hug.

She didn't pressure him about what was wrong, because nothing could be gained either by insistence or gentle probing. When he was in this mood, he turned further inward on himself, and he would come out of it only when whatever issue caused it — some fear or sadness or confusion — had resolved itself.

At times like this, she didn't know if holding him made any difference in his emotional state. She had never seen evidence that it did. Holding him, however, made a difference for *her*, made her feel that she was doing something essential.

When you loved someone as much as she loved Woody, and when you were helpless to console him when he seemed to need consolation the most, you could at times feel miserably inadequate. She had known that feeling.

Now she counseled herself to remember that Woody always came out of these funks sooner than later. He didn't lie stricken like this for days or even for longer than an hour or two. Whatever might cause these withdrawals, he was resilient

138

enough to overcome it. And when he did return from emotional isolation to mere detachment, he would find her and, in that shy way of his, touch her and, smile to let her know that whatever had devastated him had now relented.

As she held him and smoothed his thick black hair with one hand, she sang to him — softly, softly — one of those songs that he would sometimes play over and over for hours on his iPod while he read or used his computer. 'When you're weary, feelin' small . . . '

She heard Verna Brickit's car leaving the driveway and turning onto the state route. The housekeeper had a key; she would have locked the back door. She was reliable.

' . . . when tears are in your eyes, I will dry them all . . . '

30

Lee Shacket stands at the window at the end of the side hall, watching as the older woman in the Toyota follows the driveway to the two-lane blacktop, turns south toward Pinehaven, and quickly cruises out of sight.

Ravens appear again in the sky, as they had just before he shot to death the owner of the Shelby Super Snake. They wheel through the air less like ravens than like seagulls. For such usually solemn birds, they appear to be celebrating.

Previously, there were three ravens. This time,

seven engage in this aerial ballet. Throughout history and across all cultures, the numbers three and seven have had supernatural meaning. The ravens are for him, to encourage him in his becoming.

He jams the pistol under his belt and takes from a pocket of his jeans the feather that had fallen to his hand as he'd pursued Justine. The soft barbs sprouting from the shaft to form the vane are glossy black, inky yet with a hint of midnight blue, as if the bird that shed it was an emissary of some ancient god of darkness and, in the name of its master, had stolen the color of the daytime sky to ensure eternal night.

After returning the feather to his pocket, he draws the pistol.

He steps to the door on the right and eases it open and enters a room where the only illumination issues through tall windows in the north wall. Because the overcast is thicker, because the false twilight is becoming the real thing, and perhaps because rain is impending, the quality of light suggests an underwater realm, as though he is not in a house but rather in a submerged vessel.

And yet he has no need to turn on a lamp. When he moves from the brighter hallway into this room, his eyes adjust as they never would have before. His vision has been improving. Now his eyes take what light is available and somehow multiply it, so that he sees at once that he is in Megan's studio.

A large canvas appears near completion, and he is drawn to it. This is yet another of her works that, in spite of the photorealism with which it's

140

rendered, is incomprehensible to Lee Shacket. What is it supposed to mean? What feelings is it intended to evoke?

In the foreground stand three deer and a boy. The boy is Woody. He's feeding slices of an apple to the deer. The pale moonlight is eerily diffuse, strangely reflected, in counterpoint to the realism of all else.

For reasons that he can't explain, he is profoundly irritated by this image. He wants to go to the kitchen and find a sharp knife and slash the canvas to ribbons.

Not yet. In time, he will destroy every one of her paintings in this house. Once she has submitted to him, once she has been reduced to the essence of what she is and understands her place, Megan will destroy them herself, at his direction.

The only meaning, the only truth, he can see in this painting is that the deer and the mentally deficient boy are weak, nothing but prey that are destined to be taken by a predator.

31

After she sang to Woody and thought she felt him relax slightly in her arms, Megan said, 'Meat loaf, potato-and-cheese casserole, one of your favorite dinners. And for dessert, Verna's best muffins with ice cream. I'll be in the kitchen, whenever you're ready. Take your time, honey.'

She got off the bed and stood over him and smiled and bent down and kissed his cheek. The

141

boy still stared at nothing, as though in a state of shock, but she was pretty sure that he was coming around.

His computer and desk lamp were off. A thick sheaf of papers, held together by a spring clip, lay to the right of the keyboard.

Megan wondered what he had printed, but she didn't take a look at it. Every child needed privacy and trust, but that was especially true of Woody, who had an extreme aversion to his personal space being invaded. For all of his limitations, he was a good kid, and whatever he'd been doing, he would sooner or later share it with her.

After switching on one of the nightstand lamps, she left the room, quietly closing the door behind her.

She went down the narrow back stairs, which terminated in the kitchen.

The meat loaf stood on a wire rack, in a pan, beside the ovens. When it cooled and firmed, she'd cut two servings to be reheated. Covered with foil, the finished potato-and-cheese casserole waited in the warming drawer. The back door proved to be locked, as she'd known it would be. Verna Brickit was an entertaining curmudgeon, but she was also as reliable as the rising and setting of the sun.

Megan put plastic place mats and paper napkins and flatware on the breakfast table.

For whatever reason, Woody ate with less haste and was more content at dinner if the meal was served by candlelight. Megan put six small, red votive glasses on the table and inserted a four-hour candle in each. The candle glow must always be filtered through red glass. If the holders were clear, the flickering flames agitated Woody. If the glass was blue, he lost his appetite. If it was green, he grew depressed.

She didn't put china on the table, but set it on a counter for later service. She required one plate, but Woody needed a plate for his meat loaf and three shallow dishes, one each for servings of the potato-cheese casserole and the two accompanying vegetables. If one food touched another, he could not eat it. She didn't know why, and perhaps neither did he.

When Woody came down from his room, she would put the carrots and the cauliflower on the stove to cook and pour his 'cocktail.' If Megan was drinking a white wine, Woody wanted a clear, flavored water. If she was drinking red, he wanted grape raspberry to match the color of her cabernet. Trapped as he was within his condition, he nevertheless sought connections between them, however awkwardly.

She allowed herself one or two glasses of wine in the evening. Now, as she waited for Woody, she poured Caymus cabernet.

At the window in the back door, she stared at the yard where, in her current canvas, Woody stood feeding the deer. Only a few of her works featured the boy, but once she painted him in a setting, the place never seemed right again without him in it. In spite of his autism or perhaps because of it, he possessed a gravity that she couldn't explain, that bent the world around him, reshaped any venue and colored it anew and gave it fresh meaning. The yard now, without

143

him, looked incomplete, like a simple sketch, a study for a more serious scene. She supposed that it wasn't Woody who transformed those places where she'd painted him, but rather her love for him that made her see a mystical quality in them.

At the end of the lawn, in the gathering dusk, the forest darkled into a castellated architecture of turrets and battlements, just as she portrayed it in the current painting. She hadn't quite known why she'd given it an ominous character, but now she realized that it represented the evils of the world that contrasted so starkly with Woody's innocence, which would be such a threat to him if anything happened to her and she was no longer here to protect him.

She went to the table, where earlier she'd left a half-read novel. She sat and found her page and began to read again. The day had been one of accomplishment, and her pleasure felt earned. The story was good, and the wine was better.

A theme of the novel seemed to be the power of solitude. She assured herself that she wasn't lonely, and she knew that assurance for a lie. She told herself that life was good, that there were worse things than loneliness, and those were truths.

32

The hallway light passes through the living room archway and lays a faint golden arc across floor and furniture, but the deeper reaches of the large room are veiled with shadows as the day recedes beyond the French windows.

Shacket's strange augmented eyes conjure an eerie light by which he crosses the room to the Steinway. He had forgotten that Megan played the piano.

The lid is down on this parlor grand, and upon it stands an artfully arranged collection of photographs, the silver frames of which attract what light reaches this part of the room. His new way of seeing makes the silver seem to be in motion, molten and flowing even though the frames retain their shapes.

The photographs are from happier days when the family remained intact: Jason and Megan, Jason and Woody, Megan and Woody, three of them together, Jason by himself, and another of Jason, and another. Mom and Dad always smiling, but the kid only sometimes. The brain-screwed kid, the mental case. Jason steals Megan from Shacket, and he saddles her with the useless boy, and then he dies, and *still* the treacherous sonofabitch is here, *still* in possession of her heart.

One by one, Shacket turns the photos facedown. Later, when the boy is dead, when Megan understands who owns her now, he will watch while she takes the photos from the frames and throws them in the fireplace and burns them.

Noises arise from the back of the house, probably from the kitchen. He is not concerned. The sounds remain at a distance. He can smell her back there, the moistness of her, such a hot bitch, and she isn't approaching.

This house is his now. She doesn't know it, but this house belongs to Shacket. He can burn it down if he wants. If after the boy is dead, if after Shacket has slipped into Megan's bed in the night and shown her what she's been missing all these years, if *still* the slut refuses to submit, he will do to her what he did to Justine. Then he'll set the house on fire and leave for Costa Rica, where there are a lot of hot women, the jungle and the sea and more hot women than he will ever need.

In his becoming, he amazes himself, for he has not previously been so decisive in all matters.

He leaves the living room and steps into the hallway and goes to the front stairs. As he ascends, he runs his tongue back and forth over his teeth, back and forth, across the lowers and uppers, not over the molars and the bicuspids, but over the canines and the incisors, the canines and the incisors.

33

Embarrassed — worse than embarrassed, mortified and ashamed that he had nearly revealed himself to the murderers behind the Dark Web site called Tragedy, that he had come close to endangering himself and his mother — Woody Bookman retreated to Castle Wyvern, where he often found solace in solitude and sought to regain confidence in his worst hours.

Castle Wyvern was a structure of his imagination, but in times like these, it seemed more solid and convincing in its details than the so-called real world. The outer curtain wall was fourteen feet wide: parallel two-foot-thick courses of native sandstone, the ten feet between them filled with a rubble of loose rocks and mortar. Ten formidable towers soared into a perpetually stormy sky, including two each at the outer gate-house and the postern gatehouse. The outer ward was separated from the inner ward by a second and more massive curtain wall with an even more impregnable gatehouse and six larger towers. The wall walks featured merlons with narrow arrow loops and embrasures from which boiling oil and buckets of stones could be poured down on enemies attacking from below. Each gatehouse had to be approached on a twenty-five-foot-high ramp guarded by archers. Each ramp ended at a drawbridge spanning a moat. Every gatehouse featured a heavy timber portcullis plated with iron, which could be lowered to deny entrance, and beyond each portcullis stood a pair of iron-bound wooden doors that could be closed in an emergency and reinforced by double drawbars.

The name of the castle had been chosen with care. A wyvern was a particularly ferocious two-legged dragon with a wicked barbed tail. Bad people were likely to be reluctant to try to force their way into a place named Castle Wyvern, Castle Dragon.

In times of deepest mortification and shame, Woody took refuge in his high redoubt, a round chamber at the top of the southwest tower of the inner curtain wall. A timbered ceiling. Narrow windows looking to the four points of the compass. Stone walls, stone floor. He had only a pile of reeds to lie on, because there should be no comforts to reward a boy who had brought shame on himself by his foolishness and stupidity.

When he had paid a sufficient price for his errors, he would receive a sign permitting him to leave the castle and return to Pinehaven in the so-called real world, which was how things worked in stories about castles and high redoubts and lands where dragons roamed. Although the windows of the buildings of the inner ward had glass in their frames, there was none up here in this tower; in bad weather, cold wind blew in and rain slanted through the empty panes to shatter on the stone, depending on what punishment his actions required. And when his sentence had been served, he received a sign in the form of a bluebird or a soft-furred white rat that came in through a glassless window. The former sang his reprieve, or the latter danced amusingly to indicate that he was free.

Now, as he curled upon his bed of reeds, he heard the door of the high redoubt open behind him. If the door opened before he had seen the bluebird or the white rat, the visitor would be his mother who had come to the castle to check on him. He couldn't leave until he'd done his time, not even if he would please his mother if he rose from the bed and went to her. If he left before he received a sign, the shame that he'd earned would still cling to him, and his mother would see the truth of her son, and she would then share his humiliation that she had given birth to such a child.

She had been here earlier, too, had held him and sung to him. He was surprised that she

148

would return so soon. She always allowed him privacy. Mother didn't know about Castle Wyvern, but the door to Woody's high redoubt and the door to his real-world bedroom were, for her, magically connected; she saw the physical Woody on his bed, while the spirit of Woody lay abashed in the castle tower. That was how things worked in the fantasy land to which he could escape from the hard world in which he had been born and in which he so often screwed up.

Behind him, his mother stood in the open door for the longest time. Because it could be no one but her, he thought she intended to come to him again and smooth his hair and sing to him in her pretty voice. When he was withdrawn into the castle's high redoubt, she had never before visited him more than once. She knew that he could only return according to his own schedule and that by appealing to him, she was only ensuring that he would remain in retreat longer.

Finally she closed the door and went away.

Woody curled tighter on his bed of reeds, drawing his knees toward his chest.

34

The useless boy lies with his back to the door, motionless on his bed, with no deer in attendance, bathed not in moonlight, but in the glow of a nightstand lamp, as the day dies beyond the windows.

The child is easy prey, but the time isn't right.

Shacket trembles with the desire to bite. But the time isn't right.

He wants Megan first. Wants to slide deep into her and, by taking her, at last pay back Jason Bookman, who had stolen her from him, stolen her and then set Shacket up to take the fall for Dorian Purcell. Megan must be his, as she was always meant to be, and with her he can then father a superior child, which Jason's damaged seed could not produce.

If she submits and recognizes his extraordinary power, realizes what he is becoming, and understands that, without him, there is no future for her, then they will ravage the boy together. But if she resists, he'll paralyze her and, as she lies in helpless witness, he'll bite the life out of the little freak and then set the house afire.

His newfound decisiveness thrills him. He no longer must ask for anyone's advice or waste time in consultation, or seek approval. No one is the boss of him. Neither the law nor any code of morality constrains him, because he knows them to be fantasies of order. In truth, the only rule by which anyone can live successfully, either in the wilds or in civilization, is the sole mandate of cruel Nature: Prey shall submit, and predators shall reign supreme.

Farther along the hallway, he finds the master bedroom. Ashen light at the windows. Glowing green numbers on the bedside clock radio. This meager illumination is barely adequate even for his dark-adapted — and still adapting — eyes, but he makes his way to the king-size bed without turning on a lamp.

He can see just well enough to realize that the spread has been removed and folded on the padded bench at the foot of the bed. The bedclothes have been turned back for the night, most likely by the housekeeper who departed in the Toyota. Shacket drops to his knees to smell the fitted sheet and the top sheet between which Megan's lithesome body has lain. The linens have not been changed today, sparing him the disappointment of nothing more than a residue of laundry detergent and fabric softener. By smell, he can distinguish between the shampooed freshness of her raven hair and the slightly salty creaminess of her lustrous skin and the moistness of the cleft between her legs where later he will make their future.

He puts his pistol on the nightstand and sits on the edge of the big bed. He unties his shoes and slips out of them but does not undress before lying where she spent the previous night, first on his back, with the top sheet and thin blanket drawn to his chin. The high-thread-count cotton that has clung to her long legs and snugged her mons veneris and draped her breasts now wraps him, and he feels cocooned in the essence of her.

35

In the house above Lake Tahoe, Rosa Leon had phoned Roger Austin, Dorothy's attorney, using his cell number now that office hours had

151

passed. She hadn't called him to confirm that she was the sole heir; there was no reason for Dorothy to have deceived her with a false promise. But Mr. Austin was supposed to come to the house the day after the death, and that appointment needed to be changed.

Roger Austin had the deep yet mellifluous voice of a gifted speaker who could charm audiences, and everyone said that, as a man, his character was the equal of his fine voice: He was principled and trustworthy and a reliable rock in all circumstances. When he spoke of Dorothy Hummel's passing, this rock's voice fractured a few times, and once he had to stop for a minute to gather himself, which made Rosa regard him even more highly. He knew that she'd seen the video, but nevertheless he told her all that the estate contained, after taxes. He wanted to share her wonder in the change that had been wrought so suddenly in her life, and she had no difficulty giving him a taste of it. He wished also to assure her that, in association with him, Dorothy's accountant would provide her with guidance in the days to come.

'But can we delay tomorrow's meeting until perhaps Friday?' she asked. 'I've some important things to attend to, and I can't delay dealing with them.'

'Certainly, Rosa. How about three o'clock Friday afternoon?'

'That should be fine,' she said. 'And thank you, Mr. Austin, for having been such a good friend to Dorothy.'

'Please call me Roger, as she did. Being a

152

friend to Dorothy was the easiest thing in the world.' He laughed softly, perhaps to keep his voice from faltering again. 'She was one of a very small number of people in this world whom I've loved as much as myself.'

With the call concluded, Rosa was eager to get on the road in pursuit of Kipp. If he had fled in grief, she would share it with him and, by sharing, relieve the poor creature of some of that terrible weight.

However, she worried that he hadn't fled at all, but had been snatched instead, as melodramatic as that sounded. Dognapping was in fact the thing that Dorothy had most feared. At the moment, Kipp was in the vicinity of Olympic Valley, approximately twenty-eight miles from here, and it seemed to Rosa that he couldn't have traveled that far afoot in the time that he'd been gone.

His special collar issued a unique signal tracked by a state-of-the-art service, Pied Finder. The company supplied wristwatches and other items for children in which a transponder was embedded, making it possible to follow them by GPS if they should be taken by a kidnapper, by some Pied Piper, or be lost. They supplied, as well, collars for dogs.

The Pied Finder app allowed Rosa to track Kipp on Dorothy's smart-phone. Her greatest fear at the moment was that the little lithium battery powering the transponder might go dead before she recovered the dog. It needed to be changed twice a month, and she didn't know when Dorothy had last inserted a new one in the collar.

She had not mentioned this crisis to Roger

Austin, because he knew nothing of Kipp's secret. There was no one but Rosa to go to the dog's aid.

Guilt and worry weighed heavily on her. She should not have left Kipp alone during the cremation and later. She hadn't at that time known his magical nature, but she'd been acutely aware of how important he was to Dorothy.

Rosa owed her good fortune to the golden retriever. Although Dorothy was fond of Rosa, she would not have left the entire estate to her caregiver if Kipp hadn't existed. A generous measure might have been bequeathed to Rosa, but the larger portion would have gone to charities that Dorothy had long supported.

Now Rosa Leon set the alarm and locked the house and departed in Dorothy's Lincoln MKX. She steered the vehicle slowly through a forbidding fog like one of those in which sailors on a blinded sea sometimes glimpsed ancient ghost ships with torn sails or legendary monsters of the deep that breached, glaring with glowing eyes, only to dive beneath the waves, never to be seen again.

With visibility reduced to twenty feet, she took almost fifteen minutes to follow surface streets to State Route 89, which was no more than a four- or five-minute drive on a clear evening. She went north on highway 89, hoping that the fog would lift or at least thin out. If it remained as it was, the forty-minute trip to Olympic Valley might take two hours or longer, with the constant risk that some damn fool, trusting to wits he didn't possess, would crash into her at the posted speed limit.

The blinking red signifier on the navigation map, presented on the smartphone screen, indicated that Kipp hadn't moved since she'd located him. Wherever he might be, with whomever, he apparently had settled down at least for the night.

Like the probing beams of a bathysphere exploring a murky oceanic trench, headlights of an oncoming vehicle appeared at first hazy and dim but swelled in brightness. Southbound on the undivided highway, the vehicle itself was invisible until it swept past, a crew-cab pickup, as white as the fog from which it manifested. The driver carved through the night at perhaps half the speed limit, but that was still too fast in these conditions.

In his wake, Rosa slowed further. The primary pattern of this momentous day unnerved her. She had lost her dearest — her only — friend, she had inherited a fortune, she had sat through a long and dispiriting cremation, she had learned a miraculous and uplifting secret about Kipp, the dog had gone missing, and then she seemed to have located him by extraordinary means . . . A loss followed by a blessing, followed by a loss, followed by a blessing. A hard life had prepared her to expect that nothing good could last.

36

Everyone who was murdered in Pinehaven County or died by accident received the personal attention of Carson Conroy, who had come here to escape the senseless violence of the city. But first:

Having been discovered by a deputy sheriff on regular patrol, the bodies of Painton Spader and Justine Klineman were extensively photographed in situ and removed in such a manner as to disturb the scene as little as possible. Rural law enforcement did not always show such respect for potential evidence.

Because the deep overcast throttled the afternoon light, and because there was a 60 percent chance of rain that, if it came, might erase evidence, a generator and klieg lights were brought to the scene in an expeditious manner and judiciously positioned an hour and a half before nightfall. Under the direction of a deputy with special training in the discovery and handling of forensic evidence, a crew of the sheriff's men searched the graveled shoulder of the highway, the slope beyond, and the swale at the foot of the slope in which the victims had been found.

The perpetrator had not returned directly to his vehicle after killing the woman, but had angled through the meadow to a stream, trampling the tall grass and leaving drops of blood on some of those flattened green blades. They found his discarded bloodstained shirt, plus a shoulder holster without a firearm.

The bodies were taken to the county morgue.

A tow-truck operator who had a contract with the county loaded the Shelby Super Snake onto a flatbed and, always in the company of a supervising deputy who could testify that the chain of evidence had not been broken, conveyed the vehicle to an impound garage in the same complex as the sheriffs department HQ and the morgue.

The bloody shirt and the shoulder rig were brought to Carson Conroy in a brown paper shopping bag.

At forty-two, after he'd risen through the ranks of the medical examiner's office in Chicago, murder capital of the nation, Carson had become dispirited because homicides so often went unsolved. Most of the murders were gang related, and the city's governing elite had proved unable or unwilling to deal with the gangs.

The violence became as personal as it could get when his wife, Lissa, was killed in a drive-by shooting that had all the signs of a gangbanger initiation, some wannabe thug offing a civilian to prove that his balls were big and his heart was too small ever to trouble him with doubt. That was the hardest kind of case to solve, because no rational motive existed, no provable cause and effect. Carson knew Lissa's killer would never be found, and he couldn't live in a city where the triggerman who took her life still enjoyed a life of his own.

That was five years earlier, and still her murder had not been solved. Some nights, in canyons of restless sleep, Carson sought the satisfaction of bloody vengeance, scenarios in which he prowled mean streets, as though he were Denzel Washington in an *Equalizer* movie, found the shooter by dream logic, and cut him down dead. However, he had zero expectation of justice in the waking world.

Four years ago, having moved from an elected-coroner system to the establishment of a medical examiner's office, Pinehaven County had hired Carson from a wide field of applicants. His task had been not merely to do professional forensic autopsies, the discoveries of which would stand up in court, but also to establish an adequate crime lab that would free the sheriff's department from the need to farm out aspects of its investigations to state-level authorities. The county's coroners had nearly always been retired doctors or active morticians who did their best, although none of them had sufficient training to understand the precise procedures necessary to avoid contaminating evidence derived from an autopsy.

During his first year on the job, Carson worked eighty-hour weeks and thrived on the schedule, which allowed him the forgetting that he sought. Year by year, he remained busy, but he settled into his position with confidence and pleasure. Born and raised a city boy, and black, he had expected that adjustment to this rustic environment would be taxing, to say the least; but it was smooth beyond all expectation. He enjoyed the modest scale of life here, the majesty of the Sierra Nevada, the natural beauty. He loved that deer sometimes wandered along Main Street as if they were tourists who were curious about the ways of Pinehaven's inhabitants, loved even the nasty but industrious raccoons that worked assiduously to defeat each new and more complex latch that he installed on the lids of his trash cans. The people were not as he had been warned to expect. For forty years or longer, in most of the country, there had been a sophistication and fair-mindedness in rural counties and small towns about which many city dwellers and members of the media seemed clueless. Carson was happy here, charmed by the quiet flow of events, grateful to be free from the metropolitan bustle that made life a competitive marathon race without end.

In the past year or so, a disquieting change had come slowly to Pinehaven County: occasional outriders from MS-13 and other Central American gangs, scouting for opportunities like remote and easily concealed locations for meth labs, checking out the strength and determination of local law enforcement. There had been incidents between them and a few deputies, nothing too alarming. But a pretty teenager, Jenna McCall, had vanished without a trace; she'd been a good student, a devoted daughter, not the kind of girl who opted to be a runaway. And Jimmy Talbert, thirteen, had been riding his bike on an unpaved forest-service road when he'd been struck by a hit-and-run driver and left to bleed to death. There hadn't been a case of hit-and-run in Pinehaven County in thirty-six years. So everyone had suspicions informed by common sense.

Carson Conroy's suspicions and fears failed to prepare him for the condition of Justine Klineman's corpse.

The morgue had two autopsy tables, each with scales and sink, and the woman's companion, Painton Spader, occupied the first. He had been

159

shot four times point-blank with hollow-point rounds. The devastation to flesh and bone were only what could be expected.

Initially, Carson thought that Justine had likewise been shot, and that wild animals, perhaps coyotes, had savaged her after she'd been left for dead. When he could not find a bullet wound, he looked for evidence of knife work, but he found none. Her skull remained intact; no blunt instrument had put her down.

Only when the likeliest of weapons had been ruled out did he, of necessity, look more closely at her face. Little was left of it. She might have been a beauty once, but there was no way to know from these remains. Most of her face had been eaten, as had one of her breasts and part of the other. Carson had seen many gruesome things in his profession, and the horrors to which victims were vulnerable had long ago ceased to chill him. However, a chill climbed his spine now and fluttered through him like some insect horde. The bite marks along the perimeter of the remaining tissue were not those of an animal; they had the curvature and tooth pattern of the human mouth.

37

By the time Megan read three chapters of the novel and finished the glass of cabernet, Woody had still not appeared in the kitchen.

When he seemed to have difficulty returning from one of his deeper retreats, she could sometimes encourage him with music. He liked to listen to her play the Steinway and always watched her as if amazed that she could conjure music from its keys.

Sometimes she left a handwritten note for him. A recent one had asked, *Would you like me to teach you to play the piano?*

He never answered that one or any of the others, but she hoped one day he might. Exchanging notes would not be the same as two-way speech, but it would be a more satisfying form of communication than she'd yet enjoyed with him.

She went along the main hallway to the living room and turned on the lights. At the piano, Megan halted at the sight of all the silver-framed photographs lying facedown on the lid.

Verna Brickit polished the silver and glass once a week. But she'd never before left the photographs like this. Nor would she. Verna was meticulous almost to the point of obsession.

Woody must have done this. But why? The obvious answer seemed to be that the sight of his father in all those photos had suddenly pierced him. After three years, she'd thought he had accommodated himself to the loss, but evidently not as much as she had believed. He was a genius, and people tended to think that geniuses were less emotional than other people, but she knew this was not true of him; he felt things profoundly. Sometimes she wondered if he remained silent because he feared that, if he dared to speak, his long-repressed emotions would erupt with volcanic power, that he would be unable to control them and would say things that would

161

shock by the very rawness of the passion with which he said them.

She left the framed photos as they were and didn't raise the piano lid. She would ask him about the pictures later.

She sat on the bench and put up the fallboard, uncovering the keys. Flexed her fingers.

The dozen or so songs Woody liked the most, each of which he could listen to over and over for hours, were a varied catalogue. While the words had meaning for him, Megan suspected that the melodies were what spoke the most directly to his soul.

After considering choices, she played 'Moon River,' and that beautiful melody, drenched in yearning and gentle melancholy, flowed through the living room and into the hall and up the stairs, perhaps to call the boy out of the shell in which he had closed himself.

38

In the vividly imagined high redoubt of Castle Wyvern, lying on a bed of reeds, Woody stared at the glassless panes of the southern window, which was where the sign always appeared, the bluebird or the soft-furred white rat, to certify that he'd suffered enough for his errors. Iron-dark clouds scudded fast across the sky. Waves of lightning throbbed through those curdled masses without thunder, the forces of these heavens as silent as the boy who conceived them. If he'd

162

done even worse than he thought, if he'd drawn the murderers out of the Dark Web and all the way here to Pinehaven, if they were even now in transit, no amount of penance could earn forgiveness or safety, and he would be condemned to this tower room forever.

Then a sound came that he'd never heard before, a curious whine followed by a sigh and a series of heart-wrenching whimpers.

When he lowered his gaze from the southern window to the floor, he saw a golden retriever curled in a ball and sleeping, whimpering because it was caught in a bad or perhaps sorrowful dream.

Nothing like this had ever happened before, and Woody didn't know what to make of it. Might the dog be a sign, like the bluebird and the white rat, a sign that he had atoned for the mess he'd made and could now leave the castle to rejoin his mother in their cozy house?

While that question remained unanswered, an unseen presence spoke to him, the disconnected words whispering along the stone walls of the tower: '*Smile for Dorothy . . . dear, sweet Kipp . . . my special boy . . . my mystery . . . Mysterium . . .*'

Woody sat up on the thick bed of reeds and surveyed the chamber, where shadows hung that, with each pulse of lightning, billowed as draperies would when disturbed by a draft. The speaker, a woman, remained invisible.

A harder, scary male voice was almost a snarl. '*I know . . . your kind . . . teach you . . . a lesson.*'

Three oil-burning sconces flamed and smoked

163

where none had been, because he willed it so, and in the dancing light no other presence but the dog revealed itself.

A third voice, another man. '*Never . . . never hit a dog. Clover . . . cancer . . . eating her alive . . . the hardest thing . . .* '

And now all three voices issued forth: '*Teach you a lesson . . . cancer . . . Clover . . . Dorothy . . . my Kipp . . . my special boy . . . special boy.*'

The oil-fired sconces ceased to exist, and shadows stirred by the storm light shivered into the room. Woody rose to his feet as the sleeping dog became as transparent as golden glass and then vanished.

Somewhere a piano played 'Moon River.'

As surely as Castle Wyvern was of Woody's creation, so were the blue-bird and the white rat that came as signs to free him from his self-imposed isolation. He knew this. The bird and the rat were expressions of his conscience when he felt that he had done enough penance for his offenses. And he knew as well that the beautiful dog was *definitely not* his invention, that it had been inserted into his fantasy by . . . someone else. The voices had not been his, and the words had not originated with him. He didn't understand how that could be or what it portended, but it seemed to him that this was the first *real* sign that he had ever received. A gladness overcame him, and he was greatly relieved of his fear that denizens of the Dark Web would find him and his mother.

He didn't need to throw open the massive bolts on the door of the high redoubt, did not need to descend the tower stairs and make his way through the inner ward and raise the portcullis and exit the inner gate. He merely turned in a full circle, and in his turning, the medieval chamber became his modern room, where he stood beside a bed not made of reeds.

The familiar, haunting melody rose from the piano downstairs, and as always it spoke to him of all the things he would never do. He would never travel as free as a flowing river, would never be crossing it in style someday. He would never be 'off to see the world,' because the world in its immensity and complexity was too much for him. Although the lovely melody encircled Woody as surely as did the fence of his autism, he didn't find it to be a sad song. Quite the contrary. The song endorsed the value of dreaming of doing things when actually doing them wasn't possible, and for all of his limitations, Woody was a dreamer of the highest order.

He crossed the room and opened the door and stepped into the upstairs hall, where the music called him back to a world he knew and with which he could cope most of time, to the house in the pines and the mother whose graceful hands made beauty from all that she touched.

39

Although Shacket does not intend to sleep in Megan's bed, the sensorial treasure that she imparted to the sheets merely by lying between them overwhelms his increasingly acute senses, an intensely fragrant erotic sachet that inspires vivid visions of the bitch's naked form that are arousing and yet strangely soporific. Though at first awake, he is floating in a sea of lascivious images, like a pubescent boy swept into a dream that will end in a night emission — the swell of full young breasts, smooth thrusting buttocks, silken limbs encircling him — a thrilling suffocation of flesh. He can smell the particles of skin she's shed in sleep, the moistness that her labia imparted to the cotton during *her* dreams of gratification, the faint traces of colostrum that, though she is not pregnant, have for some reason leaked from her nipples, as if she has anticipated him and is readying herself to feed him as her own. He can smell the place on her pillow where, in sleep, a thread of drool has unraveled from a corner of her ripe lips, and he works the luxurious fabric with his tongue to lick up the taste of her mouth. In his fantasies, her elegant hands caress her curvaceous body, offering its pleasures to him. He wants to suck her fingers, lick the delicate webs between them, and bite the thenar eminence, the plump ball of the thumb. His senses are sodden with lust, so he cannot think, and this sensory overload, this incogitant drowning in sensation, is a kind of sedation that sends him sinking into sleep as whiskey might a dizzied drunkard.

His dreams are unlike any he has had before. A wildness informs them, an almost frantic sense that anything is possible, that just ahead lies some revelation that will satisfy his every need

166

and put an end forever to all his fears. Urgently he races through a gothic forest and then across a moonlit meadow, in a body other than his own, four-legged and quicker than a man, his breath steaming from him in a night coldness that he can't feel because he is hot-blooded and burning with exertion. He is with others of his kind, lean and long-limbed and sharp-toothed beasts, and when they glimpse the lame and hobbling deer, there is a howling that is a celebration to them but horrifying to the gentle object of their passion. At this peak of excitement, the dream morphs, *he* morphs, and no longer understands what he is or knows what he wants, only that he must feed. He is something that crawls and scuttles in a blinding dark, consuming filth, something that is driven by a mindless agitation, to which the slightest draft is a threat, and sudden light sends him into frenetic flight, into crevice and hole and descending rot. And he finds himself now something else altogether, drowned and yet alive, creeping across the floor of an ocean, under tremendous pressure that would kill a man, far below the reach of the warm sun, where phosphorescent plants weave tentacles of eerie light. Through the fathoms comes a familiar music that draws him toward wakefulness. As he ascends, he understands that these dreams were shaped not out of the ordinary experiences of life, but perhaps issued from genetic memories installed by whatever DNA billions of archaea have carried with them when he inhaled them in Springville, Utah.

He wakes.

From below issues 'Moon River,' which irritates Shacket in the same way that the painting in Megan's studio irritated him. Both her art and this song are too soft, too richly layered with the useless emotions that cloud the mind and prevent a recognition of the truth that life is hard and dark and meaningless. Life is about nothing but desire and its fulfillment, hunger and its satisfaction, hatred and the violence that it requires: It's about the power to take what you want by any means necessary. Theft, rape, and killing are no less natural to humankind than breathing; they are the essential serum of the species, and in Shacket that serum will achieve a purity heretofore unseen.

He turns back the covers and sits on the edge of the bed. He slips his feet into his shoes and ties the laces. He picks up the pistol he left on the nightstand and crosses the room to the door.

40

Woody stepped into the living room, and Megan's heart lifted at the sight of him. When he came to the piano, she hoped that he might have recovered from his sorrow sufficiently to put right at least a few of the photographs of his father that he'd overturned. However, though she gave him 'Moon River' yet again from the top, he only stood listening, with a dreamy expression.

When she finished playing and quietly closed the fallboard, she said, 'Honey, why did you turn these photographs facedown?'

The boy turned his attention to the toppled frames and frowned.

'You still miss your dad, I know. I miss him, too, very much. I always will. He was the best man I've ever known.'

Woody looked at her, still frowning, but she could read nothing in his face or eyes.

'Putting away pictures of him won't also put away the painful memories. Keeping your dad in our lives with pictures and memories, keeping him in our hearts where we never really lose him — that's the best way to come to terms with what happened. Do you understand, sweetie?'

Still frowning, the boy nodded. As she suggested that they set the photographs upright together, he left the living room.

There would be no point in calling him back. He was neither thoughtless nor disobedient, merely a prisoner of his condition, impelled to act according to an interpretation of the moment and the circumstances that was logical to him but beyond her understanding.

Very likely, after they ate dinner, as Megan cleared the table, Woody would return to the living room on his own and would set all the silver frames upright, the meaning of her request having been received by him as if her words were in a foreign language and required laborious translation. Such delayed compliance to a request was not unusual.

She followed him along the main hallway to the kitchen. He went to the table and settled in the chair where she'd been sitting and picked up the novel she'd been reading. Careful not to displace her bookmark, he began reading from page one.

The book had nothing in it that she would wish to censor from him, so she said only, 'It'll be a late dinner now, but a good one.'

Before she retrieved the sliced carrots and cauliflower from the refrigerator, potted them, and spiced them for cooking, she decanted a second glass of cabernet. For Woody, she poured grape-raspberry-flavored Sparkling Ice. She served it to him in a wineglass just like hers.

41

Shacket stands at the head of the stairs, his back against the hallway wall, so that he is gazing down into the foyer as the boy and then his delectable mother exit the living room. Having heard their one-sided conversation, he wonders if the woman suffers her son's mental disability in a milder form. It makes no sense to talk to a mute with half a brain as though he understands and might at any moment respond, when in fact he's never spoken a word in his stunted life.

When the soft creak-thump of the swinging door signals that they have entered the kitchen, Shacket quickly descends the stairs to the foyer with a catlike silence that inspires a Cheshire grin. His becoming thrills him. The subtle smell of her wet vagina, which trails after her, is a promise that floods his mouth with saliva. He licks a modest overflow from the corners of his lips.

In the living room, his smile fades as he recalls what she'd said to the boy, all that treacly crap about Jason. One line in particular incenses Shacket: *He was the best man I've ever known.*

The slut has probably known countless men, but she has never known Lee Shacket, not really *known* him. She has never let him through her gate, never given him the chance to prove that he is able to satisfy her as no other man ever could.

That will soon change.

At the Steinway, he considers the silver frames. He picks one up, turns it over, and stares at Megan and Jason, the prize and the thief who stole it, the hot bitch and the treacherous bastard.

His first impulse is to throw the photograph to the floor, stamp hard on it, smash the glass that protects it, shatter all of her treasured memories, just as she and her treacherous husband shattered Shacket's hopes.

But she will hear, she will come to investigate — and this is not the place or the time that he wishes to impose the future he intends for her. Having been in her bed and previewed, in fantasies, the pleasures of her, he is intent on easing between the sheets as she sleeps, waking her by taking her. In the dark of her bedroom, while in her blindness she wonders who has mounted her and filled her as never before, he will watch with his mothy vision as Megan's shock and fright quickly give way to rapture, her long shapely legs encircling him to pull him deeper. Archaea isn't a bacteria, and the changes those billions have brought — and are still bringing — to him can't be passed like influenza. If the new genetic information that has been installed in him is in his sperm, however, he'll impregnate her with a child who will be as superior to other children as Lee Shacket is now superior to all other men.

Instead of smashing the glass in the photograph, he pries up the tabs on the frame, removes the thin cardboard backing, and extracts the picture. One by one, he removes the nine photos from the other frames.

His intention is to tuck them between the ceramic logs in the gas fireplace, where eventually he will burn them. But he decides to keep them for a better purpose. He folds them and tucks them in a hip pocket of his jeans. In the night, when he settles atop her, if she rejects him, if she fights, if she mocks and demeans him, if she prefers her dead husband and her idiot child to a new life with Shacket, he will knock her senseless and wad each photograph and force them down her throat one by one, until she chokes to death on her precious family.

42

The cold, white, smoky masses surged sluggishly through the night like the enormous shoulders and haunches of dream beasts that wouldn't quite take form. Judging by all available evidence, the world had vaporized. No trees presented themselves, no structures, no more oncoming traffic. If pavement existed under the tires, Rosa Leon couldn't glimpse it. The vague, rectangular shape of what might be a sign was briefly blind-stamped in the murk but appeared blank, as though no community existed anywhere ahead to be announced in this world dissolving. The headlights smeared an icy glare up the wall of fog but penetrated it no more than a few feet.

From the murk emerged a phantom, casting balls of sputtering red brightness to the ground. Rosa slowed even further, and the figure hurrying toward her clarified: a highway patrol officer laying down flares. A moment later, mysterious nebulae of hazy light swelled in the beclouded night, white and red and blue, diffused beams and blinking points and swiveling-pulsing beacons, as though a colossal alien ship had landed on the highway. As she drew to a stop behind a waiting line of vehicles, she saw that all lanes of the highway were blocked by a jackknifed eighteen-wheeler, a mangled sedan, an SUV turned on its side, police vehicles, and at least one ambulance, all of them floating in the thick mist like the flotsam of a shipwreck on a fogbound sea.

The GPS map on the dashboard screen indicated that she was north of Meeks Bay, south of the town of Tahoma. In clear weather, with the highway unobstructed, she might reach her destination in twenty minutes. Now she would be stalled here for hours.

When she checked the Pied Finder service on Dorothy's phone, she saw that Kipp was still where he had been in Olympic Village.

173

She considered turning around and driving back to the south end of the lake, across the border into Nevada, along the eastern and the northern shores, to reconnect with highway 89 at Tahoe City, a couple of miles south of Olympic Village. But if the fog was likely to be thinner on the Nevada side, there was no guarantee of that, and because of the casinos over there, traffic would be much heavier.

She decided to wait where she was. Maybe the authorities would get the highway cleared sooner than she expected. Maybe Kipp was settled in and safe for the night.

In spite of her difficult life, she'd never been an anxious person. Adversity was best overcome by positive thinking and hard work. Foreboding, let alone full-blown anxiety, distracted the heart and mind, making progress less likely. However, Kipp was the most important responsibility that Rosa had ever been given, his welfare her sacred duty. If he died or were cast into a miserable situation from which he could not escape, she would not only have failed him but also Dorothy, and not just the two of them. If anything bad happened to that remarkable dog, she would have failed . . . something else, something larger that eluded definition. She felt almost as if to fail Kipp would be to fail humankind as well and somehow imperil the destiny of the world. She was not given to grandiose notions of her importance, quite the opposite, and yet Kipp's fate weighed more heavily on her by the minute. As she waited, run aground in this sea of fog, anxiety tore at her.

174

43

When he finished dessert, Woody got up from his chair and came around to his mother's side of the kitchen table and stood next to her, his head bowed, waiting expectantly. He could do nothing more to indicate that he wanted to return to his room. Attending to her like this was his way of saying both thank you and good night.

Remaining in her chair, Megan took his right hand, brought it to her lips, and kissed it. She pulled him close and kissed his cheek, his brow.

As always, he was unable to return her kisses, emotionally constrained by his condition, but he liked being kissed. She held fast to the hope that a day would come when Woody's storehouse of unspent kisses and unspoken words would spring open, that she would hear him say he loved her, would feel his lips press to her cheek.

Holding his hand in both of hers, she said, 'You're the best boy, sweetie. You know that?'

He didn't always indicate that he heard what she said to him. Some days his responses were rare or nonexistent. But now he shook his head.

'But you are,' she insisted. 'You really are. You're the best boy that you can be, and I appreciate how hard you try. I love you, Woodrow Eugene Bookman.'

His embarrassment was palpable. His eyes remained downcast, and he chewed on his lower lip.

'You brush your teeth and floss. Only two minutes with the Sonicare. No matter how badly you might want to brush for ten or twenty

175

minutes — only two.'

Woody nodded.

'I'll stop by later to tuck you in and make sure you're all right.'

When she let go of his hand, he crossed the kitchen and went through the swinging door, not with the exuberance of a young boy, but with the gravity of a little old man. He was not just a small and vulnerable child imprisoned by his developmental disorder. He was also a prodigy with a high IQ, and the chains of his condition thwarted his great promise. For the sake of her own well-being, Megan dared not consider the intensity of Woody's frustration.

She got up and went to the keypad beside the back door. To allow Woody the freedom of the house, she set the alarm system in the at-home mode, arming the doors and most windows and all the glass-break sensors, but not the motion detectors. The upstairs windows, those that were beyond easy reach from the ground or a porch roof, had not been wired.

44

Woody changed into his pajamas and went into his bathroom and brushed his teeth for precisely two minutes. He flossed especially well around those teeth that were secured by transplanted tissue donated by a dead man.

No, it hadn't been as spooky as that. The guy hadn't been dead when he made the donation.

He made arrangements while he was living. Or maybe his family had authorized the taking of the tissue after the man had died. If the latter was the case, Woody hoped that the donor's family wouldn't show up here someday and want to have their pictures taken with him because their loved one's gums were in his mouth. He didn't know the name of the dead guy, so the family had probably not been given Woody's name, but they could always go to court and try to find out. Courts were unpredictable because judges were people. There were a lot of things in life to worry about, but people were the biggest source of problems, especially when you had a developmental disorder like he did and you found a lot of people embarrassing and you knew they would find you embarrassing, too, if they knew anything about you. Not everyone was simply embarrassing. Some were also scary. The scary ones had a subtle smell. He couldn't describe it, but he could detect it. He'd done some reading on the subject, and he learned that many dogs could smell extreme cases of schizophrenia and homicidal psychopathology, so maybe he had a bit of dog in him. When he was around too many people who wanted to interact with him, whether they were scary or just embarrassing, he wanted to scream and scream until they went away with their hands over their ears. But he couldn't scream any more than he could tell them to leave him alone. So instead he got a killer headache, and he grew so nervous that he couldn't think. Sometimes he was nauseated, his stomach and intestines and everything in his abdomen felt as if it came loose and sloshed around, and he became terrified that he was going to start farting like a machine gun. Nothing was more embarrassing than farting, not even having your dead gum donor's family show up to take pictures with you.

After he finished in the bathroom, Woody turned out the light and went into his bedroom and stood staring at his computer. After some deliberation, he got on his hands and knees and crawled into the knee space of his desk and plugged everything in again. The bad men at the Tragedy website could not have tracked him. And he was never going back there again.

His report — 'The Son's Revenge: Faithfully Compiled Evidence of Monstrous Evil' — lay on his desk. He'd meant to give it to his mom, but then he'd had an episode and needed to go away to Castle Wyvern.

He would put it on the breakfast table first thing in the morning.

He thought now of the words that had appeared on his screen when he'd been deep in the Dark Web. You AGAIN. And then YOU ARE NOT ALEXANDER GORDIUS. And finally WE WILL FIND YOU.

That last one had been a bluff. They couldn't have tracked his signal to source, not after all the precautions he'd taken.

Nevertheless, he felt pretty sure that he wouldn't fall asleep right away. He lumped his pillows into a pile and sat up in bed with a novel by Patrick O'Brian, a seafaring adventure set in the eighteenth century. It was a rousing tale about courage and honor and steadfast loyalty, qualities that Woody admired and believed were important, but that he doubted he would ever possess to any significant degree, considering what a mess he was. One way you learned things, however, was by example, which was the reason he read books like this, in addition to the fact that he loved a rattling-good story. For the same reason — that you might become what you read — he avoided novels about vampires, were-wolves, and zombies.

45

After Megan washed and dried the dishes, she indulged in a half glass of wine to follow her first two. She sat at the kitchen table to savor the cabernet while reading two more chapters of her novel.

In these latter hours of the evening, a wind had risen out of the northwest, filling the night with whispers and moans. From time to time, a series of soft thumps on the back porch were not evidence of a prowler, merely one of the rocking chairs as a gust of wind bumped it against the house. And the hanging basket of trailing fuchsia swung back and forth, the friction of chain link on hook raising a creak-croak that might have been a hacksaw determinedly chewing through something as hard as bone.

Noises within the house sometimes suggested the presence of an intruder — phantom footsteps, the creak of a door — but they were only the usual settling noises, on this occasion exaggerated by the structure's resistance to the wind's insistence.

In the weeks immediately following Jason's death, when Megan and Woody moved to these acres on the outskirts of Pinehaven, the nights had not seemed romantic, as she remembered them from when she'd been growing up here. At best, the falling darkness brought with it an air of strangeness, of an alien realm, as if Nature knew of her years in the city, thought her a traitor to the land, and no longer welcomed her. At worst, the nights sometimes seemed full of menace, for the world had deteriorated since her childhood, even here in Pinehaven County. It was easy to imagine a nightmare gallery of decadents — meth-lab operators and half-crazed end-times loners — who had taken refuge deep in the wilderness and might at night venture nearer to watch her from the trees. For the first few months after they moved in, she closed all the draperies and blinds with the setting of the sun.

But the locals welcomed them at once, and in time the land seemed as benign as it had been in her youth. These days Megan no longer suspected the forest of harboring a nastywork of degenerates, and nightfall brought with it only stars and the moon either in full or fragment. For some, the loneliness of widowhood would have been magnified by the solitude of this property, by sharing it only with a boy who never spoke. For Megan, solitude allowed contemplation and introspection, which led to acceptance

180

of her loss, and peace came upon her sooner here than it might have elsewhere.

She finished a chapter in her book and the wine in her glass, closed the former and rinsed out the latter at the sink.

She went through the downstairs, double-checking door locks and turning out the lights in her wake.

In the foyer, at the living room archway, as she reached for the wall switch, she saw that Woody had been here before going to his room. The silver-framed photographs were no longer facedown on the Steinway. They were all facing the piano bench, so she could see them when she played. But they should be turned in this direction, toward the room. She would rearrange them in the morning. Right now, it was enough to know that he had heard her earlier, understood what she'd told him about keeping his father in their memory, and agreed.

She doused the living room lights.

At the front door, the deadbolt was engaged.

On the security-system keypad, a red light glowed under the word HOME, just as it did on the control unit by the back door. A third keypad was in the master bedroom.

With her book in hand, intending to read herself to sleep, Megan climbed the stairs.

The wind was a testing wind that rattled sheet tin somewhere above — perhaps the flange on a chimney spark arrester — whistled along empty rain gutters, pillowed its fists against window glass, pressed creaks and muffled groans from attic rafters, collar beams, and joists much as a rolling sea made the timbers of a ship's hull speak.

After rapping softly on Woody's door, she opened it. In the light of a nightstand lamp, he was sound asleep, half sitting up against a rampart of pillows, an open hardcover book splayed on his lap.

She plucked a Kleenex from the box on his nightstand, used it to mark his place in the story, and set the book aside. She took two pillows from the stack against which the boy leaned, eased him into a better sleeping posture, and pulled up the blanket.

Although Woody seldom slept more than five or six hours, he was a deep sleeper. Megan's ministrations failed to wake him.

She kissed his smooth, cool brow and adjusted the three-way lamp to its lowest setting.

As she stepped away from the bed, the boy muttered in his sleep. She turned to study him and listened and decided that his dream, whatever its subject might be, was not a nightmare. He didn't seem to be distressed. She was almost to the door when she thought she heard a word escape him, not the meaningless murmurs and whimpers of a dreamer, but in fact a *word*. His first in all his life.

For perhaps a minute, she stood rock still, listening. But if he had spoken, he did not speak again. Indeed, the muttering and murmuring had ceased. He lay in silence.

She must have heard something in his dreamy ramble that hadn't been there. After all, neither he nor she knew anyone named Dorothy.

46

The guest bedroom at the end of the upstairs hallway lies in darkness, the door ajar. Shacket watches the bitch through the gap as she raps lightly on the door to the boy's room and then goes in there.

When she appears maybe two minutes later, she comes toward him, unaware that she is observed and desired. She switches off the hall light and enters the master bedroom.

That door has no deadbolt, only a flimsy privacy latch engaged by a button in the knob. Most likely, she won't even use that. The perimeter of the security system is armed, the doors and windows. She feels that she is in no danger.

Earlier, while she and the boy ate dinner, Shacket returned to her bedroom, suddenly wondering about the possibility of a gun. A woman alone was likely to have a weapon.

He found the gun safe attached to the bed rail, which he had previously overlooked. To open it, he required a four-digit number.

He knew several important things about Megan, and one of them was likely to provide what he needed. When programming such devices, people tended to resort to a sequence of numbers they weren't likely to forget. He knew her birthday, Jason's birthday, Woody's birthday, and the date of her wedding, at which he had been a guest but not of course the best man. He had tried the numbers in that order. The wedding date did the trick.

The ten bullets are now in the toilet bowl in

the spare-bedroom bath, waiting to be flushed.

He leaves the guest room and makes his way along the hall to the master suite. He puts one ear to the door, listens, and hears running water.

When he turns the knob, the privacy latch is not engaged. He opens the door several inches. Both bedside lamps are aglow. The door to the bathroom stands half-open. He can't see Megan, but he can hear the buzz of an electric toothbrush.

On the bed is a book. Apparently she intends to read for a while.

If he is to fulfill his fantasy of settling atop her when she is asleep, entering her as she wakes, he needs to give her a couple of hours before he returns.

He closes the door quietly and makes his way down through the light-less house, which is not dark to him.

47

In her first few months in this house, when the Sierra night seemed to harbor imminent existential threats, Megan lay awake, in anticipation of shattering glass and the piercing shrillness of the alarm. Because she slept in a T-shirt and panties, before retiring each evening, she laid out a pair of jeans and a crewneck sweater on the other half of the king-size bed, where she could quickly snatch them up and slip into them. Three years later, though she now found her initial paranoia amusing, she remained in the habit of having clothes near at hand.

After placing the jeans and sweater like the form of an imaginary bed-mate, she went around to her side of the bed, turned back the top sheet with the blanket — and discovered a three-inch-long smear of some kind on the bottom sheet. This was Wednesday, and Verna Brickit routinely changed the linens midweek, so they ought to be spotless.

When Megan wiped a finger across the substance and brought it to her nose, it smelled like earth, dirt. A few small flecks of chaff were in it, bits of golden grass or weeds.

She couldn't imagine how this had gotten here or why Verna hadn't noticed it. Nearly all of it brushed off with the sweep of her hand. She returned to the bathroom to get a fresh wash-cloth, dampened a corner, and used that to remove the last traces of dirt without leaving a significant wet spot.

After washing her hands, as she settled in bed to read, her back against the padded headboard, she smelled something alien to herself and to the room, a thin, acrid odor. She turned her head left, right, leaned forward to smell the blanket, but the strange scent had been faint and transient. She could no longer detect it.

She picked up her book and opened it.

48

As restless as the wind that chases its many tails through the night, Lee Shacket wanders the dark rooms on the ground floor of the house.

He is frustrated not merely by the need to wait for Megan to fall asleep, but also by the slow pace of his becoming. When this horizontal gene transfer is complete, he will be a more formidable man than he is now, above all men and all laws, including the laws of nature, and he is eager — impatient — to fulfill his singular destiny. He intuits that the programmed archaea will effect further changes, rendering him powerful beyond all human dreams of power, but he lacks the imagination to foresee what his new strengths and capabilities will be. He wants them *now*.

As the wind combs dead needles from the pines and slings them through the night to prickle like sleet against the living room windows, Shacket circles the grand piano, the very presence of which angers him for some reason that he can't define.

She won't play the damn thing when she is his collared and obedient bitch. She will not be allowed music or painting. She will be allowed only to submit, to service him in all the ways he likes, and *she will enjoy it*.

The ten empty silver frames stand testament to a past that he will erase, to a husband and son who will be purged from her memory, so that her life will begin tonight, under him. He feels the folded photos in the pocket of his jeans and realizes that his previous intention to wad them and shove them down her throat to punish her for resistance is not necessary.

There will be no significant resistance. By the

hour, he grows stronger. He is aware of an increasing density of his muscles and a previously unknown tensile strength. He will easily be able to pin her beneath him. At the least provocation, he will bite off one of her ears and chew it and spit it in her face, terrifying her into submission without materially damaging her beauty, which she must retain to be worthy of him.

She must as well remain worthy of being the mother of the new race, for she will bear many offspring, children who will be formed in Shacket's image, blessed with his superior genes. They won't be merely children, but demigods incorporating the diverse attributes of many species. He no longer has any doubt that he will pass along what the billions — *trillions!* — of archaea have installed within him. His testicles feel swollen with the seed of a new world.

From his pocket he extracts the photographs. They slip from his fingers. He tramples them underfoot as he leaves the room.

His metamorphizing vision amplifies the most meager sources of light, so that he navigates the rooms and hallways with increasing agitation, but without knocking against anything, as silent as a silverfish that has slithered out of a crack in the baseboard to explore in the darkness that it prefers.

In spite of the wondrous nature of his becoming or because of it, he cannot sit and wait. He fidgets even as he moves from one place to another, wringing his hands and running them through his hair, plucking at the spots on

187

his T-shirt that are crusted with Justine's blood, sucking at his teeth for a remaining taste of her.

He finds himself in Megan's art studio, standing at a window, with no memory of having come here. Tall, slender yard trees are bent severely toward the southeast, as though the very rotation of Earth has so violently accelerated that all things rooted in its crust will be torn loose and sent tumbling. The wind's ferocity excites Shacket, calls for him to break things as it shatters fragile limbs, to tear things as it shreds leaves and sends them swarming through the night like colonies of deformed bats.

Then he's on the move again, through a bizarre architecture, as if the house is transforming in sympathy with him. Hallways are now tunnels, although not carved out of earth or rock, but rather shaped by legions from some secreted organic material resembling coarse paper, windowless rooms roughly rounded like chambers in an enclosed nest. As strange as it is, he nonetheless feels he belongs here, and he is drawn toward some communion with a horde of his own kind.

But that proves to be a hallucination — or a memory born not of experience but of instinct — because then he finds himself in the kitchen, hungrier than he has ever been. He puts his pistol on the table and searches through the contents of the freezer drawer in the bottom of the refrigerator. He finds four steaks — filet mignon — in sealed packets bearing the name of a high-end mail-order purveyor of meats. He tears open one package and chews on the raw product, but it is frozen and doesn't satisfy.

Not bothering with a dish, he places the steak in the microwave and presses the control labeled DEFROST and stands looking through the oven window while the carousel turns in the bath of radiation. As the filet begins to weep a watery serum tinted with blood, Shacket hears himself making a thin keening sound similar to one of the many voices of the wind.

Taken from the microwave, the meat is cool but no longer icy, malleable in his eager hands, wet and tender between his teeth. The taste does not offend, the texture is not repulsive, but it also is not what he hoped it would be, what he needs. The limp mass of beef doesn't struggle in his hands, nor does it cry out as it is torn, nor does it satisfy as did Justine in the meadow grass.

He wanders the house again, window to window, coveting the wind and the dark, wanting to be out there in the tumult, which speaks to him, excites him. His heart races. His pulse pounds in his temples.

He finds himself in the kitchen again, staring at the steaks that are defrosting on the floor.

He finds himself at the front door, staring at the word under the tiny red indicator light: HOME.

He turns away from the keypad, from the door.

He ascends the stairs.

In the upstairs hall, following the Persian runner, he arrives at the master suite. A blade of light slices through the quarter inch between the door and mahogany floor. The bitch is still awake, reading. He wants to take her while she sleeps. *While she sleeps.*

He stands there for a while, staring down at the light that shines like a razor's edge, his thoughts urgent and lustful and chaotic. With one hand, he rubs the crotch of his jeans. His other hand pulls at his face as though it's a mask he feels compelled to strip off, clamps over his trembling mouth to repress a cry that he yearns to let out. The wind that harrows the night encourages him to join it in a rampage, and multiple hungers besiege him.

He turns from her suite and retreats toward the front stairs.

He halts at the door to the boy's room, where only a strip of pale light purls on the polished mahogany floor. If any sound rises from within, it is too faint to be heard above the wind.

Change of plans. The boy first. Shacket opens the door. He steps inside. He quietly closes the door behind him.

49

The Four Square Diner stood directly across the town square park from the Pinehaven County courthouse, sheriff's department HQ, and morgue. At peak business hours, the mélange of aromas could make anyone on a strict diet weep, but at this late hour, the air was redolent of only bacon and coffee.

A sheriff's deputy, Bern Holland, who was on

duty from 8:00 p.m. until 5:00 a.m. and therefore ate according to a contrarian schedule, sat at the counter, having a lunch of bacon-and-egg sandwiches with fries. The other two men at the counter were here for the coffee.

Carson Conroy sat in a window booth with black coffee and a wide slice of raisin-and-plum pie.

By the time he'd finished the autopsies of Painton Spader and Justine Klineman, the dinner hour had long since come and gone — as had his appetite. Over the years, the condition of people killed in accidents or murdered had ceased to sicken him or to have any effect on him other than sometimes to elicit pity. The morgue was a world of the dead, who were beyond help and hope, as segregated from the world of the living as any dream was separate from reality. When he left work, he did so as if arising from a sleeper's phantasms, and in his busy after-work life, Carson usually didn't dwell on what he'd seen on the autopsy table any more than he would repeatedly rerun a dream in memory after waking from it. Usually. But this one was far from an ordinary case. He had no appetite for his long-delayed dinner, certainly not for meat of any kind or for anything savory, only for coffee and the sweetness of fruit pie.

With the wind gibbering and howling past the windows and the park trees shaking their shaggy shadows in the frosty light of the tall lampposts, Halloween seemed to have come six weeks early. When a van-type morgue wagon, a converted ambulance with roof-mounted lightbar, cruised

191

past the diner, bearing on its door the seal of the attorney general's office of the State of California, the sip of coffee Carson was just then taking seemed to go from hot to cold in an instant. The vehicle could not have been more ominous if it had been a long black Cadillac with tinted windows and a license plate that bore seven zeros. A chill stepped down his spine, for he knew intuitively that this had something to do with the two corpses in the morgue's cold-holding drawers.

Sacramento, the state capital, was two hours away, but the trip could have been made faster if they used their lightbar and siren.

Although some show windows glowed warmly, the shops around the square were closed, and no one was afoot at this moment.

The morgue wagon slowed at the north end of the square, turned left, slowed further, and turned left again, no doubt bound for the county buildings on the west side of the park.

That narrow greensward, about eighty feet wide, featured a three-tiered central bowl fountain and a few benches. Seven pines graced the park, all of them so old that their lowest branches were above an average man's head. Carson had a clear view of the attorney general's vehicle as it braked to a stop, hesitated, and then turned right into the service alley between the sheriff's headquarters and the morgue, its headlights washing the brick walls of the buildings.

Leaving his pie and coffee unfinished, Carson put enough money on the table to cover the check and the tip. On his way out, he told the young waitress, Angela, that he was wanted in the zombie

192

vault, which was what she insisted on calling the morgue.

Although summer officially still had another week to rule the mountains, the chilly wind previewed the autumn, scented with pine and the filtered woodsmoke that issued from fireplace chimneys. It buffeted Carson, forced him to tuck his head down and squint against the threat of the dead pine needles and fine grit that it carried in its currents.

He crossed the street, the park, the street again, and entered the alley-way as the van hearse turned right and out of sight into the municipal parking lot behind the morgue. As he was approaching the side entrance to the sheriffs headquarters, the door opened, and Sheriff Hayden Eckman stepped into the alleyway.

His face ghastly white in the fall of light from the security lamp directly over his head, Eckman appeared not merely surprised to encounter Carson, but unsettled. The office of county sheriff was an elected position, however, and being a consummate politician, Eckman instantly converted his startlement into a smile that seemed to say, *Ah, what a relief to have you here.*

'Carson! I thought you were home in bed. I'd have called, but you've had such a long day, I didn't want to bother you.'

Hours earlier in the evening, Carson had met with the sheriff in the morgue to go over the results of the autopsies. They agreed to delay a press announcement until the families of the deceased could be found and notified, and until the department's community-relations officer had time to craft a statement that conveyed the facts of the murders without using language that would unduly alarm the public.

Considering the extreme violence and the cannibalism, Carson thought the public *ought to be* unduly alarmed. But his position was not elected, and having come from a city in which political power mattered more than any other force in society, he knew the folly of asserting the full truth of anything when those who had ascended through the ballot box preferred to support a version of the truth made more palatable to the voters.

Now, as the blustering wind rattled an empty beer can along the alleyway, Carson said, 'What's happening?'

'Damnedest thing,' said Hayden Eckman. 'Come with me, you'll see.' He hurried along the alley to the municipal parking lot, into which the morgue wagon from Sacramento had disappeared.

50

In the strange dream, Woody and some old woman named Dorothy were riding in the back seat of a car, and a younger woman whom Dorothy called Rosa was driving, and they came upon this hitchhiker by the side of the road, a tall and strong-looking guy. Woody knew that it was very unwise to pick up a hitchhiker, especially one who was a tall strong-looking guy, but Rosa stopped for him nonetheless. When he got into the car, Rosa said, 'We need protection from Frank the Hater. He's going to put us in cages and never let us out.' The man smiled — he had a very appealing smile — and said, 'I've dealt with Frank the Hater before. Don't you worry about him.' From outside the car came the sound of wind, although there hadn't been wind before, and Woody felt it in his face, though all the windows remained closed. Then the tall, strong man looked into the back seat and winked at Woody and said, 'How're you doing, Scooby-Doo?' Rosa pulled the car onto the highway again, and the wind in Woody's face increased, blowing on his eyelids and lashes, and Dorothy said to the man, 'My sweet boy's just fine now that you're here,' and she put an arm around Woody. Although he didn't mind being touched by nice people, Woody was surprised when he licked Dorothy's hand.

The wind made him blink, blink, blink, and when he opened his eyes, he found himself lying in bed on his left side. A man was kneeling next to the bed, clearly visible in the low light of the lamp, leaning close and blowing on Woody's face.

For a moment, Woody felt disoriented, wondering what happened to the car and everyone in it, and then he realized he had been dreaming. For another moment, he thought he might still be dreaming as the kneeling man stopped blowing and smiled at him.

And then he caught the scent of the intruder, the subtle odor that he couldn't describe, that he'd experienced a few times before, the scent that maybe smelled stronger to dogs, like they said in those articles he'd read. This man smelled scary.

Worse than scary. What was worse? Evil?

Fear paralyzed Woody, so he couldn't even lift his head from the pillow.

The stranger spoke softly. 'Hey, little dude, what do you say?'

Woody said nothing.

'Cat got your tongue?'

Their faces were maybe six or eight inches apart.

The man's left eye was gray, his right eye brown, as if he wore colored contacts and one of them had fallen out.

Something was odd about the left eye, a soft glow deep in it. 'You hear me, *Woodrow*?' the stranger whispered. 'Are you mute *and* deaf, you little freak?'

51

The ice-white fluorescent radiance in the cold-holding room fell on bone-white ceramic-tile walls and floor, on the stainless-steel fronts of two banks of cadaver drawers, four above and four below, on Carson Conroy and Sheriff Hayden Eckman, and on the two men from Sacramento. The hard light made no one look young or handsome, or kind.

Of the men from the state capital, the one

named Frawley was supposed to be an assistant medical examiner. Even at this hour of the night, he wore a well-tailored suit, white shirt, and silk tie. His wingtips looked English, maybe by Crockett & Jones, which meant they probably cost six or seven hundred dollars, and he sported a gold Rolex watch.

The other guy, Zellman, was a blocky individual with a face like one you might find frowning eternally in a deep-jungle temple, carved from stone by worshipers and meant to represent a god of the wrathful variety. Thick neck. Long arms. Enormous hands. He claimed to be a morgue attendant and driver.

Carson didn't believe either man was what he presented himself to be. Frawley looked like a fixer, a slick operator who had friends in all the highest places and knew how to take care of any screwup they committed. Zellman had to be muscle, plain and simple.

They were here to take possession of the bodies of Painton Spader and Justine Klineman, which were zippered tight in cadaver bags and snugged in two of the stainless-steel drawers.

'We'll remove them to the morgue in Sacramento,' said Frawley.

'I don't understand this,' Carson said.

'We're asserting jurisdiction. Sheriff Eckman has agreed to relinquish investigative authority to the state.'

To Carson, Hayden Eckman said, 'The AG called me himself, a few hours ago. He made a persuasive argument.'

'What argument?'

197

Frawley turned to an attaché case that lay on a gurney employed to move cadavers through the morgue. Opening the case and extracting a sheaf of papers, he said, 'One of Sheriff Eckman's men found the killer's wallet near Justine Klineman's body. It must have fallen out of his pants when he was . . . savaging her. ID in the wallet is for Nathan Palmer, who's a fugitive wanted for murder.'

'When we had the ID,' Hayden Eckman told Carson, 'we went to the National Crime Information Center website to see if there was any posting for this guy. There was. State and federal authorities are after him big-time.'

'When did this happen?'

'Earlier this evening.'

'While I was doing the autopsies?'

'You and Jim had just started the first one.'

Jim Harmon was Carson's one assistant.

'And you didn't tell me?'

Eckman didn't meet Carson's eyes, but instead stared at the papers Frawley had produced. 'The want on this Nathan Palmer creep is intense. It's not something to dick around with. I've been on the phone working things out with the attorney general and the FBI for hours. We have a good lab here, but nothing like the state and feds can provide in Sacramento.' He stepped to the gurney and began to sign the documents where they were marked with brightly colored stick-on plastic arrows.

For the past nine months, Carson had been trying with some difficulty to get a fix on Hayden Eckman, who wasn't the sheriff who'd brought him to Pinehaven County four years earlier. Eckman was a competent lawman and department manager, but more political than his predecessor, perhaps with one eye on a higher elected office.

'He urinated on the bodies, on their clothes,' Carson said.

Frawley looked at him as if to say, *And your point is?*

'I have the clothes, other evidence. We'll find a few hairs of his, other DNA. Everything's ready for the lab in the morning.'

Frawley nodded. 'We'll take all that with us tonight. Our lab operates twenty-four/seven.' He presented a new document. He said to the sheriff, 'Signature there, initial here.'

'But what about finding him?'

'It's inevitable, Mr. Conroy.'

'You seem very laid-back about this. Palmer bit the woman to death. *He ate her face, her breasts, for Christ's sake.*'

'Nothing's to be gained by panicking the public,' Frawley said.

'Leaving them ignorant is leaving them vulnerable.'

'We release sensational details like that, we'll get hundreds of call-in tips, people sighting Palmer everywhere he isn't. We'll have to investigate them when we should be tracking him down.'

Carson said, 'Sheriff, if this lunatic sonofabitch is loose in Pinehaven County — '

'His pattern,' Frawley said with a note of condescension, 'is to keep moving. Especially after a kill like this. There's virtually zero chance he's anywhere within a hundred miles of here.'

'Virtually is good enough for you? And since when do bug-shit crazy and patterns of behavior go together?'

Finished signing, Sheriff Eckman finally looked at Carson. 'Just in case Palmer is still in these parts, the state AG is lending us manpower for the search. We're a small department and cover a lot of ground, Carson. For a case like this, we need that help.'

Producing a second set of documents, Frawley said, 'Mr. Conroy, I need you to sign cadaver and evidence releases plus an NDA.'

'A nondisclosure agreement for a medical examiner? I've never heard of such a thing. If I have to testify in court — '

'You won't. You're out of this when you sign. It's not just a murder case, Conroy. It's a matter of national security.'

'Palmer may be a monster, but in court he has the right to call as witness anyone whose name is in the chain-of-evidence file.'

'Not this guy. Not this case. Different rules apply,' Frawley declared.

He cited federal statutes allowing Carson to be prosecuted for failure to cooperate.

Whether they were real laws or fabricated, Carson didn't know. However, for years the country had seemed to be morphing from a representative republic into something worse.

Throughout this, stone-faced Zellman had never taken his eyes off Carson, as though he was prepared to break a knee whenever that might be required.

'Sign it,' Sheriff Eckman said, the coldness of

angry authority in his voice. 'It's late. It's the right thing to do. *Sign it.*'

Strictly speaking, Hayden Eckman wasn't Carson's boss, but he had considerable influence with the county board. There was no doubt that he could get Carson fired for cause — and ensure that no other jurisdiction in need of a medical examiner would hire him.

Affronted, Carson signed where the brightly colored stick-on arrows indicated, although he said, 'I consider this under duress.'

'Consider it what you wish,' Frawley replied as he returned the documents to his attaché case.

52

The skirling wind whipping the night. The low lamplight. Gray eye, brown eye, the gray one somehow *wrong*.

The stranger's breath smelled megabad. His teeth were stained. Ragged tissue peeled from his chapped lips, as if he'd been chewing on them.

With one finger, the guy stroked Woody's right cheek, the side of his nose, and it was like being touched by something that had slithered out of the closet or from under the bed in a scary story, so that his hammering heart felt as if it might be rising into his throat, and he wanted to scream and scream, but he couldn't make a sound, nor could he move, only lie paralyzed with fear and gaze into the intruder's fierce eyes and smell his stinky breath. And wonder what next, what next?

201

'You look just like your treacherous father,' the stranger whispered. 'Good thing you don't have a brain. The world doesn't need another scheming, selfish piece of shit like Jason.'

This must be someone from the Dark Web, from the Tragedy site. Who else could it be? But how *fast* they tracked down their quarry! He should have left the computer unplugged.

'Are you really a dummy? You don't look like a dummy. Maybe you fake being a dummy.'

With his finger, the man drew circles on the ball of Woody's chin, around and around.

'In the world becoming, there won't be any room for dummies. Not for dummies and cripples and people with wrong ideas.'

He slid his finger over Woody's lower lip, the upper, the lower again, and Woody wanted to bite him hard.

'Very tender,' the intruder said.

Rapidly, repeatedly, the man blinked his right eye, and the colored contact lens popped out. It stuck on his lower lash. With thumb and forefinger, he plucked it up and stared at it as though puzzled, as though he had no idea what it might be. He flicked it away.

Now both eyes were gray, and both were *wrong*. When the man focused on Woody again, there seemed to be a radiance in his eyes that wasn't a reflection of the lamplight. The eyes were pools of gray, like rainwater puddled on weathered wood, and the pools were deep and cold, and from far down in them emanated a phosphorous glow.

Woody desperately wanted to go away to

Castle Wyvern, climb the tower stairs, shoot home the massive lock bolts, and curl up on the bed of reeds until this man wasn't here anymore. He wanted to look up at the glassless windows and watch the dragons flying across a sky thick with dark clouds through which lightning pulsed but from which thunder never issued. If he fled to Wyvern, however, he would be leaving his mother alone with this man, this *thing*.

53

A few minutes past midnight, Megan closed the novel and put it on the nightstand. She was about to switch off the lamps when she realized that she hadn't gotten her pistol from the gun safe that was attached to the rail of the bed frame.

She slid out of bed and knelt and entered the four digits of her wedding date. The door of the small metal box clicked open, and she retrieved the 9 mm Heckler & Koch — and went suddenly, absolutely still.

Always, she stowed the pistol with the muzzle toward the wall, toward the head of the bed. That was how the box was designed. The safe could accommodate the weapon in either position, but it was specifically designed for the grip to be toward the foot of the bed. Now the gun was reversed.

Never before had she locked the pistol away in this position.

Verna Brickit didn't have the combination. Only Megan could open the gun safe.

The weapon didn't feel right, either. Fear fine-tuned her senses, so that she could hear distinctly every instrument of the wind's symphonic performance and every response of the house, see her ghostly reflection in the farthest window and the dark lashing yard trees and the darker woods that should have been beyond her ken, feel every subtle current of air that breathed across her bare legs and also feel a lightness to the gun.

She practiced at a shooting range monthly, often two hundred rounds in a session, and she knew what the Heckler felt like when it was fully loaded. She released the magazine. Empty.

The pistol had held ten rounds when she put it away the previous morning. Someone had come into the house before the alarm had been activated for the evening. Someone was still here. But who?

Although she felt naked in her sleepwear, she went first to the walk-in closet. As she turned the knob, she realized that she hadn't entered the closet when she'd come to bed, and she thought, *He's in there!* That was an irrational thought, and she knew it for what it was, fear borne, and indeed no one lurked in the closet. She turned on the light.

The metal canister was stored at the back of a deep drawer filled with running shorts and sweatpants. She retrieved it, screwed off the lid, took out a box of Gold Dot ammunition, opened both ends of the box, pressed out an egg-crate plastic container in which were nestled twenty bullets, and hurried back to the bed.

Hands trembling, she fumbled bullets out of the container and dropped three on the carpet. She told herself to get a grip, shape up. She thought, *Woody, nothing can happen to Woody, please God.* Her hands steadied, though inserting the rounds in the magazine wasn't as easy under these circumstances as on a shooting range. *Come on, Megan, load the damn thing, all ten rounds, might need every one.*

When it was done, she glanced at the phone on the nightstand. The numbers for fire and police and ambulance were printed on a community-supplied card adhered to the cradle, between the handset and the keypad. No. Woody first. Sheriff's deputy would take five minutes, maybe ten, to get here. No time to pull on the jeans she'd laid out, either. Straight to Woody, bring him back here, lock the door, brace it with a chair, call the police, then slip into the jeans and the crewneck.

She went to the hallway door, grabbed the knob with her left hand, holding the pistol with her right. She couldn't do this and keep a preferred two-hand grip on the gun.

Doors were the worst. No way to know what waited beyond one. If an intruder stood ready on the other side, if he rushed her as she pulled open the door, he could unbalance her, strike her, tear the gun out of her hand. Except he thought the gun was unloaded, not a threat, so even if he knocked her off her feet, she still had her own advantage of surprise.

Maybe it shouldn't have taken her this long to understand, but she only now realized that he hadn't come in her room and somehow opened the gun safe and unloaded the Heckler if his intention was to burglarize the house without risk to himself. He had disarmed her and bided his time, hiding somewhere in the residence, waiting for her to go to sleep, so that he could easily overwhelm her and rape her.

Her heart knocked violently against its caging ribs as she opened the door to the hall.

54

Kipp erupted from a dream about riding in a car with Dorothy and Rosa. The boy was screaming on the Wire.

He was a boy, no doubt about that now, not another dog but a special boy who could use the Wire, whether he knew it or not, a boy like no other, and he was in peril.

Springing to his feet on the bed, Kipp barked twice.

Startled, Ben Hawkins switched on a night-stand lamp and sat up, blinking away a residue of sleep. 'Hey, what?'

Kipp jumped down from the bed and padded to the motel room door and reared up on his hind legs and pawed at the deadbolt.

But that wasn't good enough. He seemed to be saying that he needed to potty. He didn't need to potty.

He dashed to the nightstand, where Ben had left his wallet and the electronic key for the Range Rover.

He stood on his hind legs again, bit the key chain, and hurried back to the door with the key dangling from his mouth.

Getting out of bed, Ben said, 'What's gotten into you?'

Not having an alphabet wall and a laser pointer made life a lot more difficult.

Kipp dropped the key at the door.

He hurried to the small table by the window, stood again, and got his mouth on the hardcover book Ben had been reading.

He took the book to the door. He dropped it beside the key.

He turned to look at his new companion.

'You don't like the motel? You want one with more amenities? Listen, Scooby-Doo, I've only gotten like an hour of sleep.'

On the Wire, the boy was screaming in abject terror.

Ben had brought a shaving kit in from the Range Rover. It was in the bathroom. He would have to pack that himself.

He had also brought in a suitcase, but he had not yet opened it. The suitcase stood near the mirrored closet door.

Panting with frustration, Kipp went to the bag and knocked it over. He looked at his companion.

Ben had hung his jeans in the closet. As he took them out and pulled them on, he said, 'All right, you're trying to tell me what? That you need to pee?'

He had been a Navy SEAL. He couldn't be stupid. Maybe he just woke up slowly.

Kipp took the handle of the overturned suitcase in his mouth and, backing up, dragged the Samsonite across the room to the door.

Sitting on the edge of the bed, pulling on the socks he'd left balled up in his sneakers, Ben said, 'You're a very strange dog.'

The motel key was lying on the table where the book had been.

Kipp got it, brought it to the door, and dropped it on the suitcase.

'Weird things happen in a war zone. There are times you ought to die, you don't, and it's impossible to explain why you don't.'

After putting on his shoes without further comment, Ben came to the door and stood looking at the suitcase, the book, the keys.

'Like, you turn a corner, there's a bad guy with an automatic carbine ten feet away. He pulls the trigger, the rifle jams, and you shoot him dead instead of he you.'

Kipp wagged his tail.

'About the third time something like that happens, you start to think the world is a stranger place than you always thought.'

Kipp nodded.

'Or maybe I'm losing my mind.'

Kipp shook his head: *no*.

'Well, I guess there's no going back to bed.

Maybe you don't need to pee, but I do. Then we're out of here.'

55

Megan pulled the door open, let it arc under its own momentum, shielding behind it as it moved, and no one burst into the bedroom. She had both hands on the pistol as the door swung past her to reveal the hallway.

As she cleared the threshold, the spill of light issuing from her suite proved barely sufficient for her to see that the hall was deserted.

Woody's quarters lay to her left, toward the front of the house. To her right were two guest rooms, a bath, and a hall closet. The intruder could be in any of them, door ajar, watching through the gap. Opposite Woody's suite was a sewing room that she used for storage, and maybe the door stood ajar, maybe not. She didn't dare turn her back on the guest wing, and she needed to keep an eye on that sewing room, so she put her back to the wall, just to the left of the door that she'd come through.

Before she began to move, she listened, trying to hear through the lamentations of the wind that, in their volume and quality of distress, might have been a threnody for the death of the world itself. But the rainless storm was a mask of sound behind which footsteps or any other telltale noises could not be heard.

Her heart knocking to the frantic tempo of the

wind, she eased sideways, turning her head left and right, the one eye of the pistol tracking where her two eyes looked.

She came to Woody's room without incident. As she stepped inside, she urgently whispered his name.

Before she could close the door behind her, she saw her son on the bed, lying on his left side, his back to her, a man kneeling in soft lamplight at bedside, face-to-face with her boy.

'Here comes Mommy,' the intruder said. 'You know how hot your mommy is? Way too hot to waste her life with a dummy like you.'

56

The wind was a mad spirit, howling along the alleyway as though through the halls of Bedlam, flailing against the brick walls of the buildings.

The guy named Zellman, surely experienced in the handling of the dead, whether as an assistant medical examiner or otherwise, drove the morgue wagon with two cadavers aboard. Frawley the fixer followed in the Shelby Super Snake that had belonged to the late Painton Spader, which had been transferred to the custody of the state attorney general along with the bodies and other evidence. Both vehicles turned right into the town square and out of sight, taking their light with them.

In the wind-shaken gloom, Carson Conroy said, 'This is so not right.'

Sheriff Eckman shrugged. 'It is what it is.' He went to the side entrance out of which he'd come earlier and disappeared into his elected domain.

Carson heard that expression more often these days — *It is what it is* — and it nettled him every time someone spoke it. He wanted to say to Eckman, *You are what you are, and now I know what that is.* He held his tongue, because in the next election the voters might wise up and cast their ballots for a new sheriff. In the meantime, Carson didn't want to be forced out of his job.

In spite of the late hour, he left the wind to its raging and returned to his office. At his computer, he accessed the National Crime Information Center website and went to the list of people for whom arrest warrants were outstanding. He sought the name Nathan Palmer — and began to make a list of curious facts.

57

For an instant, Megan didn't recognize the intruder, but then she identified him by his voice, which she had heard earlier in the day, on the phone. Lee Shacket.

His hair was no longer blond, but brown. His neatly trimmed beard had been shaved off. Other changes in his appearance were too subtle to pinpoint, but he had about him a disturbing *otherness*.

211

Woody lay motionless, and when she spoke his name louder than before, he didn't respond with any movement. Her thundering heart pounded faster, and she thought, *What have you done to him, you sonofabitch?*

Shacket's right hand was on Woody's head. On Woody's *face*.

Megan had the Heckler in a two-hand grip, just like she'd been taught, the front sight fixed on Shacket's face, the only thing she could see of him as he knelt at the other side of the bed, the boy between them, but her knocking heart shook her arms, something that never happened on a shooting range. At twenty-some feet, even when you were ready steady, a head shot was a tricky deal, a chest shot always better.

'Mommy wants to shoot the hundred-million-dollar man,' Shacket said. 'Your mommy doesn't know what's good for her, but she'll learn soon enough.'

She gave voice to her fear. 'What have you done to him?'

His smile was wolfish. 'Just touched him. Being touched seems to traumatize the little dummy. He's stiff as a board, petrified. He doesn't like being touched, at least not by me.'

As Shacket stroked Woody's face with one hand, Megan said, 'Get away, get away from him.'

'He doesn't like being touched by me,' Shacket repeated, continuing to touch the boy. 'The little freak is a big snob, just like his mommy. Mommy Megan thinks she's so much better than other people. Even a hundred-million-dollar man isn't

212

good enough to touch her.'

She dared to take a step closer to him, another step, but she couldn't yet keep the front sight where it needed to be, her heart beating so loud in her ears that she could no longer hear the windstorm if it still raged. Even in her paranoid days, when she'd first moved here and imagined a hundred scenarios in which nothing but a gun would save her and Woody, she hadn't foreseen a situation like this, with the boy intervening between her and a threat, the only possible shot too dangerous to take.

'I called the police,' she lied.

'That would be too bad if you did. That would be a big mistake. We all make mistakes though, don't we, Megan? I made one when I left my pistol in your kitchen earlier, after I ate that hot bitch's tits.' He snickered and shook his head. 'No, that's not right, it was a steak. In your kitchen, it was a steak, and it wasn't as good as Justine's breasts.'

Maybe drugs fueled Shacket, but he was also inarguably insane. He began to lose control of his face, features failing to cooperate in a coherent expression. Twitches and ticks and squints and crooked grins and ill-formed frowns contested ceaselessly.

His increasing instability and his claim of cannibalism were force magnifiers for Megan's fear. Her chest became tight, and she drew breath in ragged inhalations.

He said, 'There would be no future for any of us if you really did call the police. But you're a terrible liar, Megan. I smell the deception as surely as I smell your twat. Now let me tell you what's going to happen. I'm going to have my fantasy, after all. You and me, just like it always should have been. You know where my right hand is?'

'Get away from him.'

'*Do you know where my right hand is?*' he shouted, the lamplight lending an eerie glow to his eyes.

'Your hand's on his face,' she said.

'But you can't see precisely how it's placed. The dummy's eyes are closed, Megan. My thumb is on his right lid, my forefinger on his left. Can you picture that, Megan? I could press hard, dig deep, take out his eyes in two seconds. Then he'd be mute, blind, stupid, three times useless.' He put his left hand to the back of Woody's head, to prevent him from pulling away. 'You want me to gouge out his eyes, or you want to stop where you are and discuss options?'

'You fucking creep. You're dead if you hurt him.'

'Megan, Megan, Megan. You're in no position to be so rude. Get off your high horse for once.'

She didn't dare take another step, still didn't have the shot she needed. Blood sang in her ears as shrill as tinnitus.

'You want to take a shot, Megan? Go ahead and take a shot.'

He thought the pistol wasn't loaded. If she took a shot and missed, he would blind Woody.

'Do you feel lucky, Megan?'

'No.'

'Do you still think you're better than me?'

'I never said I was better than you.'

'But you thought it. Don't lie to me. I smell your lies. Be truthful with me, or the dummy pays.'

'All right. Yes. I thought I was better than you.'

'But now. Now I've been in your cozy house all afternoon, all evening, doing what I please, and you were clueless. Do you still think you're better than me, smarter than me?'

'No.'

'Say it.'

'I don't think I'm better than you. Or smarter.'

'I hope that's true. For the dummy's sake, I hope that's true, Megan. I hope you've learned and you're chastened. I feel his eyes moving under the lids, like when a dreamer dreams and there's rapid eye movement. So there are three things I want you to do, Megan. Are you with me?'

'Yes. I'm with you.'

'First, I want you to put down the gun. Second, I want you to take off what you're wearing. Third, I want you to lie down on the bed and spread those long lovely legs for me.'

'Here?'

'Of course here. Are you worried about corrupting a minor?' That juvenile snicker again. 'The dummy won't even understand what we're doing. He'll lie here sucking his thumb while we make a better baby than him, a baby for the new world becoming.'

'Don't hurt him.'

'Don't *make* me hurt him, Jason's little freak. You understand how much I would like to hurt him, Megan?'

'I think so, yes.'

'For you, just for you, I'm not hurting the little dummy. We're making a bargain here. You're not as smart as you think you are. You don't know what you think you know.'

By that he probably meant that she didn't know he had taken the ammunition out of her pistol. He was taunting her. He wanted her to pull the trigger, experience the shock of its failure to fire.

'Where do you want me to put down the gun?'

'On the bed. Be very, very careful, Megan. If you try anything, you'll be surprised how badly it works out for you and him. You try anything, and it doesn't work out, I'll take his eyes, and that will be on you, his blindness on you forever.'

The moment had come. The boy was his shield, even though he didn't believe he needed a shield. He had an animal cunning. She wasn't going to get a clearer shot than the one the next minute might offer.

As she approached him, she didn't lower the pistol, hoping he would tempt her by rising up just a little, putting slightly more space between his head and Woody.

Fear of what might happen abruptly became an abhorrence of allowing it to happen, and in an instant her tremors stopped, her aim steadied, the front sight fixed on his face, and as she reached the bed, she squeezed off a shot.

Maybe he smelled her deception. He juked as she was about to fire, and the bullet tore his left ear. He howled like an animal, didn't blind the boy, but instead, as fast as a skink, inhumanly

216

fast, he swept Woody off the bed, into his arms, using him as a shield. She didn't dare another shot. The bathroom door stood just three steps away, and Shacket was through it, slamming it behind him — *Sweet Jesus, so crazy fast* — so supernaturally fast she knew in an instant he hadn't been warning her just that her pistol might be empty when he had said *You don't know what you think you know.* Something else must be going on with him, something beyond easy comprehension.

She tried the door, it was locked, he was going to blind Woody, she fired two rounds into the latch, shouldered the door, crashed through into a tumult of wind rattling the medicine cabinet door, flapping the towels on the rack.

Woody on the floor, in the corner by the shower, his beautiful eyes wider than they'd ever been, staring at something far beyond this room.

To her right, the lower sash of the tall double-hung window open, Shacket going through, no alarm wailing because no porch roof beyond. A fleeting glimpse of him, hunched and troll-like on the sill, under the sash, looking over his shoulder, his eyes wild and shot with light, hissing at her through clenched teeth, hissing like some reptile, then dropping away into the dark.

She stepped to the window, saw he'd landed on all fours maybe fifteen feet below, like a cat, clad in black in the black night, looking up at her, his face a pale oval, as ghostly as that of a spirit wandering between worlds. Then quick across the lawn, toward the front of the property, the highway, and out of sight.

She put her pistol down on the vanity, slammed the window, gasping for breath as if she'd been running for her life. She went to Woody, knelt before him on the cold bathroom tile. Blood. Oh God. Spatters of blood. Yes, but not his. Blood from Shacket's torn ear. She touched Woody's face, smoothed his hair, picked up his hands and kissed them, all the while telling him it was all right, they were safe, the bad man was gone, she was so sorry, sorry this happened, but it was over.

Woody wasn't here with her. Sometimes he withdrew and there was no reaching him, no indication that he saw her or heard her. He went away somewhere when he was badly stressed, although she seldom knew what stressed him, couldn't get in his mind to learn the source of his upset, though of course *she knew this time.*

She sat on the floor and put her arms around Woody, pulling him into her lap as best she could, rocking him. 'It's all right, baby. Everything's okay now.'

Glass shattered in a downstairs room and a glass-break sensor set off the security alarm. Shacket had returned.

58

One lane of highway 89 was finally cleared, and the highway patrol allowed southbound and northbound traffic to get past the remaining wreckage in alternating waves. The heavy fog began to lift as Rosa Leon drove inland from the lake, toward Tahoe City. By the time she found herself two miles from Olympic Village, the last rags of mist raveled into the darkness behind her, and the night ahead lay clear but starless under an overcast.

She had dozed off twice during the hours she'd waited in line for the overturned eighteen-wheeler to be moved to one side of the highway, and now she yawned extravagantly. This had been a long day, wearying not just because of its length but because of the sadness attendant to it. But the wonder of Kipp and her responsibility for him kept her in motion.

A couple miles short of Olympic Village, she consulted the Pied Finder app again. She was dismayed to see that, after remaining for hours in the same location, Kipp had gone on the move once more. His blinking signifier placed him on Interstate 80, west of Truckee, heading toward Donner Summit. The speed at which he moved meant he must be aboard a vehicle.

Perhaps he was in the company of a good person, or maybe someone not so good. Whoever his companion might be, that person couldn't know that Kipp was more than a dog, that he was a treasure. Anyway, this wasn't anyone whom Dorothy had chosen for the role of caregiver, and Rosa would, by God, not fail Dorothy.

Although she was already doing the speed limit, she pressed down on the accelerator.

59

Pistol in hand, seven rounds remaining in the magazine, Megan hurried barefoot across Woody's bedroom, into the upstairs hallway, as Shacket threw open the front door with such force that it banged hard against its stop. He had shattered the sidelight and reached through to twist the thumb turn on the deadbolt.

Wind seethed into the house, huffing and wailing, and the alarm shrilled, and Megan reached the head of the front stairs in time to see Shacket snatch a large vase from the foyer sideboard and throw it against the wall in a rage before he disappeared panther-quick into the hallway, heading toward the back of the house.

He was insane, but he was something stranger than crazy: wild and weird and powerful and unpredictable. If he had charged up the front stairs, she would have shot him repeatedly. But as bold as he might be, he wasn't improvident.

She recalled something that he'd said: *We all make mistakes though, don't we? I made one when I left my pistol in your kitchen earlier . . .*

He'd returned to get his gun. He could ascend one set of stairs or another, probably from the kitchen, firing as he reached the top.

She went back into Woody's room, pushed the button in the door-knob to engage the privacy latch. A hard kick would spring that flimsy lock. *Brace the door.* No straight-backed chair. Just Woody's wheeled desk chair and an armchair.

Shacket was coming, and coming fast.

220

Left of the door, a seven-drawer highboy stood on four legs, too heavy to drag across the carpet. She tipped it, and it crashed onto its side, blocking the door to the height of the knob.

The phone ringing. Alarm shrieking, wind jamming the house, and *the phone ringing*. She snatched the handset off the cradle, knowing it must be the alarm company, and didn't even listen, just shouted, 'Man with a gun, in the house, *now, now, now!*'

She didn't hang up but dropped the phone and moved to the bathroom doorway.

Woody was where she had left him, but on his side now, in the fetal position.

She turned her back to the boy and faced the hallway door, on the farther side of the room, wanting to kill Shacket for what he'd already done to Woody, for terrorizing the boy, for *touching* him. If the bastard suddenly had a come-to-Jesus moment and threw down his gun and begged forgiveness, she'd shoot him anyway, shoot him again and again, kill him with great satisfaction.

He should have been here by now. The howling wind, the creaks and rattles and thumps it raised, the insistent bleating of the alarm, again her heart thundering, but she heard no gunshots, no pounding on the braced door.

She wondered where he was, thought of how he'd gone out the window and landed on all fours in the yard, his eyes like burning coals in his moon-pale face. Her imagination brought her a mental image of him climbing the house wall with the alacrity of a spider, raising the

221

double-hung window from outside and entering the bathroom behind her.

Help was on its way, armed deputies, although not likely just around the corner, still a few minutes away, when a few minutes was an eternity.

Suddenly Shacket rattled the doorknob but only for a moment, then fired two shots at the lock, disintegrating it. He tried to shove the door open, but the highboy was heavy. He pushed harder, and the door arced an inch, two inches.

She was at an angle to the gap, couldn't see him, but she fired at the jamb, fired again, and saw the pressure on the door relent.

She had five rounds left.

How many did he have — six, eight?

Again he shoved hard on the door, moving the toppled highboy another inch, two inches. If it came to a firefight, maybe his aim would be as uncanny as his animal physicality. The solid-core door was two inches thick. Trying to shoot him through it was likely a waste of ammunition.

The door moved two inches, then another two. Soon he would force entry. Judging by his rabid behavior thus far, he'd enter fast and low, firing as he came, and he would expect her to be where in fact she was, defending the entrance to the bathroom in which her troubled boy lay immobile.

Megan shrank back, using the doorjamb for what little cover it might offer, the pistol in a two-hand grip, aiming at the widening gap across the room, where the sonofabitch would soon appear.

The distinctive waffling wail of a patrol-car siren spiraled through the cacophony of wind and shrilling alarm, sooner than she had expected and swelling fast.

'They're coming!' she shouted at Shacket. 'They're coming, you ass-hole, you're finished, they're coming!'

Shacket heard them, too, and he ceased forcing his way into the room, maybe only for the moment, maybe permanently.

Megan stood ready, acid rising in her throat, vision pulsing with the violence of her heartbeat.

60

Shacket in a fury, so strong in his becoming that he believes he can kill them all, the two cops responding and the bitch and the boy. He starts boldly toward the front stairs, but cunning tamps his fury down into rage, tamps rage down into mere anger, and instead he pivots and hurries along the hallway to the back stairs, plunges down them two at a time.

The response to the alarm might involve more than two cops. Even if there are only two, they'll have pistols *and* shotguns, and they can call for backup. He's better than any of them, but a pack of wolves can defeat a single tiger.

Across the kitchen, through the back door, onto the porch. The tempest welcomes him, as does the night, and he leaps off the porch, over the steps, into the yard.

They will mount a search. He might not be able to go directly to his Dodge Demon on the forest-service road and flee the area before they begin stopping cars on the highway, looking for him. He must be indirect.

There are no deer, no dummy boy feeding them apple slices, no moonlight emanating from things instead of being reflected by them, just the rampaging wind with the first chill of autumn on its breath and all around the forest, a citadel from which the night arose and to which it will return at dawn. He races across the deepest part of the yard, toward the woods in the west.

They will come into the forest with bright Tac Lights, seeking his spoor. But in his becoming, with his increasing night vision and enhanced sense of smell, guided by an intuitive understanding of the wilderness that no other man has ever known, he will be fleet when they are fumbling, confident when they are uncertain, and he will leave them far behind, lose them, and send them home defeated.

Among the trees, both by sight and smell, he quickly finds the wandering paths that generations of deer have beaten through the underbrush, their route marked by the scent of their shed hair and musk and urine and fecal droppings. The winding trail leads through pine, cedar, fir, buckeye, soon ascending to an outcropping of rock smoothed by millennia of weather. Beyond the rock, the trail resumes and in time descends toward a stream, where the crisp night air is redolent of sedges, mosses, wild onions.

What once would have been an arduous trek

does not for a moment test his resources. His muscles stretch and flex with ease. As he moves through the wilderness, he is lithe and limber as he's been before only in the dreams of his youth. He fears nothing, neither bear nor mountain lion, and he senses that his passage spreads fear through the hearts of all the creatures that live here, paralyzes the small animals that might be his prey if he chose to take them.

Wind rages less here on the floor of the forest than in its higher boughs, shaking down dead needles and pine cones and birds' nests, the primeval equivalent of confetti to celebrate his passage.

His sense of dominion, of sovereign authority over all that he surveys, might be expected to slake the anger that has burned in him through the previous day and now into another. Instead, the farther he gets from his humiliation at the Bookman house, the deeper into the gothic spires of cedars and pines, the more the postmidnight darkness infuses itself into his blood. Anger escalates once more into rage, rage into fury. Escape accomplished — or the need for it forgotten — he stalks the night in hope of repeating the experience that had been more exciting and more satisfying than anything else in his life, sniffing the air for the wealth of information it carries, licking the darkness as he remembers that singular taste, gnashing his teeth and wishing they were sharper.

Bella on the Wire

Dogs of the Mysterium needed less sleep than ordinary dogs. They even required less sleep than the average human being.

Bella rose hours before anyone else in the Montell family.

She considered herself something of a guard dog.

From time to time, she practiced baring her teeth before a mirror. She scared herself a little.

She preferred to sleep in one of her beds on the ground floor, to more quickly become aware of any smelly intruder forcing entry.

No intruder had ever breached the sanctity of the Montell home.

That didn't mean it couldn't happen.

Although Bella was an optimist like all of her kind, she also knew that the world was awash in evil.

She could remain an optimist because she understood that the world was made exclusively for the innocent.

Rooms to house the wicked weren't included in the original architecture.

Eventually, the world would be remodeled to restore it to its original purpose.

Now, in the early hours of Thursday, she rose from her bed in the kitchen and went into the family room and stood on her hind feet and used the wall switch to turn on the lights.

She had been caught at this a few times. The family thought it was cute.

Larinda, the oldest of the children, had said, *She's afraid of the dark. I don't blame her. Just look at the news!*

Sam, the next to the oldest, said, *Boys aren't ever afraid of the dark*, though he always slept with a night light aglow.

Dennis, younger than Sam, said, *Maybe we have mice, and Bella needs light to catch them.*

We don't have mice, Larinda declared. *And Bella's not a cat. Anyway she's never produced a mouse.*

Maybe she eats them, Dennis said.

Bella is every inch a lady, Larinda objected, horrified by her brother's suggestion. *Ladies don't eat mice, for God's sake.*

Milly, the youngest, said, *You're all full of pishposh.*

Bella wasn't afraid of the dark. She just couldn't read in it.

The Wire wasn't merely a communications system. It was also an educational tool.

Other members of the Mysterium could share their knowledge of language with a young dog in mere minutes.

Solomon and Brandy, two of the more philosophical members of the Mysterium, called this ability 'brain-to-brain data downloading.'

In the family room were shelves and shelves of books.

Although she was a big girl, Bella was pretty much limited in her reading to the volumes on the lower four shelves.

There was a wheeled ottoman she could push across the room and stand on to reach the fifth shelf, but she rarely used it because of balance issues.

She could paw a book off a shelf and return it with her teeth.

If she heard footsteps and needed to ditch a book quickly, she shoved it under a skirted chair or put it on an end table, to shelve it later.

Sometimes Bella forgot, in which case the children were blamed for leaving books off the shelves.

All but one child rightly denied it. On a few occasions, after favoring Bella with a long stare, Milly had taken the blame.

Milly suspected. One day, the girl might seek the truth.

Bella hadn't decided what she would do then. Probably play it by heart when the time came.

Now, in the wee hours of Thursday morning, she was lying in the family room, reading *The Magician's Elephant* by Kate DiCamillo.

The story was funny and sad, magical and strange, but true.

True in the sense that, strange as it was, it described the matrix underlying life, a matrix of unsuspected connections among people, places, and moments widely separated in time.

Bella turned the pages either by snorting out a blast of air or by the careful brush of a paw, so as not to crinkle a page.

Stories were as delicious as food. As important as food.

Bella could not live without stories.

Stories were the greatest blessing of intelligence. They were food for the soul. They were medicine.

You could live a thousand lives through stories — and learn to shape your own life into a story of the best kind.

She had just finished chapter five and sighed with contentment when the most amazing thing happened.

A new voice came on the Wire.

He called himself Vulcan.

He claimed to be a three-year-old German shepherd.

Thus far the Mysterium had been limited only to retrievers, golden and Labrador.

Vulcan was of course telling the truth. He was a dog.

But there were other details even more astonishing.

He was transmitting from a great distance. He had been seeking contact for a year, straining ever outward.

Bella didn't know how widely the transmission had been received throughout the Mysterium.

She returned *The Magician's Elephant* to the shelves and composed an announcement for immediate urgent distribution.

Bellagram. Something exciting is happening out there. Until moments ago, no transmission on the Wire has ever been received from beyond a 120-mile radius of Sacramento. Vulcan, a German shepherd living in La Jolla, just north of San

229

Diego, has broken through to us with the news that there is a community of our kind in San Diego, Orange, and Riverside Counties. Mostly German shepherds and Bernese mountain dogs. There are seventy-two of them, residing in various conditions. What we call the Wire, they call the Radio. They have no name for themselves, but we can hope they adopt the Mysterium for themselves. Where have we come from? Why are we here? Our story is at last unfolding. Our time seems to have come. Rejoice. Be true. Stay tuned.

A DOG
AND
HIS BOY

THURSDAY 1:00 A.M. – 4:00 A.M.

61

In his first year of service, Sheriff Hayden Eckman had never before been in his office past midnight, in fact seldom after six o'clock in the evening. He was there now, and worried.

Still young and attractive, he could speak eloquently about the rule of law and public service, winning over any audience, but his current position was not his life's work, only one step on the staircase of a career that would take him far.

He had been a deputy, rising through the ranks for five years, and before that he'd been a lawyer with a less than grand practice. He still thought of himself as an attorney rather than a lawman. During the next three years, he intended to network tirelessly and take advantage of all the legal and quasi-legal ways a sheriff could enrich himself, and then run for the district attorney of Pinehaven County. With the ultimate goal of becoming attorney general of the State of California, he had already begun using the resources of his office to obtain information damaging to a list of public servants who he anticipated would be his competition in future elections.

Therefore, this business with Dexter Frawley — transferring the bodies of Painton Spader and Justine Klineman to Sacramento, that nest of vipers, and relinquishing jurisdiction in this case to the state — left him uneasy. On the one hand, the attorney general, Tio Barbizon, now owed him a favor. On the other hand, if this situation couldn't be contained and if it blew up on them, Hayden might suffer some damage to his image for having acceded so quickly to Barbizon's request.

What most disturbed him was that he couldn't be sure he was getting the straight story from Barbizon. The AG claimed to be working in conjunction — unofficially — with the National Security Agency, which was eager to keep its connection to the case secret. But Barbizon withheld large parts of the story, and he had a reputation as a sharp operator.

There was reason to think the claim of NSA involvement was legit. When the wallet containing the Nathan Palmer driver's license was found near the woman's corpse, Hayden had gone to the NCIC website to check if there might be a criminal history or an outstanding warrant on the guy. The warrant had been issued by a court in Salt Lake City, at the request of the attorney general of the State of Utah, rather than by a court in the county or the town, Springville, where the crime had been committed. Palmer was wanted for suspicion of larceny, arson, and murder. While Hayden was reading what little was in the Nathan Palmer file, the screen of his computer had blanked to white, and a silhouette of his shoulders, neck, and head appeared in black. His screen remained locked for maybe three minutes before control was returned to him. He knew this meant his photograph had been taken and his location identified, which was a capability only of the nation's major security agencies. One of them had a watch on the NCIC's Nathan Palmer file, to see who might check it out.

Twenty minutes later, before he could contact the attorney general of Utah, Hayden had received the call from Barbizon, who surprised him by asking why he had been inquiring about Nathan Palmer. When Hayden described the double homicide and the horrific savaging of Justine Klineman, Barbizon put him on hold for five minutes while he conferred with others. When he returned, he'd suggested that in this matter he was a front for the NSA, which wanted the Pinehaven case against Nathan Palmer transferred to Barbizon for prosecution. He was permitted to reveal more than the details in the warrant issued by the Salt Lake City court: Palmer had been a highly placed executive employed by Refine with oversight of the Springville facility where ninety-three people died in the fire that had been big news for two days; the Palmer ID was in fact false, one of several that the man had obtained prior to events at Springville and thought were known only to him. Barbizon wasn't permitted to reveal the fugitive's real name. Nathan Palmer had bought a custom red Dodge Demon via an offshore shell corporation that he had formed; although he thought his employer didn't know about the vehicle, he was wrong. Apparently after purchase, the Dodge had been stripped of its GPS, so that it couldn't easily be tracked; that was something his all-knowing employer *hadn't* known. Any lead that Hayden might develop on the Dodge would be welcome. Finally, this was a matter of national security, and Hayden was enjoined by law from repeating to anyone what little had been dis-closed during this conversation.

Now that Frawley and Zellman had come and gone, Hayden Eckman sat in his office, working on a pot of black coffee, wondering why Nathan Palmer, under his real name, had thought it necessary to acquire false ID and a hard-to-track vehicle. It sounded as if he either planned to sabotage the Springville plant and go on the run or anticipated a disaster for which he might be blamed. Whatever work might have been underway there, it sure as hell hadn't been the cancer research that the media reported, in which the NSA would have had no interest.

And why would Palmer's boss, knowing of his preparations to go on the run in a crisis, have kept him employed at that facility? What a snake's nest this seemed to be — a tangle of threats, yes, but also, for a man like the sheriff, a squirming mass of opportunities.

Now, following the departure of Frawley and Zellman with the bodies of the victims and all associated evidence, Sheriff Eckman had settled at his desk to write a memo describing that transfer, giving special attention to the behavior of Dr. Carson Conroy. The medical examiner had questioned the propriety of the transfer, had raised issues of protocol and ethics, infuriating the sheriff. If this ever ended up in a court, Hayden wanted a version of events, composed immediately afterward and time dated, that would diminish Conroy's credibility. According to Hayden's reimagining of events, the medical examiner hadn't shown up uninvited, but had been called to assist in the transfer and had arrived inebriated; Conroy hadn't questioned anything about the procedure, but in fact had been both confused and abusive toward the men from Sacramento.

Hayden enjoyed writing dialogue for the drunken medical examiner and inventing convincing details of his erratic behavior, careful not to make him unbelievably clownish. If ever he needed to present this memo in court, he would first share it with Frawley and Zellman, so that they could corroborate it in their testimony.

Hayden had just finished the memo, printed it, and personally filed it both electronically and physically, when Carl Fredette, the watch commander currently on duty at the front desk, buzzed him on the intercom to report a home invasion with shots fired at the residence of Megan Bookman, on Greenbriar Road.

Home invasions hereabouts were as rare as incidents involving elephants.

Although Hayden always put his own interests above those of the community and defined corruption less strictly than did the law, he had a cop's good intuition. He suspected at once that Nathan Palmer, whoever he might really be, had not moved on from Pinehaven County.

62

Like all members of the Mysterium, Kipp could turn the Wire on and off as if it were a radio, though emergency transmissions always came through.

He didn't turn it off now, because the boy's cry of emotional pain and desperation was a signal to home onto.

Giving directions to Ben Hawkins could be accomplished without words because the man was smart enough to believe in the impossible when evidence showed him it was possible, after all.

Sad to say, not all human beings were that open-minded.

Some believed the most ridiculous things without a shred of evidence, but wouldn't believe a truth even when it stuck its fingers in their eyes. So to speak.

Anyway, when they came to an intersection, Ben pointed and asked, 'That way?'

If he pointed the right way, Kipp barked once enthusiastically.

If he pointed the wrong way, Kipp whined with disapproval.

As always, there was much he would have liked to say if he'd had the physical apparatus necessary for speech.

He would have said, *You're a really good driver*.

He would have said, *Faster, faster*, though Ben already exceeded the speed limit, aware that this was urgent business, whatever else it might be.

Given speech, Kipp would have asked a thousand questions about Ben Hawkins's life, what kind of books he wrote, whether he'd read Dickens, whether he believed those physicists

238

were right who said there were parallel universes perhaps infinite in number.

Dorothy had been fascinated by quantum mechanics and string theory and all that.

She had a way of making you interested in what fascinated her.

This was a theory of Kipp's: There are parallel universes, and when we die, we go on living in other realities.

Dorothy was lost here, but not lost everywhere.

He took comfort in that.

He wouldn't go so far as to say that Heaven was a parallel universe where everyone lived forever. He wasn't a theologian.

From Olympic Village, they went north on State Route 89 and then west on Interstate 80.

They left 1-80 for State Route 20, still heading west.

If he were just an ordinary dog, he would as often as possible ride with his head out the passenger-door window.

But he understood the danger of flying debris causing serious eye damage.

Sometimes, being a supersmart dog was less fun than being an ordinary dog.

Maybe not just sometimes. Maybe a lot of the time.

Dorothy would let him ride with his head out the window, but then she would drive only very slowly. Not so much fun.

Thus far he had assumed that others on the Wire heard the boy, but suddenly he wondered at their lack of comment.

He sent, *Do you hear the boy on the Wire? He screams and he cries.*

The answers came quickly from all points of the night. No one else heard the boy. They were excited to think that a human being might ever be on the Wire.

He wondered why they didn't hear the boy. Life was full of things to wonder about.

When Kipp growled to warn of an upcoming change of direction, his companion said, 'Go right?'

Kipp barked, *Yes.*

Just then the Bellagram about Vulcan in La Jolla flared in his mind, the news bright with Bella's joy.

Bella was right. Something was happening out there. Something monumental.

And somehow the boy must be as much a part of it as was Vulcan and Bella and Kipp and all the smart dogs who had thus far believed themselves to be strangers in a world that had spawned them for no certain purpose and set them loose to live outside of nature in perpetual longing for answers that never came.

63

After carrying Woody from the bathroom to his bed, Megan had pulled on her jeans and crewneck just as the police arrived.

She was reluctant to leave Woody, who appeared to be entirely detached from reality, traumatized and withdrawn into a world of his own. This was not the first time he had traveled afar like this, of course, but she sensed a new quality to his withdrawal this time. She prayed it wasn't despair.

She had gone to the head of the stairs to call down to the arriving officers, but refused to descend to the ground floor, instead insisting the deputies come to her.

As she told the first officers her story, she rolled Woody's desk chair beside the bed and sat in it and held one of his hands, gently opening his clenched fingers and ceaselessly stroking them, with the hope of relaxing him.

She strove to remain calm, to recount events without letting the anxiety that possessed her be evident in her recitation, for fear the boy would understand that her sense of safety had been forever stolen from her by Lee Shacket. Woody needed her to be a rock on which he could stand, not a sea of dread in which he might drown.

As the men listened to her, they examined the door lock that had been damaged by gunfire and explored the room without touching anything. With their solemn expressions and deadpan stares, they seemed to regard her with suspicion, which perhaps their experience and training required of them. Nevertheless, she found it difficult to conceal her exasperation that they were not urgently seeking Lee Shacket wherever he had fled into the night, assuming he had fled and wasn't nearby, waiting for them to investigate and leave.

She supposed that her quiet recounting of this mad and violent encounter might have made them wonder about her veracity. Where was the residue of terror that should still leave her agitated? Where was her anger at the violation of her home?

Of course they were coiled deep inside her, as tight as the internal windings of a golf ball, so that they wouldn't be conveyed to her son. Being the parent of a developmentally disabled child who was unable to express his emotions but felt them deeply, a child who had no defense mechanisms to cope with fear, Megan needed at all times to consider how *her* expressed feelings affected him. He had been so traumatized by Shacket that he'd retreated into a stillness that she found disturbing if not itself frightening, and she dared say nothing in a tone that might wind tighter the clock spring of Woody's terror.

A second pair of deputies arrived within a few minutes of the first, and for whatever reason, perhaps seniority, they seemed to take charge, though they hadn't been the first-responding officers. One of these was a thirty-something woman, DEPUTY CARRICKTON according to the black letters on the white name bar clipped to the breast pocket of her uniform shirt.

Carrickton was a cross-trainer with solid forearms, attractive, with Scandinavian features, blond hair cropped short, and Wedgwood-blue eyes. She seemed efficient, producing a notebook and pen to memorialize Megan's statement, which the first two deputies had not done.

Megan was relieved to have a woman in the

242

room, someone who could better relate to what she'd been through. Soon, though, she began to realize that, however capable Carrickton might be, she seemed to have a visceral dislike of Megan and therefore distrusted her without reason.

After Megan gave them a shorthand version of what had happened, Deputy Carrickton said, 'What's wrong with the kid?'

'He's a high-functioning autistic.'

'What's that mean — 'high-functioning'?'

'He's a natural autodidact, reads at a college level, doesn't act out, not ever. But he can't bear to be touched by anyone other than me or Verna Brickit, the housekeeper. And he doesn't speak.'

Carrickton stood too close, violating Megan's personal space, staring down at her and Woody. 'The way the kid's just lying there, as though he doesn't even know I'm here. Is he always that way?'

'No. Shacket traumatized him, like I said.'

'Did he molest the boy?'

'He threatened him, tormented him. When I found Shacket here, he had control . . . he was touching Woody's face. That's the worst for him, having his face touched by a stranger.'

'I'm asking is he traumatized because he was raped?'

'No. Shacket meant to rape me. And torment me by terrifying Woody.'

'We'll have to get the boy examined by a physician within the next few hours.'

'He wasn't raped,' Megan said. 'We don't need to put him through an exam.'

243

'We'll see what he says. I'll need a statement from him.'

'As I told you, he doesn't speak.'

'Not ever?'

'It's not uncommon in autism.'

Carrickton's partner, Deputy Argento, alternated between watching the interrogation and returning to the hallway to confer with other deputies. A third car had arrived. The flashing red and blue beacons of the lightbars washed the wind-shaken night beyond the windows. Perhaps six deputies were in the house. The night crackled with traffic on police-band radios and on the various deputies' belt-clipped walkie-talkies. Megan wondered into what rooms they were venturing, what they were examining. She was glad they were here, that they had arrived in time to frighten Shacket away, but she felt violated all over again.

'You dated this Lee Shacket,' Carrickton said.

'A few times, yes, many years ago.'

'You had a relationship with him.'

'Not sexual, no. A few dates. Nothing more. A long time ago.'

'You said he called you earlier today.'

'Yesterday now. He wanted me to go to Costa Rica with him. It was crazy. I turned him down.'

They had been through this before. Megan understood that Carrickton was using a circular technique, repeatedly returning to ground already covered, to see if Megan's story changed, but it was nonetheless annoying.

'If Shacket didn't have a key, how did he get in the house?'

'I think he came in while Verna was here. She leaves the back door unlocked sometimes because she has to go in and out.'

'And Shacket just hid somewhere until you went to bed?'

'That's what I assume.'

'Hid out for hours. That sounds awfully patient for a guy who's as crazy as you say.' She made a note. 'You were sleeping, but he didn't come straight for you, he came here to the boy's room.'

'Like I said, I wasn't sleeping. I was reading, and then I got sleepy, decided to turn in. That's when I realized my pistol had been put back in the gun safe in the wrong position and the magazine had been emptied.'

'Was the gun safe locked?'

'Yes. I don't know how he got the combination.'

'How long have you owned the weapon?'

'Three years.'

'You purchased it legally in California?'

'Yes.'

'I'll need to see the registration.'

'I'll get it when you're done with your questions.'

'You took a safety course in firearms?'

'Like I said, I practice with it once a month. And, yes, I took a safety course.'

'Did you get the weapon because of Lee Shacket?'

'No. Why would I? By the time I bought the gun, it had been years since I'd seen him. And he wasn't batshit crazy back then.'

245

'So you said you wounded him.'

'Not severely. Maybe tore off part of his left ear.'

'The kid was present then?'

'Lying right here, as he is now.'

'You shot toward the kid?'

'I had to. Shacket threatened to gouge out his eyes.'

'Is he blind?'

'What? No. He's not blind.'

'The way he's just lying there, that fixed stare.'

'He's not blind.'

'High-functioning autistic. So have you had him evaluated to see if this is the best environment for him, he shouldn't be in some special care facility?'

Megan needed to change the dynamics of this. She let go of Woody's hand and stood up, eye-to-eye with Carrickton. 'This isn't about whether Woody is in the best environment. Is anyone looking for Lee Shacket? He's crazy and something worse than crazy. Is a search party being organized?'

'That's not my job,' Carrickton said. 'My job is to get your statement, which I'll need if we're going to convict this guy.'

'All right. But let's stay focused on what happened here tonight, what Lee Shacket did and tried to do.'

Carrickton met Megan's stare in silence for perhaps ten seconds, her Wedgwood-blue eyes as brittle as a china plate, and then said, 'You've got a nice big house filled with all the best stuff. But with a problem kid like him to look after and unstable boyfriends from the past liable to show up, the best stuff doesn't mean much.'

Inexplicable animosity, emanating from a total stranger who presumed to know you, was not a frequent occurrence when you were face-to-face with someone. Social media was a hotbed of it, which was why Megan didn't go online every day. However, in a situation like this, in the physical presence of the apparent hater, she could not just click off and shut down her computer.

'I'm not going to go over this endlessly. I'm not a suspect in this. I'm the victim. I'll give you five more minutes, that's all.'

Two minutes later, Sheriff Hayden Eckman arrived.

64

In the high redoubt of the southwest tower of Castle Wyvern, Woody was lying in abject self-disgust. This time he knew that he would never be able to pay penance for his weakness, that he would never be going home again. No bluebird would appear to sing a song of forgiveness, and the furry white rat would never dance in delight as a sign that he had paid a proper price for what he'd done — or, as was more often the case, *hadn't done.*

The bad man had called him a dummy, but Woody was no dummy. No one could make him believe that he was stupid just because he never talked. But the bad man also called him useless.

Although it was a bad man who made the accusation, that didn't mean the judgment had no merit. It was true, all right. The man had insulted Woody's mom, had worse than insulted her, had told her to take her clothes off, had been going to force her to have sex. Woody was innocent, but he wasn't naive. He knew what sex was. Sex could be a beautiful thing when it was making love, or it could be as ugly as murder when no love was involved. That's what he knew.

Through all of it, Woody had done nothing. Nothing. The crazy man's light touch — stroking his cheek, his nose, drawing circles on his chin, tracing his lips with one fingertip — had so shocked Woody, embarrassed him because of his helplessness, that his arms and legs became leaden, and he couldn't lift his head. Though he hadn't at once gone away to Wyvern, he had remained as paralyzed in his own bedroom as he was now here in his crude bed of reeds.

He had finally traveled to Wyvern after the shooting was done, when he couldn't rise from the bathroom floor where he'd curled in a corner. His mother had to lift him and carry him and put him on the bed, and his helplessness had never been more mortifying.

Now he lay gazing up at the high windows, at the swollen black bellies of the clouds behind which lightning pulsed without shaping itself into bolts, like waves of acid eating through the impending storm. Dragons were in flight in numbers he'd never seen before, flocks of them with long spiked tails and scalloped wings, fearsome harbingers of some apocalypse. No thunder followed the lightning, and no shrieks escaped the dragons, for all was ever silent in this realm, as silent as Woody, until the bluebird sang or the white rat danced, allowing him to go home, but neither of them would appear this time.

When there was so much you wanted to say but the words wouldn't form, when you had never spoken to anyone but a few deer in the back-yard, you learned to live with your voice locked inside you. What he said to the deer — 'You're beautiful. I love you' — was what he wanted to say to his dad, before his dad was gone forever, and it was what he wanted to say to his mother, who might one day be gone forever, too, but he was such a mess that he could only say it to the deer, so he learned to live with that, too.

When your mother's arms around you were the best feeling in the world, then you knew that, if you could just put your arms around her in return, it would be even better yet, but you learned to live with not being able to hug anyone. He had told himself that she knew how he felt even without the hugs, and most of the time he really believed she *did* know. But sometimes, like now, he thought maybe she didn't know, that she only *hoped* he loved her — and he'd even learned to live with that doubt.

He wasn't able to live with *this:* that his mother was almost raped, almost shot, and he did nothing. *Nothing, nothing.* Not only was he incapable of helping her; in his paralysis, he had been a burden to her, had almost gotten her killed because he couldn't bring himself to touch — to strike out at — the bad man. He couldn't even run for help. And all this that had happened was maybe because he had visited Tragedy on the Dark Web and had written 'The Son's Revenge: Faithfully Compiled Evidence of Monstrous Evil.'

Something else the bad man said was true.

You know how hot your mommy is? Way too hot to waste her life with a dummy like you.

If he never went home, she would be free of him. If he stayed here in Castle Wyvern, his mom could have a better life with someone who could tell her that he loved her. She could travel places she liked to go and not worry anymore about what might happen to her dummy child. He was smart, but he was nevertheless a dummy: dumb, mute, speechless, full of learning and full of so many feelings that mattered not at all because he couldn't share any of what he knew and felt with anyone.

In the throbbing of the silent storm light, under the soundless flights of dragons, in the unearthly quiet of the high tower room, where he could no longer hear the crackle of the reeds under him or his own heartbeat or his breath drawn and expelled, he suddenly heard a voice.

'*I'm coming, boy, I'm almost there.*'

He lowered his stare from the windows without glass panes and saw the dog again, not curled on the floor this time, but sitting up, a harness around it as if it was riding in car.

'*Don't cry, boy, don't be afraid. I'm almost there.*'

65

Upon being told of the extraordinary home invasion and violence at the Bookman residence, the sheriff had assumed that this incident and the Spader-Klineman murders might involve the same perpetrator. He at once ordered blockades on Greenbriar Road. They were looking for a red Dodge Demon fleeing the scene, a high-end aftermarket job with the power to outrun any vehicle in law-enforcement's fleet.

Four men had been assigned to each roadblock, the first one approximately two miles south of the Bookman property, the other a mile and a half to the north. The southern post was fully manned almost at once, and two deputies with one car established a half-adequate barrier at the northern position.

Nathan Palmer, if it was Nathan Palmer, had been harried from the Bookman house by the sound of approaching sirens. It was thought that he had gone west on foot, across the backyard of the property and into the forest rather than risk the highway with patrol cars swarming it. He'd surely arrived in his Dodge Demon, however, and secreted it somewhere in the vicinity; he would attempt to circle through the trees to the vehicle.

For the past half hour, traffic on Greenbriar Road had been halted and subjected to inspection. Now deputies Walter Colt and Freeman Johnson, the first to arrive at the Bookman residence, departed the house and drove north to

251

fortify that roadblock.

Freeman rode shotgun. An ardent woodsman — hiker, fisherman — as well as a deputy, he possessed an acute awareness of the patterns of nature. The forest-service road they passed on the right appeared as dark in its depths as the bowels of a leviathan. The sidewash of the headlights penetrated only a few feet, yet Freeman detected a visual discordance amid an otherwise vertical blackness of night-shrouded trees.

'Hold it, turn around,' he said. 'Something back there on that forest-service road.'

Walter Colt slowed, hung a U-turn, cruised south for a short distance, turned left onto the narrow dirt lane, and clicked the headlamps to high beams. With the light boring directly into the woods, what had been concealed to all but Freeman's intuition now stood revealed approximately sixty or seventy feet from the paved highway: a red sedan.

As the patrol car coasted slowly through the trees and the sedan before them was revealed to be a Dodge, Walter Colt snatched up the police-radio microphone and reported the find. He stopped ten feet short of the perpetrator's vehicle and shifted into park and put on the emergency brake, but he left the engine running.

Neither Johnson nor Colt had been at the scene of the Spader and Klineman murders the previous afternoon, but they had heard that the woman had apparently been ravaged by animals or carrion-eating birds, perhaps vultures, after her death. They realized that if the attack at the

Bookman house involved the same perp, he was both reckless and uncommonly violent, although they were not yet aware that he was something far beyond their combined thirty-six years of law-enforcement experience.

In addition to a shotgun clamped muzzle up to the dashboard, left of the front passenger seat, there was also a four-foot-long cattle prod for use on animals only. Pinehaven County was home to more wild animals than people, and some of the former were powerful predators, most notably mountain lions, but also bears and coyotes. In Freeman Johnson's experience, there had also been a runaway bull twice, a tiger kept illegally by an idiot who thought it would always be as gentle as a kitten, and a badly abused pit bull that understandably turned savagely against all humankind. Deputies didn't encounter such dangerous creatures every day or even weekly. But because it had long been the policy of the sheriff's department not to shoot any animals except in the most extreme circumstances, there were times when the electric prod was essential.

Although the Dodge Demon was dark and silent and seemingly untenanted in the headlight beams that pierced its windows, Colt and Johnson exited the patrol car with guns drawn.

To an extent, the wildwoods raised walls against the power of the wind, although these ramparts weren't impervious. A lesser but still-insistent tempest shivered across the forest floor, thrashing whatever undergrowth it found, and a stronger gale fiercely shook the higher boughs of the evergreens. Translated by the deep canopy of needled branches, the upper currents of air sounded like rushing water, as though a great river surged overhead, and within that susurration arose thin shrieks, hollow groans, cries of seeming anguish, as if the river were the Styx, sweeping legions of souls from the world of the living to the land of the dead.

Freeman and his partner approached the Dodge with caution, but they also ceaselessly surveyed the eclipsed woods beyond the light provided by their car. That gloom seemed somehow different from any that Freeman had known before, like the fabled outer dark beyond all hope of Eden.

If the moment felt fraught with unnatural or even supernatural threat, then the attack came in harmony with the mood, the assailant dropping from a branch high above their line of sight, like a winged devil. He crashed hard into Walter Colt and drove him to the ground at the back of the Dodge. The deputy's gun flew from his hand, hit *spang* on the bumper of the car, and spun away into the shuddering brush.

In shock, Freeman reeled back a step, two steps, as Colt heaved and rolled to get atop of — or cast off — his attacker. The deputy was the bigger of the two, but it was at once evident, from the snarling ferocity of his assailant, that size and combat training might not be enough to beat back the assault.

The tangled, thrashing bodies in a frantic struggle allowed Freeman no easy shot, in fact no shot at all. He stepped forward to join the fray, intending to club Nathan Palmer on the head with the barrel of his pistol. He halted when Walter Colt screamed. As long as he'd known the man, Colt had never shown fear, never issued a complaint about pain, remained always the definition of *stoic*. This wasn't merely a scream of pain, but also of pure terror, and carried on it were words: *'He's biting, he's biting!'*

In the glare of the headlights, Colt's left hand was gloved in blood — not just his left, both hands — blood on his face, too, the assailant snapping at his throat, Colt fending him off with bleeding hands, attacker slamming a knee into his victim's crotch, slamming and slamming. Palmer glanced once at Freeman, and a slick mass of bloody saliva slid from his mouth, across a curve of grinning teeth, *his fierce glare bright with animal eyeshine.*

With no clear shot, in the clutches of fright, Freeman returned to the patrol car, grabbed the cattle prod, which would deliver a high-voltage low-amperage charge, enough to dissuade a bear or bull, maybe enough to kill a man if applied relentlessly. He was back at the scene in three seconds. Colt was still screaming. Department rules forbade the use of the prod on a human being. Fuck the rules. He jammed the copper prongs into Palmer's back.

In contact with his attacker, Walter Colt would receive a hard but less disabling subsidiary shock, but there was no helping that. The maniac howled, and Freeman stung him again, and Palmer fell off his victim, facedown on the dirt track.

Gasping, groaning, Colt tried with only a little success to overcome the shock, to hitch away from his assailant.

Palmer should remain paralyzed for twenty to thirty seconds and be disoriented, largely helpless, for a minute or more after that.

Freeman slipped a thick plastic zip-tie handcuff from his utility belt. He dropped to one knee beside the prostrate attacker, intending to bind the bastard's wrists tight together behind his back.

Palmer flailed, rolled over, tried to sit up, hissing with the fury of a taunted serpent.

Heart knocking so hard that it shook his arms, zip tie slipping from his sweat-slick fingers, Freeman scrambled backward, snatched up the cattle prod. He jammed the copper terminals into the maniac's abdomen. Palmer clawed the hard-packed earth, scoring it as if his fingers were talons and the ground mere sand. Freeman shocked him again, again, and Palmer tossed his head, the cords in his neck standing out like steel cables, and Freeman gave him yet another jolt, a longer one. At last Palmer collapsed, unconscious or dead; Freeman didn't care which.

He knelt and rolled Palmer facedown and zip tied the man's hands behind his back. He drew the plastic straps tighter than regulations allowed, then used a second zip tie, even though he'd never heard tell of anyone breaking free of one. He tightened a zip tie around each of the man's ankles and connected them with a third.

At last, he felt for a pulse in Palmer's neck and regretted that he detected one.

256

During all of that, Walter Colt had managed to crawl to the patrol car and sit with his back against the front fender on the starboard side. He was bleeding from both hands, and the little finger on his left had been bitten off. The forefinger hung loose but was still attached by a shred of flesh. The ball of his chin had been bitten so severely that it wobbled as though it would fall off the bone. He was crying like a child, maybe in physiological shock.

Freeman Johnson hurried around to the driver's door and got behind the wheel and grabbed the mic. He called for an ambulance — 'officer down, critical wounds' — gave his position, and asked for backup — 'as much damn backup as you can get me' — because the batteries in the prod must be nearly depleted. The plastic cuffs would hold; they always held. But someone was going to have to get a bite block in Palmer's mouth before they transported him, and Freeman wasn't going to do that without plenty of assistance.

He got out of the car, retrieved the emergency medical kit from the trunk, went around to Walter, and knelt at his side. The hands were bleeding but not so bad that a tourniquet was required before the EMTs got here. He gave Walter two spools of gauze to squeeze lightly in his fists, to apply pressure to the wounds in his palms. Nothing could be done about the chin.

'Ambulance in route, buddy. They'll be here in a five minutes, not long, sooner than five.'

'Jesus God,' Walter said, his voice breaking.

Already, Palmer was stirring. He cursed and

tried to turn over. He strained his bound wrists and kicked his shackled legs. He arched his back impossibly, as if he might be able to lock his vertebrae in sequence, like a snake, and curl his upper body erect, but he could not, and so he cursed more furiously.

'For God's sake, what is he?' Walter asked. 'Shoot the freak, kill him while you can.'

His partner's uncharacteristic fear further chilled Freeman. He rose to his feet and retrieved the cattle prod and stood ready as sirens rose in the distance. Backup.

No moon or stars above the narrow service road, the cool wind roaring overhead like the caissons of Armageddon, the forest deep and black and crawling with mystery as it had never previously been for Freeman Johnson.

66

Police car lightbars flung off glisters of red and blue that washed across the windshield and the dashboard of the Range Rover.

Kipp and Ben sat in a line of cars at a blockade, northbound on Greenbriar Road.

Ben waited more patiently than Kipp, who panted with anxiety.

'What's wrong, fella?'

Ben didn't know about the boy, that the boy had been screaming and was now almost silent on the Wire, issuing only a pitiable sound of perfect despair.

258

Two species on this planet had been bonded for many thousands of years. Maybe more than a hundred thousand. Dogs and people.

Dogs had been at the side of human beings for millennia before horses or cats.

They had hunted together when hunting had been essential for survival.

They had protected each other from all threats in a primitive world where nature was even crueler than it was now.

Of all the creatures on Earth, only people and dogs engaged joyfully in play all the days of their lives.

In the relationship between humanity and dogs, some mutual destiny existed that had not yet been fulfilled.

That was what Dorothy had believed.

She had been sure that Kipp and the others in the Mysterium must represent the next stage in that human-canine destiny, that they would change the world.

And now this boy, unknowingly, was able to use the Wire. Which might mean that, in the near future, the human-dog bond would knit the two species more tightly together.

Kipp felt that an event of historic importance loomed.

The police went slowly from vehicle to vehicle, questioning the drivers, looking in the trunks of the cars.

A historic event loomed, and the police delayed traffic on Greenbriar Road, and if Kipp became any more frustrated, he would need to get out and pee.

67

Deputy Carrickton and her partner, Deputy Argento, were gone, Megan's statement having been deemed adequate by Sheriff Hayden Eckman.

With the assistance of Argento, the sheriff had set right the overturned highboy and settled on the edge of the armchair, to speak with Megan while she remained at Woody's bedside.

Having entered the room with a sense of the antagonism between Megan and Carrickton, he apologized for his deputy's aggressive style of questioning, but also excused it by asserting that the woman was one of the best in his department.

Megan had once met the previous sheriff, Lyle Sheldrake, a low-key folksy man with a leathery face and white hair that glowed as if irradiated. She hadn't known him, but those who had long experience of him said that he was a dedicated and honest man — whom Eckman had run against and defeated in a campaign of low character. Now, even as the new sheriff sought to smooth away what irritation Carrickton had caused, he struck Megan as oleaginous, not trustworthy. These days, Americans seemed attracted to such politicians if they were exceptionally gifted at virtue signaling while they slandered their opponents.

Eckman didn't want to rehash all that Megan told Carrickton, but he was intently interested that she knew her attacker and that his name was

Lee Shacket. 'To the best of your knowledge, Ms. Bookman, has he ever used the name Nathan Palmer?'

'No, not to my knowledge. But I wouldn't know, really. The last time I saw him was at a corporate affair with my husband eight years ago, and before that . . . thirteen years since I knew him socially.'

'You said he was the CEO of Refine, Inc., part of Dorian Purcell's empire?'

'That's right.'

'Are you aware of the catastrophic fire at Refine's operation outside Springville, Utah?'

'No. I avoid the news, Sheriff. There's nothing I can do about the people who make it, and I'm determined to keep my art positive in a world that increasingly isn't.'

'Well, he may be on the run from responsibility for the deaths of ninety-two people at that facility.'

She grimaced, but there was nothing she could say about such a tragedy that would mean anything to anyone. 'Then you've even more reason to find him quickly. There's something gone very wrong with him.'

'Do you have a photograph of this Lee Shacket?'

'I'm sure you can find one online.'

'No doubt. But all we have now is a driver's license he was carrying. It's in the name Nathan Palmer. If you have a photo, Ms. Bookman, I could confirm in a minute that they're one and the same.'

'It's Mrs. Bookman.'

261

'Yes, of course. If you prefer.'

'Lee Shacket was at our wedding. The album I kept has a few snap-shots of him. He still looks much the same — except he's dyed his hair. He had a beard for a long while, though not back when I knew him, so it's just the hair that's changed from the photos.'

'Could you show that album to me?'

'I'm not leaving Woody. Go downstairs to the study. On one of the bookshelves are eight or ten photo albums. It's the white one with gold trim. Bring it to me, and I'll find Lee Shacket for you.'

In the sheriff's absence, she spoke softly to Woody, assuring him that they were safe now, that Shacket would be found and would not be returning. Those assurances, however, were hopes rather than certainties, and perhaps the boy detected the difference, for he did not return from whatever deep place in his psyche he had gone.

The wind howled down on the house, not a nature sound empty of meaning, but a shriek of blackest madness, conjuring in Megan's mind a painting by the eighteenth-century Spanish master Francisco Goya, *Saturn Devouring His Children*, a nihilistic image of such insane violence that it was capable of inspiring genuine fear in the viewer and weeks of nightmares.

Shacket had shattered one of the sidelights flanking the front door. Sam Brickit could fill the frame with plywood till a glazier came to replace the glass. The alarm would continue to function in the meantime. She would arrange to have *double* deadbolts installed on every door. Key

262

locks on the operable sash windows rather than thumb-turn latches. She had a spare magazine for the pistol. From now on she'd keep it loaded and always with the weapon. She would draw shut the draperies at all the windows, day and night, so that activities in the house could not be observed by anyone outside.

And all of that would be for nothing.

She wouldn't feel safe, wouldn't *be* safe, not for a minute, until Shacket was apprehended.

In truth, she wouldn't feel safe until he was dead.

We all make mistakes though, don't we, Megan? I made one when I left my pistol in your kitchen earlier, after I ate that hot bitch's tits. No, that's not right, it was a steak. In your kitchen, it was a steak, and it wasn't as good as Justine's breasts.

The temptation was to take everything he'd said as the ravings of a madman, but he'd indeed left his gun in the kitchen. And Deputy Carrickton had asked about the raw steaks on the kitchen floor.

The sheriff returned with the white-and-gold photo album.

Megan paged through it and found a good snapshot of Shacket in suit and tie, at the reception following the wedding, proposing a toast to the newlyweds.

'Nathan Palmer,' Eckman said. 'Everything but the blond hair.'

Rising from the chair, Megan said, 'Come with me.'

She put the album on the bed and led Eckman

into the upstairs hall.

Easing the door most of the way shut between them and Woody, she spoke hardly louder than a whisper. 'Is Lee Shacket wanted for something more than the fire at the Refine facility?'

His eyes were abacus beads of calculation. He followed her example and spoke softly. 'What do you mean?'

'Just what I said.'

'I'm sorry, Ms. Bookman, but I'm not at liberty — '

'A woman named Justine,' she interrupted. 'Did he murder a woman named Justine?'

After a silence, Eckman said, 'There's been no media yet.'

'He made a reference to something . . . sick. I wasn't sure if it was true or not. Did he kill her here or in Utah?'

Eckman relented. 'It'll hit the news tomorrow. This couple had a flat tire on highway 20. Wouldn't have been much traffic at the time. Palmer . . . Shacket evidently came along. He shot the man four times, killed them both.'

The sheriff was clearly still tabulating the pros and cons of sharing more than he'd already revealed.

Pressing the issue, Megan said, 'How did he kill Justine?'

Eckman hesitated as the wind played Saturn, crying progenicide down the ever-darker night, and then he said, 'He bit her.'

'To death?'

'Yes. But I must ask you, Ms. Bookman, to please — '

264

'Did he . . . eat part of her?'

Eckman frowned. 'Apparently cannibalism was involved.'

Megan looked away from him. The horror was of such an intimate nature that she could not meet his eyes to discuss it. 'Was it her breasts?'

'So he told you.'

'Indirectly.'

'One of her breasts. Part of the other. And most of her face.'

'Oh, my God.' Her once white-hot fear, which lately had been simmering, suddenly flashed bright. She remembered how Shacket had touched Woody's face, how close his face — his mouth — had been to the boy. 'We can't stay here. We're getting out tonight. Now.'

'I can assign you protection.'

She met his eyes once more. 'You don't have enough men. There aren't enough police in the world to keep me here.'

'It would be helpful if you didn't mention this to anyone. We don't want to panic the public. We need to manage the release of the information, probably by noon tomorrow, maybe as late as early afternoon. We need time to craft answers to assure — '

A deputy, thundering up the front stairs, shouted, 'Sheriff! You up there?'

As the man appeared at the head of the staircase, Eckman said, 'What is it?'

'They got him. Johnson and Colt got the bastard. Colt's hurt bad, ambulance on the way. Johnson's all right, and the perp is under restraint.'

Eckman smiled broadly at Megan, as though the abominations so recently revealed were no longer of any consequence. 'You're safe, Ms. Bookman. Perfectly safe. My men have done their job. You can stay the night without concern. Now if you'll excuse me . . . '

His shoulders back and a bounce in his step, as though the terror visited on Pinehaven County was an opportunity seized, a political crisis become a career enhancement, he walked away.

To his back, she said quietly, 'It's *Mrs.* Bookman.'

68

The ambulance was capable of carrying two injured persons, but Walter Colt refused to be taken to the hospital in the same vehicle as Nathan Palmer, even though the EMTs intended to tranquilize the killer with chlorpromazine.

Freeman Johnson totally understood. He persuaded the first responders to put in a call for a second unit for Palmer, and Walter Colt was whisked away, the ambulance's lightbar flashing and its siren wailing as if it were some woodland banshee chasing through the trees.

Backup had arrived before the ambulance, so that Freeman didn't have to wait alone with the prisoner. He had his cattle prod ready, and Deputy Argento had one as well. Carrickton armed herself with a shot-gun, and she looked as though she would enjoy using it.

Facedown on the ground, the perp struggled tirelessly to free himself from the zip ties that bound his wrists behind his back. He was so persistent that he had rubbed the skin away and was bleeding slightly. The pain seemed not to matter to him.

69

Hours past his usual bedtime, fueled by black coffee and two glazed doughnuts, beginning to consider using the next cup of brew to wash down a caffeine tablet, still at his computer in the morgue, Carson Conroy had gathered more information than he had hoped to acquire.

When he'd gone to the National Crime Information Center website to look for any warrant issued for Nathan Palmer, his screen had gone white except for a perfect silhouette of his shoulders, neck, and head. He knew this meant that some security agency — most likely the NSA — had an interest in who researched Palmer and had taken his photograph with the camera in his computer. He was not concerned, because this had happened twice before on other cases, without any subsequent consequences.

Although Nathan Palmer was wanted for larceny, arson, and murder, the specifics of these crimes, the what-when-where, were missing from the writ issued by the court in Salt Lake City. That data had been put under seal, which

Carson found decidedly strange. Palmer's photo, taken from a Montana driver's license, showed a reasonably attractive man in his midthirties, clean-shaven with brown hair and brown eyes.

Something about the photo resonated with Carson. He had never met Nathan Palmer, yet the man looked familiar.

Lyle Sheldrake, the previous sheriff and the one who brought Carson to Pinehaven, had anticipated a moment when his successor, Hayden Eckman, would get himself into a situation where he would feel it necessary to set up a fall guy. Because Carson was not an Eckman loyalist, he would always be a prime candidate for the new sheriff's scape-goat. Consequently, Sheldrake had created a secret back door into the department's computer system and left instructions for its use only with Carson. Sheldrake had said, 'Maybe Hayden's not the snake he seems to be, but you best have some antivenin just in case.'

Now Carson Conroy swam secretly through the shallow lake of data maintained by the sheriffs department and found his way into the cloudy backwater of Hayden Eckman's personal files. The one that looked most interesting was labeled UNOFFICIAL CASE NOTES. Therein he found an entry made this date, regarding his supposed inebriation, argumentativeness, and generally unprofessional behavior when Frawley and Zellman had arrived from Sacramento to effect the transfer of jurisdiction in the Spader-Klineman murders.

Carson was angry, but not enraged. In such a situation, an element of surprise, a sense of

268

unexpected betrayal, must be present for anger to escalate into something stronger. He had thought Eckman capable of both deceit and treachery, so that his anger was hardly more than indignation, lacking violent passion and vindictiveness. Anyway, the lie about his being drunk was not the most interesting thing in the file related to the recent murders.

Of greater interest were Eckman's notes on his conversations with Tio Barbizon, the attorney general of California. The National Security Agency was not only interested in the case, but was trying to run the investigation — and keep it quiet — through Tio Barbizon's office. The suspected killer's Nathan Palmer ID was false. Although Barbizon didn't share Palmer's real name, he did reveal to Eckman that the fugitive had been a highly placed executive at Refine, Inc., with oversight of the Springville, Utah, facility where ninety-two had died in a ferocious fire.

Carson backed out of the sheriffs department computer system. He knew why Nathan Palmer looked familiar. The previous day, he had seen a bit of film on the news, a clip from a two-year-old speech that the CEO of Refine had given concerning the company's cancer research at its labs outside Springville. He googled it, found it. At the time of the speech, the guy sported a neatly trimmed beard, and his hair appeared blond, not brown. Although his name was Lee Shacket, the resemblance was strong enough that Carson had no doubt the guy was also Nathan Palmer.

According to some news reports, Refine, Inc., was a subsidiary of Parable, which had been founded and was still controlled by Dorian Purcell, the multibillionaire. Instead, Refine was a separate company entirely, private rather than public, largely but perhaps not entirely owned by Purcell.

They said Lee Shacket had been at the labs in Springville when the catastrophic gas leak had destroyed the complex and everyone in it. Given the inaccuracy of that information, Carson made a fearsome assumption: Whatever work Refine might be doing in Utah, cancer research was the least of it or perhaps not a part of it at all; they were preoccupied with something of a much more exotic and dangerous nature, and the explosion had been no accident.

After he brooded about the situation for a few minutes, he made three more assumptions. First, whatever else Refine might be doing in Utah, it must have contracts to perform research for the National Security Agency or for other government entities that relied on the NSA to cover their tracks for them. Second, no accidental explosion and fire at such a large facility could be so sudden and complete as to leave not one survivor; the intensity of the blaze suggested a doomsday device designed to halt the spread of highly contagious pathogens that might inspire a plague for which no cure existed, and the lack of a single survivor implied that a biologically secure lockdown program had intentionally trapped the ninety-three people in the facility. Ninety-two. Third assumption: Lee Shacket had

270

slipped out seconds before he, too, would have been imprisoned.

And something was seriously wrong with him. Extreme violence and cannibalism weren't symptoms of disease. Rabies? No, not even that retrovirus. In humans, the symptoms of rabies were high fever, muscle spasms, thirst, the inability to swallow liquids, seizures, eventually total paralysis. Outrageous violence and cannibalism suggested mental illness rather than a physical disease.

Or . . .

As Carson recalled the ravaged face of Justine Klineman, it seemed that Shacket must be shedding the customs, conventions, and practices of civilization, descending into a primitive moral state. Not just descending. Plummeting. Carson could think of no condition, physical or mental, that could lead to such an abrupt collapse — until the word *devolution* occurred to him. He didn't know what he meant by that, why the word hung stubbornly in his mind. Then halfway through another mug of coffee, he found himself considering genetic engineering, by which some enthusiasts in the scientific community believed human *evolution*, the opposite of devolution, could be facilitated to improve the health and longevity of the species — and even to give it superhuman powers. *Transhumanism* and *posthuman* were words that thrilled them, that engendered visions of humankind raised to a godlike condition.

In recent years, momentous advances had taken place in genetic engineering. That technique of gene editing known as CRISPR had been used in China and elsewhere to edit out a disease-causing

271

gene from the parental sperm and egg. But little was known about how genetic information was expressed in the individual or what the consequences of editing anything out might be. A grave danger existed that those engaged in such experiments might introduce inheritable changes in the genome that could lead to a cascade of faults that, over a few generations, might result in a new humanity of critically diminished physical and mental capacities. Or even bring on the extinction of the species. Some of the cooler heads thought it the most reckless practice of science in history, but there were always the true believers for whom a new trick of science became their religion.

And CRISPR was only one of several new techniques. If it or something even more effective was the subject of research at the Springville labs of Refine, might Lee Shacket be sliding down the evolutionary ladder into a terrifying primitive state? Or was it even possible that some material had been *added* to every cell in his body with the result that he was . . . What? Neither moving up nor down the evolutionary ladder? But somehow sliding . . . *sideways*?

Less than half an hour earlier, Carson had considered washing down a NoDoz tablet with his black coffee. He no longer needed any help staying awake. Cold dread did the job better than caffeine ever could.

He switched off the computer and got up from his chair and stood listening to the silence of the morgue. A line from T. S. Eliot came to mind: *I will show you fear in a handful of dust.*

Room by room, he turned off the lights. He set the alarm and stepped outside and locked the door.

The wind sang requiem for the world, and it seemed to Carson that the chilly currents of harried air were more than that, were also time itself racing toward some plug that had been pulled, to drain away and leave the world eternally still, silent, and dark.

In the postmidnight alleyway, as he turned toward the town square, intending to walk home, he heard the sirens of ambulances. One seemed to be coming, the other going.

70

When Ben and Kipp were nearing the front of the line, the officers stopped inspecting vehicles. They removed the roadblock.

'I started to wonder if they were looking for you,' Ben Hawkins said. 'Seems like someone should be trying to find the smartest dog in the world.'

Kipp wasn't the smartest. Not nearly.

Someday Ben would have to meet Solomon to learn what a really smart dog was.

Solomon and Brandy. They were mates and very wise.

Leaning forward, Kipp panted and whined. They needed to move faster.

The boy hadn't begun screaming again. But he was suffering, crying and miserable and alone.

They had hardly gone any distance north from the roadblock before an ambulance appeared ahead of them, in the southbound lane.

As it shrieked past, lightbar strobing, Kipp clenched his teeth and repressed a howl, though his ears were ringing painfully.

After another minute or so, a second ambulance came flashing and wailing, this one from behind them, heading north.

Pulling off the pavement to let the vehicle pass, Ben said, 'Lassie helped people get out of trouble, but I have this feeling you're leading me straight into it.'

After returning to the pavement in the wake of the ambulance, they had not gone far when a large white house, ahead on the left, drew Kipp's attention.

He popped the safety-harness release with one paw, slipped out of the restraint, and stood with his forepaws on the console.

He craned his head forward, staring at the house.

Even at this hour, the place blazed with light at most windows.

The boy waited in that house full of light.

The unique boy.

The boy who could send on the Wire.

Kipp was not a barker, but he barked. He barked and barked at the house, and he barked directly, urgently in Ben's face.

'Hey, take it easy. Are you telling me this is the place?'

Kipp stopped barking and wagged his tail as fast as he could.

Although he slowed the Range Rover, letting it coast, Ben seemed hesitant. 'There's a patrol car in front.'

So Kipp barked and barked again.

'All right, okay, whatever.' Ben turned left, crossed the southbound lane, and pulled into the driveway.

The sight of the police car and the memory of the ambulances alarmed Kipp. Maybe the boy had been hurt.

Switching off the engine, opening his door, Ben said, 'You better wait here while I check this out.'

As Ben exited the Rover, Kipp scrambled onto the driver's seat. He leaped through the open door before it could be closed.

He wasn't being disobedient. Ben wasn't his master any more than Dorothy had been.

They were companions. That was how things were between dogs of the Mysterium and their people. If they had people. If they weren't alone, as a few were.

Nevertheless, because he was still a dog and always would be, he regretted that a higher duty to the anguished boy required him to leave Ben with even the temporary perception that his instructions were not valued.

Wind thrashed through the woods and across the yard, scented with squirrel and rabbit and raccoon and fox, with pine and cedar and woad-waxen and golden sedge and wild mushrooms clustering in the rotting trunk of a fallen tree.

The porch steps boomed hollowly under his paws.

A policeman at the top. Another coming out of the open front door.

They cried out as Kipp dashed, tail tucked, between their legs and off the porch and across the threshold.

A woman in the foyer reeled back and cried —

275

'No, stop!' — as if Kipp were not what he appeared to be but were instead a wild beast of ill intent.

Drawn as if the Wire must be on a reel that pulled him in like a helpless catch, Kipp could only whine meekly to reassure the woman as he raced to the stairs and bounded up them.

The woman charged after him, as did one of the officers, but he was far faster than they were.

71

The high redoubt in the great tower at Castle Wyvern was a refuge of the mind, not the body, a place where Woody Bookman came and went without ever really using the stairs or a door. He was there when he needed to be and gone when he was ready to be home again.

On this occasion, however, he found himself clambering up from the bed of reeds and scrambling to the door as he heard the thunder of footfalls on the spiral stairs. Overcome by an excitement that he couldn't explain, he threw back one great iron bolt on the heavy timber door, a second bolt, and a third.

As he stepped across the threshold, he found himself sitting up in bed, in his room in the Pinehaven house, as through the door came a panting dog, a glorious golden retriever.

Be not afraid. I'm here, I'm here!

The voice issued from the dog's mind to his, as if by an act of telepathy in a story.

The retriever sprang onto the bed and threw

itself against him, so that Woody fell back on his pile of pillows, laughing.

Good boy, good, the dog declared. *You're safe now. I'm here now. We are family now.*

72

Megan had heard Woody laugh before, but the cause of laughter had never been clear. It often seemed to arise from some internal cause, some private observation, never from something amusing that happened and that she could share with him.

When she rushed into his room and saw the boy overwhelmed by the dog, embracing the dog and laughing, her heart was snared in such a tangle of emotions that she could have laughed, could have wept, should have been able to step away from her fear in the wake of Lee Shacket's arrest, but she couldn't do any of that. Woody was happy, and the dog seemed harmless, but the dog had *teeth*, and she thought of what Shacket had done to that poor woman, to her face, and fear would not relent.

The deputy who entered the room immediately after Megan didn't know what to do, either. He asked if this was her dog, and she said it wasn't, and he asked if it was a neighbor's dog, and she said she didn't know. They stood there, uncertain of what needed to be done, and the boy's giggles and the dog's apparent delight seemed to argue that nothing needed to be done, that all was well.

The stranger who followed the deputy into the room possessed a presence that none of the deputies nor even the sheriff could claim, a calm demeanor and an easy way of moving that suggested that little surprised him and nothing rattled him.

'Ma'am,' he said, 'I apologize for my dog. He's a good boy, and he means well, but sometimes his enthusiasm gets the best of him.'

Before Megan could reply, the man spoke to the retriever. 'Hey, Scooby.' The dog looked at him. 'Is everything okay?'

Megan thought she must have imagined it, but knew that she didn't: The dog nodded.

'Everything's all right,' the newcomer said to the deputy. Without being asked, he extracted a wallet from his hip pocket and produced a driver's license. 'My name's Brenaden Septimus Hawkins. Friends either call me Ben or Hawk. My mom and dad are great people, but they've got a tin ear about names. My brother's Willie Willard Hawkins. My sister's Eulalia Ermintrude Hawkins. Fortunately, she's smart, pretty, and damn tough, so everyone knows better than to call her anything but Trudie.'

73

Perhaps the booming wind has fallen into an unlikely rhythm, but the red-blue strobing of the ambulance beacons seems to beat like a fatalistic drum. The nearer trees flare in carnival colors, though the deep darkness of the farther forest swallows the light, refusing to reveal its secrets. All of it is exciting, the wind and the dark and the pulsing light, the frightened men calling out instructions and warnings to one another, so that Shacket feels exhilarated rather than defeated.

In spite of his shackled ankles and his wrists cuffed tightly behind his back, two EMTs from the second ambulance and two deputies are required to restrain him enough to inject chlorpromazine, and then a few cubic centimeters more when the first dose has less effect than they expect.

Even when they think he is at last unconscious, he is not. He's helpless for the moment, unable to struggle anymore, but he can hear everything they're saying. He knows where they intend to take him, how they expect to manage him in custody. The powerful drug has left him physically incapacitated, but he is still rapidly becoming, and his mind is not affected, though his captors are certain that he is subdued beyond all awareness. He keeps his eyes closed, so that they will not suspect his true condition. He listens, and he schemes.

74

The county jail didn't have a cell suitable for a suspect in an extreme psychotic state, nor did the staff have sufficient medical expertise to protect such an individual from himself and others. Therefore, Shacket was transported to the county hospital, on the southeastern edge of the town of Pinehaven.

Sheriff Eckman waited with Deputy Rita Carrickton under the portico roof of the emergency entrance. Because she was meticulous in all things and unfailingly loyal, he trusted her more than anyone else to use her iPhone and his to obtain an adequate video record of the calm authority with which he would oversee the arrival of Lee Shacket. They would secure this serious threat to public safety in one of the four hospital rooms that doubled as regular patient-care spaces and, in a crisis, as units of a psychiatric ward.

He and Rita were lovers, in violation of departmental rules against intimate relations between uniformed personnel. They risked raising suspicions each time he chose her for a task that any deputy could do, especially since he'd appointed her undersheriff. They were pledged to each other, however, not just romantically — in fact, not primarily for romantic reasons — but because they understood each other's single-minded aspiration. Those possessed by truly ruthless ambition were rare, and rarer still were those who understood that a tightly bonded couple were more powerful than a hundred loners. They would rise in status together, protecting each other at all costs, until they could marry and then openly destroy their competition, whom they'd previously worked secretly, each on behalf of the other, to eliminate via character assassination and other means.

Speaking above the wind, Rita said, 'She's not an innocent victim. I'd bet on it.'

'Who isn't?' he asked.

280

'The Bookman bitch. She drew him to her.'

'Who? You mean this Shacket?'

'She drew him to her somehow. Just look at her.'

'Who knows how he thinks? He's a psychopath,' the sheriff said.

'Tell me you wouldn't like a piece of her.'

'I've got you. More than enough for me.'

Rita spat and the wind carried the spittle onto Eckman's pant leg. 'Heard that from other guys. Then one like her comes along.'

'She's not my type.'

'She's got it all, and she sells it hard.'

'Sells what?'

'You make me suspicious when you play dumb. That face, that body, she's all, *Look at me, I'm the perfect piece of ass.*'

'She doesn't wear makeup, she dresses in jeans, and she seems all about that screwed-up kid, not much about herself.'

'Don't you ever touch her.'

'I have no interest in her.'

'I've been through shit like this before with sluts like her.'

'You've never been through it with me. We're in this together. All that matters is getting ours, and we can best do that together.'

A keening siren needled through the wind's chorus.

'Here they come with him,' Eckman said. 'Be sure to video me directing the unloading of Shacket on his gurney.'

Just then, to the left of the portico, a rat came out of the shrubbery, half-blind and bloody-eyed, confused. It hitched across the pavement

281

on three feet, left-back leg dragging behind it. The hospital tucked poisoned feeding stations in the shrubbery, to decimate the rat population before any might find their way inside. This specimen had obviously dined heartily on warfarin. Thirst was driving it in search of water. If healthy, the rodent would have shunned the light and scurried away at the sight of Eckman and Carrickton, but it ignored them, making its way in a pitiable crawl. Without comment, they watched it cross the portico and disappear into more shrubbery. The ambulance appeared on the approach lane in cascades of flaring light, its siren dying from shriek to moan.

'Showtime,' Eckman said, and Rita readied her phone to video.

75

The exuberant greetings had been concluded. On the bed, Woody was lying on his side, facing the golden retriever. The retriever was lying on his side, facing Woody. They stared into each other's eyes, seldom blinking. This was an age-old posture for a boy and his dog, and yet it was different from merely that, somehow singular.

Megan stood at the foot of the bed with Ben Hawkins, wondering. This was Woody in a state of detachment, transported, whatever you wanted to call it. He was here physically but perhaps not mentally or emotionally. She'd seen him in this condition many times. What seemed strange, if not extraordinary, was that the dog appeared to be in the same condition, lying as still as the boy, neither seeking the touch of an affectionate hand nor restless, nor reacting to any rattle or clang or whistle raised by the wind. Boy and dog were breathing in perfect synchronization.

'There's something different about him,' said Ben Hawkins.

'He's high-performing autistic with a genius IQ.'

'I meant Scooby. He's not autistic, but I think maybe he and the boy have the smarts thing in common.'

'You really call him Scooby?'

The dog did not react to his name, as he had earlier.

'I had to call him something, and he didn't like Rin Tin Tin. He hasn't found a way to tell me his real name yet, but I expect he'll figure out how to do it.'

Megan looked at Ben and liked him, and warned herself to be cautious. 'But . . . how long have you had him?'

'I found him yesterday afternoon. I began to realize there was something special about him when he wanted to know why the name Clover was on the water bowl I gave him.'

Her smile was tentative. 'What do you mean, he wanted to know?'

'It's quite a story. But you evidently have one, too. The lock on that door has been shot out. There's a bullet hole in the wall by the window over there. Scooby and I had to wait at a roadblock, and there were deputies here when we arrived.'

'It's been a weird night,' she acknowledged.

'You've got a broken-out window by the front door. This wind is gonna blow everything from leaves to raccoons into your front hall if we don't get a temporary fix on that window. If you have a heavy plastic painter's tarp, anything like that, and some small nails, we can amaze each other with our stories while we get the job done.'

The deputies were gone. She looked at Woody, loath to leave him alone, even though Lee Shacket was in custody.

Ben Hawkins said, 'Don't worry. He'll be all right. Scooby's gonna look after him.'

'It's just that . . . he's everything to me.'

'Ma'am, that dog woke me after only an hour's sleep, harassed me into driving — heck, I don't know — maybe eighty miles, giving me directions all the way, just so he could get to your boy. Damn if I can understand it, but your son seems to be everything to him, too. What we've got here is mystery and strangeness and a broken window, and maybe when dawn comes, we'll still have all three, but at least there won't be owls flying through the house trying to eat the mice the wind chased inside.'

'Let's nail up that tarp,' she said. 'Don't be spooked, but I'm going to the nightstand to get a gun I put in the drawer.'

'If you think you need it.'

'I can't leave it here with Woody.'

'Does he have a tendency to play with guns?'

'No. He's too smart for that.'

'So's the dog. But get it anyway. I won't draw down on you.'

She retrieved the gun from the nightstand.

Even at a distance, he recognized the make and model of the weapon. 'Heckler and Koch USP, nine-millimeter, ten-round magazine, twenty-eight ounces, four-and-a-quarter-inch barrel. That's a good one. You hit the intruder?'

'Tore off part of his right ear. Not a clear shot. He was using Woody for cover.'

'What were you aiming for?'

'Dead center on his face.'

'Close enough.'

'You know guns,' she said.

He smiled. 'I was a Navy SEAL for eight years. In training, they expect you to do more than learn to swim.'

76

Blood calls to him. His own blood sings through his arteries, whispers home to the heart through his veins, and both its voices are cries for freedom. The blood of others speaks to him only as a scent, which he smells strongest when they're here with him, though he also smells them in the corridor beyond the closed door.

He is fully awake now, with only a small light above the head of his bed, the room draped with gathered shadows, which do not in the least obscure anything from him. In his becoming vision, all details are revealed in shades of red, for he sees not just by the light of the visible spectrum but also by the light that others cannot see, the infrared radiation that is produced by the molecular vibration occurring in all solid matter — the floors, the wall, the ceiling, the furniture, his own body — and by the molecular rotation of the gases in the air.

His damaged ear has been treated and bandaged while they thought he was entirely unconscious.

For his comfort, the bite block has been removed from between his teeth. Any time they feel the need to reinsert it, they will dose him with a tranquilizer first.

The zip ties have been removed. A wide strap across his chest binds him to the bed, his arms at his sides. Another wide strap runs across his thighs.

He is hooked up to an IV to keep him hydrated and to allow for the quick administration of drugs through the port in the drip line. He's catheterized and is urinating into a bottle.

He isn't concerned about his situation.

The wide straps across his chest and thighs are not leather, but rubber, allowing just enough elasticity to afford him minimum comfort and avoid obstructing circulation. An average man could not struggle successfully against the four-inch-wide restraining bands, but he is not an average man.

He is thinking this through, working out the *how* of escape.

A deputy is stationed in a chair outside the room door. Shacket has heard people talking to this guard. He can smell the deputy: the hair cream he uses, the dried sweat in his armpits, his sour breath born of acid reflux from a fondness for food heavy in garlic.

They do not know what they have done, to whom they have done it, and Shacket will not forgive them. He will rise again, and he will teach them humility. The world is at the end of an age, and Lee Shacket is the embodiment of the new age being born. He is progress, remade by science, which is the only force on Earth with both the right and the obligation to change everything always and forever.

77

Carson Conroy in his Ford Explorer, in a far corner of the hospital parking lot. Waiting for Sheriff Hayden Eckman to be gone. Fortified by a thermos of black coffee from the Four Square Diner. One caffeine tablet consumed, a tin of others in one jacket pocket.

Having made a life of working with the dead, of documenting the extreme cruelty that murderers had visited on their victims, Carson had ceased to believe in justice. Justice was nothing but a concept, not a fact, manipulated and ceaselessly redefined by everyone from the manufacturers of pop culture in Hollywood to politicians to self-appointed deep thinkers who were as susceptible to intellectual fashion trends as the average teenager was driven to want whatever sneakers and jeans were the cool gear of the moment.

What he sought in his new life in Pinehaven, in the wake of his wife's long-unsolved murder, was not justice but truth. Truth could not be redefined. Truth was what it was. The simple task of finding the truth was complicated only by the haystacks of lies you had to sort through to find the shiny needle.

He had no illusions that he would ever learn the identity of Lissa's drive-by killer, or that any forensic autopsy would provide him with the full truth of *any* human act of violence. The truth he sought in this new life was both the truth of nature and of himself. He spent much of his leisure time hiking ever deeper into the Sierra Nevada, observing — studying — the natural world with increasing care and intimacy. A marvelous order existed in nature, a damn harsh but rational order, and no deception was involved other than, in some cases, the camouflage of fur or feathers, or chameleon scales. In the wilds, no lies were told by tongue or pen. He hoped that the better he understood the way of nature, the better he'd understand the way a man needed to live to have respect for himself and others that included no self-delusions or equally egregious errors.

He couldn't say why he believed that the truth of the Spader-Klineman murders and the truth of Lee Shacket, alias Nathan Palmer, were inextricably linked to whatever ultimate truth he expected to find in nature. That was just what he felt, and he felt it strongly.

Earlier, in the alleyway between the morgue

288

and the sheriffs station, when he'd heard an ambulance arriving in Pinehaven just as another was leaving, he'd intuited that the sirens had something to do with Shacket. He'd gone next door to speak with Carl Fredette, the watch commander on the current shift, and had learned about the events at the Bookman house.

Now, through binoculars, he watched as Hayden Eckman and Rita Carrickton came out of the emergency entrance and stood talking for a minute or two under the portico. Their patrol cars were in the no-parking zone, and they departed one after the other, without sirens or lightbars.

Carson finished his current cup of coffee, screwed the cup onto the thermos bottle, and set out across the parking lot toward the hospital. According to Carl Fredette, Shacket had been captured and would be restrained at the hospital until the sheriff could speak with the district attorney in the morning.

Because Carson knew the four rooms that could be adapted as psychiatric-care units, he didn't have to make an inquiry as to where Shacket was being held. He went straight to the third floor, the highest floor, and to the end of the east wing.

A straight-backed chair and small folding table had been placed in the hall, to the left of the door to Room 328. On the table were a sweating carafe of ice water with a glass, a can of Coca-Cola, a bag of peanuts, and magazines about hot rods.

Thad Fenton, a young and earnest deputy, put down a magazine and rose to his feet when he

289

saw Carson approaching. He had been in service only about six months. That was good. He would be uncertain about this unprecedented situation and respectful of Carson's authority.

'Dr. Conroy,' he said too loud, caught himself, and spoke softly in respect of the patients in that wing. 'What're you doing up and about at this hour?'

'I finished the Spader and Klineman autopsies, and I can't sleep. Hell, I might not sleep for a week.'

'I heard about the Klineman woman. It's straight out of *The Walking Dead*. I sure don't know how you do what you do.'

'Somebody's got to do it. Listen, I need to see this crazy sonofabitch.'

'Shacket? Well, Doc, nobody told me you'd be coming around.'

'I have a few questions for him.'

The deputy frowned. 'Should he have an attorney present?'

'He hasn't been charged with anything. He's on a psychiatric hold. When he's charged, he'll need an attorney.'

Fenton remained dubious, although evidently not because of any doubt about Carson's right to be there. 'He's dangerous, Doc. He was on enough drugs to knock him out for hours. Instead he came around while they were still restraining him, and they had to shoot him up again. They wanted to zap him a third time, but they were worried about him overdosing.'

'He *is* fully restrained?'

'Oh, yeah.' Fenton took a key from his pocket.

290

'Just be careful 'cause he bit off Walter Colt's finger. And when you go in there, I have to lock the door after you. That's the rule.'

'I understand.'

'I'll be watching through this little window here, but I still have to lock the door after you.'

The window in the door was about eighteen inches wide and a foot tall, multiple panes with layers of wire between them.

Deputy Fenton looked into the room as he inserted the key in the lock.

He glanced at Carson again. 'What they do here is they go in two at a time, never one alone. Usually it's a nurse and some big guy who's an orderly or something.'

'I'll be fine,' Carson assured him.

'Oh, and about how his eyes glow like animal eyes. They think he's wearing some crazy contacts, like people do at Halloween. They were gonna remove them after they finished everything else with him, but then he came out of the sedative or whatever, came out of it *again*, tossing his head and fighting the restraints, so they just left the contacts for tomorrow.'

'He tries to spook me,' Carson said, 'I'll put in my wax fangs and give him a scare right back.'

78

Megan and Ben worked well together, cutting a double thickness of painter's tarp and nailing it over the tall sidelight next to the front door, stretching it taut enough so the wind couldn't billow it like a sail and thereby either strain the nails or tear the thick plastic. The molding would have to be repaired and painted after the glazier replaced the glass. Because the sidelight wasn't an operable window, there were no security-system contacts related to it, and the alarm could be set again whenever Megan wanted. They swept up the broken glass and the in-blown debris, cleaned the mess that Shacket had left in the kitchen, and throughout these tasks, they shared their stories.

She hadn't believed that anything Ben Hawkins needed to tell her could distract her from the terror Lee Shacket had brought into her life and the stain of horror that his assault had left in her memory. However, the incredible story of the golden retriever's seeming intelligence and his insistence on guiding Ben all the way from Olympic Village to this house outside Pinehaven filled her with wonder and raised countless questions beyond answering. For the moment at least, Lee Shacket faded from immediate consideration.

She made coffee, and they took two mugs upstairs to Woody's room, where they settled at the small round table at which Megan and the boy sometimes worked a jigsaw puzzle together.

The blustering night pressed its featureless face against the windows, its voice groaning in the glass, seeking admission, and the attic creaked as though some intruding weighty presence coiled among the rafters in that high realm. The night was no less strange than it had

292

been since the hard wind had risen in the latter hours of the previous evening. However, now the rainless storm seemed to be blowing not just a fusillade of threats but also a promise of something amazing and agreeably transformative.

The boy and the dog lay as before. Neither seemed to have moved as much as an inch. This was not necessarily curious behavior for Woody, but it seemed highly unusual for a dog that wasn't sleeping.

'Woody has some kind of connection with animals,' Megan said. 'He feeds deer that come on the property. They almost take apples from his hands. Rabbits, squirrels — small things don't run from him.'

'I had dogs as a kid. I had Clover until recently. They were wonderful, but they were nothing like this one.'

'What's happening between them?' Megan wondered.

Ben shook his head. He got up and stepped to the foot of the bed and said softly, 'Scooby?'

The dog thumped his tail once, emphatically, but didn't move otherwise.

Megan went to the bed as well. When she spoke her son's name and received no response, she said, 'Scooby?'

Again the dog responded with one hard slap of his tail against the mattress.

Without breaking eye contact with the retriever, speaking in a whisper, Woody said, 'No. His name is Kipp.'

79

Carson Conroy stepped across the threshold. The door fell shut behind him. Deputy Fenton locked it.

The prisoner was on his back, arms at his sides, restricted by wide straps, the upper half of the bed raised at about a thirty-degree angle.

Currently, the only light in the room issued from a sleep-hours luminary on the wall behind the bed, directly above Shacket's head. Even the low wattage of this lamp streamed down on him in an eerie, mocking approximation of the mystical light that some painters of Christendom had portrayed as descending on the crucifixion, though this was not a portrait of self-sacrifice and redemption bathed in the light of love. This grotesque, demonic figure brought to mind the poet Yeats, who had written of some 'rough beast, its hour come round at last,' slouching toward Bethlehem to be born.

As Carson approached the foot of the bed, he saw what seemed to be animal eyeshine in Shacket's hateful glare, fluxing continuously between yellow and red. He suspected that, in the morning, when the staff calmed the prisoner with another injection and attempted to remove the contact lenses, they would discover only eyes that in some hideous fashion and with terrifying rapidity had become other than human eyes.

'I'm Dr. Carson, the county medical examiner. I performed autopsies on the man who was shot yesterday and on a woman who was bitten to death.'

If there had not been wicked cunning in this creature's stare, Carson would have imagined it; so he knew that he couldn't trust himself to discern with full confidence what Shacket might be thinking or the true condition of his mind.

'I don't have any intention of testifying against you in a court, only as to the condition of the bodies of Justine Klineman and her companion.'

Shacket made no attempt at a reply.

The air carried a subtle but peculiar smell. The scent was neither foul nor pleasant. Just different. Carson had never smelled anything quite like it, and he couldn't give it a name.

'No one here is operating on a worst-case scenario. They think you're just psychotic, had a total mental breakdown. I'm afraid it's not that, not in the way they mean. I think something extraordinary is happening to you.'

Shacket's arms lay above the blanket, under the straps. The pale light was just bright enough to reveal the muscles tighten and the hands claw into fists.

'Do you know the word *transhumanism*, Mr. Shacket?'

The prisoner's nostrils flared, possibly a sign of excitement.

Carson said, 'It's too puerile to be a philosophy, too barren of foundational facts to be called a theory. It's just a high-tech religion.'

'What would you know?' the prisoner said. 'You're not a doctor in any meaningful sense. You're a butcher of the dead.'

'An article of the transhumanism faith,' Carson continued, 'is that human beings will soon have the ability to transform themselves physically and intellectually, acquire much stronger bodies, vastly increase our intelligence, gain powers once dreamed of only by the folks at Marvel Comics. This is expected to happen through a melding of man and machine or by breakthroughs in genetic engineering.'

'You have eyes to see, and you see not,' Shacket said.

'Was it truly cancer research that was being conducted in Springville?'

'Nothing so inconsequential as that. Why are you here? To thank me for bringing business your way? Without murder, you would have no work. Have you ever given thought to how complicit you are in crime, Doctor?'

Whatever Carson had been expecting, this was not it. Where was the out-of-control subhuman beast who had grossly assaulted Justine Kline-man and bitten off Walter Colt's finger?

Declining to take the bait, Carson continued. 'Dorian Purcell has said that, considering the medical advances being made, there are people alive today who'll live two hundred years, three hundred, maybe longer. Did the research in Springville involve the issue of longevity?'

'It involved the human genome, horizontal genetic transfer, the destiny of humanity, the fate of the earth — much more elevated work than carving up corpses to see what made them stop ticking.'

Carson persisted. 'Something went wrong?'

The skirling wind protested loudly. Shacket turned his head to the left, regarding the window with what might have been longing for the tumult of the night.

'Something went wrong?' Carson repeated.

Smug satisfaction pulled Shacket's features into a sardonic grin. 'Something went wrong *and* something went right.'

'You were contaminated?'

In Shacket's eyes of light, blue irises floated like gentian petals in moonlit pools.

Carson Conroy believed he was in the presence of something profoundly alien. He could not prove it, but he knew it.

In a voice astringent with contempt, Shacket said, 'You say contaminated, I say coronated.'

'Coronated? Crowned? Made king of what?'

'Of all that will come to be.'

Those seven words were spoken with quiet confidence that either confirmed Shacket's insanity or belied it. Carson was disturbed to find that he could not be sure which.

'Whatever happened to you,' Carson said, 'whatever you've been coronated with — are you communicable?'

'So this is why you're here. Ready to inflame the population with fear of a plague.' Shacket shook his head and looked again at the window. 'You're getting tiresome, Doctor.'

'No bacteria, no viruses?'

'When a king coughs, does he then infect those around him with royalty?'

'The ninety-two killed in the fire — they were contaminated?'

'Coronated. Try not to be dense, Doctor. No bacteria, no virus. Just . . . an agent of change programmed to invade every cell.'

'What agent?'

'Archaea. If you don't know what that is, look it up. It won't do you any good to know. In my becoming, archaea isn't kryptonite to me. I have no fear of it.'

'Your 'becoming'?'

'Before your eyes, I am changing. But you haven't the capacity to see.'

'They were burned to death — why? Because they were liable to undergo . . . changes, genetic changes?'

'Precisely.'

Carson thought about that. 'Uncontrolled changes. So they were a publicity disaster. And the source of potentially hundreds of millions in lawsuits.'

'Ah.' Shacket smiled at him. 'Associating with the deceased has not left you entirely brain dead.'

'Did those people know when they signed employment contracts that they were essentially working atop a bomb, that they were all expendable in a crisis if this altered archaea somehow escaped whatever isolation lab it was confined to?'

'If they didn't know, they suspected. They all signed off on the risk. Scientists can be true believers, too. In fact, perhaps more easily than others if they haven't yet found something they can call true and worth believing. Dorian pursued and signed up only those with a passion

298

for the transhuman future, who wanted to be *there* when the ultimate break-through occurred — who wanted to be among the first to be guaranteed centuries of vigorous life free of disease, with new capabilities. We all live for the fulfillment of one promise or another — love, wealth, fame. But what could be a promise more worth pursuing than the promise of physical immortality?'

Of all that Shacket had said, this speech was the first that, to Carson, had the unmistakable flavor of insanity.

To Carson's best knowledge, archaea could horizontally transfer genes between species but were not known to be carriers of disease.

He assumed that altered archaea programmed to deliver a genetic package into the cells of a test animal would die after fulfilling that function or would resort to a preprogrammed natural condition and would become agents of only *natural* processes.

His concern about a plague receded to the back of his mind.

'Becoming what?' he asked.

Again the wind drew Shacket's attention to the casement window, where the glass vibrated and the metal frames of the two tall panes rattled against each other.

When the wind subsided slightly, Shacket brought his radiant gaze back to his visitor. 'I am becoming the king of beasts.'

Here was the more obvious evidence of insanity that Carson had expected when he'd first entered the room. 'King of what beasts?'

'This is a world of beasts, Doctor. Human beings are just one of the many in the zoo. I'm becoming king of them all.'

Delusions of grandeur. Megalomania. The eerily articulate and considered Lee Shacket, with whom he'd been speaking, now seemed to be revealing a more recognizable madness heretofore concealed.

The scent that Carson had never smelled until entering this room was less subtle than previously. For a moment he was reminded of raw onion, but then wasn't, and for an instant he thought of the vapors from rubbing alcohol, but only for an instant, nor was this the astringency of the urine in the collection bottle.

It was evidence of his dread that he wondered what the smell would be like in a warren of raw earth where a snake curled among the wriggling lengths of its recent offspring. Maybe like this?

'Considering your circumstances,' Carson told Shacket, 'you were deposed from the throne before you could occupy it.'

The prisoner didn't rise to an argument. He only smiled.

Carson turned to the door, where Deputy Thad Fenton's face was pressed to the view window.

In the hallway, as the deputy relocked the door, he said, 'So how crazy is he, Doc?'

'Crazy enough. If he were to get out of that room — '

'No way he can,' Fenton interrupted. 'He can't even get out of bed to piss.'

'But if he *were* to get out of there,' Carson

300

said, writing his phone number on a hot-rod magazine, 'shoot him dead, stay away from the corpse, and call my cell at once.'

'Shoot him dead, just like that? Department rules — '

'Your life is more important than your career, Deputy. Shoot him dead, and I'll do my best to ensure you aren't disciplined too severely.'

Fenton thought about that. 'I wish Sheriff Sheldrake was still sheriff.'

'Stay awake, stay sharp.'

'The head nurse, she brings me coffee.'

'You have to leave your post to use the bathroom.'

'I'm quick about it,' Fenton assured him. 'Not that I don't take time to wash my hands. I wash them, all right.'

'When you go to the bathroom, don't first look through the view window in the door here. He might figure it's a check before you step away.'

'You're spooking me a little, Doc.'

Carson said, 'Good.'

80

No. His name is Kipp.

Those words brought to full life in Megan something that she hadn't realized was dormant: an exhilarating sense of possibilities that perhaps had shut down with the death of Jason. The precious sound of her child's voice — sweet, mellifluous — awakened in her a hope that she'd put to bed in a deep chamber of her mind, with no expectation of returning to it. Eleven years of waiting, eleven long years of coming to accept that the waiting would be for nothing — and now those five simple words.

Beside her, at the foot of the bed, Ben Hawkins said, 'What's wrong? You're shaking.' And then he remembered what she'd told him as they worked together in the foyer. 'He's never spoken.'

Her heart knocked no less forcefully now than when Lee Shacket crouched beside the bed, thumb and forefinger positioned to blind Woody, but this time it was the ardent pulse not of fear and anger, but of gladness and astonishment. And more than astonishment: Awe gripped her, a sense of the miraculous and transcendent, so that suddenly she was as mute as Woody had been before.

She found herself moving around to the side of the bed until she was standing over the boy, his back to her. She dared to put a hand on his shoulder, as tentatively as if her touch might turn him to dust.

Neither Woody nor Kipp moved, still engaged in whatever strange communion had conveyed to the boy the retriever's name and had freed his tongue to share that knowledge with Megan and Ben.

The boy, the dog, the bed, the room blurred and melted warmly down her face. Even when she wished that Jason had been there to hear his son's voice for the first time, the fabric of the moment included not one thread of sadness.

Over the years, when she had wondered what Woody's voice might sound like if ever he spoke, she'd sometimes thought his enunciation might be unfortunate, distorted. He had spent his life listening to the speech of others, but he'd had no practice at it — as far as she knew. However, though these five words of his shook her and moved her more than she could ever explain, far out of proportion to the information they conveyed, he sounded as natural as any child his age.

She recalled the moment, earlier in the night, when Woody had been murmuring in his sleep and, turning away from his bed, she had thought she heard him say *Dorothy*, though they knew no one by that name. She had assumed that she'd misheard. Now she suspected that in fact he'd spoken the name. With her hand on his shoulder, eager to hear him speak again, she said, 'Honey, who is Dorothy?'

The dog's tail thumped three times against the mattress, and from Woody issued words that were musical to his mother. 'Dorothy was his human mom. She raised him from a puppy. She died yesterday of cancer, and Kipp loved her more than anything, anything, the way I love you more than anything. Don't ever die, don't ever, it's too terrible for those you leave behind.'

All her life, Megan had been strong. Fate could throw no punch that would knock her down and keep her down. Life was a racing river of many currents, yet all the undertows and raging rapids were not merely survivable but were also experiences that made her still stronger. She should not have been surprised, therefore, when it wasn't a mortal threat that unraveled her heart, but instead Woody's declaration of love, against which she had no — nor wanted any — defense, after waiting to hear those words for eleven years. Her legs abruptly grew so weak that she couldn't stand, and the trickle of tears became a quiet flood. She sat on the edge of the bed and told him she loved him, too, loved him desperately, and although Woody said nothing more just yet, Kipp slapped his glorious plume of a tail three times against the mattress.

81

Kipp and Woody were eye to eye but also mind to mind, as they could be only on the Wire.

Their connection was private. They sent, and they received, but only between each other.

Kipp offered the boy the world as he experienced it.

Here I have been, this I have seen, these people I have met, this I conclude from all of that.

He revealed what he treasured, what he feared, all he knew.

The boy knew much the same, though less of many things, but also otherwise, and he, too, shared.

Kipp knew — and Woody Bookman knew but now came to understand in mind and heart and soul — that simplicity in human affairs was the way of truth, and complexity the way of deceit.

That envy and coveting were poisons from which arose the lust for power and all evil.

That love was the antidote to envy and coveting.

That truth was essential for the flourishing of love.

That love was essential to maintain innocence.

That peace of mind and perfect happiness could be achieved only through the truth of innocence and the simplicity of truth.

Neither was embarrassed by his numerous personal revelations or by any of the many thousands of things that he discovered about the other.

What might have been awkward revelations were instantly purged of mortification in the sharing.

For one thing, both Kipp and Woody were innocent and had been inoculated against the loss of innocence, the former because of his canine nature, the latter because of his developmental disability.

Furthermore, both understood that all creatures with high cognitive ability, to one degree or another, were often fools and should embrace their foolishness rather than deny it.

That understanding ensured humility.

Humility was the foundation for all lasting achievements.

By this telepathy, two lives, in their intricate simplicities of facts and emotions, flowed as freely as information from a computer onto a flash drive, but with more profound effect than a mere transfer of data.

The bond between humanity and dogs had flourished for maybe a hundred thousand years.

In this hour, at least between these two, that bond had grown stronger and deeper than mere millennia could have made it.

What might come of this, Kipp did not know. Nor did Woody.

They would find out.

The *what* was always revealed.

The *why* of things, however, was more often shrouded in eternal mystery.

82

Two o'clock in the morning. On the outskirts of Sacramento. An abandoned shopping mall. Reconstruction would eventually transform the site into upscale apartments with numerous amenities.

A chain-link fence encircled the large property, emblazoned with red-lettered signs warning of hazards and against trespassing. Although nothing remained in the mall worth stealing, a guard was usually stationed in a car inside the only gate in the fence, less to deter thieves than to dissuade adventurous urban explorers — those self-described concrete spelunkers — who engaged in explorations of everything from abandoned hotels to the maze of service tunnels underlying major cities. Such exploring was illegal, but if some catacomber or amateur city archeologist were injured in one of their adventures, there was every reason to be concerned that a jury of the ignorant and a judge with issues would award millions to the trespasser.

On this night, the graveyard-shift guard had been instructed not to show up for duty. The abandoned mall offered an ideal venue for a meeting between two parties who both insisted on a rendezvous where an accidental witness was not only unlikely but virtually impossible.

Haskell Ludlow got out of his Lexus SUV and, in the beams of his headlights, making a spectacle of himself, used a key to unlock the gate, as if he were the first to arrive.

A few hours earlier, he'd been sharing a penthouse suite in Vegas with twenty-two-year-old twins, Zoey and Chloe, who surprised him by knowing more perverse practices than he did, although he had been immersing himself in perversity almost as long as they had been alive. He had been tight with Dorian Purcell for twenty-five years, his quiet partner, but he'd stepped away from the business two years earlier to devote himself to pleasure. Now Dorian was occupied with the cover-up of the truth of Springville and needed Ludlow for this one task, and Haskell was back to do his part for the team.

The sagging chain-link sang eerily in the wind: Hell's harp strings strummed by a demon hand. Plastic bags of numerous origins, in a variety of conditions, caught in the gaps between the links, flapped and fluttered, producing a sound like swarming wings, as if a colony of bats were passing low overhead.

The gate rolled aside, wheels stuttering on the cracked and pitted blacktop. After driving onto the grounds, Ludlow closed the gate behind him, but he didn't lock it. Two men, arriving together, would supposedly soon follow him.

He drove around the east flank of the immense building, entered an open-air four-story parking garage, and slotted the Lexus in a handicapped-only space. His was the sole vehicle in sight.

A brick-paved promenade separated the parking structure from an entrance to the mall. Ludlow's flashlight revealed a few score of cracked and tattered plastic cups shivering along the pavement like schooling fish condemned to swim these bricks until demolition day.

The pneumatic glass doors had been removed and salvaged and replaced by a formidable plywood barricade and a single metal door. Using a second key, he unlocked the door and went inside, and did not lock up behind himself, pretending that events would unspool precisely as arranged.

The escalators had not yet been removed, though they were no longer operative. He climbed the grooved treads to the main floor. At most of the shops, the signage had been taken down, but here and there a retailer's name and logo appeared above empty show windows.

Birds had gotten in somehow and had not found their way out. Sparrows and crows. Lying here and there in seemingly organized configurations of feathers and fragile bones. As if voodoo cultists had made patterns out of their remains as a prelude to a ceremony. Pinions and bones quivered with the illusion of movement in the traveling flashlight beam.

Midway along the main promenade of the structure was a large round pool in which lily pads had floated and colorful koi had once swum. The pond was waterless and fishless now, half filled with a random origami of paper debris.

He sat on the wide coping that capped the two-foot-high wall of the pool, shielding the lens of the flashlight with two fingers of his right hand and directing the beam at the floor between his feet, as it had been stipulated that he would.

Haskell Ludlow and Dorian Purcell had been friends since junior high school, when they had both been kick-ass hackers and beardless code writers, planting rootkits in the poorly defended computer systems of major corporations, gleaning all manner of compromising information from the emails of reckless executives who didn't yet understand the eternal nature of electronic correspondence. There were unlimited potential income streams if you were too young and too clever to be daunted by the word *extortion*. Balzac had written, 'Behind every great fortune, there is a crime,' which was both a cliché and a lie. However, Haskell and Dorian had taken steps to ensure that if ever an origin story of Parable were written, no author would be able to follow a single thread back to the clichéd truth in their case. Haskell Ludlow, though always keeping a low profile, owned the second-largest block of voting stock in Parable, and he would take nearly any risk, as he was doing now in this crumbling mall, to protect his fortune and his good name.

Dressed in black, wearing night-vision gear that penetrated the darkness, as silent as souls that had shed their bodies and had no weight to strike footsteps from the floor, the two men from Tragedy materialized before Ludlow at 2:15 a.m. According to the agreed-upon plans for the meeting, they were to follow him into the mall at two thirty. In fact, they had been here since half past midnight.

He did not look up from their shoes, but held out the driver's license in his left hand. It was an excellent forgery in the name of Alexander Gordius, an identity used by him and Dorian Purcell, one buried under more shell corporations and sedimentary layers of false data than the geological strata that overlaid Jurassic-era fossils. It was the phantom Gordius who paid the Dark Web masters of Tragedy to perform five carefully crafted exterminations over the years.

Returning the driver's license, one of the agents of Tragedy said, 'What kind of name is Gordius?'

'My dad's,' said Ludlow, getting to his feet and leaving the bright flashlight on the pond coping.

The two men were lithe bulls, the kind who looked like they could crash through walls or slip through cracks, whichever method of attack was required. They wore black hoodies, and their faces were smeared with a nonreflective black grease. Their night-vision goggles now dangled from their necks.

Their Tragedian names were Keith Richards and Roger Daltrey, but their real names — which they thought undiscoverable — were Frank Gatz and Boris Sergetov. The entire Tragedy staff consisted of only six people, for it was wise to limit a murder-for-hire operation to as few potential rats as possible, and these two were the founders of the organization.

Having informed their client of the breach of security that made them vulnerable to exposure, they were prepared to kill — for no fee — the hacker who had jacked the Gordius ID and had evidently been trying to put together evidence regarding Tragedy's activities, in particular seeking details related to one of the five hits for which Gordius had contracted.

The 'real' Alexander Gordius — alias Haskell Ludlow and Dorian Purcell — had insisted on this meeting to learn the identity of the hacker and to devise a mutually agreeable plan for the extermination of same. Tragedy operated out of a warehouse in Stockton, and this shuttered shopping mall, little more than fifty miles from their headquarters, served as a convenient rendezvous point. They surely researched the ownership before coming here; but they couldn't have found any tie to Dorian or Parable among the American divisions of a trio of foreign conglomerates that each had a piece of the property.

Working off nervous energy, Ludlow paced as he talked. 'So who is the bastard?'

With a Russian accent as rich as beluga caviar, Sergetov said, '*Gospodin*, the deceiving bastard person is indeed a bitch.'

'Say what? Are you serious? Some geek twat was almost able to get a knife to our throat?'

'No offense, man,' said Frank Gatz, 'but that kind of thinking is prediluvian.'

'It's what?'

'Prediluvian — out of date, ancient, before Noah and the Flood, white male thinking at its worst.'

'I'm not white.'

'All I'm saying is that women can do anything a man can do.'

'Piss standing up?'

Gatz sighed. 'If that's the way you want to be.'

As if making a philosophical point to all present, Sergetov said, 'Woman is possible to be both brilliant and still *svoloch*.'

'Whatever. I'm not the one who screwed up here,' Ludlow said, pacing ceaselessly. 'Tragedy screwed up here. You screwed this up. Where is this bitch?'

'She exists not two hours from here, *gospodin*,' Boris said, 'but you might never to have heard the village called Pinehaven.'

Indeed, Ludlow had never heard of the place.

'Her name,' said Gatz, 'is Megan Bookman. You may recall her husband, Jason, was a problem we solved with a helicopter crash.'

Suddenly the mall had a Gothic quality. If it had seemed like the ideal venue for a highly private meeting beyond the eyes of any chance witnesses, it now struck Ludlow as more sinister, a nexus where past deeds and consequences met at last. Could it be that Megan Bookman — looker, painter, pianist — was a quadruple

312

threat, also a white-hat hacker, a data pirate who was buccaneering through the Dark Web in search of justice?

Jason had learned about — and been radically opposed to — the research into genetic engineering via archaea. He hadn't understood how central transhumanism was to Dorian's view of the future — and what the consequences would be of threatening to resign and go public with his boss's plans, which were even then far advanced. If he'd shared his concerns with Megan, might she have viewed with suspicion the helicopter crash that killed him?

Ludlow, who had never been interested in Refine's research, who wasn't a transhumanist, had not criticized Dorian. He knew nothing of the work in Springville and didn't want to know.

Gatz said, 'Mrs. Bookman lives there alone with a mentally disabled boy of eleven.'

'Just because he is child and stupid, the *nevezhda* should not be spared,' Boris Sergetov declared. '*Krugovaia otvetstvennost* — collective responsibility. She popped him from her oven, fed him from her tit. He is our enemy no less than she. They are turds from the same bowel. Flush them both away.'

To Frank Gatz, Ludlow said, 'Your friend is so eloquent. Does he write poetry for the corporate newsletter? If not, you ought to let him have a page, see if maybe you have another Robert Frost among you.'

'Sir, excuse me, but could you stop spinning like a top?' Gatz said. 'Man, you're making me dizzy.'

'I'm not spinning. I'm pacing,' Ludlow insisted. 'I've got a serious case of nervous tension. I'm drowning in stress hormones, thanks to this colossal screwup. Pacing is how I clear my head and think. It doesn't help that the two of you don't seem to be stressed at all, don't seem to think there's any risk in offing this bitch and her brat.'

As he said *brat*, Haskell Ludlow hit the mark he had previously selected when he'd staged this with Hisscus, Knacker, and Verbotski, which was their cue to step in from the wings, so to speak, now that they had the information they needed.

Leroy Hisscus, Bradley Knacker, and John Verbotski had come to the mall at 10:30 p.m., four hours before the boys of Tragedy were supposed to show up, two hours before they *actually* showed up. Leroy, Brad, and John had embedded themselves in nearby abandoned stores, so cleverly concealed that the cursory search for hostiles undertaken by Gatz and Sergetov detected no trace of them. Gatz and Sergetov had weapons, but their guns were holstered. When Hisscus, Knacker, and Verbotski materialized like spirits at a séance, their pistols were drawn and Ludlow was safely out of their lines of fire. Even if Gatz and Sergetov were wearing Kevlar vests, they were doomed, as three extended magazines containing forty-eight rounds were emptied in less than a minute, with a number of head shots that would have won all the biggest stuffed animals at a duck-shooting game booth in a carnival.

All the pistols were fitted with sound suppressors, which never totally silenced a weapon. This much gunfire might have been heard beyond the walls of the mall, even on a night of explosive wind, although probably not as far away as the one-story elementary school across the street from the construction-fence gate by which Ludlow had entered the property.

A third Tragedian, Cory Holmes, was stationed on the roof of that school, watching the gate, to be sure Ludlow came alone and that no one followed him. By now, Holmes was probably dead from a bullet to the back of the head, because an associate of Hisscus, Knacker, and Verbotski had secreted himself on that roof before Holmes got there.

If the muffled gunfire didn't still echo through the desolate shopping mall, it still rang in Ludlow's ears as he approached Bradley Knacker and his partners. Brad wore an earpiece walkie-talkie, one finger pressed to it to tighten the fit, listening intently. He said 'Ten-four' to the man on the elementary-school roof. To Ludlow, he said, 'Sherlock has gone over the Reichenbach Falls for real this time,' by which he meant that Cory Holmes was dead and would not later be resurrected as Arthur Conan Doyle had resurrected his detective after killing him to the dismay of his readers.

Ludlow wondered when it was that men in this line of work had concluded that part of their job was to get off a half-baked quip in the midst of action. Blame the movies.

The other three agents of Tragedy, asleep in their Stockton homes, had been or were now being likewise dispatched. No bodies would remain to be found either here or there. Six men would just disappear. The website and all records of its

315

operation, if any, would cease to exist by dawn.

If Frank Gatz and Boris Sergetov had been aware that the seed money with which they had launched Tragedy some years earlier had not come from mob sources, as they thought, but from Dorian Purcell, by a most indirect route, they might have marveled at the irony of their fate. Or perhaps at least Gatz might have had the capacity to marvel. Sergetov not so much.

Hisscus, Knacker, Verbotski, and five associates had formed *their* Dark Web operation two years ago, with seed money they thought had been arranged through certain international arms dealers that did business with mercenaries worldwide. In fact, Dorian was the murder-for-hire equivalent of a Broadway angel, backing their Dark Web play, which had a fifty-two-character address of letters and numbers, and which they called Atropos & Company, after the most ominous of the Three Fates in classical mythology. Atropos was the goddess who cut the thread of life. The name had been provided by John Verbotski, who was perhaps overeducated for his profession.

Behind many great fortunes there was no crime, only hard work and intelligence and obsession, but Balzac was not entirely wrong. Fourteen-year-old boys, well rewarded for extortion, would always learn from that experience the efficacy and profitability of well-considered crime.

The man who had killed Holmes on the schoolhouse roof would deal with that corpse and then assist Leroy Hisscus in the cleanup here at the mall. John Verbotski and Bradley

316

Knacker would set out shortly for the Bookman house on the outskirts of Pinehaven, which lay less than two hours away.

Being of more delicate sensibilities than the agents of Atropos, Haskell Ludlow moved farther away from the perforated, leaking corpses of Gatz and Sergetov, which smelled of blood and feces and urine and stomach gas.

'Mr. Gordius,' Verbotski said, moving with him, the brassy clink of expended cartridges rolling away from their shoes, 'we've done good business with you in the past, and we'll make all this go away. We'll make what's in Stockton go away, too. But I want to be sure what you want us to do in Pinehaven. We don't operate the way these two meatheads did.' With disdain, he indicated the riddled bodies of Sergetov and Gatz. 'A town like Pinehaven, strangers are noticed and remembered. We just wouldn't storm a house in a quiet hickburg and blast away.'

'You wouldn't, and you shouldn't,' Ludlow said. 'I want Megan Bookman and her son alive, and within the next twelve hours. I want to break her down, take her apart piece by piece, find out what she knows and who she's told, if anyone. If I've got the boy, I'll break her by breaking him.'

Verbotski suggested approaches, involving two men in addition to him and Knacker, and Ludlow offered refinements.

Being Alexander Gordius, Haskell Ludlow made his way out of the decaying mall, where the reflections of his flashlight in the dusty shop windows shaped stalkers in his peripheral vision. He knew his imagination was plaguing him, but he kept nervously turning his head left and right, to confront what wasn't there.

Although he had paid for killings before and thought little of it, he had never until this night been present when the contract was fulfilled. He found the experience far more unsettling than he had imagined he would.

When he returned to the open-air four-story parking structure in which he'd left his Lexus SUV, a sudden rattling noise inspired him to pivot and play his flashlight across the forest of concrete columns. Out of the darkness swooped several sheets of a discarded newspaper, animated by the wind, whirling together along the parking row, like some creature of pale wings and hooded form, with lethal purpose. This storm-crafted presence lacked a scythe or sickle, but with a sudden seeming leap, it sprang on Ludlow, enwrapped him in crackling crispness, masking his face, blinding him. He cried out and thrashed free of its embrace, slashing viciously with the flashlight as if the thing could be wounded.

He clambered into the SUV, pulled the door shut, started the engine, switched on the headlights, locked the doors, and sat in a cold sweat. He watched the sheets of the newspaper billow away into the dark, embarrassed by the panic that had seized him.

Stress. He was stressed out. The violence in the mall. The possibility that Megan Bookman had linked him and Dorian to Tragedy on the Dark Web. Since he had nothing to do with Refine and knew nothing about what had happened in Springville, he didn't worry much about that, except to the extent that he was concerned how Refines troubles would affect Parable's stock price.

Ludlow drove out of the parking garage, off the mall property, into the street.

It would be three thirty by the time he returned to his hotel. This Tragedy job had cost him sleep he badly needed after days of playing with Zoey and Chloe in Vegas. He wanted a martini with the merest whisper of vermouth, followed by a superb cabernet with an early breakfast, although not breakfast food, dinner fare instead, so that he might reset his circadian rhythm. Then eight hours of sleep to prepare himself for the interrogation of Megan Bookman. He had a suite at a four-star hotel. Sacramento, the capital, was home to a wonderfully corrupt state government, with an ocean of dark money washing around, which meant there were a great many good hotels to choose from. His suite had three bedrooms; when he woke in the night and went to the bathroom, he liked to return to a fresh bed with crisp, clean sheets, where he hadn't yet left any bad dreams under the pillow.

83

Behind the sheriff's department headquarters and town jail lay a city-employee parking lot. Beyond the parking lot stood a brick building, a garage, with small, high-set barred windows that were at the moment full of pearl-gray light, a backwash from the hooded lamps that hung below the glass line.

In this structure, vehicles associated with a serious crime and permitted to be seized for investigation were impounded until they must be released according to timetables established in the law or until a court ordered that they be returned to the rightful owners. In generally peaceful Pinehaven County, law enforcement was not impoundment crazy or reliant on income from using asset-forfeiture statutes. Currently the garage contained only two vehicles in addition to Eckman's personal patrol car: a Ford F-150 pickup involved in a DUI hit-and-run and the red Dodge Demon in which Lee Shacket, alias Nathan Palmer, had fled Utah.

Having come directly from the hospital to the impoundment garage, Sheriff Eckman was too excited to sleep. He worked alone on the Dodge and its contents. Because of the extraordinary nature of the crime and the connection to a company owned by Dorian Purcell, he would not alert the media to the arrest of Shacket until noon, which would give him time to determine how to exploit this situation to his very best advantage. This case would provide him with statewide name recognition in the days to come and add momentum to his career. If he played this right, there might also be a way that he could ingratiate himself with Purcell that would result in a large financial benefit.

Ask and you shall receive.

The second of two suitcases in the trunk of the

vehicle contained packets of hundred- and twenty-dollar bills. Never before had he seen so much cash in one place. A quick count suggested there might be as much as $100,000.

After careful consideration, he put the suitcase in the trunk of his patrol car.

Clearly, the money was intended as a run-for-it fund. This suggested that Shacket had been aware that whatever work was being done at the Springville facility might suddenly go bad and put him in serious legal jeopardy.

Megan Bookman had said that Shacket spoke of Costa Rica, where he apparently had prepared a secure retreat under a name other than his own or Nathan Palmer. If he hoped to live anonymously, he would need to get there indirectly, by a transportation scheme complex enough to be untraceable. There would be costs involved, not least of all bribes. Shacket would have millions in offshore accounts, beyond easy reach. It seemed to the sheriff that $100,000 might not be adequate cash for an escape when even the all-powerful National Security Agency was involved in a search for the guy. Given his resources and considering his dire legal liabilities in this case, Shacket would not have scrimped on his getaway stash.

Eckman walked around the Dodge, studying it. Cars were often rebuilt to create compartments in which drugs could be transported. In this case, it would be cash, and it would have to be somewhere that it could be quickly accessed. Shacket wouldn't want to have to cut away a fender to get at the money. Which meant it would probably be inside the vehicle.

The Dodge Demon was a highly customized work of art, not merely an assembly-line vehicle with a souped-up engine. Interior finishes were equal to those in any Mercedes. A hidden compartment would be cleverly integrated, but the perfection of the upholstery stitching and other details made it more difficult for the craftsmen to hide an accessible cavity.

In ten minutes, he found the pair of pressure latches that released a concealed panel on the back of the front passenger seat. A quick tabulation, based on counting the hundred-dollar bills in one of the plastic-wrapped bundles, suggested that he'd found an additional $300,000.

He almost transferred the entire sum to his patrol car. Then he realized that once he went public with the arrest of Lee Shacket, Tio Barbizon would send Frawley and Zellman from Sacramento, this time with others, not just to claim custody of Shacket, as they previously assumed possession of the bodies of his victims, but also to take with them the additional gathered evidence, including the Dodge Demon.

They would go over the car with great care. They would discover the hidden compartment. If they found it empty, they would wonder why Shacket had gone to the trouble of having the hiding place crafted without stashing anything in it.

Reluctantly, Hayden Eckman transferred only two-thirds of the cash to his cruiser, leaving $100,000 to be found by the attorney general's investigators. Shacket might later claim there had been three times as much, plus $100,000 in a suitcase. But he was insane, a degenerate cannibal, and not to be believed.

Anyway, by the time Eckman announced Shacket's arrest, the prisoner might be dead. Considering Shacket's extreme violence, a scenario could be imagined in which he'd free himself enough to attack either a deputy or someone on the hospital staff, whereupon lethal force could be rightly used against him. Sheriff Eckman had been thinking about how to engineer such an event ever since he'd overseen Shacket's commitment to the psychiatric ward.

Leaving the $100,000 for Tio Barbizon's investigators to find would have anguished Eckman if, mere moments later, he had not found another fortune sewn into the lining of the leather sport coat lying on the front passenger seat. The stylish garment offered nothing of interest in the pockets, but in checking it out, he felt something odd in the hem. He ripped out the silk lining; sewn to it was a plastic sleeve with thirty-six small compartments, each containing what appeared to be a diamond. At a guess, he valued this collection higher than the $300,000 he had transferred to his vehicle.

Hayden Eckman had seen Pinehaven as nothing but a stepping stone, his office just one tread in a climb toward a more powerful position. But the town was proving to be a trove of opportunities.

84

Woody's mom sitting on the edge of the bed. Woody in her lap, in her arms, holding fast to her.

Ben in the armchair, Kipp standing at his side, tail lashing with excitement, delight.

Kipp had never known another human being as he now knew Woody.

He loved the Woody he knew. He loved Woody's mom, whom he knew through Woody.

Although Kipp loved Dorothy, she had never been completely known to him, not down to the deepest roots of her psychology, as Woody was known.

Woody Bookman had never known another human being as he now knew Kipp.

Furthermore, in coming to know Kipp through communion on the Wire, Woody had come to know himself as never before.

Kipp could still not talk and never would — except by the use of his sixth sense, telepathy.

But the boy now talked, freed from the crippling inhibitions that had silenced him.

Maybe this meant that the cause of his developmental disability was largely psychological.

But probably not.

Kipp knew that, without a Sonicare, Woody would still brush his teeth until he had no gums.

Woody knew it, too.

And Woody would still be aware of useless things like that he was born at 4:00 a.m., July 26, and July was the seventh month, and twenty-six multiplied by seven was 182, and then if you added four, representing the hour he was born, the total was 186, which happened to be his IQ.

There in the boy's bedroom, with Kipp and Ben looking on and everyone in the grip of wonder, Woody talked in explosive rushes. He revealed profound feelings and thoughts trapped in him for a lifetime, not least of all that he loved and adored his mother.

That he hoped one day to meet a girl who, like him, had a dead person's gum tissue in her mouth, so they would have something to talk about and might eventually kiss.

That deer had families, too, and found it just as hard as human beings did to keep their families together.

That his mother was his bridge over troubled water.

That when she played 'Moon River' on the piano, he didn't find it sad that he would never be crossing it in style someday or be off to see the world.

That instead of following Moon River around the bend to see what lay ahead, he could read about the world in books and could *imagine* the whole world, which was good enough for him, which he thought she needed to know.

That his dad had died 164 weeks earlier.

He said that he had been investigating his dad's death for sixty weeks.

That 164 minus sixty equaled 104.

That 104 was exactly the number of pages in 'The Son's Revenge: Faithfully Compiled Evidence of Monstrous Evil.'

Kipp hurried to the desk. Stood on his hind feet. Gripped the spring-clipped report in his teeth.

He took the document to the bed and put it beside Woody's mom.

If things had been already kind of crazy, they became really crazy now.

85

When Deputy Thad Fenton returned from a quick trip to the bathroom, he heard a loud clattering in Room 328. Since taking up his post, the only noise he'd expected to hear was the prisoner screaming and cursing and shouting nonsensical things that a wildly homicidal psychopath might be expected to shout, but there had been none of that. Now this.

Fenton looked through the view window in the door. The lighting in there wasn't good, but it was adequate for him to see that the impossible had happened. Shacket had escaped his restraints, torn the cannula from his arm, freed himself from the catheter through which he urinated into a jar, and cast off his backless hospital gown. Naked, he stood at the sole window, trying to force his way through it.

The casement window featured two tall panes that were hinged to the upright jambs. The mechanized panes could be opened outward only with a detachable crank, which usually lay on the sill, so that it wouldn't be protruding if

326

the pleated shade needed to be lowered. The crank had been removed when the room was requisitioned for a psychiatric patient.

Skinned in shadow, Shacket was a surprisingly powerful figure, straining against the metal-framed panes, neither of which was wide enough to allow him passage. He needed to force both halves of the window open by stripping the gears in the mechanism, a feat that required greater strength than any man possessed. Yet abruptly the panes shuddered and, with a metallic snapping and shrieking, began to part where the flange of one overlaid the lip of the other. A bronze frame torqued and glass burst. Shacket let out an inhuman roar. A hinge popped and cracked, squealed like a wounded thing.

A nurse approached quickly along the corridor, and Thad Fenton warned her to stay back. He drew his pistol and tried the door, but of course it was locked. He keyed the lock, gripped the pistol in both hands, and entered the room with a shout, ordering the prisoner to drop and stay down.

Just then the left half of the window sprang outward, and the right half tore away from the jamb. Shacket flung the glassless metal frame at Fenton, who ducked to avoid being struck in the face.

When the deputy straightened up, bringing the pistol to bear once more, Shacket was crouched on the stool of the open window, no less terrifying than a raging ape, a hairless ape that glared with eyes as red as if his skull were filled with fire. The autumn wind screamed around the naked creature in his gargoyle pose and blew a winter chill through the room, flapping the torn rubber restraints on the bed and rattling the IV-drip rack. Because Shacket was more than thirty feet above a concrete walkway, it seemed that he had nowhere to go — and then he launched himself into the night as though he could fly.

Stunned, Fenton crossed the room to the window and leaned into the howling wind and peered down, certain that he'd see the crazed prisoner lying broken and unmoving in a widening pool of blood. But Shacket was neither immediately below, nor to the left, nor to the right. Incredibly, the man seemed to have survived the fall. Deputy Fenton shifted his gaze farther out from the building, past a planting bed of low shrubbery, toward a visitor's parking lot that wasn't in use at this hour, searching for a pale, naked figure making its way toward the street. Shacket wasn't out there, either.

Whether Thad thought first of the Edgar Allan Poe story that had scared the bejesus out of him back in the day, when his teacher had read it to his ninth-grade English class, or whether instead the two words came first through the wind and reminded him of the story, he would never know. Words and memory — or memory and words — followed each other with but an instant between. The words were 'See me,' issued like a serpent's hiss, and the story was 'The Murders in the Rue Morgue,' about a violent orangutan trained to commit murder. Thad turned his head and, in defiance of all logic, he looked up. Like

328

some spider to which vertical surfaces were no different from those horizontal, clinging impossibly to the simple limestone lintel and the decorative brickwork around it, Shacket was pressed to the wall, legs splayed behind him, gazing down, eyes bright and teeth bared, face-to-face with the deputy.

The fugitive let go of stone and brick, dropped on Fenton, and dragged him out of the window. Together they fell from the third floor, through a wind that buoyed them not, the pistol slipping from the deputy's hand, Shacket crying out in triumph. Thad Fenton landed on his back, on concrete, and all the breath blew out of him. Pain tore along every neural pathway in his body, as if a thousand knives had been thrust through him. But the agony was brief, a cruel flare of torment and then no pain at all below his neck, only in his head, his face. Paralyzed.

Gasping with excitement, making eager wordless sounds, seeming no worse for the fall, Shacket crouched upon his prey.

The deputy felt a ribbon of warm blood unraveling from a corner of his mouth and down his chin.

Murmuring like an enraptured lover, Shacket licked up that red essence. He lowered his mouth to the deputy's throat and bit away his ability to scream or speak, and then bit away his ability to breathe.

For Thad Fenton, there was nothing but the chilly wind and tossing trees and extreme terror — but only for a moment.

86

At first with astonishment and pride in her son's initiative, but soon with growing alarm, Megan paged through 'The Son's Revenge: Faithfully Compiled Evidence of Monstrous Evil,' while Ben Hawkins asked Woody about the Dark Web and the site calling itself Tragedy.

Sitting in Woody's office chair, Megan felt a little dizzy. In one hour, she'd had her mind opened to the possibility of dogs with enormously enhanced intelligence, witnessed her son ascending from high-functioning autism to very-damn-high-functioning autism, heard him speak for the first time in eleven years, and learned that some murder-for-hire outfit on the Dark Web might be seeking him. Wonder was rapidly darkening into confusion and dread.

Because Jason had been disturbed by Dorian Purcell's passionate interest in transhumanism, not merely by the financial risks being taken by the billionaire to fund research, but by the nature of the research itself, he had made plans to leave his position at Parable. When he had died in the helicopter crash, suspicion had simmered in Megan, although not for long. When the initial shock of his death passed, she decided that suspicion was merely part of the anger that gripped her upon receiving news of the loss — anger at the injustice, at fate, at God. When anger gave way entirely to grief, and when grief became sorrow, and as she bootstrapped herself out of sorrow for Woody's sake, the suspicion gradually faded. Anyway, it made no sense that a man of Dorian's wealth and fine reputation would risk everything to remove a subordinate by violence, unless that had been part of his successful modus operandi from his earliest days. But no evidence of such a dark side existed.

Except that evidence *had* existed, after all, so deeply hidden that no one but an obsessive-compulsive autistic genius, motivated by acute grief, could possibly have the time and the focus to devote to the uncovering of it.

For all of his formidable brainpower, however, Woody was a naif. He lacked the street smarts to realize the risk he was taking by penetrating Dorian's cover as Alexander Gordius and by snooping around on the Dark Web.

To the boy, Ben Hawkins said, 'So . . . what was the last thing you saw on the screen before you backed out of the Tragedy site?'

Woody looked at the dog rather than at the man. He said, 'Four words came up. They said 'We will find you.' I crawled under my desk and unplugged the computer, unplugged everything, even my work lamp. I was scared. I'm still scared. I did a stupid thing. I'm sorry I did such a stupid thing.'

Listening to him, Megan found it remarkable that he spoke now as if he had always spoken, as if he'd already forgotten that eleven years of silence had been lifted from him.

Ben said, 'Listen, Woody, you didn't do a stupid thing. You did a brave thing, an amazing thing. Any time you do a brave thing, see, there's always a possibility of pushback from bad hats who don't like people with courage. Now that we know what we're dealing with, we can handle them. Putting bad hats in their place is easier than you think. It can even be fun.'

As the boy stared intently at the dog, Megan watched Ben — until she realized the retriever was watching her and wagging his tail.

She reminded herself that the dog wasn't just a dog. Kipp was also . . . a person. She had to get her head around that. He saw how she was watching Ben, and he was perceptive enough to guess what she must be feeling.

Abruptly, Kipp slipped away from Woody and padded across the room to the open door and stood staring into the hallway.

The doorbell rang. It was a quarter past three in the morning, and the doorbell rang. It rang again.

87

After his interview with Lee Shacket in Room 328, Carson Conroy was discomposed, too agitated to go home, even though he was strung out on caffeine and bad news, eyes burning from lack of sleep. He drove the town, seeking something, but not sure what he sought.

He'd fled Chicago for Pinehaven, left the madness of metropolis for the comparative sanity of the Sierra Nevada range. But the truth of contemporary life was that distance no longer insulated anyone from the cancers of calculated modernism. Gangbangers like those who killed Lissa for sport had begun showing up in small towns. Social-media mobs could as easily destroy the life of a schoolteacher in rural America as that of a celebrity, for transgressions either real or imagined. Dorian Purcell, working with a federal agency, funded a reckless research project into the engineering of the human genome and sited the work in rural Utah — but now people were dying here.

Progress was *real* progress only when it evolved naturally and thoughtfully from the history of human experience and accumulated wisdom. When it was imposed in contempt for that experience and wisdom, then progress was in fact radical destruction.

Cruising the picturesque streets of his beloved Pinehaven, Carson began to understand that what he sought was an escape from the hubris of humanity, from the endless discontent of those who believed in one utopia or another in spite of the fact that history showed utopian thinking to lead inevitably to disaster and often to mass murder on an industrial scale. But of course there could be no escape from the overweening pride and arrogance of the species. You could withdraw, remake your life with a small circle of friends who didn't wish to silence and punish their fellow countrymen with whom they disagreed, who knew the grievous threat to peace that arose from contempt for others, from an inflated self-esteem that became vainglory. But there was no town remote enough, no fortress walls high enough to protect you from mad ideas with mass appeal.

Immortality had mass appeal. Even if it became public knowledge that Purcell had financed research that had led already to ninety-four deaths and counting, perhaps in the current climate he would still be celebrated for his good intentions.

As Carson drove again through the heart of Pinehaven, the wind-shaken night was assailed by sirens. A patrol car that was parked in front of the Four Square Diner swung away from the curb, lightbar blazing. Another cruiser erupted from the alley beside the sheriffs station and followed the first vehicle.

Carson pulled to the curb and phoned Carl Fredette, the watch commander on duty. He expected bad news. He didn't expect that it would be as bad as it was. Lee Shacket had escaped his room at the county hospital. Deputy Fenton was missing, presumed captive, and judging by the blood at the scene, either gravely wounded or dead.

In this case, with the perpetrator being unique in the world and fast 'becoming' a threat of unknown dimensions, the law offered no real and lasting protection, only an illusion of it.

The sheriff would never admit as much. Nor would anyone working for him. Nor would any higher authority above those in Pinehaven County. Megan Bookman needed to know that truth, and perhaps there was no one but Carson to convey it to her.

88

The doorbell rang, and the dog raced into the upstairs hall, out of sight, and Megan picked up her pistol from the nightstand.

As Ben followed the retriever, he said, 'You won't need that. Kipp's excited, but it's positive excitement. He knows who's at the door, and it doesn't scare him.'

'How can he know who's at the door?'

'Smell, I suspect. Once a dog knows your smell, he can pick up your scent a mile away, a lot farther than just a mile. That's why they're always waiting for you at the door when you come home after leaving them alone.'

Nevertheless, she told Woody to stay put and she followed Ben into the hallway. 'Just the same, I'll be on the landing with the gun.'

Already, Ben knew her well enough to be sure that she wouldn't be careless with a firearm. Descending the stairs two at a time, he said, 'I'm always happier with backup.'

Kipp was at the undamaged sidelight to the left of the front door, not just wagging his tail but also wiggling his entire body and prancing in place with excitement.

A thirtysomething woman crouched on the farther side, looking in at the dog, smiling broadly and saying something. Ben couldn't make out what she said, except that she knew the retriever's name.

He opened the door, and she looked up. 'Oh! Hello, my goodness, you found Kipp. My name's

Rosa. Rosa Leon, I'm Kipp's ... I'm his guardian.'

Although Ben was happy that the dog took such obvious delight in this reunion, a sense of loss overcame him. In less than a day, a bond had developed between him and this amazing retriever. He didn't want to be cut out of Kipp's life, his story.

In the foyer, Rosa Leon went to her knees, and Kipp nuzzled her, and Ben said, 'How on earth did you find him?'

'His special collar. It has a GPS.'

As Ben started to close the door against the insistent wind, a white Ford Explorer pulled to a stop behind the Lincoln MKX in which Rosa Leon evidently had arrived. The driver doused the headlights.

'He's no ordinary dog, this one,' Ben said, closing the door and watching the Ford Explorer through the sidelight.

Rosa continued rubbing behind Kipp's ears. 'Oh, yes, he's very well trained. Kipp is quite remarkable. He knows ever so many clever tricks.'

'He knows a lot more than tricks,' Ben said, watching a man get out of the Explorer. 'This fella's no circus dog. He's something else altogether.'

Rising to her feet, frowning, the woman said, 'I'm not sure I know what you mean.'

'I'm pretty sure you do,' Ben said, using his best smile to take the edge off the words. 'You're protecting him . . . his secret.'

The newcomer was approaching the house.

Ben was licensed to carry, but his pistol remained in the Range Rover. 'Megan, we have another visitor. Can you come on down here?'

When he turned his head to confirm that she was descending from the landing, he noticed Woody at the top of the stairs.

Seeing the pistol in Megan's hand, the woman rose to her feet. 'What's happening here, what is this?'

'We're not the problem,' Ben assured her. 'Maybe the guy coming up the front walk is. Step aside. Get behind Megan.'

As the man came onto the porch, Ben said, 'Megan, do you know him?'

She looked at the visitor through the sidelight, and he nodded at her, and she said, 'I've seen him around a few times. I think maybe he works for the city.'

'Stay ready,' Ben said, and he opened the door.

The guy had a business card. 'I need to see Mrs. Bookman. It's an urgent matter.'

According to the card, he was Dr. Carson Conroy, the medical examiner for Pinehaven County.

'See her about what?' Ben asked.

'Lee Shacket has escaped psychiatric confinement at the county hospital.'

Kipp pivoted from Rosa Leon and raced up the stairs to Woody.

From a distance came the rising scream of sirens.

Bella on the Wire

Santa Rosa, California. The family room of the Montell house.

Bella finally had to return *The Magician's Elephant* to the bookshelf from which she'd removed it.

The story was so good, she didn't want it to be spoiled by all the interruptions.

And there were a lot of interruptions.

Something was definitely happening out there.

History was being made tonight.

The Mysterium culture and history were not conveyed generation to generation in written texts. Their kind had no hands with which to write.

Their culture was vocal, if telepathic conversation qualified as vocal.

They passed their stories from generation to generation on the Wire, as if around a campfire.

Their history, such as they knew it, dated back only four generations. Or about fifty years.

Even as smart as they were and even though they considered the maintenance of their oral history to be a sacred duty, they knew that not everything in it was reliable.

When a story was passed from one friend to another, details inevitably changed in the retelling.

This wasn't because anyone lied.

Anyway, dogs didn't lie. They couldn't.

They weren't sure why they couldn't, but they couldn't.

Yet details changed in the retelling, because their memories were, like those of human beings, not perfectly reliable.

Their history, therefore, had a certain quality of myth.

Regarding their origins, every story attributed their genesis to human beings.

The first of their kind came, so the legend had it, from a genetics laboratory. Born from experiments in enhanced intelligence.

They said the Pentagon funded this research.

The military was hoping to create intelligent dogs to serve as spies and perform reconnaissance in urban warfare.

Legend identified several places in California where those experiments might have taken place.

Devoted Mysterians had visited every potential cradle of their civilization, but found no laboratories.

They found housing developments. A supermarket. A shabby minimall. An athletic club. A tract of marshland.

They found a retirement home. A cheesy strip club with pole dancers. A sports park with baseball and soccer fields.

Of course the facility might be secret, lying underground or otherwise disguised.

Nothing, however, could be concealed from canine olfactory perception. Their noses revealed to them more clues than all the wits of all the detectives ever born.

But they found no hint of a hidden laboratory.

Now, on this night of nights, when the Wire hummed with news, Bella sensed history in the making. A history different from any they had ever imagined.

Something was happening out there.

Something big. Something wonderful.

Just today, in Pinehaven, Kipp had found a boy who could use the Wire.

Vulcan, a German shepherd, had reported a previously unknown community of their kind in Southern California.

Caesar and Cleo Ishigawa of San Jose had produced a healthy litter of six.

Just half an hour earlier, word came that Lucy and Ricky, companions of Nancy Peltz, of Vallejo, were parents of five pups.

More of their kind had been born in one day than in the past three or four years combined.

And now, from out of Oregon issued a transmission on the Wire alike to that from Vulcan in distant La Jolla.

According to a mixed breed named Ginger, a community of forty lived in and around the town of Corvallis.

The Oregon group had long hoped to make contact with other communities on the Wire, which they called 'the Network.' They had tried for years without success — until now.

Event by event, Bella became more excited.

While the Montell family slept, Bella moved restlessly through the house.

She went to her water dish.

She went to the kitchen drawer where her cookies were kept.

She went to her toy box in a corner of the family room.

She didn't want water or cookies or a toy.

At first she didn't understand *what* she wanted.

And then she knew. She wanted to *run*.

All of the good news had incited in her such joy that she could not be still.

Bella ran through the family room. Sprinted along the first-floor hall.

She raced around and around the living room, leaping on and then off sofas and armchairs.

Into the kitchen. Through the pet door. Across the porch. She circled the yard again and again, as if it were a racetrack.

When she returned to the house, she collapsed on the cool tile of the kitchen floor, tongue lolling, panting, happy.

Later, after she'd recovered and had a drink, she considered sprinting upstairs.

She wanted to wake Andrea and Bill. Larinda, Sam, Dennis, Milly. Her people. Her loves.

She yearned to share her joy with them.

But she could not share.

They didn't know how very intelligent she was, and she could not speak, and they weren't on the Wire.

She loved them, and they loved her, and if she could have no more, what she had was more than enough.

Yet right now, her great joy rested on the quiet sadness of loneliness.

Nature was a green battlefield where the weak were forever preyed on by the strong. Nature did not care, nor did the earth, which for all its beauty was nonetheless a hard place, indifferent to its creatures.

It was *mind* that mattered, mind that cared, mind that loved, the best works of the mind that changed this hard world for the better.

Mind — and the heart — had bonded people and dogs for tens of thousands of years. They had formed an alliance for survival and a covenant of affection against the darkness of the world.

If the minds of dogs were undergoing change, enlightenment, then the bond between them and people might one day be even more satisfying than it had been for millennia.

As she composed another Bellagram to report the existence of the community in Corvallis, Oregon, she hoped that one day more people than just the boy Woody would be on the Wire.

She hoped that, when the time was right, Andrea and Bill and Larinda and Sam and Dennis and Milly would know her in her fullness.

She hoped that she would live long enough to see the mystery of the Mysterium solved.

She hoped to know why she'd been born as she was, what it all meant, where it was all going.

From her toy box, she retrieved a hard rubber bone infused with an interesting flavor.

For all that she was, she was no less a dog.

The toy bone was conceived by the human

mind, crafted by human hands, given to Bella as an expression of love, so it comforted her even when she was alone, while her family slept.

THE MYSTERIUM

THURSDAY 4:00 A.M.–EVER AFTER

89

Woody was in the world as he had never been before, embarrassed neither by himself nor others. As he'd shared his *fear* of closeness with Kipp, the dog had shared his *need* for closeness, for touching and sharing. Knots deep in Woody had been untied. He could not say what kind of knots they had been, whether psychological or physical, or both. He could not say how they had been untied, except that the means by which he and Kipp opened each to the other — the Wire — served not merely two purposes but as well a third; it wasn't just a means of communication and swift education, but also a mysterious instrument of change. He intuited that Kipp understood the third purpose and how the Wire functioned to fulfill it. He wanted the golden retriever to explain it to him, how the Gordian knots of autism had been untied, but this was not the right time for that.

At the moment, in addition to himself, the house contained four people — his mom, Ben Hawkins, Rosa Leon, and Carson Conroy — three of whom had been total strangers an hour earlier, plus a dog who was no longer a stranger and as well-known to Woody as Woody was known to himself. Furthermore, there were deputies everywhere outside: two in a patrol car in front of the house, on Greenbriar Road; two in an all-wheel-drive SUV at the end of the

347

backyard, near the forest; two more in another SUV that was parked at the foot of the back porch steps.

After what had happened earlier with the Shacket thing, all of this activity and all of these people would once have spooked Woody, so that he would have gone away to Castle Wyvern. He didn't want to go away now. He thought maybe he would never want to go away again.

All of these people, minus the deputies, were gathered in the living room, where the draperies were closed over the windows. No one had been offered coffee yet or Mrs. Brickit's excellent muffins, because everyone had something urgent to say, especially Mr. Conroy, who told them about Shacket's escape and archaea and ninety-two dead in Springville, Utah. Ms. Leon told them about Dorothy and Kipp and the Mysterium, about the enormous inheritance and her legal custody of Kipp. It was all very exciting, like something in an adventure story, but also scary. Sitting on a sofa with Kipp's head in his lap, Woody expected to embarrass himself when they asked him about the Dark Web and the site called Tragedy, but it all came rushing out of him without hesitation, everything he'd discovered over the past sixty weeks, the satisfaction he took in seeking justice for his dad. He was amazed by himself. He wondered . . . if his vegetables and potato and meat were all served on the same plate the next time he had dinner, would seeing the different foods in contact with one another sicken him as before, or would he be able to eat like a normal person?

When everyone had said what most urgently needed to be said, an uncomfortable silence settled over them, as though they had become autistic, though it was most likely amazement that left them briefly speechless, for they had fallen down a rabbit hole for sure. Then everyone but Woody started talking at once. They were in agreement about the situation in which they found themselves. Woody had kicked a hornet's nest, and he was in deep shit. If Woody was in deep shit, so was his mom. Kipp wasn't going to be separated from Woody, the only human being who could use the Wire, so Kipp was in deep shit. Because Rosa Leon was legally and morally responsible for Kipp, she, too, was in deep shit. And because Lee Shacket, in the hospital, told Mr. Conroy about the true nature of the Springville experiments, the medical examiner was in deep shit. All of them were now enemies of Dorian Purcell, who had a zero tolerance policy when it came to people he believed were a serious threat to him.

The only person in the room who wasn't in deep shit, who could walk away and get on with his life, was Ben Hawkins. But he said that he had been in deep shit many times before, had gotten out of it, and in retrospect had enjoyed the experience and always learned something from it. They were forming a mutual-defense society here, or maybe an extended family, and Ben insisted on having a role in it because, he said, he wanted to be part of the magic that was Kipp. The magic-of-Kipp part was surely true, but the way he looked at Woody's mom was how Woody imagined he himself would look at a girl he wanted to kiss, if one ever entered his life, so it wasn't all about Kipp.

Mr. Conroy said, 'Right now, Megan, the sheriff is flooding you with protection because he thinks this is where Shacket might go. He doesn't care about you and your boy, only about his career. If they find Shacket and take him down, he'll pull these deputies out of here. Then if someone shows up from this Dark Web operation . . .'

'We're on our own,' she said.

Conroy shook his head. 'It's worse than that. Hayden Eckman is already doing the bidding of someone — maybe the NSA, maybe Purcell — by making no objection to the transfer of jurisdiction to the state attorney general. If Purcell wants these Dark Web killers to have a clean shot at you — at us — and he attempts to corrupt Eckman, he'll find the sheriff eager to be bought. Then we won't be able to rely on local law enforcement. Any deputy hired by the former sheriff, Lyle Sheldrake . . . well, I'd trust them. But Eckman has been purging Lyle's best people and expanding the force as much as he can afford. There are some of his men, if they showed up to protect me . . . I'd want to be anywhere but here.'

'Should we leave?' Woody's mom wondered. 'Where would we go? I don't like the idea of running.'

'There's nowhere you can go that you can't be found,' Ben said. 'Not if someone with Purcell's resources wants to find you.'

'We need a plan,' Woody said. 'That's what people do in stories when they're in really bad trouble. They make a cool plan.' He slid off the

350

sofa, and Kipp jumped to the floor with him. 'Mrs. Brickit made some totally great muffins. Would anybody like one? Should we make some coffee?'

Although obviously tired and worried, Woody's mom seemed to surprise herself with a quick laugh. 'Woodrow Eugene Bookman, just look at you. The host with the most.'

A blush warmed his face, but this was a far different kind of embarrassment from that under which he had so long suffered. 'I know how to make coffee,' he declared, and hurried off to the kitchen, with the dog close at his heels.

90

The wind was the voice of madness, and Hayden Eckman thought he heard deep within it the rabid-coyote cry, demonic-hyena call, evil-clown laugh of Shacket. The fugitive now seemed to be as swift and unrestrainable as the wind, as elusive as the rain that had been impending since the previous afternoon, as dark as the night into which he'd vanished much like Dracula, in those old movies, swirled his cape and became a bat and was *gone*.

The blood trail petered out along the south side of the hospital, only forty feet from the impact point below the third-floor window. The sheriff stood at the end of it, his back against the wall of the building, waiting while three deputies with Tac Lights searched the concrete sidewalk and the blacktop parking lot for a telltale crimson drop.

Being an attorney had entailed no risk other than potential disbarment, and during his five years as a deputy in generally quiet Pinehaven County, he'd never needed to draw his gun. Nor had he even once faced the muzzle of an adversary's firearm. He anticipated that a four-year term as sheriff would be a pleasant ride with numerous opportunities for self-enrichment, various civic honors bestowed by organizations of grateful businesspeople and charities, the respect accorded law enforcement, and the special attention of those women who were enchanted by men in uniform.

Instead, not quite nine months into his first year in office, here he stood with his back to the wall, his hand on the grip of the pistol in his belt holster, nervously surveying the night, expecting to be suddenly assaulted by a naked maniac. Not just a naked maniac. A naked maniac who had torn loose of restraining straps that were guaranteed escape proof, overpowered an armed deputy who stood six feet four and weighed two hundred ten pounds, survived a fall from the third story onto a concrete walkway, and carried off a dead or crippled lawman for some purpose that didn't bear contemplation.

With $300,000 and a fortune in diamonds in the trunk of his patrol car, the sheriff was pondering a different future from the one he had planned when he ran for office.

Given the chaos of the past twelve hours — three murders, one deputy badly bitten, Megan Bookman and son terrorized, all of them victims of the sole escapee from the catastrophe

352

at Springville — there would be investigations at the state and perhaps even the national level. As long as Hayden Eckman remained in office, he would have some ability to influence the results of those inquiries. If he left office, he'd become an easy scapegoat for the bureaucrats and politicians who cared even less about the truth than Hayden did.

He was spared further consideration of an assuredly bleak future when a deputy, Freeman Johnson, hurried to him with the news that a uniform shoe, evidently belonging to Thad Fenton, the missing deputy assigned to guard Lee Shacket, had been found toward the east end of the hospital grounds.

Although he was accompanied by Johnson, each with his right hand on his holstered pistol, and although two more men were waiting for them at the shoe, Sheriff Eckman didn't want to be part of this investigation. He preferred to call a higher authority, relinquish jurisdiction, but he was the highest officer of the law in Pinehaven County, an unfortunate consequence of winning an election.

The particular parking lot east of the hospital was reserved for the staff of the institution. The wind whistled and hissed off the polished flanks of at least two dozen vehicles, among which — or in one of which — Shacket could have been hiding. The two deputies who had run a quick search of the cars and SUVs assured him that the fugitive was not here. But they were men Eckman had hired for their lack of curiosity and blind loyalty, and he didn't trust them to have done a thorough job.

Freeman Johnson, a holdover from the Sheldrake administration, who had earlier cattle-prodded Shacket into submission, inspired more confidence. He was the one who had found the shoe, and he led them past the vehicles, out of the parking lot, onto a service road that encircled the grounds.

The shoe lay on its side in that road, the knot in the laces having slipped loose. In the beam of Johnson's Tac Light, the shoe was a pitiable sight, like that of a snatched child whose parents would never see him again, except this shoe was a size twelve.

Directly across the road, a separate building housed the gas-fired heating and cooling plant that serviced the hospital through a four-pipe fan-coil system, allowing every patient room, surgical unit, and office to be set at a different temperature from the others.

Freeman Johnson said, 'That's where he is. That's where he took Thad Fenton. I'd bet my pension on it.'

The heating plant was built of slumpstone painted gray, with a metal roof. Inside were boilers and chillers and a maze of other machinery, including a cooling tower. Through a tunnel under the road and parking lot, one large pipe carried superchilled water to the HVAC equipment in the hospital, and another carried superheated water; two return pipes brought exhausted water back to the building to be filtered, chilled or heated again, and recycled. There weren't many windows, and at this hour,

354

half were dark. A thick corpus of steam, rising from a cooling-tower stack, was dismembered by the wind and harried through the night like a withering procession of damned spirits.

Sheriff Eckman didn't want to go into that place. The building might as well have had a neon sign on the roof that said COME HERE TO DIE. Because Freeman Johnson had always done what was required of him during a long career of service, he was ready to draw his pistol and search the building. Deputies Hardy and Drew were not merely game, but eager to bring Shacket to justice, because they were stupid.

Hayden Eckman made two phone calls, the first for backup. He wanted two more men, both with shotguns. He also called the night administrator of the hospital to find out who might be at work in the heating-cooling plant at this hour.

The administrator, Janet Fegin, said, 'There are three during the day, but only one on the graveyard shift. Eric Norseman.'

As the sheriff waited with his team for the deputies bearing shotguns, the words *graveyard shift* echoed in his mind.

91

By the time that John Verbotski and Bradley Knacker arrived on Greenbriar Road, after driving from the abandoned shopping mall in Sacramento, their associates in Atropos & Company had researched the situation in Pinehaven. They provided necessary information acquired by hacking into the county sheriff's communications system, the property-title records in the tax collector's computer files, the county voter rolls, and the records of births and deaths.

At 4:43 a.m., Verbotski and Knacker cruised north on Greenbriar in their Cadillac Escalade, past the Bookman house. The presence of sheriff's department vehicles and deputies sitting sentinel didn't surprise them because they learned en route about the fugitive Lee Shacket, his violent acts at this residence, his arrest, and his subsequent escape. Their client, Alexander Gordius, hadn't mentioned this complication; he was evidently not aware of it.

As they passed the house a second time, heading south, Bradley Knacker called the current number for Gordius. No answer.

'He was going back to his hotel, hit the sack.' Verbotski said.

'We might not be able to reach him for a while.'

'You know the hotel?'

'No. He's not going to give me that, figuring I might try to get the registration records, learn his real name or whatever other fake name he used to register.'

For Atropos & Company, the only business more profitable than murder-for-hire was blackmailing selected clients who had paid them to kill people. Gordius, whoever he might be, was always careful not to provide a lead on his true identity. He always contacted them on a different

356

disposable phone. And though they had tried to get his fingerprints, he seemed to have none; perhaps they had been removed with acid and CO_2 laser treatments, a process that Verbotski had been considering for himself.

'So now what?' Knacker asked. He was the younger of the two and had less patience when the timing of a plan had to be revised. 'We just wait around until we can get hold of this asshole?'

'No. Let's secure our base of operations. Be ready to make our move. And never call a client an asshole.'

'Not even if he is?'

'Especially not if he is.'

The murder-for-hire operation that had called itself Tragedy had been thuggish. Atropos & Company styled itself as a refined person's option for aggressive problem solving. Maintaining this image required a certain restraint, a sense of decorum.

Because they were here to invade the Bookman house, take mother and son prisoner, assist in their interrogation, eventually kill them, and dispose of their remains where they would never be found, they must be discreet. In a small town like Pinehaven, registering in a motel, even under false ID, would be leaving an easy lead for investigators to follow later.

Instead, from the tax assessor's records, their associates had identified a potential property on Greenbriar Road, almost a mile south of the Bookman residence. The title was held in the name of Charles Norton Oxley and had been in his name for forty-nine years. Mr. Oxley had been on the county voter rolls for fifty-six years, so by all indications, he was at least seventy-seven years old.

The single-story ranch-style residence stood well back from the high-way, shaded by cedars. Even a few minutes before five o'clock in the morning, lights were aglow in the windows.

On Interstate 80, south of Colfax, they had pulled into a rest stop that provided bathrooms as filthy as any in the state's most deteriorated public schools. After carrying suitcases into the men's lavatory and assessing the chances of contracting a life-threatening infection, they returned to the parking lot and stripped to their underwear at the open tailgate of the Escalade. They had dressed in black suits and white shirts and black ties, their basic FBI look, which served them well when they needed to deceive people, which was most of the time.

Now, in Pinehaven County, with dawn more than an hour away, looking uncommonly present-able for this time of night, they went to the front door of the Oxley house, unfazed by the wind. Knacker's hair was short, incapable of being mussed, and Verbotski's full head of hair looked even better windblown than combed. Their suits were well tailored and of the finest wool blend, capable of holding their shape through a gale.

The lighted doorbell escutcheon was half a century newer than the house and obviously included a camera.

Verbotski smiled at it.

Knacker was too impatient to fake a smile. He

was a reliable partner and well trained in the mortal arts, but he looked and acted too much like an assassin. Verbotski was dedicated to mentoring Bradley Knacker, however, because he believed the younger man truly wanted to be the best that he could be in his profession. These days, many of the younger generation lacked a serious work ethic and, having been hooked on tech and social media most of their lives, had the attention span of a Chihuahua with ADHD. Knacker was able to focus, and hard work didn't daunt him. If he could lighten up, develop a credible smile of some kind, and temper his gung-ho attitude with patience, he would be the perfect partner with whom to go killing.

A stoop light came on and a voice issued from the doorbell speaker. 'What do you want?'

'Mr. Oxley? Mr. Charles Oxley?' Verbotski asked, raising his voice against the wind.

'Who wants to know?'

Holding his expertly forged badge and photo ID to the doorbell camera, Verbotski said, 'Special Agent Lewis Erskine, FBI. We need to ask you a few questions.'

'Before the damn sun is even up?'

'We saw your lights were on.'

'What the hell questions? Questions about what?'

'There was a serious event at the Bookman residence earlier tonight.'

'Damn sirens all night, so a man can't sleep. I don't know a damn thing about what happened up there. I got enough damn problems of my own, what with the social security not paying me for fourteen months. Go away.'

Bradley Knacker looked as though he might shoot out the lock and break down the door.

Smiling, nodding, Verbotski said to the doorbell, 'What problems with your social security, sir? Maybe we can help.'

'They stopped sending my check fourteen months ago, said I was dead. Do I sound dead to you?'

'It was your wife who died fourteen months ago.'

'How the hell do you know?'

Verbotski faked a convincing little laugh and shook his head and said, 'We're the FBI, sir. We know just about everything. We're here to help.'

For a long moment, Charles Oxley said nothing. As a citizen of the modern state, he had uncountable reasons to understand that a slight excess of power rapidly became a lethal excess, that when an agent of the state insisted he had come to help, there was at least a 70 percent chance that he had come to punish or pillage. In the human heart, however, there was a perverse desire to surrender control to those who claimed a right to power and advertised their good intentions, to *believe* in something, even if the something was a hive lacking human order or a machine without a face. As Verbotski had known he would, Charles Oxley unlocked and opened the door, and welcomed them inside.

Oxley stood perhaps five feet six, a lean bantam rooster of a man. His face was dramatically seamed either by loss and hardship or by hard living, his nose a broken beak, his blue stare defiant.

In spite of his short stature, he might have been a successful scrapper in his day, never an

360

easy target. But he was half a century older than Bradley Knacker and at least seventy pounds lighter, and one punch in the gut from the younger man all but lifted Oxley off his feet, sent him crashing backward into the wall.

Before Knacker could throw a punch or two into Oxley's face, Verbotski said, 'We don't want blood all over the carpet if someone comes visiting and won't go away and we absolutely have to open the door.'

Knacker grabbed the dazed and retching old man by the shoulders and steered him into the kitchen at the back of the house and shoved him into a chair at the breakfast table.

Verbotski found a door to a cellar, turned on the light, and went down to have a look around. There was an oil-fired furnace. An explosion and fire could be easily engineered.

When Verbotski returned to the kitchen, Knacker said, 'He tells me there's no children, and there's no neighbor he's friendly with.'

Adult children and neighbors were the most likely to drop in unannounced.

In a mudroom off the kitchen, Verbotski found a long woolen scarf hanging on a hook, but better yet were a few extension cords in a utility drawer. He took one of the extension cords into the kitchen and strangled Oxley to death.

Together, he and Knacker threw the body down the cellar steps. Verbotski turned off the light. Knacker closed the door.

The two of them went through the house, closing blinds and draperies where they weren't already closed.

The two-car garage contained only a Ford Expedition. Verbotski drove the Escalade into the empty stall and closed the segmented door with a remote he found in Oxley's vehicle.

By the time Verbotski came inside, Knacker was making coffee.

Because four men would be necessary to fulfill this contract, two of the additional principals in Atropos & Company would soon leave Reno in a black Suburban packed with the necessary gear. They would be here in three or four hours.

Verbotski made a phone call to Reno. He listed the items they would need to rig the oil-fired furnace for an unfortunate accident.

As cover and to launder money, the Dark Web entity called Atropos & Company did business as a high-tech security firm, under the name Supersafe Tomorrow. Their headquarters was in Reno because of the considerable advantages of Nevada tax laws.

Verbotski said, 'The coffee smells great.'

'The old guy had a good Jamaican blend,' Knacker said, 'and I spiced it with a teaspoon of cinnamon.'

92

In less than a day, Rosa Leon had traveled from the middling finances of the middle class to wealth, from a quiet acceptance of the hardness of the world to a belief in the magical nature of it, from a mundane life to one of high adventure, and she marveled at her flexibility.

Mrs. Brickit's muffins had been eaten, and coffee had been drunk. Especially because of Ben Hawkins's expertise in the strategy and tactics of war, a plan of sorts had been devised with surprising speed. They were proceeding on the premise that bad people from Tragedy would be coming soon — WE WILL FIND YOU — and that, because of incompetence and corruption, Sheriff Hayden Eckman would provide them with no useful protection.

Sitting on the bed in one of the two guest rooms, Rosa had already done her part by using her iPhone to call Dorothy Hummel's attorney — well, *her* attorney now — Roger Austin, whom she knew to be an early riser, up before dawn. She said nothing of Kipp, because Roger didn't know the dog's secret. But she succinctly laid out the incredible story of Woody's investigation of his father's accident. She didn't mention the threat issued by the Dark Web operators behind Tragedy. She asked Roger to keep safe the document — 'The Son's Revenge: Faithfully Compiled Evidence of Monstrous Evil' — that was even then being emailed to him by Megan. She asked him to read it and then share it with two people in the legal system, judges or lawmen, whom he knew for certain were not corrupt and could not be corrupted.

'But how did you meet Mrs. Bookman and her son?' Roger asked in that deep, mellifluous voice that might have given her confidence in the attorney even if she hadn't known him. 'I never heard you speak of them before.'

'Oh,' Rosa said, 'I've known them quite a while. It seems like forever. Listen, Roger, I haven't said who was responsible for the death of Woody's father. You'll discover the name when you read his research, and it's a shocker. The man is powerful and very wealthy. You might be tempted to wonder if it's a fantasy that Woody has spun. But I swear to you it's not. There will be additional proof coming.' She couldn't resist adding, 'It's not a shaggy-dog story, Roger. Anyway, once you've read the document and thought about it, we very much need your advice about how to proceed in such a way that what Woody's discovered will be believed and acted upon. Until the story is out there in the press, it doesn't seem that Megan and the boy will be safe.'

When she concluded that call, her immediate contribution to the plan had been made, although she had a role to play when the coming day ticked into the afternoon. Now she stretched out on the guest-room bed, hoping to get some rest for what lay ahead, though she doubted that she could quell her excitement enough to sleep. In spite of her doubt, she slept.

93

While Rosa Leon spoke on the phone to Roger Austin, Carson Conroy was on the east side of Pinehaven, at the home of his friend Harry Borsello, who was about to drive into town to oversee the morning rush at his restaurant, Four Square Diner, and grab some breakfast of his own.

Carson and Harry were friends not just because they relished bacon, but because they were in the same poker club and attended the same church and shared a love of nature and were widowers. Three years earlier, Harry lost his wife, Melissa, not to a senseless drive-by shooting, but to a senseless cancer, and Carson helped him make it through the worst of his grief.

Now, as he followed Harry to the barn at the back of the property, the low clouds churned, the pines thrashed, and all the creatures of the night cowered in their warrens and roosts as if the slowly approaching dawn would be the last day of Earth.

The previous owner had used the barn as a stable. Because Harry Borsello had a fear of horses, a love of horsepower, and an interest in comfortable camping, he had removed the stalls to make room for his collection: a 1970 Ford Mustang Mach 1 Twister, a fastback coupe; a 1976 Corvette Stingray; a 1968 Pontiac GTO; a 1971 Dodge Charger Magnum V8; a new Ford F150 crew-cab pickup; a thirty-six-foot Fleetwood Southwind.

Together, they had twice taken off for a week in the motor home, once south to Yosemite, once north to Shasta Lake for some good fishing, and Carson had borrowed the vehicle for a solo run across Nevada and into Utah. He wanted to borrow it again.

When Harry switched on the barn lights and closed the man-size door behind them, he said, 'Where are you lighting out for?'

'I haven't finally decided,' Carson said, regretting the lie even though it was in Harry's best interest not to know what use his vehicle would serve. 'Just a few days, maybe over to Mendocino. I feel a need for the coast.'

'Should be a hell of a lot less wind there,' Harry said. 'And if the rain comes, it's moving south-southeast, so you'll have clear weather.'

As Harry handed the key to Carson and used a remote to roll aside the big door, the massive rafters groaned. At the pinnacle of the roof, a large weather vane, in the image of a galloping steed, spun with a shriek and a rhythmic clatter, as if it were ridden by one of the fierce horsemen of the Apocalypse.

'I'll pull your Explorer in here after you're gone,' Harry said. 'If you wrack up the Fleetwood, for God's sake don't kill yourself. I'll need you alive to buy me a new one.'

'You're a real pal, Harry.'

'Plus poker night won't be fun anymore without you losing your shirt to me on a regular basis.'

'I'm well aware you don't make any money from that pathetic greasy-spoon joint of yours,' Carson said. 'That's why I let you win at cards. It's a charity thing.'

He drove directly home in the Fleetwood Southwind and parked it in the driveway. He made several trips between the house and the motor home, stocking the vehicle's refrigerator with bottled water, Coca-Cola, and four pepperoni-and-cheese pizzas from his freezer.

From the mantel over the living room fireplace, he retrieved one of the smaller photographs of Lissa to take with him. He removed the picture from the frame and slipped it into a jacket pocket without folding it.

Although the coming showdown might be violent, Carson didn't believe he would be killed before Thursday became Friday, eighteen hours hence. Nevertheless, he wanted Lissa's picture with him, so he could look at it in the moment before his death, if it should come.

94

While Rose Leon settled down to sleep and while Carson Conroy was borrowing Harry Borsello's motor home, Ben Hawkins moved his Range Rover and then Rosa Leon's Lincoln MKX into the two empty stalls in the four-car garage attached to the Bookman house.

Perhaps Carson's acidic assessment of Sheriff Hayden Eckman colored Ben's reaction to the deputies, but something about their manner and deadpan expressions and ice-pick stares suggested they were here not just to guard against the return of Shacket, but also to maintain surveillance of the occupants of the house.

He removed a suitcase from his Rover. He carried it into the residence and upstairs to the second guest bedroom. In addition to clothes and toiletries, the bag contained his pistol, a Nighthawk Custom .45 ACP. The frame, slide, barrel, extended magazine well, magazine release, and slide stop were forged rather than cast. It looked like a solid artifact, like a machine produced by some 3-D printing process that would be perfected in another hundred years. It was the most accurate and reliable handgun he had ever used.

He sat on the bed to load the weapon and a spare magazine. He threaded a Kydex holster onto his belt and inserted the pistol in that scabbard. For the time being, he had no intention of wearing a jacket to conceal the gun. He was licensed to carry, and if any of the deputies assigned to the property or any who relieved them might have sinister motives, the prospect of resistance would discourage them from doing anything foolish.

He'd slept only one hour at the motel in Olympic Village before Kipp woke him. He would need more sleep soon if he were to be on his game when the Dark Web killers arrived. If the thugs behind Tragedy did not come to clean up their mess, someone else would. After all, if Dorian Purcell was capable of dealing with murder-for-hire types, he was capable of taking extreme action through other surrogates.

Before he slept, Ben wanted to tour the house to familiarize himself with its rooms, check the doors and windows for adequate locks, and scope out the most likely approach that an enemy would take if they intended to make a surprise entrance.

368

He didn't bother Rosa Leon in the first guest room, but as he checked out other rooms, he discovered that second-floor windows were not connected to the security system unless they overlooked a porch roof. Those that could be reached only with a ladder weren't wired for an alarm, which was a common but foolish practice of many security companies. He'd need half an hour — and Megan's approval — to nail the moving sashes shut, as there wasn't time to have the alarm company work those windows into the system.

She was in the downstairs study, at the desk, reading Woody's 104-page report, and Ben didn't want to bother her. He found the ground-floor doors and windows reasonably well secured. Glass would have to be broken to gain entrance; there were glass-break sensors, as well as backup batteries that might keep the system functioning for a few hours if the public power were cut.

In the side hallway, he became enchanted by the examples of her art that hung on the walls, and he was most captivated by the canvas in progress in her studio — Woody feeding the deer in moonlight.

When he saw the painting, he dared believe that he had found the woman he had been looking for all his life. He was a romantic; he didn't deny that or make excuses for it. In spite of their many eccentricities, Brenaden Septimus Hawkins's parents had loved each other and had raised three well-balanced and happy, if oddly named, children. He didn't want a woman like his mom, and he was different from his father, but he hoped for a match as right as theirs had been. He had been taken with Megan on first sight, but he wasn't a man for whom looks mattered most. He'd had too much experience of women whose exterior beauty masked an inner ugliness or, almost worse, a vapidity that would make a life together too empty to endure. Already he'd seen evidence that Megan possessed uncommon fortitude, wisdom, wit, a good heart, and other qualities that he had not before found so concentrated in one person. Now this painting suggested that she saw the beauty of the world in its fullness, not just its surface dazzle, because what she rendered on this canvas was reality as the eye perceived it but enhanced by what deep insight and intuition told her about the layers of reality that the eye alone could not perceive. In spite of the subject, the work wasn't sentimental; it presented a scene of moonlit wonder, yes, but it was a composition that also conveyed both the fragility of the peace we seek and the darkness that could at any moment close in upon us.

As a Navy SEAL, he had fought for his country and would have died for it. In these last few hours with Megan and Woody and Kipp, however, Ben had been overcome by a rapidly growing sense of family as strong as what he had felt in his parents' home. It was this, after all, that made a country worth fighting and dying for, and life worth living.

95

Ben stopped in the open doorway of Megan's study just when she would have had to go searching for him. She swiveled away from the computer and said, 'I put in the address, and I got to the Tragedy site on the Dark Web. It was just like the screenshots in Woody's report. Then it suddenly went dark. Now it doesn't seem to be there anymore. I can't reconnect with it.'

'They've taken it down? Folded up the tent and gone away?' he asked as he approached the desk.

'I think maybe they have.' She found hope in that prospect. 'If they know they've been found out, wouldn't they want to close shop and skip? With their client list, they can open with a new address, a different name. Maybe what Woody did doesn't matter that much to them. Maybe from their point of view, it's an inconvenience, not a catastrophe, not worth coming after us.'

Ben shook his head. 'If they got a track-to-source fix on Woody's computer, they know who lives here, and they know that one of their hits was your husband. They don't know for sure what all you might have learned about them. What they'll be most concerned about is that you might have their client list.'

'We don't. Woody found them by hacking into Purcell's email and working out the connection between Purcell and Tragedy through the Gordius identity. He doesn't have a complete client list, only proof against Purcell.'

'They have to be sure of that. They're going to come here to find out.'

'Not with the place protected by six deputies.'

'Probably not. But what if Shacket is found and killed or arrested again? Then the sheriff's gonna withdraw the protection.'

Megan was tired. She drew one hand down her face, as if she might be able to wipe off her weariness. 'So we stay with the plan.'

'At least we have a plan,' he said. 'And there's no way in hell they can anticipate what's going to happen to them.'

96

While Rosa Leon was sleeping and Carson Conroy was driving away from Harry Borsello's house in the Fleetwood and Ben and Megan were conferring downstairs . . .

Kipp and Woody were in the boy's room. Sprawled on the floor and in the lap of history.

Historians often presented turning points of civilization as loud and bright, full of boom and flash.

In fact, decisions to make war or seek peace were often made in quiet rooms.

Cures for diseases were developed slowly, in laboratories that lacked both TV and piped-in music.

Kipp and Woody were on the Wire.

In the wake of all the recent Bellagrams, they were now at a turning point of history.

They *were* a turning point of history.

Kipp knew it, and Woody knew it, and everyone on the Wire knew it, and there was no boom or flash.

Although Kipp explained the situation and made the appeal, per the plan that had been devised, Woody was the star.

Many Mysterians, though not all, lived with people who shared their secret.

They had invented clever ways to communicate, similar to what Dorothy had arranged with the alphabet wall.

This was the first time, however, that they were able to speak directly to a human being.

Their excitement level was high, but they didn't all speak at once.

They were disciplined and considerate. They were dogs.

Each Mysterian's voice, being imagined and telepathic, was either like that of one of its human companions or was based on the voice of an actor on television.

Woody on the Wire sounded like Woody face-to-face, the Woody released from a lifetime of silence.

Kipp sounded like a certain game-show host on TV.

Historic moments were no less likely to include an absurdity or two than were moments about which historians cared nothing.

When the appeal had been made and responses received, when Kipp and Woody disconnected from the Wire, the dog bit the boy.

It was a play bite, no skin broken.

Woody growled and bared his teeth.

Kipp growled and bared his bigger teeth.

They wrestled with much flailing of paws.

Woody sprang up. He dashed into the adjacent bathroom.

Kipp scrambled into the bathroom after the boy.

Woody pivoted out of the bathroom and pulled the door shut.

Kipp's black nose appeared at the one-inch gap between door and floor, sniffing frantically.

Woody lay prostrate, teasing the nose with a finger.

When Kipp issued a woof of frustration, Woody opened the door.

The boy leaped onto the bed, pulled the covers over his head.

Kipp sprang onto the bed and thrust his snout into every fold of blanket that he found, seeking a route to his giggling, cocooned companion.

Such were the ways of dogs and boys, even after they had been the lever that turned history on its fulcrum, even as a night of violence was about to end in the dawn of a day that promised worse.

97

As the sheriff and his three deputies waited for two more men, those bearing shotguns, the heating and cooling plant behind the county hospital acquired an ever more ominous air,

374

becoming for Hayden Eckman the repository of all evils, the vault of his fate. Beyond the dark windows seemed to be something more disturbing than lightless rooms, a bottomless void from which no escape could be achieved once you had entered. The bright windows were no more reassuring than the dark panes, the quality of light otherworldly, witchy.

The incessant wind not only stung his eyes and parched his skin and chapped his lips, but also abraded his nerves, as did the memory of Justine Klineman's ravaged face, as did Thad Fenton's blood on the pavement below that third-story window. He began to think he had made a mistake when he'd closed his law office. He had needed three attempts to pass his bar exam, and he'd been little more than a slip-and-fall personal-injury shakedown artist, and his income had been limited by the frequency with which his own clients took him to arbitration and won a refiguring of his fees. But at least none of them ever bit him in the face or anywhere else.

In cascades of red and blue pulsations, but without a siren, the expected patrol car arrived. Two men clambered out, fresh-faced and lanky and, in spite of their shotguns, about as reassuring as a couple of Hollywood's more callow young actors playing at being real men. They were among the hires that Eckman had made, chosen in part because they seemed too slow-witted ever to notice or even suspect their boss might be corrupt. They looked like potential fodder waiting to be mulched.

The sheriff instructed one of them to lead the way, the other to bring up the rear, and he patiently, repeatedly stressed that they were to take special care not to discharge their 12-gauge semiautos if any of their own people were within the arc of fire. He could only assume that their solemn nods meant they understood and were not merely the organic equivalent of the mechanical action of bobblehead dolls.

The small parking area that served the heating-cooling plant contained not a single vehicle, though it seemed there ought to be one belonging to Eric Norseman, graveyard-shift maintenance man.

As a first sign that something might be amiss, the main door to the plant stood open, held that way by the wind, which caused it to thump softly against the exterior wall.

The lighted vestibule offered three doors.

A deputy opened the one on the right and cleared the threshold. Beyond lay a large chamber with boilers, chillers, holding tanks, pumps, a maze of machinery the sheriff couldn't identify, and a labyrinth of PVC pipes of various sizes running both vertically and horizontally. The room resonated with the humming, throbbing, ticking of exquisitely coordinated machines and with the susurration of rushing water under pressure. The place resembled the set for an action scene in a James Bond film, with too many blind corners to turn, too many hulking objects to look behind.

Sheriff Eckman didn't want to have to search there unless absolutely necessary, and they wouldn't know if it was necessary until they checked behind the remaining two doors.

He felt as if he desperately needed to pee. He told himself that the urge was entirely psychological. It had better be if any hope remained for him to one day become state attorney general.

The door on the left of the vestibule opened onto a balcony overlooking the twin stacks of the immense cooling tower. This construct of sheet steel, condensation coils, and drum fans stood three stories high, the first third of it below the ground-level balcony, and was serviced from catwalks at various levels. It, too, looked like the set in a James Bond film and was no less daunting than the first chamber.

The third door, directly opposite the front entrance, opened into the plant manager's office. In addition to the main desk, two smaller work-stations were provided. A refrigerator. A microwave. Two filing cabinets. At the back of the room, the door to a bathroom stood open, no one in the small space beyond. Another door, closed, might have led to a supply closet.

Because he was all but certain that Lee Shacket wasn't lurking in the supply closet, that the killer fled in Eric Norseman's vehicle, Sheriff Eckman followed a deputy into the office, another man close behind him. His confidence — and a diminishment in his need to urinate — resulted from the fact that the body of Thad Fenton lay facedown on the floor to the right of the door and the corpse of another man was sprawled across the desk, each cadaver in a condition suggesting Shacket thought of them as trash that he'd discarded during his flight from the premises.

Bristling with blood-clotted hair, pieces of Thad's broken skull lay separate from his body. His brain appeared to be missing.

The body of the man on the desk, approximately the size of Shacket, had been stripped of everything, including his shoes.

Evidently the naked fugitive was now clothed.

This second victim might have been Eric Norseman, although identification would have to rely on fingerprints, as he had been crudely decapitated, and his head was missing.

98

As the first gray light of dawn dissolved the stain of night from the low clouds, Carson Conroy parked the Fleetwood Southwind on a paved lane to nowhere that dead-ended in a meadow.

Five miles outside the town of Pinehaven, a former trailer park had once occupied nine acres of this forty-acre tract that was known locally as the Big Windy. Where mobile homes had once stood side by side, there were only cracked blacktop streets, concrete foundation pads, and weeds. The state had acquired the trailer park and the additional acreage as a site for a wind-power farm. Unfortunately, studies had claimed that the windmills would be standing in the migratory path of several species of birds, with the consequence that an estimated fourteen thousand of our feathered friends would be killed each year by the huge churning blades. Those who supported the project cited experts who believed the birds would eventually learn that windmills were a threat and would, in seven or eight years, alter their semiannual flight path, after the loss of hardly more than a hundred thousand specimens. Sadly, the experience of other wind farms seemed at odds with this optimistic assessment of the avian ability to reprogram instinct, as fields at most of those facilities were routinely littered with so many downed aviators that it looked as if all the gods of old had engaged in a pillow fight.

To await his first visitor, Carson went to the bedroom at the back of the motor home and took off his shoes and stretched out on the mattress.

He had never been so physically weary from lack of sleep and stress. At the same time, he'd never been so mentally invigorated, his mind flying through a wonderland of possibilities. He was fearful and joyful in equal measure, as he once would have thought impossible.

Shacket — and what Shacket was becoming — terrified Carson, and what research might have occupied the staff at the Refine labs in Springville was a source of dread. It was human nature to obsess on negatives, to worry the smallest of sparks into infernos. And yet as he waited for sleep, he dwelt less on the horrors of genetic chaos than on the amazing Kipp and on the other dogs of the Mysterium that he had yet to meet.

As a student of the natural world, he knew that nature was a green machine, indifferent to the creatures — from mice to men — that struggled to survive within it. Every machine is made to be used, however, and whatever power employed nature to a purpose, it was able to produce wonders, humanity being one of them, the Mysterium being another.

Dorian Purcell, through the work at the now destroyed labs in Springville, sought to find a path toward a transhuman future, when current and future generations would shed their limitations. Maybe he was right to believe that human beings could become something superior to what they now were. But he was woefully wrong to believe that such change could be forged by the application of sciences that were, for all their recent advances, still crude instruments.

Carson was charmed by the thought that whatever power used the machine of nature might be in the process of elevating human beings and improving the quality of their existence, though in a way more elegant and astonishing than the blunt hammer-and-anvil method that Purcell had funded at Refine. What if it had always been the destiny of humanity not to stand alone and lonely at the pinnacle of nature, but instead to share that exalted position with another species that didn't compete with it, but in fact *completed* it? Tens of thousands of years ago, when dogs and people first made an alliance against the cruelty of indifferent nature, what if a process had begun that would lead inevitably to the gradual increase of canine intelligence as the bond of love between the species drove dogs to strive ever harder to understand, to know, their benefactors? What if, as the human-dog bond intensified, the very intensity itself became a force magnifier that sped up the changes in our four-legged companions until one day, among them arose individuals who developed telepathy to serve in place of the articulated vocal apparatus they lacked?

Until a knock on the door of the motor home would eventually wake him to a new and astonishing world, a river of what-ifs carried Carson Conroy into sleep. He dreamed of dogs, a glorious panoply of breeds, and of a world transformed in the most magical way.

99

Morning. Sheriff Eckman had thought that the interminable night would never end, that morning would never come, but now that it had come, he wished it hadn't. The cloud-filtered morning sun at the windows of the heating-cooling plant was the light of blame, the light of accountability, and it could not be escaped.

Here a jigsaw skull, there a headless Norseman. The wind raving like rabid wolves outside, the building seeming filled with machine sounds, as if the robots of the Apocalypse were being manufactured here.

Sheriff Hayden Eckman felt his world

fragmenting just like Thad Fenton's skull had been cracked into pieces and pried apart.

Nobody could locate Carson Conroy. He was supposed to be on call at all hours if a crime scene required his presence. But he wasn't answering his phone, and he wasn't at home.

Jim Harmon, Conroy's assistant, took photos, gathered evidence, attended to the dead, but he wasn't Dr. Carson Conroy, he was only Jim Harmon, just thirty-four years old, damn it, a mere *assistant* medical examiner, and this was the biggest crime in the history of Pinehaven County, a *murder spree* that could destroy more than the killer's victims, that could also *vaporize Hayden Eckman's career.*

He couldn't tolerate being in the plant manager's office with all the blood and biological debris. When he had run for sheriff, it had never crossed his mind that he would have to wade through a damn abattoir, that he would see things that would give him nightmares for the rest of his life. The urgent need to pee that had almost embarrassed him earlier, when he had barely avoided soiling himself in front of his deputies, was nothing compared to the compulsion to vomit that surged anew each time that he thought he had repressed it; his throat burned with the tides of stomach acid that washed up and down, up and down.

Pretending only that he wanted to stay out of Jim Harmon's way, the sheriff stationed himself in the large room with the boilers and chillers. He was sitting on the top step of a three-step ladder. The throbbing pumps pushing water through the maze of insulated pipes sometimes matched the rhythm of a strong impulse to regurgitate, but that was better than the sights and smells of the scene in the plant office.

When Freeman Johnson came to report on Eric Norseman's missing vehicle, which Lee Shacket had surely stolen, he had more bad news. Norseman was a hot-rodder who drove a black '48 Ford pickup that had been chopped, channeled, sectioned, and further customized. Although the truck might be easily spotted once an APB had been issued, it had no GPS, which meant it was not emitting a signal that could be located almost immediately.

'By the way,' Johnson said, 'there's no doubt about it now.'

'No doubt about what?'

'Fenton's brain is gone.'

Eckman grimaced. 'I thought that was already obvious.'

'Well, Jim Harmon had to make a thorough search.'

'Did he expect to find it in a desk drawer?'

'You never know with a lunatic like this.'

'Is Harmon nearly finished?'

'He'll need another hour. You know Norseman's head?'

'I never met him. I wouldn't recognize his head.'

'Jim says it's definitely gone, nowhere on the premises.'

Sheriff Eckman didn't want to talk about the missing head.

'You know what some of the guys are calling it?' Johnson asked.

The sheriff answered the question with silence and hoped that Johnson would take the hint.

Johnson didn't take the hint. 'They're calling the missing head Shacket's lunch pail.'

Hayden Eckman shuddered. 'I am so screwed.'

100

In his sleep, Woody went to Castle Wyvern, but Kipp went with him, their dreams as synchronized as their snoring. Together, they walked the ramp to the drawbridge and crossed the moat and entered under the portcullis of the first gatehouse, into the outer ward. The sky was blue and without lightning, and no dragons flew as the boy and the dog passed through the second gatehouse, into the inner ward. They climbed the spiral stone stairs in the southwest tower of the inner curtain wall and went through the iron-bound door into the high redoubt with its timbered ceiling and narrow windows at each of the four points of the compass.

The dog and boy turned in a circle, gazing at the high windows.

The sky remained blue.

All dragons had been vanquished.

As they completed a full turn, the castle disappeared.

In the dream, they stood in a meadow overlooking the sea.

From the sea, in all other directions, the meadow stretched a hundred miles, a thousand.

Out of nowhere appeared a foil balloon, buoyant with helium.

It floated across the field.

The words HAPPY BIRTHDAY were printed on it in red.

Although this was neither Kipp's nor Woody's birthday, they found the balloon irresistible, for it was strange to see it adrift here in the wilds. The bright, mirrored Mylar, trailing a red satin ribbon, seemed important. It must mean something. They pursued it with exuberance. Kipp leaped to bite at the long ribbon, and Woody leaped higher and missed, but they would not give up. They would never give up. Laughing, barking, they raced across the meadow. Through knee-high golden grass they ran and ran, ran and ran.

101

At ten o'clock Thursday morning, after three hours of deep though nightmare-riddled sleep, Megan came downstairs to a kitchen redolent of baking cheese and tomato sauce and basil, where Ben Hawkins was at work, on both guard and culinary duty.

She stood in the doorway, watching as he finished layering a second pan of lasagna, getting ready to put it in the oven after the first pan came out. He was unaware of her, softly singing an old Boyz II Men song, '4 Seasons of Loneliness,' though he somehow made it sound upbeat.

She said, 'You even cook.'

Glancing at her, he said, 'That's what I call it. Cooking. Not everyone who tastes it thinks the term is appropriate.'

'You really believe we'll have something to celebrate.'

'Lots of people have shot at me, nobody ever hit me, so there's precedent to expect a need to celebrate.' He spooned sauce over the top layer of noodles. 'Anyway, I looked through your pantry, it's a massive pantry, all those packages of pasta, plus all the treasures you packed away in that humongous freezer — enough choice sirloin hamburger patties and fine steaks for half a dozen Independence Day parties — and I was inspired. Well, first I said to myself, 'Ben' — I call myself Ben — I said, 'Ben, this woman must be seriously worried that cattle are going extinct,' and *then* I was inspired to start making use of all that stuff, because I've got it on good authority that cattle will be around for at least another millennium.'

'I have this need to be prepared for anything,' Megan said. 'We have a generator, runs on propane, so we can power the entire house for a month if the electric company goes down.'

He nodded. 'In case it's taken out by terrorists.'

She said, 'Or in a cattle stampede.'

He was covering the top layer of noodles with mozzarella. He knew what he was doing. 'I assumed Woody likes lasagna.'

'As long as it and each vegetable is in a separate dish.'

'Maybe that's all behind him.'

'Amazing if true. But whatever happens, he's

the best, a great kid. My turn for guard duty. Get some sleep while you can.'

'Six deputies left and six new ones came about two hours ago.'

She looked toward the back door, at the police SUV parked athwart the porch steps.

He said, 'I've just begun to cook. There's still a lot for you to do.'

'Good. It'll keep my mind off . . . everything.'

'The first pan comes out of the oven in five minutes.'

He washed his hands, dried them on a paper towel.

As she stood at the oven, peering in at the baking lasagna, he said, 'I like your paintings. They're very good.'

She shrugged. 'They're all I know how to do.'

'I doubt that. I'd like to talk with you about them, when this business is over.'

'I hope it'll be over soon.'

'It will.'

He went to the door. As he was about to step into the hallway, Megan said, 'Which was your favorite? Of the paintings.'

He turned and smiled. 'Everything. I like everything I've seen.'

102

In his three-bedroom suite in the hotel in Sacramento, after only five hours of sleep, at 11:10 a.m. Haskell Ludlow woke from a dream about the murders in the abandoned shopping mall. He got out of bed and went to the nearest of three bathrooms. After he relieved himself, he intended to go to a different bedroom, where the sheets were fresh and no nightmare lingered to enfold him again.

Bad dreams were such a dependable part of his sleep for so many years that he had begun to wonder if a supernatural entity, perhaps the evil twin of the Sandman, had taken a disliking to him and was targeting him with horrific visions. At first this was a frivolous thought; maybe it still was, but as the years passed, he came to take it more than half seriously. By changing bedrooms in the middle of the night, Haskell Ludlow was taking evasive action. In his house in Menlo Park, where he lived alone when not traveling, there were nine bedrooms through which he cycled.

Now, as he was crossing the living room of the hotel suite, the disposable phone, which he'd left on a coffee table, began to ring. Only John Verbotski and Bradley Knacker, of Atropos & Company, had this number, and Ludlow would destroy the phone once the business with Megan Bookman, in Pinehaven, had been concluded.

Being Alexander Gordius, he sat on the sofa and picked up the burner on the third ring and said, 'Yeah?'

John Verbotski said, 'We've been trying to get you for hours.'

'I was wiped out, sleeping.'

'We've gotten some sleep, too, but we're taking turns at it.'

388

'Yeah, well, I've got no one to take turns with me. What's happening?'

'We're in position, four of us, but we can't visit the lady because the sheriff's got six deputies at her house as protection.'

Bewildered, Ludlow said, 'Six deputies? How did he know she'd need protection?'

'Not protection from us. We're monitoring police radio traffic here. They're protecting her from some guy named Nathan Palmer, he went after her.'

'Who the hell is Nathan Palmer?'

'He killed a couple of people yesterday afternoon. His real name seems to be Lee Shacket.'

Ludlow was for a moment speechless. Lee Shacket? The CEO of Refine? Because he only knew what the media was reporting about events in Springville, he said, 'But Shacket is dead. Everyone's dead there.'

'Everyone's dead where?' Verbotski asked.

Ludlow bit his lip and finally said, 'Shacket knew Megan Bookman a long time ago. Why the hell would he go after her now?'

'Why do crazy guys go after women all the time?' Verbotski said. 'That's a rhetorical question.'

'Who're the two people Shacket killed?'

'Four. There've been two more since he went after the lady and failed to get her.'

After Verbotski listed the killings and gave what details he knew, Ludlow could not suppress his astonishment. 'He *beheaded* a guy? He bit people? He *ate* people?'

'Parts of people, not whole people,' Verbotski

clarified. 'He's some kind of freak. You knew this freak?'

Ignoring the question, Ludlow said, 'And he's still there in Pinehaven?'

'They don't know. He stole a pickup. He's on the run. It's a '48 Ford pickup, custom hot rod. So it should be easy to spot.'

'Holy shit, this must be big news. I never listen to the news, I'm done with news. But this must be wall-to-wall on cable.'

'Not yet. The sheriff hasn't released a statement.'

'Hasn't released a statement about four murders and the suspect on the loose? That's insane. The first murders were yesterday when — afternoon?'

'Yeah. But it looks like, last night, jurisdiction on those was transferred to the attorney general in Sacramento.'

Ludlow rose from the sofa. 'To Tio Barbizon?'

'Yeah, I think that's the name.'

Shacket was supposed to be dead in Springville. He wasn't. Tio Barbizon had taken jurisdiction in the first two murders — and had not yet conducted a press briefing or issued any statement. Tio was in Dorian Purcell's pocket and always had been.

Ludlow stood in silence with the phone pressed to his ear so long that Verbotski at last said, 'You still there?'

'Yeah.'

'We can't move on the lady with all those deputies there.'

'Stay put. She's still on the agenda. I've got to

make another call. Then I'll be back to you.'

Ludlow pressed END.

He picked up another disposable phone from the coffee table. This one had been purchased solely to report to Dorian Purcell on the situation with the murder-for-hire operation called Tragedy. Taped to the unit was the number of yet another disposable that was in Dorian's possession. When the Tragedy website and the breach of security related to it were erased, along with everyone involved, Ludlow and Purcell would destroy these two burner phones.

Considering the ever-escalating criminal activity in this country, Haskell Ludlow congratulated himself on having long ago invested significant capital in the disposable-phone business.

He keyed in Dorian's number.

103

Parable headquarters in Sunnyvale, California, included an eight-thousand-square-foot apartment in which Dorian Purcell could be in the heart of corporate affairs when a new acquisition was pending or when a new product launch was being fine-tuned, or when any politician on the make insisted on a secure face-to-face sit-down with Dorian himself to work out the terms under which the public servant would sell out his office and constituents. On this Thursday in September, Dorian was not residing in this apartment.

Slightly farther up the coast, in Palo Alto,

Dorian owned a twelve-thousand-square-foot estate on a two-acre parcel with a view of San Francisco Bay. He lived in this resplendent house with his fiancée, Paloma Pascal, who was highly educated and charming and stunningly beautiful, who could move with confidence and grace in the most rarefied social circles, who made a positive and lasting impression on everyone, and who would remain his fiancée as long as she never insisted on getting married. Dorian was not at the moment in this residence.

In a stately building atop Nob Hill, in the heart of San Francisco, Dorian owned a fourteen-thousand-square-foot, two-floor apartment with spectacular views of the city, from some of its most glorious and iconic architecture to its homeless encampments and feces-strewn side-walks. He lived in this exquisitely appointed penthouse with Saffron 'Sunny' Ketterling, twenty-three, who was even more stunningly beautiful than Paloma Pascal. Sunny was also remarkably lithe and supple, because she had been a devoted gymnast since the age of six. Currently, at 11:40 a.m., Sunny was sleeping. She and Dorian had gone to bed at 1:15 a.m., but they hadn't settled down to sleep until six o'clock, when there had been no further positions to explore.

Dorian had awakened at ten thirty, after little more than four hours of sleep. Since late childhood, when he had fully understood death, he had not slept more than five hours a night and had been driven to embrace excess as a rebuke to the Grim Reaper. Now Dorian was in his study on the lower of the two floors of the apartment, at an immense stainless-steel and blue-quartzite desk, having breakfast that had been served by the butler, Franz. He was also consuming the first 40 of the 124 vitamin-mineral supplements that he downed every day, and composing the eulogy that he would give at the memorial service for the employees of Refine who perished in the tragic fire at the Springville, Utah, facility.

When the disposable phone rang, he knew who was calling, for only Haskell Ludlow had the number.

He took the call. 'Life is good.'

'Life is complicated,' Haskell said.

'Tell me.'

'Our old friends in the pest-control service located that troublesome cockroach. Now they're out of business.'

So the principals of Tragedy were dead. But they had found the cockroach, the hacker.

'Our new friends in pest control,' Haskell continued, 'are ready to do the job.'

That would be Verbotski and the boys from Atropos.

'But the problem I've been dealing with,' Haskell said, 'and the problem you've been dealing with have become the same problem.'

'How so?'

'You didn't tell me that one of the ninety-three beat the big bang and hit the road.'

Shacket.

Dorian said. 'You didn't have a need to know. And how did you find out?'

393

'Yesterday, Mr. Ninety-three was a bad boy. You know how often he was a bad boy?'

'Twice,' Dorian said, referring to the murders of Painton Spader and the Klineman woman.

'Twice yesterday afternoon. But what you evidently don't know is then he went to her house, made a scene, had to be restrained, but that didn't work, and now he's been bad twice again.'

Dorian pushed aside what remained of his breakfast. 'Her house? Her who? Can we stop being too cute about this?'

'I don't feel cute, actually.'

'No one can be listening, and if anyone is, he can't know who the fuck we are.'

Still being half-cute, Haskell said, 'You remember the guy who wanted to shit all over your archaea business?'

Jason Bookman.

'I remember.'

'His widow is in that town. Ninety-three has a thing for her. On the way to her house, he's bad twice. Then he makes a try for her, ends up in bracelets, so he's bad twice again and loose.'

'Why don't I know about more than the first two he did? We own that jerkwater through our friendly AG. We're supposed to be kept informed. This is supposed to be quashed, like it never happened.'

'That jerkwater isn't Mayberry RFD, and apparently this particular khaki-ass bastard is a bad piece of work, wants to make himself a lawman star.'

A sludge of vitamin pills rose in Dorian's

throat. He swallowed hard and washed the resurgent wad down with a kale smoothie.

He said, 'I'll break that fucker down to dogcatcher. But I still don't get how our two problems are one.'

'Our pest-control friends, the ones who aren't in business anymore, they tracked the hacker to source. The widow.'

'Are you shitting me?'

'Somehow she got the Gordius ID and your Tragedy password, and she's putting together a case.'

'The ungrateful bitch,' Dorian said.

'Maybe you should have let her have that block of shares.'

'By my calculations the option wasn't vested yet. I'm not fucking Santa Claus. What's holding you up from finishing the job?'

'The future dogcatcher is providing her with protection in case your bad boy comes back. Six men. They need to stand down, go away and eat some doughnuts.'

'I'll get right on it. And what about Mr. Ninety-three?'

'He beheaded some hapless sonofabitch, jacked his pickup, a fancy hot-rod truck, easy to spot. So now they figure he's long gone from that area, although they don't want to take a chance with the widow. Something totally *X-Files* is going on with this guy. You have any idea what?'

Staring at the congealing eggs and avocados and crabmeat on his breakfast plate, Dorian said, 'No. I don't. Not a clue.'

104

Sheriff Hayden Eckman retreated to his residence on Sierra Way, the nicest street in Pinehaven.

The house provided ample space for a single man, was pleasantly furnished, included all the latest appliances, but the sheriff was not proud of it. Because he'd known that one day he would live in a much larger, much grander home, this place embarrassed him, not for any inadequacy in it, but because when eventually he achieved the status he deserved, he would not be able to say that he'd always lived at such a pinnacle, had always been among the elite. To a degree roots could be faked, the past papered over with lies, but some people would remember it was here that the great man had once lived, when he'd worn a uniform and been far too close to common.

Now he had to cope with the recognition that perhaps this was the grandest residence he would ever know. Which was so unfair. He had done everything right. He used his law degree to promote himself into the role of sheriff and salted the department with loyalists who were supposed to make sure everything occurring in Pinehaven County law enforcement would redound to his credit, even to his glory. He networked assiduously with leaders in adjacent counties and in Sacramento. He used far less campaign funds for personal expenses than he would have liked. He had $300,000 in cash, taken from Shacket's Dodge Demon, when he could have been greedy and taken the other $100,000 that he had left in the car. And in spite of doing everything right, he now stood on the brink of disaster, ruin.

His deal with Tio Barbizon required him to keep the attorney general informed about any developments in the case. But he had agreed to that condition and passed the Spader-Klineman murder investigation to Sacramento only because he thought that the killer was long gone from Pinehaven County, that there would be no further developments in Hayden's jurisdiction.

Then chaos. Event by violent event, until the disaster at the hospital, the sheriff believed he could control the situation to his benefit. He intended to craft a brilliant statement to the press, taking sole credit for the capture of the crazed fugitive — who was not just a homicidal psychopath but also the former CEO of Refine, responsible for the catastrophe in Springville! At that public briefing, Hayden planned to turn the fiend over to the attorney general, whom he would inform only moments before making his statement to the press, to ensure that Tio didn't hog the credit.

But now. Oh, now. Now, two more were dead and Shacket was loose and the sheriff failed to keep the attorney general informed. The shit hadn't hit the fan; it was far worse than that. A *cannonade* of shit was about to erupt, a long barrage of it, and Hayden Eckman would be the sole target.

He had come home ostensibly to write a

statement for the press. He couldn't do it because it would be tantamount to a suicide note.

In truth, he had come home because, with Lee Shacket loose, he didn't feel safe anywhere else in Pinehaven. He had a first-class security system. He had a handgun secreted in every room, and he was still in uniform with a pistol on his hip. He closed all the blinds and draperies.

As an attorney representing charlatans who were willing to fake their injuries or fantastically exaggerate the effects of genuine injuries, the most dangerous clients he had faced were those quick to seek redress in court or through arbitration when they discovered he had in one way or another skimmed more from their settlements than the terms of his basic agreement allowed. As if everyone didn't do it. None of them had ever tried to kill him.

Having made such a show of overseeing Shacket's arrival at the hospital and the man's commitment to the psychiatric ward, with Rita Carrickton using their smartphones to film key moments, the sheriff now felt that perhaps he had unwittingly made himself the focus of the mad-man's rage. He had only been an officer of the law, doing his job. But who knew what irrational resentment might have formed in the mind of a homicidal maniac like Shacket?

Thad Fenton's brain had been missing.

Eric Norseman's head had been taken away. Shacket's lunch pail.

Restlessly, the sheriff prowled his house, upstairs and down, again and again, half-convinced that he was not alone. With all the window coverings drawn shut, he needed to turn on lamps everywhere, and yet the rooms were infested with shadows that sometimes appeared to move in his peripheral vision, so that he pivoted with a start, hand on the grip of his pistol.

Every sound the wind wrenched from the house, every creak and pop and rattle, seemed not to be the structure protesting the storm, but instead suggested to Hayden that a stealthy stalker was but a room or two away.

He was terrified of turning a corner and encountering Shacket with a grin full of bloody teeth. He told himself that this was not a realistic fear, that he needed to calm himself. But was it really unrealistic to expect this particular fugitive to accomplish what was thought impossible? If Shacket had been able to escape from inescapable psych-ward restraints and exit by a third-floor window as if capable of flight, who was to say he couldn't get into a locked, alarmed, fully secured house as easily as an ant entering through a keyhole?

Although the sheriff wasn't much of a drinker, his anxiety grew until he began to treat it with Macallan Scotch, first on the rocks but then neat because he didn't like the way he couldn't stop the ice from rattling in the glass. He might have been concerned about insobriety compromising his senses and making him more vulnerable to attack, but fear accelerated his metabolism to such an extent that whisky seemed to have no effect on him.

Slotted on his utility belt along with his

department-issued phone, his personal smart-phone rang as he was circling the kitchen island to no purpose. His five closest deputies had personal phones of their own, provided by the sheriff, and had been instructed to call him on *his* private line in some circumstances, to ensure that certain sensitive subjects did not become part of the official — public — record. The screen said NO CALLER ID, which meant this wasn't one of those deputies.

He was tempted not to answer it, but he intuited who must be trying to reach him. He knew that to dodge this caller would only increase the amount of shit he had to endure when the crap cannon began to fire.

He put down his drink and backed up against the refrigerator and slid down to sit on the floor. He didn't think he could handle this on his feet.

Intuition proved reliable: The caller was Tio Barbizon, though he didn't identify himself. He knew that Shacket had been captured and had escaped. He knew about the two additional murders. He was not the same Tio as he had been before. He no longer treated the sheriff as an equal, but as an inferior, and he was furious.

'You understand how totally you screwed yourself?' Tio asked.

'Yes.'

'Do you think you have a way out?'

'No.'

'Because right now there is no way out for you.'

'I understand.'

'We had a deal. You pissed on it. You decided

400

to grandstand, be the glory boy, and you let him get away. You haven't just fucked me over. There's an interested party you don't know about, someone who could crush you like an ant and enjoy doing it. You've fucked him over, too. If the worst that happens to you is you wake up some morning to find your balls have been cut off, you should spend the rest of your life thanking God nothing worse was done to your sorry ass. But because something is needed from you, there is one hard way out, only one way.'

Tears welled in Hayden Eckman's eyes. 'Tell me.'

'Some men from my office will be coming to see you at six o'clock this evening. You will turn over to them all evidence, including the bodies of the victims.'

'Yes, of course.'

'They'll have a long statement for you to sign, explaining all that happened. The names Nathan Palmer and Lee Shacket won't be anywhere in the statement. The perpetrator will be identified as a drug-addled MS-13 gang member.'

'What MS-13 gang member?'

'We'll produce a likely candidate later. Not your concern.'

'But Shacket's still out there.'

'We'll find him. Anyway, he'll self-destruct.'

'I don't think he'll kill himself,' said the sheriff.

'I didn't say he would. I said he'll self-destruct. He won't be able to stop it. Now do you want to take this one chance, or are you determined to blow up your life?'

401

As fat, warm tears rolled down Hayden Eckman's face, he said, 'Will I be allowed to continue being the sheriff?'

'As long as you understand I own you, the interested party I mentioned owns you, everybody owns you.'

'All right,' the sheriff said without hesitation. He was no longer sitting on the floor. He was lying on his side, in the fetal position. 'Would it be possible . . . Will I be allowed eventually to run for higher office?'

'Allowed? Hell, you'll be *required* to run. Once you're owned by the right people and you acknowledge being owned, that you're in the game just to do what you're told, you're an ideal candidate. There's one more thing you have to do to earn all this.'

'Tell me.'

'Those six deputies providing protection. Pull them off that duty. Send them home. They aren't needed anymore.'

'But what if . . . '

'They aren't needed anymore.'

'What if Shacket . . . What if this MS-13 gangbanger goes back there?'

'Nothing bad is going to happen. Nothing that will cast blame on you. There are elegant ways to deal with these things. Now are you owned or are you not? It's comfortable being owned, Hayden. It makes everything so much easier. You'll become a valuable asset and be well taken care of. Your progress will be assured.'

'That sounds nice.'

'It *is* nice.'

'Well, if they aren't needed anymore . . . '

'They aren't.'

'I'll pull them off that duty.'

'Welcome home, Hayden.'

'That sounds nice, too.'

'It *is* nice,' Tio said and terminated the call.

Sheriff Hayden Eckman continued lying on his kitchen floor, in the fetal position, for perhaps another quarter of an hour. He felt as if he were descending through a narrow passage, forced forward by contractions through a birth canal, toward a new life. These weren't contractions of his conscience, for his conscience wasn't muscular enough to get the job done. These were contractions of desire, the same desire for status and power that had driven him as long as he could remember. If the exalted status he might one day achieve was unearned, conferred on him because of his obedience to the biases and preferences of the ruling class . . . well, he could revel in the prestige of his position nonetheless. He wouldn't be alone; probably three-quarters of those who enjoyed acclaim and high renown had achieved nothing to warrant it, other than to follow slavishly the ideology currently required of the anointed. And if the power that he acquired was not real power, if he was only doing to others what he was told to do to them, it was far better to be the whip that the powerful used than to be one of those lashed by it.

I'd rather be a hammer than a nail.

Furthermore, he was well suited for the new life Tio Barbizon offered him because he was a superb liar. He was such a convincing deceiver, he often found that in time he came to believe that the truth he invented was the truth in fact, and could occasionally be surprised to discover that he had even deceived himself. Once his new masters had lifted him up several rungs of the ladder, he might well believe that his power was his own, real and earned. If one believed something with all one's heart, that made it enough of a truth on which to base a life, at least one day at a time.

Finally he got up from the kitchen floor, born fully clothed, with no messy afterbirth.

He finished the Scotch in the glass he'd left on the island.

Then he used his personal phone to call the personal phone of one of the deputies at the Bookman residence, and he ordered an end to the protection he had provided for the widow and her child.

105

At 12:46 p.m., as a recently awakened Rosa Leon was assisting Megan in the kitchen, the deputies stationed in an SUV at the west end of the yard, near the forest, and those in another SUV near the back porch drove away into the wind.

Megan doubted that Shacket had been apprehended. Her experience and Carson Conroy's assessment of Hayden Eckman convinced her

404

that the Pinehaven County sheriff's department was corrupt. The very fact that no one informed Megan that her protection was being withdrawn suggested that someone working on Dorian Purcell's behalf had gotten to Eckman. She was being left vulnerable to Lee Shacket but also to whoever might be coming from Tragedy, the Dark Web operation.

Rosa said, 'I should wake Mr. Hawkins.'

'Let him sleep a while longer, Rosa. He said that when and if our protection was withdrawn, the men from Tragedy won't come right away. That would be too obvious. We've got a few hours. But go see about Woody and Kipp. If they're sleeping, wake them and bring them down here. Let's keep them near us.'

As if it were just another culinary tool, her 9 mm Heckler & Koch lay on a nearby cutting board.

As Rosa hurried upstairs, Megan picked up her phone and keyed in Carson Conroy's number. He would be waiting in Harry Borsello's Fleetwood Southwind in the former trailer park that had never become a wind-power plant.

Carson answered on the second ring, and Megan said, 'All the uniforms are gone. No one to see you. Are you ready?'

'Be there in fifteen,' he promised.

106

Dorian Purcell in the transit station on the roof of the Nob Hill building. At a window, staring impatiently at a helicopter landing pad. Waiting for his air taxi.

The two bodyguards, one at the elevator and one beside Dorian, would not be making this trip with him. His destination was secure.

In addition to the large apartment at Parable headquarters in Sunnyvale and the larger estate in Palo Alto and the still larger two-floor penthouse here in the heart of San Francisco, Dorian had an additional property in his Bay Area residential real-estate portfolio. His house in Tiburon, on the north shore of San Francisco Bay, encompassed forty thousand square feet and stood on five prime acres. The mansion provided a south-southwest view of the Golden Gate Bridge and the fabled city, which lay at an aesthetically pleasing distance, across almost five miles of water, a dazzling sight in its nightdress, and at all times inoffensive to the sense of smell.

His fiancée, Paloma Pascal, who lived with him in Palo Alto and sometimes joined him in the Nob Hill penthouse when they were in the city for a cultural event, did not have an article of clothing or even a toothbrush in the Tiburon house. Saffron 'Sunny' Ketterling, gymnast and contortionist extraordinaire, who lived with Dorian in the penthouse except on the rare occasion when Paloma was visiting, also had spent no time in Tiburon.

Dorian had acquired three side-by-side properties, had torn down the existing mansions, and had commissioned the current ultramodern residence, which had been completed sixteen months earlier. It was a wonder of steel and granite and quartzite and glass, with secret staircases and hidden rooms and all kinds of other gee-whiz features that every thirteen-year-old boy, besotted with fantasy and science fiction, would include in a mansion if thirteen-year-old boys had the wherewithal to spend $80 million on a house.

Four days a week, a staff of fourteen cared for the new mansion and the grounds, but no one was there from 5:00 p.m. Thursday until 8:00 a.m. Monday. Although he decamped to Tiburon only one or two weekends a month, Dorian valued the property as a retreat. The absolute privacy allowed him the freedom from distractions and the clarity of thought to speculate about where culture and high tech were going, to apply his singular genius as a futurist to conceiving new businesses and technological innovations that would keep Parable growing.

He saw himself as the Thomas Edison of his time, although with none of Edison's primitive moralism, and with a keen sense of how to maximize profits that the vaunted Wizard of Menlo Park could only have dreamed about.

Although he didn't mind being alone in Tiburon, he had built the house with the expectation that it would eventually be staffed with a conjugal partner, some different flavor from either Paloma or Sunny. He was a highly sexual person and thought of himself as the human equivalent of a prize breeding bull, though only in the sense that he was always ready; the thought of fathering a child chilled him to the bone, and he didn't tolerate scheming in that direction by Paloma,

Sunny, or anyone else.

In all the months since the mansion was completed, he had not settled on a woman to install among its many comforts. During the design and construction process, he never consciously considered the subject. When the contractor handed him the keys, however, Dorian realized that subconsciously he had been thinking of this place as not merely a retreat from the distractions of his busy daily life but as a retreat, as well, from the stifling rules and petty social norms of a world that was fast changing, though not fast enough to suit him. During his monthly visits to Tiburon, he had conceived of a few ways that he might venture into exciting new sexual territory. He hadn't yet settled on a course of action; as a most ambitious yet prudent man, he was still considering his options, debating with himself as to how outrageous he could be and still count on getting away with it.

Bearing the Parable logo, the twin-engine eight-passenger helicopter with high-set main and tail rotors, with an advanced-glass cockpit, floated down out of the sky. In fifteen minutes, Dorian would be in Tiburon.

107

Kipp knew they were entering a period of great danger.

The lives of those in this house were at risk.

But not just their lives.

He had smelled the scent of Shacket on the things the man had touched in Woody's room and elsewhere.

It was the scent of a man but also not the scent of a man.

It was the scent of something new and terrible. The odor sickened Kipp.

The Shacket thing was out there somewhere.

The science that had made him would not be abandoned.

More death would come of it in the years ahead.

The killers from the Dark Web were out there, too.

Nevertheless, Kipp was in an olfactory ecstasy in the Bookman kitchen.

Much cooking was underway. All of it delicious.

Although his nose was a blessing, it complicated his life.

A dog's nose had forty-four muscles.

The human nose had just four.

The number of scent receptors in a canine nose might not exceed the number of stars in the sky, but sometimes it seemed that way.

Humans had less than 1 percent as many scent receptors.

However poor their sense of smell might be, their compensation was that they had thumbs.

Amazing, really, that Kipp could endure beef chili simmering in a pot on the stove, a potato casserole baking in one oven, a cake in another —

— and still be alert for a fresh whiff of the Shacket thing —

— and smell the Dark Web killers if they got out of a car on Greenbriar Road —

— and know that Ben was still sleeping upstairs, know it by the rhythm of his uniquely scented exhalations —

— and detect the pheromones of happiness that beclouded the air around Woody —

— at the same time receiving the psychic blast of a Bellagram about the contact, minutes earlier, with a community of sixty-four in Coeur d'Alene, Idaho.

Something was happening out there.

And something was happening here.

Kipp smelled the exhaust of the motor home turning into the driveway.

He raced — and Woody raced — to the living room in time to see the big vehicle cruise slowly past, toward the rear of the house.

They sprinted to the kitchen, to the back door.

Megan said, 'Wait. Let's do this in an orderly fashion.'

The Fleetwood Southwind pulled off the driveway, into the backyard, out of sight of the county road.

So much hung in the balance now.

108

At one o'clock Thursday afternoon, four hours ahead of the usual quitting time, Amory Cromwell, the estate manager for the Purcell residence in Tiburon, released the house and

410

landscaping staff of fourteen until 8:00 a.m. Monday.

The Great Man had decided at the last minute to come here for the weekend and to arrive early. Everyone must do what the Great Man wanted, and without complaint, even though it upended half a day's scheduled work. Cromwell had harried the employees into their cars and away, as if chasing out a pack of uninvited feral cats, because the Great Man did not like having to greet or even acknowledge with a glance anyone who worked here other than his estate manager.

Cromwell used the sobriquet 'Great Man' only in his thoughts, never with the staff, who must not be encouraged to mock their employer. Born in London, educated in Britain, having worked on some of the finest estates in Boston, New York, and Philadelphia, where there were different antique silver services for breakfast and lunch and dinner, where his employers came from old money and spoke fluent French as a second language and were steeped in the myriad rules of etiquette, Cromwell felt that he was not only entitled but obligated to mock a poseur like Dorian Purcell. So what if the Great Man had more money than the combined wealth of all the families for whom Cromwell had worked heretofore?

Two years previously, Cromwell had given his notice in Boston, in order to accept this position at $350,000 per year plus benefits, twice what he'd been paid before. Unfortunately, he hadn't foreseen that a man worth as many billions and as acclaimed for tech wizardry as Purcell could

411

be both a case of arrested development and a boor. In Tiburon, the Great Man never threw parties, never entertained house guests. He wanted nothing to eat but frozen pizzas, frozen waffles, and ice cream, in addition to an entire delicatessen's worth of lunch meats, cheeses, and sandwich fixings left for him in a Sub-Zero. There were so many big-screen TVs that the house felt like an extremely elegant Best Buy store. Twenty video-game consoles were distributed through the thirty-four rooms. An arcade contained forty-six pinball machines. Nearly one thousand hard-core porno DVDs were stored in a walk-in safe, which Cromwell had discovered only because Purcell accidentally left that vault open when he'd departed hastily one Sunday.

Cromwell's current intention was to stay here three years before seeking another job. He was only forty-eight, and he could not possibly endure Purcell until retirement.

Now, he hurried through the ground floor of the sprawling residence, checking to be sure that all the doors were locked. He could have engaged them all from the house computer, except that some on the staff broke the rules and overrode the automatic-lock system while working, propping open a door here and there with a wedge, because they had too often been locked out of the house and refused reentry by a facial-recognition system that stubbornly refused to recognize them. Sometimes the through-house music system turned itself on, always blasting forth Taylor Swift, of all things. Now and then, in the garage, the carousels of collectible cars — none of which Purcell ever drove — began to turn of their own accord, as if the vehicles were bored, just sitting there day after day. On occasion, the charming female voice of the house-management program reacted to the sound of a vacuum cleaner by inquiring over and over again, 'Do you need medical assistance?' None of these systems was a product of Parable or one of its subsidiaries, but Cromwell wondered if the manufacturers, knowing where the equipment was destined, had fiddled with them to mock the Great Man. He was pleased to think that might be the case.

Because the staff had been chased out so unceremoniously, Cromwell found four doors wedged. Just as he secured the last one, the clatter of a helicopter announced the imminent arrival of the Great Man.

He went out to the rear terrace to watch the craft land and to greet his employer with more dignity than would be appreciated. Then he would depart for a long weekend of golf, pampering at a spa, and fine dining in Pebble Beach. He was booked into a five-star resort where they might have enough excellent wine in stock to heal the trauma of having to spend five minutes in Dorian Purcell's company.

109

A mile south of the Bookman residence, Verbotski, Knacker, and two of their partners in

Atropos — Speer and Rodchenko — gathered in the garage of the house where Charles Oxley lay dead in the cellar. In addition to Oxley's vehicle, the garage housed the black Suburban in which Speer and Rodchenko had driven from Reno.

Among other items that the newcomers brought in the Suburban were white-vinyl stick-on block-style letters in two different sizes, large and extra large. They didn't have the entire alphabet, only multiples of *F* and *B* and *I*. They required time and patience to align the letters and apply them to the roof, each front door, and the tailgate of the vehicle. The result was convincingly official.

Alexander Gordius called to say that the sheriff's deputies were no longer providing protection to Megan Bookman and her son.

Verbotski, Knacker, Speer, and Rodchenko were in agreement that they should wait until four o'clock to proceed to the Bookman place. To act any sooner would be to make it obvious that their arrival was a direct consequence of the deputies' pullout, which might make the widow wonder if they were in fact FBI.

After they rigged the simple device to blow the furnace in the basement, leaving only one connection to be made later, they agreed to pass the time playing poker at the kitchen table. A thousand-dollar buy-in was required. They were drinking men, but not when a job was pending. Verbotski brewed a fresh pot of coffee, and Knacker set out a package of a dozen chocolate-covered doughnuts that he found in the bread box.

Having never seen the body of anyone strangled

414

with an extension cord, Speer was curious about what the ligature marks might be like. He went to the basement to have a look at Charles Oxley's throat, and he returned to say he was suitably impressed.

They had been playing poker only half an hour when Alexander Gordius called again to report that, according to a friendly deputy who had been on the security detail, Megan and Woodrow Bookman were not the only people in the house. A thirtysomething Latina woman was there, as well, and a thirtysomething man who had arrived in a Range Rover with a golden retriever. At one point, the man had moved the Latina's Lincoln MKX and his vehicle into Mrs. Bookman's garage. No one had instructed the deputies to be curious about Mrs. Bookman's visitors, and they had lacked the initiative to record the license plate numbers of the Rover and Lincoln. There was no way to know who these people were or if they would still be in the house when the boys from Atropos arrived.

After three minutes of discussion, the killers agreed that this development was of no concern. Operating in concert, they had once subdued eleven civilians for interrogation and had subsequently shot all of them to death. They were professionals.

As they returned to poker, Rodchenko said, 'These are damn good doughnuts.'

'One dozen for four of us,' said Speer. 'Your share is three.'

'What? If I eat four, you'll shoot me?'

'We could do the job with just three of us,' Speer said.

'Easily,' said Knacker.

'If we had to,' said Verbotski.

Because none of those present was a man known for his sense of humor, Rodchenko did not take a fourth doughnut.

110

From a Crestron screen embedded in a kitchen wall — they were placed throughout the house — Dorian Purcell engaged the security system, which covered not just all doors and windows but also the five acres of grounds. If anyone tried to scale the front gate or the spike-topped estate wall, combined heat-and-motion detectors would identify a human-size figure. The alarm would sound, segmented steel shutters would roll down over all windows, and the police would be summoned. Through his charitable foundation, Dorian donated $30,000 a month to the Police Benevolent Fund, so local authorities tended to answer an alarm from this property six times faster than one from any other. He had tested them.

He came here to Tiburon not merely to think deep thoughts about technology and culture, and not just to brood about what new sexual adventures he might be able to get away with in this place, but also to kick back and enjoy himself without the annoyance of people. He poured chocolate-flavored vodka over ice. With the drink in hand, he toured his sleek ultramodern palace, not sure if he wanted to play pinball or a video

416

game, or pilot an F-18 fighter in his virtual-reality flight simulator, or take his air rifle up to the roof deck to shoot crows in flight, doves if there were any.

He came to the library. An enormous, antique Kashan carpet, with an intricate pattern in shades of coral and sapphire and deep amber, seemed to float on the pale limestone floor as if waiting for the genie who knew how to spell it into flight. The bookshelves were crafted from quarter-cut anigre, a rich golden wood that seemed to glow. He had contracted with a book scout to search for and acquire six thousand important first editions at a cost in eight figures.

He meant to walk among the stacks, admiring his acquisitions. Turning a corner into the nearest aisle, however, he got a whiff of a subtle, disturbing smell. Unable to locate the source, he wondered if it was mold or another affliction of paper. His bookman would have to track it down. His enthusiasm for a tour waned.

He'd not yet had time to read any of the volumes in his world-class collection, but that didn't matter. The library served two primary purposes. It added class to the residence. Second, more important, it allowed him to have a bookcase that was a hidden door, like those in old spooky movies — Karloff, Lugosi! — that he'd thought were cool ever since he was a kid who'd been into retro films.

When he said 'Ochus Bochus,' the name of a mythical Norse magician and demon, a voice-recognition program unlocked the door and swung it open on powered pivot hinges. He stepped into a secret corridor, one of a network of such behind the walls of the house, and said, 'Hoc est corpus meum,' which instructed the bookcase door to close and lock.

At the end of the secret corridor was a secret door disguised as a wall-to-wall floor-to-ceiling mirror. No one on the staff knew of these hidden passageways, and he cleaned this mirror himself from time to time. He took a moment to admire his reflection. He thought he looked wonderfully mysterious. Then he found the concealed latch in the looking-glass frame and opened the door.

Beyond were secret stairs leading up and secret stairs leading down. He descended to a twelve-foot-square space lined on three sides with some of the most expensive books in his collection. Yet another hidden door pivoted open when he declared, 'Abracadabra,' and he passed through into a vestibule as sequestered as any forgotten catacomb sealed off a millennium earlier.

For as long as he could remember, words like secret and hidden and sequestered and mysterious and sub rosa had quietly thrilled him, no less now than when he'd been a boy.

On the wall opposite the hidden door by which he entered was an insulated steel door weighing eight hundred pounds. It could be opened either with a combination dial or the words Hola Nola Massa, an incantation used by dark magicians in the Middle Ages to ensure the success of their endeavors.

He spoke the words, and the door opened, and

he went through into a small apartment at the moment unfurnished. The front room was twenty by thirty feet. Beyond it was a full bathroom that also provided a refrigerator and microwave.

The walls and ceiling were three-foot-thick, poured-in-place, steel-reinforced concrete covered with inch-thick sound board and then dry-wall. If he were to bring an iPod in here and play the most ear-splitting heavy-metal song at the highest possible volume, the crashing chords would sound like a distant, not-quite-identifiable noise on the other side of the eight-hundred-pound door, out there in the vestibule. Beyond that, it couldn't be heard at all.

This was one of three panic rooms concealed at different points in the residence, to which he could retreat if terrorists or mere burglars invaded the house, and wait them out until police had dealt with them. The other two chambers were not as deeply placed or as thoroughly fortified as this one. None appeared on the records in the city's building department.

Not until a few weeks after the completion of the house had he begun to understand that this particular panic room could serve in a different capacity from the other two. He needed an additional month before he could admit that subconsciously he had known to what alternate purpose this space could be put. It was conceived neither by the inner child who loved spooky old movies nor by the security-conscious billionaire that child had become. It was designed instead by a more ruthless aspect of his personality that he hadn't been fully ready to

419

acknowledge, a totally free and all-powerful version of Dorian Purcell, an Ultimate I that yearned to express itself.

Now he spoke two lines of verse that he'd heard once, that appealed to him for reasons he could not entirely explain. He did not know the poet or the rest of the poem, and he didn't care to know.

'*I should have been a pair of ragged claws I Scuttling across the floors of silent seas.*'

The acoustics of the room were such that, though he didn't whisper, the words seemed to die in the air before reaching the farther wall.

To cross over from this blighted age to the transhuman future and rise above the limitations of the human species, to become as a god, it was necessary to think like a god. And gods recognized no limitations.

He stood sipping chocolate-flavored vodka over ice, surveying the room, considering what age-appropriate decor might be the most appealing, imagining what ultimate power could here be his.

The challenge was daunting, to indulge in a secret life of forbidden pleasure in this sanctum sanctorum without allowing it either to dominate him or to change in any way the face or the personality that he presented to the world above.

Slowly a measured smile formed as he considered what fun he might have rising to this challenge, as he had risen to so many others with ever-escalating success.

111

Already, by 2:05 Thursday afternoon, Sheriff Hayden Eckman had talked himself into a good mood. Tio Barbizon was right: It was a relief to be owned, to have no responsibility except to do as he was told. When Barbizon's men arrived at six o'clock to collect dead bodies and evidence, to have Hayden sign off on a concocted version of recent events that would satisfy the attorney general, then his new life could begin.

He was in a living room armchair, a third of the way through a second serving of Scotch, when his personal phone rang. The caller was Deputy Reed Hannafin, one of the loyalists Hayden had appointed.

'Sheriff, I just learned from one of our guys that Dr. Conroy was at the Bookman house last night while we were guarding it.'

Hayden sat up straighter in the chair. 'We couldn't find Carson earlier. Jim Harmon had to run the murders at the heating-cooling plant. What the hell was Carson doing at the Bookman place?'

'Nobody knows. His Explorer was parked in front. Then he left before dawn. You want me to find him? Maybe check out his house?'

After a hesitation, Hayden said, 'I'll have to ask.'

Puzzled, Hannafin said, 'Ask who?'

'I mean, I'll have to think about it, how to approach it. He shouldn't have gone there, not officially or unofficially. But he's an odd duck.

Testy. Let me deal with this.'

'Just thought you ought to know.'

'Now I do,' Hayden said and terminated the call.

Half a minute later, his phone rang. Rita Carrickton.

'I got some sleep,' she said. 'Did you?'

'No. Maybe I'll never sleep again. I'm wired.'

'I'll come over and unwire you. I'm horny as hell. All this action, this violence — I don't know, it just turns me on.'

Hayden consulted his wristwatch. He had almost four hours until Barbizon's men would show up. A tumble with Rita might be the only way he could relax enough to get maybe two hours of sleep before the Sacramento boys arrived. He needed a little rest to hold his own with them. 'Come on over.'

'Be there in twenty minutes.'

The sheriff hurried into his bathroom and downed a fifty-milligram Viagra with a swallow of Scotch.

He turned off the alarm and went into the garage. From the trunk of his patrol car, he retrieved the cash and the jacket with diamonds sewn into its lining.

In the kitchen again, he hung the jacket on a stool and dumped the cash onto the center island.

He wasn't going to tell Rita about being owned by Tio and most likely by Purcell. Being owned was a good thing. He knew it was a good thing. But Rita might need some persuading. She would want to talk it to death. Right now,

Hayden didn't want to talk; he wanted her to bang his brains out. She was already in the mood, and the sight of all that money would be like feeding her a pound of a powerful aphrodisiac.

He almost put the alarm back on while he waited for her, but she would want to know why it was engaged. He didn't want her to think he was afraid of Lee Shacket.

Instead of twenty minutes, she arrived in fifteen. She parked in the garage and came into the kitchen through the connecting door. She was off duty, not in uniform, and when she saw the money piled on the island, her nipples swelled instantly, enormously, against her white T-shirt.

She said, 'What's this, some case evidence or something?'

'No, baby, this is righteous spoils.'

Amazed, she said, 'Yours?'

'Ours. It was hidden in Shacket's car.'

She had brought a bottle of good red wine. She set it on the island and buried her face in the money, and inhaled deeply. When she looked up, she said, 'You are going to get *so* totally humped.'

'I need to take a quick shower.'

'It *better* be quick. I'll be waiting in bed with two glasses of wine, Mr. Big.'

He loved it when she called him Mr. Big. How astonishing that, only a short while ago, he had been lying on the kitchen floor in the fetal position, convinced that his life must be over or that his future must be diminished to the point that he had nothing to live for anymore. Now a bright future was assured, and he was shortly to be wrung dry by Rita, who was a fabulous ride. She would be even more fabulous if he pretended she was Megan Bookman.

112

The center of the action was upstairs now, and Woody's mom didn't have to be concerned about him and Kipp being up here alone, as she had worried when the deputies were first withdrawn.

In his room, with Kipp at his side, Woody had spent half an hour on the Wire with Bella, the golden retriever who lived in Santa Rosa with the Montell family. Of all the members of the Mysterium, she was the most experienced with the uses of the Wire, because for years she had volunteered to remain receptive around the clock, seven days a week, when others were tuned out. And when she had a major news alert to share, she forced connections with all of her kind and implanted the story in their minds. Woody's awareness of the Wire had at first been subconscious, and his initial use of it had been unintended, when he had drawn Kipp to him. Now he needed to know everything about how to use it. Bella not only advised him but also sent down the Wire a data package that in minutes made him as accomplished at transmission as any of the Mysterians.

The result of this education was a further unlocking of doors that he hadn't known were closed within his mind, a sense of freedom and completeness rising in him like a helium-filled balloon with the words HAPPY BIRTHDAY emblazoned on it. His metamorphosis had begun with the communion between him and Kipp, when they had stared into each other's eyes on the bed the previous night, and now thanks to Bella, it was complete.

When it was done, he knelt on the floor with Kipp and held his companion, their faces cheek to cheek, fur to skin, for a long, sweet moment. The boy did not speak, and the dog could not speak, but they were both celebrating thousands of years of mutual dependence and love between their species. They were celebrating as well the maturation of that bond into something magnificent and miraculous that neither of them could have imagined two days earlier.

They were poised on the brink of a radical transformation of the world, which had begun before the earliest recorded history, when an alliance had first been made between one dog and one primitive human being on some hostile plain or in some forest filled with menace. Until then, the only shelter against bitter weather and the mortal dangers posed by nature's many beasts was a cave and a carefully tended fire. But with that alliance, two predators — dog and man, working together over uncounted millennia — had made of themselves more than predators by virtue of the love that grew between them. This love was not just the instinct of one species to value its own, but a love that put dogs and human beings on a long road toward one destiny. Some might call it evolution, dogs slowly becoming more intelligent until they took a sudden quantum leap forward, and some might call it intelligent design, but whatever the agent of change, neither species was as much as it could be without the other. Dogs needed the hands and voices of human beings, and people needed — desperately needed — to receive unto themselves the innocence of dogs, to acquire their intolerance for deceit, and to seek to match their loyalty.

That it was a mute autistic boy who became the translator between the two species was an irony Woody could have appreciated even in his former condition. The responsibility humbled him now, and he said, 'Come on, Kipp. I need to talk with Mom.'

113

In the Oxley house, the agents of Atropos were finished with poker and were preparing for their visit to the Bookmans.

They were armed with pistols, but they had no intention of blasting their way into the house. A simple knock on the door and a credible-looking badge would get them inside. The Bookmans might be expecting trouble, but not trouble that arrived in a vehicle like the FBI used in movies, not trouble that wore a dark suit and spoke respectfully and presented a superbly forged photo ID with the Bureau seal.

Their weapons of choice were Tasers and small spray bottles that fired streams of chloroform. When the targets were stunned with 50,000 volts and then rendered unconscious, they would be restrained with zip ties.

Thereafter, the interrogation could begin, to discover exactly all that Megan Bookman had learned about Dark Web murder-for-hire and the clients who paid for well-staged accidents, induced heart attacks, cerebral embolisms, suicides, and fake terrorist incidents.

They would inject the widow Bookman and possibly others with the barbiturate thiopental, often called 'truth serum,' which did not guarantee she would tell them everything, only that she would experience an irresistible compulsion to answer their questions. When thiopental was administered with a cocktail of drugs developed by Russia's chief intelligence directorate, however, lying became almost an impossibility, especially when the injections were with the threat of extreme pain.

'If we're lucky,' Verbotski said, 'she hasn't yet shared what she's learned with anyone outside that house. Then we only need to gather all her evidence, bring the four of them back here, kill them with as little mess as possible, take them back to Reno, and dispose of the bodies so they can never be found.'

Atropos & Company had an unblemished record of disposing of the dead in ways that no remains were ever recovered. The liquidation lab

427

in their Reno facility was a marvel of cadaver processing.

'What about the dog?' Rodchenko asked. 'That guy, whoever he is, showed up with a dog.'

'What about it?'

'Are we going to kill the dog?' Rodchenko wondered.

'If it gives us trouble.'

'I want to kill it whether it gives us trouble or not.'

'What've you got against dogs?'

'I don't like the way they look at me.'

'How do they look at you?' Bradley Knacker wondered.

'The way a cop looks at you when his instinct is on fire. Dogs just creep me out. They always have. I've been bitten three times.'

Speer said, 'So kill the dog.'

'Everyone okay with that?' Rodchenko asked.

Everyone was okay with it.

114

Woody led his mother from the kitchen to her studio, where she sat on her stool near the unfinished painting of him and the deer.

Beyond the tall windows, the yard trees were not tossing as violently as before. The wind seemed to be at last diminishing a little, though the overcast was growing darker.

He stood before his mom and took her hands in his. He saw that she was still surprised and moved by his willingness to touch rather than just assenting to be touched.

'Something really big is happening,' he told her.

'Something enormous already has, sweetie.'

'Bigger than just me.' Of course she knew about the Mysterium and the Wire. She knew that the dogs couldn't read one another's mind, that the Wire was essentially just a psychic telephone. Now he told her about Bella in Santa Rosa and about what Bella had done for him. 'I'm still learning how to do what Bella does, how she speaks to all of them, gets through to all of them, whether they're on the Wire at the moment or not. It's cool. It's like something out of Heinlein. But I'm going to need more hours of practice before maybe I can . . . take the next step.'

Her long, graceful fingers tightened around his hands. 'What next step, Woody?'

'It's nothing scary,' he assured her. 'I just need some time to practice, to be sure I can do it right. I'm going to practice real hard. But before then, I just wanted to tell you.'

Into his silence, she said, 'Tell me what, honey?'

He knew the words he wanted to say, for he had said them to her when first he'd been able to speak after his long silence, but words were only part of it, the smaller part. Woody closed his eyes and gathered all of his feelings about her: his recognition of her love for him, of her sorrow over the loss of his father, of her grace and profound tenderness, of her devotion and commitment to him, of the sacrifices she had made for him, of her talent as an artist and a pianist, of her great heart and the purity of her intentions. He took all those bright truths about her and all the emotions they evoked in him, and he wove them into a radiant fabric and wrapped them around fourteen words — *You are an angel on earth, and I love you with all my heart* — and he transmitted everything to her with the same gentle but irresistible force that Bella used when she sent one of her Bellagrams.

The Wire had existed for thousands of years. No one knew how long. Before they'd had a word for it, without even thinking about it, dogs had used the Wire long before undergoing a rapid expansion of their intelligence, had used it in a primitive way: to establish their territories, to warn one another of threats, to alert one another to a richness of prey to be chased down. The Wire, which might simply be labeled 'telepathy,' had been part of that fund of knowledge called 'instinct.' There were four kinds of knowledge: what was taught, what was learned from experience, what was intuitively known, and matters of instinct coded in the genes.

Having trusted in their instinct far more than human beings did, dogs had been prepared to use the Wire in a more sophisticated fashion when their intelligence reached a level at which they could understand how the gift could be better employed. In Woody's case, he was unaware that the Wire waited in him for his benefit, and he unwittingly transmitted on it when his inability to speak had left him no other outlet in those hours when he'd been seized by despair, terror, and blind panic. But since the Wire was part of *his* genetic package of instinctive knowledge, surely every human being on the planet had the same potential to be telepathic.

And so he used the Wire to send his mother this valentine in September. He watched her eyes grow wide, wider than he had ever seen them, and he heard her breath catch in her throat, and he felt her hands tighten again on his, and he saw her tears come. She had cried earlier, too, when she heard his voice for the first time and he said he loved her. She was pierced more profoundly, however, by the power of the Wire and all that it could carry in addition to words. This time was different also because Woody wept, lifted by the message of undying love that she returned to him on the Wire, through the connection he'd opened for her.

During the 164 weeks since his dad died, his mom had on occasion caught him in tears. He always smiled and gave her a thumbs-up sign and, by other means, deceived her into thinking his were happy tears. But no lie, regardless of how well intended, could deceive in telepathic communication, because the truth of the sender's motives was inextricably bound up in the emotions that were transmitted with the words. Now Woody's mother knew that the tears he'd shed before had been in grief, but that these were truly tears of joy.

Suddenly she understood everything that had happened, realized what it meant, what must eventually happen, and she wired him, *OMG,*

431

baby boy, you've just scared the hell out of me.

He knew exactly what she meant. She didn't mean scared in a bad way. She meant the kind of scared that a dirt-poor person might feel if he won a billion dollars in the lottery and understood that nothing would ever be the same.

115

When the sheriff came out of the bathroom, naked and ready, Rita was still fully clothed, sipping cabernet. She gave him a full glass of wine and sat him on the edge of the bed and then slowly undressed for him.

For Hayden Eckman, watching Rita undress was as thrilling as what would follow. Avoiding the theatricality of a stripper, she removed each article of clothing slowly but with crisp efficiency and with a challenging stare that said, *I am the law, mister, and you're going to do just what I want.* As a teenager who found girls as mystifying as they found him impossible, Hayden lived with his mother next door to Mr. and Mrs. Dowling, who were police officers. His adolescent lust was so intensely focused on Joyce Dowling, whom he watched through binoculars when she was sunbathing in her backyard, that he never quite got over her. The only thing that would have made Rita's striptease more thrilling would have been if she had been in uniform and if her name had been Joyce.

432

Now, the sheriff put aside his half-finished glass of wine and welcomed Rita into his bed. She was lithe, lubricious, more ravenous than ever, she could not get enough of him, she was a *sex machine*, the ride was better than anything in his experience — until he fell asleep under her.

He woke in some confusion, for although he was naked, he was no longer in bed. He was instead in the bathtub. The water was cold. He was shivering.

Rita, now fully clothed, sat on the closed lid of the toilet, watching him.

Standing in the bathroom doorway, Deputy Andy Argento said, 'Hey, he's awake. That's not supposed to happen.'

'It's all right,' Rita said. 'There's not much left of him.'

'Whatever you say, Sheriff.'

This confused Hayden further. His voice was slurred as he said to her, 'No, you're the undersheriff.'

'And thanks for the appointment,' she said. 'I'll be interim sheriff until the special election.'

Hayden didn't think he'd had enough Scotch and certainly not enough wine to be drunk, but he sounded inebriated. 'What special election?'

'Tio Barbizon will endorse me. I've made the club, Hayden. I'm on my way.'

He smelled blood. He realized the water was discolored by it.

A lot of blood.

For a moment he thought Shacket had gotten

433

into the house and had bitten him half to death. Then he realized that his right arm was lying on the porcelain ledge of the tub and that his wrist bore a deep cut from a razor blade.

His eyelids were very heavy. Leaden. He couldn't hold them open. He said, 'But I'm owned. I sold myself I'm a valuable asset.'

'It's nice for you that you could think you were, for a little while.'

Her voice seemed to come from a distance, as if she had left the bath and spoke from the bedroom.

With effort, Hayden opened his eyes, but she remained sitting on the closed lid of the toilet.

Shadows were gathering in the room. He couldn't quite make out the features of the watching woman.

'Joyce?' he asked.

'Damn, you hear that, Andy? You know what I hated most about this asshole?'

A man who was only a silhouette said, 'What's that?'

'We'd be doing the nasty, him grunting like a pig rooting for truffles, he'd call me by her name and not even realize it.'

'Whose name?'

'Joyce. Some next-door neighbor cop he wanted to do when he was a geek teenager.'

'What a freak,' the man said.

'A freak's freak,' the woman said.

Hayden Eckman tried to protest that insult. He couldn't find his voice. And then he couldn't remember what had offended him. And then —

16

After a few hours of sleep, Ben Hawkins met with Megan Bookman to review preparations for their unwanted but inevitable visitors. In spite of her fear of what might happen, she was nonetheless eager for a chance to fight back. Ben expected her to insist that Woody be hidden away from any potential confrontation, but she understood the boy's presence was essential to convince the killers that, however traumatized she might have been by Shacket, she didn't at the moment recognize the danger she faced. If they didn't see the boy at once, they would suspect they'd been made, the guns would come out, and there would be blood.

Minutes later, Ben was in the kitchen when Carson Conroy, having returned from his third trip to the abandoned trailer park, brought in the last two bags and put them beside a pile of others.

'Not enough time to risk another run,' Ben said.

Carson shook his head. 'No need to. That's the lot of them.'

'If you'll tend to all this' — Ben indicated the bags — 'I'll tuck the Fleetwood away like we planned.'

'You really think they'll come today? It's just yesterday they tracked Woody to his computer. Or I guess they think it was Megan.'

'They'll want to move as fast as they can. They're coming, all right. They won't wait for night, because they'll expect us to be more suspicious of them if they show up in the dark. With this heavy overcast, there's only a few hours of good light left. They'll be here soon. In maybe an hour.'

Carson glanced at a window, beyond which the day was steadily dimming under a sombrous, swollen sky. 'And they'll come boldly, pretending to be what they aren't?'

'They'll see it as their best chance to get in the door and establish control. Their kind think the rest of us are suckers.'

'Often we are.'

'Yeah, but not this time.'

Although the wind was rough, it had lost its rage. It blustered now instead of shrieking, and it seemed to choke on the anger that it could no longer adequately express.

The key to the motor home lay in the cup holder next to the driver's seat. Ben drove out to the highway and turned north.

In less than a mile, he came to a mountain-view rest area with picnic tables. In respect of the wind and the threat of rain, no one currently made use of the facility. He parked the motor home and locked it and walked briskly back to the Bookman property.

As he approached the residence, he surveyed the windows. Blinds and draperies were drawn over all of them, except for the panes in the front door and the two sidelights, one of which featured glass and the other the semi-opaque plastic tarp that he and Megan had nailed in place the previous night.

In the house once more, he found everyone in the living room, waiting as had been arranged. Carson and Rosa were in armchairs. Megan sat on one of the sofas, Woody at her left side, a pistol under the decorative pillow to the right of her.

Ben stood at the fireplace, his back to the ceramic logs that were licked by gas flames. His pistol was tucked behind the mantel clock.

If it came to guns, they were dead, but neither he nor Megan felt comfortable without firearms within reach.

Coffee had been served. Platters of homemade cakes and cookies were offered on a sideboard, as if the Bookmans and their guests were in the habit of taking the equivalent of a British tea at this hour and wouldn't be deterred by memories of a recent home invasion and violence.

In the wake of what had happened here, the scene was ludicrous, really. However, their plan depended on precise timing. An important part of it required that whoever came here with malicious intentions should not act precipitously once they were through the front door, that they should come into the living room and, for a minute or two, be uncertain about how to proceed. The best way to ensure the wanted reaction was to greet them without apparent suspicion and to present them with a circumstance that surprised them and left them a little disoriented.

'Looks good,' Ben told them, 'but you're as tense as if you're waiting for root canals without novocaine. Fake a little relaxation. Check out

437

Rosa. She's got the right attitude.'

'I spiked my coffee,' Rosa admitted.

With a smile, Ben said, 'Not a solution for all of us.'

'You're sure we can't call the police?' Rosa asked.

'Someone already called Eckman,' Megan said. 'Someone he *really* serves instead of us. We're on our own.'

Carson agreed. 'So much for safe and peaceful Pinehaven.'

The boy had assumed an unusual posture, sitting back on the sofa, but leaning forward from the waist, his head cocked to the right, staring vacantly at the ceiling, breathing through his open mouth.

'Woody,' Ben said, 'is something wrong?'

'I can't talk. I'm being autistic.'

Megan put a hand on his shoulder. 'Don't ham it up, sweetie.'

Woody looked to Ben for guidance. 'You think I was overacting? I mean, I *know* this character.'

'There was a pretty thick slice of ham in that,' Ben confirmed. 'Maybe you should just smile at everyone.'

'How's this?' Woody shaped a sweet *One Flew Over the Cuckoo's Nest* smile, early Danny DeVito.

'Perfect,' Ben said.

'Don't be afraid,' Rosa told the boy. 'I thought I would be afraid, but I'm not. Well, a little. Maybe a little more than a little, but not a lot.'

Shaking his head, Woody said, 'I'm not afraid. Not anymore. Not since Kipp.'

438

Ben Hawkins hoped that wasn't true. Fearless-
ness got people killed.

He was afraid, a heaviness in his heart, a knot
of dread in his gut. His eyes met Megan's, and
he saw she was racked with misgiving. Each of
them in this room had so much to lose: not just
one another, not just their lives, but a whole
world on its way to wonder.

The sound of a vehicle turning into the
driveway drew his attention toward the drapery-
covered windows.

He went into the foyer, to the front door, and
peered through the one intact sidelight.

Four men in dark suits were getting out of a
black Suburban marked with the letters FBI.

He said, 'They're here.'

117

Kipp sitting in the upstairs hallway, alert.

He wanted to be with Woody, to be in a
position to die for the boy if it came to that.

Kipp thought it would come to that.

Even on the brink of disaster, humans
deceived themselves. They wanted to believe they
would never die.

Dogs knew better.

Kipp loved people for their hopefulness. Like
dogs, humans had been born to hope.

But if you understood the cold indifference of
nature, as dogs did, then you did not hope to live
forever in this violent world.

You tried instead to make the world better while you were here, and you put your hope in another, better world.

Oh, how fiercely, ardently, intensely, fervently he wanted to be at Woody's side in this perilous moment!

But for now his place was here in the upstairs hallway.

He knew his duty.

Because Dorothy's enemy was cancer, Kipp had not been able to do anything for her.

Woody's enemy was not cancer.

A remarkable quiet had settled on the residence.

Kipp listened and heard naught, and that was good.

At last the wind had ceased to torment the structure.

The house did not groan with either all that it contained or the weight of history.

The air was rich with scents, and so many of them were of the greatest importance.

He took no pride in being the dog chosen by destiny to bond with the boy who might change the world.

Instead, he was honored, humbled. And determined not to fail.

He heard the vehicle turn in to the driveway.

The engine died.

Doors opened.

Kipp smelled one, two, three, four Haters.

His hackles bristled.

Four subtly different varieties of evil.

He got to his feet, holding his tail low and still.

The doorbell rang.

As the chimes echoed through the house, a peal of thunder followed, a rending crash as if the crust of the earth must have cracked to its molten core.

118

John Verbotski rang the doorbell. On the porch behind him were Knacker, Speer, and Rodchenko, the last two with briefcases of a style that FBI agents might carry, in which were all the necessary drugs and instruments of interrogation.

Verbotski startled when lightning flashed as if the sun had gone nova and burned off the overcast in an instant. A fierce crack of thunder reverberated in his teeth and bones.

As a hard rain abruptly rattled on the porch roof with the icy racket of hail, the door opened, and a man loomed on the threshold with a boy at his side.

The guy must have been the unknown individual who had arrived in a Range Rover. He was tall and fit, and he had about him an air that Verbotski didn't like. Competence? Steadfastness? Whatever it was, it wasn't good.

His intuition told him to shoot this fucker now. But Verbotski had earned a university degree — or received one — in psychology. His favorite German masters of that field had written that intuition was merely a myth, that the concept had its origins in the *Volkskunde* of superstitious peasants who believed in such nonsense as natural law.

An enlightened man must be guided by cold reason based on clear-eyed observations and hard facts. When he gave credence to intuition, he was doomed as all such myth-besotted fools were doomed. He held his fire.

The boy at the man's side must have been the mental misfit, the son of Megan Bookman. He was small for his age. His blue eyes seemed to swim in their sockets, as if he couldn't quite focus on anything, and his smile was like that on a strange doll or marionette, eerie because it seemed perpetual and unrelated to any emotion.

'May I help you gentlemen?' the man said.

Verbotski had his fake Bureau ID ready, and he presented it with a smile that he was sure looked more genuine than that of the basket-case boy. 'Special Agent Lewis Erskine.' Indicating his companions, who displayed more phony ID, Verbotski said, 'Special Agents Jim Rhodes, Tom Colby, and Chris Daniels. We're here to see Mrs. Bookman regarding the unfortunate encounter she had with Lee Shacket, who's now on the Bureau's most-wanted list.'

All that didn't sound quite right to Verbotski as he said it, and he wished he'd taken more time to practice his lines. But the boy maintained his idiot smile, and the man appeared relieved. 'I'm Ben Hawkins, a friend of Mrs. Bookman's. Considering that Shacket's killed people in at least two states, we've been wondering why the hell someone at the federal level wasn't on this. Come in, come in, Agent Erskine, gentlemen.

We're all in the living room.'

Leaving them to shut the door behind themselves, Hawkins turned his back, not in the least suspicious, and started across the foyer. When he realized that the eternally smiling boy was still in the doorway, staring *through* Verbotski and crew, Hawkins halted and said, 'Come along now, Woody. Let's get a cookie, son.' When the boy still didn't move out of the way, Hawkins returned and took him by the hand. 'Sorry,' he said to Verbotski. 'Woody is a very good boy, he usually listens, but he's . . . you know, special.' With that, he gently led the kid toward the living room archway.

Being Lewis Erskine, Verbotski went into the house, and his crew followed, and Speer closed the door.

The torrents of rain came down so hard that they filled even this well-built residence with a soft drumming-rushing sound that was strangely comforting. Perhaps in the amniotic sac, an unborn child heard a susurration alike to this, the sound of his mother's life-sustaining blood circulating ceaselessly through the body that encompassed and sustained him.

Whenever a thought like that occurred to Verbotski, he wondered about himself, whether something might be a little wrong with him. Had he continued his education with a master's degree in psychiatry, he would have been required to undergo psychoanalysis to learn how to conduct such sessions, which might have been interesting. But in short order he'd gone from being a highly paid mercenary in foreign hot spots to being an

443

extravagantly paid domestic murder-for-hire specialist, and a career path in psychiatry appeared insufficiently rewarding.

Now, as he followed Ben Hawkins and the boy into the living room, he heard the man say, 'Megan, everyone, our prayers have been answered. These gentlemen are from the FBI, and they're here about Lee Shacket.'

The people in the living room were having coffee, the sideboard was laden with tarts and cookies and finger sandwiches, Hawkins went to the fireplace where he had left his cup and saucer on the mantel, Megan Bookman put her cup aside on a table next to the sofa and rose to her feet to greet her visitors, and John Verbotski was impressed that she could be so fresh and lovely and psychologically *together* after all that she'd recently been through.

She had about her a regal quality, an air of indomitability. They might need a lot of thiopental and other drugs to break her, but she would be fun to interrogate. And when the interrogation was finished, she'd be fun to use, just to see how much humiliation she could endure without cracking.

A Latina woman was sitting in one armchair, a black man in the other, holding coffee cups, and neither of them rose, which made Verbotski's work easier. He put away his phony Bureau ID and said, 'Mrs. Bookman, I'm Special Agent Lewis Erskine.' As he began to speak, his three associates moved farther into the room, getting in position to act, each within striking distance of one of the adults. They could deal with the kid after everyone else had been Tasered, chloro-formed, and restrained. Rodchenko and Speer put down their briefcases. 'And these,' Verbotski continued, 'are Special Agents — '

He intended to introduce them in this order: Rhodes, Colby, and Daniels. Rodchenko was being Daniels, and when his name was spoken, it would be the signal to pull their Tasers.

Then Verbotski hesitated because he saw the idiot smile slip off the boy's face, saw intelligence in those blue eyes, saw contempt in the black man's face, saw Ben Hawkins putting a hand on the mantel clock as though to reach behind it. Suddenly he knew that intuition was not *Volkskunde*, after all, that he should have shot Hawkins on the doorstep, that he needed to shoot the bastard now, shoot the black dude and shoot the Latina bitch and shoot the kid, shoot them all before they made a move, and take Megan captive. She was the only one they really needed.

119

Deputy Foster Bendix was assigned to a winding rural route where nothing ever happened except DUI arrests, teenagers busting themselves up while back-road drag racing, good old boys blasting away at road signs just for the fun of it, if you called that fun, and vehicle breakdowns to which he could lend a helping hand. At times, Foster thought he was more of a janitor, cleaning up messes, than he was a cop.

In the dismal gray light of the storm, through thick curtains of rain, as he passed the former trailer park, where the planned bird-slaughtering system had failed to be approved, he thought he was seeing a mirage, a fata morgana, except not illusions of cliffs and buildings, but ranks of cars and SUVS.

No one had lived there in years. The mobile homes were gone. There had once been power hookups and connections for gas and septic tanks, but the utilities had been cut off long before the decision was made not to build the windmills. The property wasn't suitable for any kind of gathering.

In fact, the county owned the land, couldn't find a buyer for it, and was liable for any injuries that anyone might sustain there. No funds had been provided for a fence, but they had staked some no-trespassing signs at the entrance.

Because it fell to Foster Bendix to pursue any miscreants who ignored the signage, he drove off the county road and onto the buckled and cracked blacktop of that forlorn property. The most vehicles he'd ever seen here before was one, always at night. One teenage couple or another with nowhere else to go, doing the Meat Loaf thing, like he sang about in 'Paradise by the Dashboard Light.'

Standing side by side in the pelting rain, these vehicles all appeared to be without drivers or passengers, unless everyone was lying down, which Foster didn't credit. There were Hondas and BMWs, SUVs and crew-cab pickups, a couple of vans with sliding side doors. Most of the license plates were from California, but three were from Oregon. He counted forty-one vehicles.

Not sure what to do, he called the current watch commander, Cecil Kalstrom, and Cecil said, 'Did you have a close-up look at 'em, see if there's maybe dead people slumped in 'em or something?'

'Why would there be so many dead people?'

'Could be some cult, like that Jim Jones thing years ago, and they all met to kill themselves.'

'You've got some imagination, Sarge.'

'All my imagination ten times over couldn't keep up with the weirdness that's really out there. Look in some of the cars.'

'The way it's raining, some Noah somewhere is building himself an ark.'

'It's a rough life being a uniformed hero.'

'Ten-four,' Foster said.

120

Thunder and rain and voices below.

Kipp in the upstairs hall, at the top of the stairs, standing ready, head raised. Every muscle tense.

Trembling with the expectation of action.

Woody on the Wire: *Now, now, now!*

Kipp howled, not just on the Wire, but for real.

Behind him in the hall, other dogs howled, as

447

did still others in the bedrooms.

The dogs he had summoned on the Wire. Before dawn of this very day. According to the plan worked out with Ben and Megan.

These Mysterians had been silent, waiting. They had been still and poised.

Now they cried their outrage and flew to the fight.

Kipp raced down the stairs.

A thunder separate from the thunder of the storm filled the house, the booming of paws pounding down the steps behind him.

121

Verbotski reached under his suit for a cross-body draw, and all the demons in Hell howled at once. As he pulled the pistol from his belt holster, the pack exploded off the stairs, across the foyer — German shepherds, golden retrievers, Labradors, Dobermans, mastiffs, rottweilers — barking, snarling, teeth flashing, a score of dogs, a double score, even more than that, a crashing sea of dogs breaking onto the shore of the living room. A mastiff leaped, a hundred-plus pounds of irresistible force, and John Verbotski proved not to be an immovable object, staggering backward as the dog slammed into him. A golden retriever seized his wrist in its mouth, the pistol flew from his grip, he stumbled sideways and collided hard with an end table, lost his balance, fell to his knees. Dogs swarmed him, nipping at his hands when he tried to reach for his Taser, for the pressurized can that would stream chloroform. When he attempted to struggle back onto his feet, they tore at the sleeves and panels of his suit coat and pulled him to the floor, flattened him facedown, flopped across his back and legs to pin him in place. A rottweiler licked the back of his neck and breathed on it, every hot exhalation a mortal threat that Verbotski, even in his bewilderment, took seriously.

★ ★ ★

Bradley Knacker had never gotten a degree in psychology, had never gone to college, had never seen any purpose for high school other than that it provided a convenient pool of targets, smaller kids he could intimidate and beat senseless and from whom he could steal. His talent and genius were for violence, from common street thuggery to the planning and execution of murders made to look like accidents and suicides, or that set up innocent people to take the fall for the crime. In spite of his high homicidal intelligence, Bradley was in other matters often slow on the uptake. When he heard the howling, he looked to the drapery-covered windows, because he could not conceive that such a large pack of animals could be in the house. When the beasts erupted into the living room, he was amazed, but he didn't at once realize that they were anything more than an uncommon number of pets, until they attacked Verbotski and took him down as if he really were nothing more than a candy-ass

449

Bureau agent instead of a hard-core blood junkie who killed people for money and fun. It was his nature to think of the animals not as defenders of home and family but instead as attack dogs trained to kill. At that instant, Bradley Knacker's homicidal brilliance kicked in big-time, and with the mathematical felicity of a certified public accountant, he required half a second to compute that the snarling horde bolting toward him constituted an overwhelming force against which a ten-round pistol and a Taser were inadequate. He then did what he had done in high school when a brute bigger than he was made a move on him: He turned and ran, this time toward the connecting door to the dining room. That didn't work out well.

★ ★ ★

Speer admired snakes. His only pets were garden snakes kept in a large aquarium and a freedom-of-the-house boa constrictor to which he fed mice and gerbils and rabbits that he bought in quantity. A tattoo of a rattlesnake twined around his left forearm and biceps; on his right arm, it was a cobra. He envied snakes their quickness, their cruelty, and he tried to style himself after them. The moment the dogs appeared, he knew intuitively that somehow they were not just ordinary dogs. Speer wasn't a complex man. He believed in only five things — violence, sex, money, snakes, and intuition — and he believed in them profoundly, passionately. The instant he saw the coordination among the scores of dogs, he hissed

450

and pivoted and took two steps and hissed and grabbed the boy, intuitively convinced that the dogs would not harm him if he was holding a knife to the kid's throat. But as he pulled the switchblade from a coat pocket, before he could push the button to spring the blade from the handle, he realized that his snake-quick response to the snarling dogs had been matched by Ben Hawkins's snake-quick reaction to *him*, when the cold muzzle of a pistol pressed hard against his right temple.

★ ★ ★

When Verbotski reached under his suit coat, cross-body with his right hand, going boldly for the pistol on his left hip, instead of reaching with his left hand for his Taser, Rodchenko knew that his partner had picked up on some tell, some detail that convinced him the operation was about to go wrong. Rodchenko reached for his own pistol, intent on killing them all, everyone except Megan Bookman. It would take about four seconds — two of them sitting down, easy head shots, easier chest shots. He actually got the weapon out of his holster, and then all the dogs in the world cascaded down the steps, through the foyer, into the living room, big bitches and big sonsofbitches, enough teeth for ten nightmares. There was supposed to be a dog, *one* dog, and Rodchenko had been given permission to kill it, a pleasure to which he looked forward. Now it seemed that the dog had known Rodchenko was coming for it and had called in backup of its own kind, more dogs than Rodchenko could kill before they took him down. Over the years, he'd been bitten three times, and every dog that had ever crossed his path had looked at him as though it *wanted* not only to bite him but to tear out his throat. All dogs looked at him the way wise cops looked at him, the way attractive women with street smarts looked at him, the way mothers with tender young daughters looked at him: with suspicion, disgust, and contempt.

Although Rodchenko had his pistol out and pointed at the head of the Latina in the armchair, Megan Bookman held a 9 mm Heckler & Koch in a professional two-hand grip, aimed at his face. Point-blank. Maybe ten or eleven feet. In spite of her grip and stance, maybe she was a piss-poor shot. If he drilled the brain of the Latina, and Megan squeezed off a round but missed him, and he pivoted and fired and took *her* out, at least he'd have the satisfaction of wasting two of them before he was dragged down and savaged. Better to go out with a double score than to die having failed to make this douchebag and her friends pay a price. This strategy made perfect sense to Rodchenko — except that all the mean-eyed dogs staring at him and that forest of dripping teeth so unnerved him, he wasn't able to keep a steady grip on his pistol. His heart boomed, shaking his arms, and the gun jumped left, right, off target, so maybe he wouldn't be able to hit even an elephant at four feet.

'Drop it, drop it now, shithead,' she said, and

as she spoke, people appeared in the foyer, having come down the stairs in the wake of the dogs. Men and women, all ages and races. Twenty, thirty, maybe more. Some of them had guns.

As dogs jostled around Rodchenko, snarling and nipping at his shoes, at his pants, he understood that something extraordinary was going on here, something stranger than just the startling number of animals, and he dropped the weapon. 'Don't let them kill me.'

'I'd love to watch them kill you,' she said. 'Give me any excuse, and I'll tell them to tear you apart.'

'I have a Taser and an aerosol can of chloroform,' Rodchenko revealed, as he dropped his weapon, eager to curry favor with this queen of canines. 'So does each of the other guys.'

122

The Tiburon house. In the third and deepest of the panic rooms, the one Dorian now understood that he'd created with a subconscious desire to indulge in a level of sexual freedom that society was not yet advanced enough to permit, he had finished his chocolate vodka. He'd been sitting on the floor, in a corner of the windowless room, fantasizing about what desires could be fulfilled here, until the ice in the glass had melted and he had drunk that, too.

He wasn't concerned about events in Springville or Pinehaven. Every crisis would be resolved, just as every past crisis had been extinguished. To ensure success, one had only to understand how the world worked: Nature set the only rules that mattered. There were predators and prey, and the losers were the weak, both the prey who could not or would not protect themselves and those predators who were incapable of fully embracing the fact that the only virtue was winning and the only vice was losing.

Some people said the arc of history led to justice, but that was foolishness. There was no justice, or very little. The word was too political to have an enduring meaning; the definition of justice was continuously changing. Those who fancied themselves champions of justice always had a price — money or prestige, or the adoration of crowds, or self-esteem — and when Dorian got them what they wanted, every one of them traded his or her cause for the price paid.

Truth was something else again. If ever a large number of people became hell-bent on knowing the truth of things, not merely a few stiff-necked crusaders but a majority of humanity, then he'd be in trouble. Never going to happen.

Because the purpose of the Tiburon house was self-indulgence, he decided to have another drink. This time he'd mix vanilla- and orange-flavored vodkas to make an adult Creamsicle.

He left the hidden room, swung shut the eight-hundred-pound door, departed the vestibule, closed the bookcase door, and climbed the stairs to the ground floor.

To his right, at the entrance to the hidden

corridor behind the library, stood the door disguised as a wall-to-wall floor-to-ceiling framed mirror on both sides. It was open. He was surprised, because his habit had always been to close every door behind him, even when it was in an already secret space like this.

He stepped into the corridor and clicked the big mirror into place and went to the door that was a bookcase on the farther side.

He said, 'Ochus Bochus,' and it opened, and he went into his library, where the words '*Hoc est corpus meum*' caused the pivot-hinged section of shelves to arc back into place, making a seamless wall of books.

Cool. He would never tire of this house.

In the kitchen, as he stood at the white quartzite island with two bottles of vodka, pouring vanilla and orange in equal measure over ice, he smelled something different from either. Although it was an unpleasant odor, it was even stranger than it was offensive, not chemical in nature, neither suggestive of rot nor ordure. He was reminded somewhat of the peculiar smell in the library, although this was stronger.

He circled the immense kitchen, trying to locate the source, opening cabinets, but the scent proved elusive, coming and going. When he arrived at the walk-in pantry, he hesitated to open the door, wondering if he might find a dead rat.

No. Impossible. The house was too soundly built ever to be vulnerable to rodents.

He opened the door, and the pantry light came on automatically. At first, the malodor was

455

stronger in this enclosed space. But it quickly dissipated, as though the cause was no longer present. He scanned the shelves of foodstuffs, but he could see nothing amiss.

Now the odor relented, and he could smell nothing unusual.

He shrugged and returned to the island and finished making his adult Creamsicle.

123

Lightning flared around the edges of the draperies. Thunder rolled and rain drummed.

It had been quite a day. Evening was coming.

Kipp was not jealous of the other dogs.

Woody remained in the living room, where three of the four killers were restrained with zip ties.

The boy wasn't interested in the killers.

He was having fun with all the dogs.

Having fun with them and talking with them telepathically.

All the dogs loved Woody and were fascinated by him.

The first human on the Wire.

In a state of excitement and relief, the visiting Mysterians and their human companions were mingling throughout the downstairs.

Everywhere but here in the study.

In the study, Rodchenko was spilling his guts to Ben, Megan, Carson, and Rosa.

Kipp sat close to the thug, staring hard at him,

456

now and then growling and baring his teeth.

Sweating as if the study were a sauna, Rodchenko was afraid that Kipp would bite off his man package.

Apparently, another dog had once tried to do this.

No doubt with good cause.

Rodchenko was willing to tell everything without the drugs.

However, Ben didn't trust him.

Aware of the proper dosages of thiopental and the Russian drug cocktail, Ben administered them.

Rodchenko became a Vesuvius of words.

He answered every question at greater length than wanted.

He answered questions that weren't even asked.

He incriminated himself and his partners and all manner of other people, including a man named Alexander Gordius.

Thanks to Woody's research, they already knew Gordius was Dorian Purcell.

Megan recorded it all.

She emailed the recording to Rosa Leon's attorney, Dorothy's dear friend, Roger Austin.

Online, Ben went to the Atropos & Company site on the Dark Web.

Following Rodchenko's instructions, he hacked their computer and downloaded everything onto a flash drive.

A copy of this was also sent to Roger Austin.

Roger would have to work out how to extract evidence from all this, as well as from Woody's report.

That was a difficult job. But essential.

When the evidence was given to some trusted authority, it must not be traceable to Woody or Megan.

Because of the Mysterium.

If the four killers were no longer a threat, they were for sure a problem.

Because of the Mysterium, which did not yet dare to be known.

'We're in something of a fix,' Ben said, 'but there's a way out that's less risky than it sounds.'

124

The lavish arcade in the Tiburon home contained forty-six pinball machines from different periods in the evolution of the game. Dorian preferred to play when all machines were lighted, because the flashing-pulsing backboard displays and the come-on music enlivened the place, made it feel like a real arcade in an amusement park or on a boardwalk somewhere. Now he activated the forty-six from a single switch just inside the arcade door.

Near the middle of the chamber, he decided to start with a kick-ass Gottlieb machine called Haunted House, which he and Haskell Ludlow had been aces at when they were kids. The deep game table had three levels: upstairs, main floor, and basement. There were eight flippers and various ramps and secret passageways for the ball, so sometimes you couldn't guess from where it was going to appear. Because the machine was set up for free play, he didn't need coins, and in maybe ten minutes, he was in the groove of it, as if he had played only yesterday.

One of Dorian Purcell's rules for living a good life was that no matter what you were doing, whether it was building a giant tech company or banging your mistress, breaking a competitor and driving him into ruin or playing pinball, you had to commit to it as if it was *everything*, as if your very survival depended on it. He leaned into Haunted House, fiercely determined to beat his previous highest score, which the machine showed as 1,340,000 points. He worked the flippers with pinball-wizard finesse no less impressive than the keyboard work of a great concert pianist, played with body language, cheering each triumph, cursing every missed chance with such fervor that spittle sprayed across the glass that covered the game table.

Because of the theme music, clattering flippers, ringing bells, other sound effects, and his own exclamations, because of his intent focus on winning, he didn't react to the words 'Ochus Bochus,' which was an early form of *hocus pocus* and which he assumed came from the machine in a raspy voice, just one of its many spooky effects. His concentration began to falter only when he slowly realized that he smelled again the malodor he'd detected but couldn't track down in the library and later in the kitchen. A ball escaped his control, slipped down the chute labeled GOODBYE, and almost at once he lost another. He realized this would not be the day when he beat his previous highest score. With that recognition came a sudden keener awareness of the stink, which had gotten much stronger than before. He was not alone.

He turned, and Lee Shacket was three feet away. Shacket had been to this house three times during its construction, Purcell proudly showing it off. But this was Shacket monstrously changed, blistered and pocked with suppurating sores, scaly patches on his face, his eyelids red and swollen, and his eyes protruding as though subject to a terrible pressure in his skull. His lips were pale. No. Not just pale. *White*. Peeling and as white as flour, as if he had pressed his mouth into some acidic powder that burned the color out of his lips. He said, 'Dorian,' his voice thick and gravelly.

The Haunted House pinball machine was at Dorian's back. He would have to slip to the right, slide out of Shacket's reach, and run for the arcade exit. He didn't believe Shacket — this *thing* that once had been Shacket — could move fast, not in its condition. Dorian could escape, as he had always escaped the negative consequences of his actions. He could escape this, lock himself in one of the panic rooms, call for help. All he had to do was fake to the left and slip to the right and run.

But he couldn't move. His muscles were locked. His body seemed to have turned to stone. 'Dorian, I'm becoming. Do you see how I'm becoming?' It wasn't just the terror of this creature that paralyzed Dorian Purcell, but something else, a greater horrific possibility that trembled at the back of his mind, that he couldn't quite name. Or maybe he didn't dare to name it, for fear that the naming of it would make actual what was at the moment only possible. 'Becoming the king of predators,' Shacket said. He grinned, he licked his teeth, his tongue was as white as his lips. His teeth were stained, the spaces between them clogged with gray material, his breath foul, rancid. The tremulous thought that Dorian strove to avoid would not be repressed. Maybe it wasn't his destiny to significantly extend the human life span, to live for hundreds of years; maybe he would not be one of the first transhumans, with vastly enhanced intellect and extraordinary powers. Maybe he would die as billions had died before him. Having lived with the conviction that the world could not evict him, he was paralyzed by the possibility of mortality.

When Shacket seized him by the arms with both hands, Dorian at last threw off the paralysis. He struggled, only to discover that this creature, even if terminal, was not weak, as he had thought, but inhumanly strong instead. The serum oozing from the sores in Lee Shacket's hands was disgusting, potentially infectious, and so gluey that it penetrated Dorian's shirt and seemed to bond with his skin. He felt something leeching into his biceps, so that the harder he strained to wrench free, the firmer became Shacket's grip on him, until he made his most desperate effort and felt his muscle fibers tearing apart. Dorian's scream of pain and fright and horror earned another grin from Shacket, who once more crowned himself: 'I have become.'

The former CEO of Refine tasted the arcade air with his white tongue and then he bit into the scream, bit and bit the tender lips.

125

Rodchenko had been taken upstairs and locked in a closet for the time being.

The humble study in the white clapboard house on the outskirts of Pinehaven did not look like the epicenter of a quake that would change the future. The storm that seared the night with lightning and shook it with thunder and hammered the house with rain might be taken, however, as a metaphor for the fury that great change often inspired.

Ben Hawkins knew this: The amazing bond between the Mysterium and humanity would change the world forever, but the world could not be radically changed overnight without widespread fear of the new and without dreadful consequences arising from that fear.

There would be profound dislocations, cultural and economic. There would be an impact on all religions and no less on science, for the majority of scientists in all disciplines were and always had been committed to theories as fiercely as political types were bound by ideology. Although science was never settled and was a perpetual process of discovery that undid past ideas, there were many who adamantly resisted all evidence that didn't support the theories on which they had built their careers. Human beings could hate to the point of killing whom they hated, based on class and race and politics and religion and mere envy. When the dogs of the Mysterium brought the Wire to other people, through Woodrow Bookman, each person who received the telepathic ability would be henceforth unable to be deceived or deceive others on the Wire. People would be forced to confront the daunting fact that the truth they claimed to pursue and cherish was in fact a burden that they most often chose not to carry, that the lies they insisted they despised were instead often preferred to hard facts and cold reality. Even such wondrous and miraculous creatures as these beautiful dogs would soon become targets, as would the boy, as would all who wished to embrace the profound change ensuing from this ultimate refinement of the human-canine bond. A potential for violence on the scale of a holocaust could not be ruled out.

Ben argued — Megan, Rosa, Carson, and Kipp agreed — that the dogs of the Mysterium must be introduced to the world slowly, over years if not decades. The people who loved these dogs, who accepted the gift and burden of the Wire, must keep the secret of the Mysterium until communities of them and their human companions were everywhere in such numbers that the world had quietly changed from one steeped in deceit to one in which truth was more prevalent in human affairs than ever before. When the balance changed, when violence and theft and betrayal had diminished, they would know the moment had come to say to humanity: *Here are the agents of the world as it has been evolving, our canine brothers and sisters on four legs, who have been our companions since time immemorial, who have always wanted nothing more from us than love and mutual defense against a cruel nature. They are not selfish or envious or arrogant. Join us for a tomorrow where the world is not deformed by the power mad, where every life matters, and where so much will be within our reach that once seemed forever beyond our grasp — even the stars.*

The immediate problem was the four men from Atropos & Company.

For one thing, there was no trustworthy authority to which they might be transferred. Sheriff Eckman had withdrawn protection from Megan and Woody even knowing that they were targeted. According to Carson, the attorney general of California, Tio Barbizon, had been bought by someone, most likely by Dorian Purcell, who had paid for Jason Bookman's 'accident' and sent Atropos to Pinehaven. In recent years, the once sterling reputation of the FBI had been tarnished. These days, no one could say with certainty who could be trusted.

For another and more important reason, Ben didn't want to turn these four men over to the law. Verbotski, Knacker, Rodchenko, and Speer didn't know much about the dogs that had defeated them today, but they were aware that these creatures were extraordinary, that they were more than mere dogs, and that their human companions knew the truth of them. This was the last thing that Ben wanted anyone to be reporting to any authorities.

Sitting in an armchair with Kipp in her lap, Rosa Leon said, 'But what do we do with them?'

'We're not going to kill them,' Megan said.

'Of course not,' Ben agreed. 'We're going to do the only thing we can do — let them go.'

Carson Conroy turned from a window, where he'd been watching the rain and lightning with perhaps a sense that they would be a long time passing through the different storm that would soon come upon them. 'Let them go? Four professional killers? What have I missed?'

Ben explained what he had in mind. 'So we turn them loose and trust that they continue to be who they have always been.'

'If it doesn't go the way you expect, we bear responsibility for whatever they do,' Megan said.

'We do, we will,' Ben agreed. 'The only way to avoid that is to kill them now and bury them here.'

After a long mutual silence, Rosa said, 'I think Ben has them figured out. There aren't any easy answers. We can't start a better future with four murders.'

Carson went out into the storm to search the black Suburban in which the killers had come, to make sure it contained no weapons.

Ben went first to talk with Verbotski, who was restrained with Knacker and Speer in the living room. And then he went upstairs to speak with Rodchenko.

126

In the second guest bedroom, Ben removed the straight-backed chair from under the doorknob and opened the closet door. Rodchenko waited with his hands zip tied behind him.

Ben directed him to sit on the edge of the bed. Rodchenko sat.

'We're letting you go.'

The killer looked surprised. 'Why me?'

'Not just you. All four of you.'

This alarmed Rodchenko. 'That makes no sense. Why are you doing this?'

'You don't have to understand. You just have to go and not come back. I've discussed it with Verbotski.'

Rodchenko shook his head. 'No. You can't do this. They know I ratted them out. They'll kill me.'

'You didn't rat them out. We used the thiopental and the other crap. You had no choice but to talk.'

'Yeah, well, they know the dogs scared the piss out of me. They know that I'd have talked without the drugs, and they don't know for sure you ever used them on me.'

Ben sat beside him and patted his knee. 'I understand, amigo. I've dealt with a lot of murderous assholes in my life. No offense. There isn't much loyalty among you folks. So because you cooperated, I'll give you a little something for self-defense.'

Rodchenko looked hopeful. 'A gun?'

'Not a chance. Verbotski and the others are already being taken out to the Suburban. After I free you from that zip tie, I'll walk you downstairs. Just before you go out the door, I'll provide you with Speer's nasty switchblade and one of those pressurized cans of chloroform you were going to use on us.'

'But there's three of them.'

'Sorry, that's the best I can do.'

'What have you given them?'

'Nothing. They didn't cooperate.'

'I hope that's true.'

'Don't call me a liar, amigo.'

'Will the dogs be downstairs?'

'I'll walk you through them.'

'There's something weird about those dogs.'

'Look who's talking.'

'And who're all those people down there?'

'Friends. We're all in the same kennel club.'

127

Megan, Rosa, and Ben had been cooking most of the day, so there was enough food for an army.

Kipp thought all these people were an army of sorts. An army of the just.

People were mingling, laughing, eating.

Making new friends.

They all smelled nice. None smelled like a Hater.

Not now that the four from Atropos were gone.

Of course, Shacket was still out there somewhere.

Maybe he would come back, maybe not.

Kipp would smell *that one* from a long way off.

The dogs were mingling, laughing telepathically, eating what had been specially prepared for them.

Hamburgers. Chicken breasts. Rice and carrots cooked in chicken broth. Potatoes.

The gathering was very nice.

It would have been so much nicer if Dorothy had been here.

And if Jason Bookman had been here.

In a way, they *were* here. In the hearts of those who had loved them.

What an amazing two days these had been. From a deathbed to the birth of a new world.

It was like a story in a book.

But the real world was more fantastic than fiction.

Everyone here this night knew how fantastic the world was.

There was a growing expectation in the house. They were aware of how the evening would end.

Some of the people were a little afraid. But only a little.

Kipp could smell how small their fear was.

As an hour passed and then another, people looked more and more often to the boy who once could not talk.

He was so small, but the future was on his shoulders.

He could carry it. Even if he did still eat each

kind of food in its separate dish, he could carry the future.

At last a silence came upon those gathered, a mutual sense that the moment had come.

Megan took Woody by the hand. 'Sweetie, are you ready?'

'I am if everyone else is.'

'They are,' she said. 'We are.'

Ben Hawkins went to Megan and held her hand.

Rosa Leon went to Ben and took his hand.

Carson Conroy took Rosa's hand.

Although there was no need for them to link hands, though it could be done with them standing apart, they joined hands anyway.

Joined hands from the living room into the foyer.

From the foyer along the hallway.

From the hallway into the dining room.

Into the kitchen.

Into Megan's studio, where the painting of Woody and the deer, the family of deer, waited to be finished.

Everyone stood hand in hand throughout the house.

The dogs pressed against their people's legs.

Now Woody did what Bella had done for him, what she had showed him how to do for others.

He did what only Woody alone in all the world could do for other human beings.

To all the people assembled, Woody gave the gift and the burden of the Wire.

Had there been people present not gifted, the house would have seemed to them eerily silent but for the storm that beat on the roof and windows.

But to those who had received, the house was filled with joyful greetings and excited conversations.

Even one who was deaf to all of those voices would nevertheless have sensed the wonder and emotion swelling from heart to heart to heart.

Later, when the rain passed, all the visitors would return to their homes in distant places.

Something was happening out there.

For the foreseeable future, the best thing the Mysterium and their beloved companions could do was wait and let it happen.

128

With the windshield wipers beating like drums in a funeral cortege and the darkness suggestive of the grave, Verbotski drove from the Bookman house to the Oxley place, where they'd left their luggage and Charles Oxley's corpse.

He'd wanted Rodchenko to ride in the front passenger seat, where he could keep an eye on him. But the bastard would have none of that. He obviously worried about being garroted from behind or otherwise wasted.

Speer rode shotgun, and Rodchenko sat in back with Knacker.

'If they drained our computers and sent all that shit to whoever, then we can't go back to Reno, we're finished,' Knacker said, because he was the stupidest among them.

'We're not finished,' Verbotski disagreed. 'Each of us has his getaway stash, plus offshore accounts, alternate identities. We fly out of Sacramento to four different cities. Change our appearance. Meet in Miami a month from today. We start over and build something bigger and better than what we lost.'

'Damn right,' said Speer. 'And a year from now, when nobody's expecting us, we go back to Pinehaven and kill that slut and her snarky kid.'

'Something weird was going on there, all those dogs, something strange,' Verbotski said. 'Better we stay away from there forever.'

Speer said nothing. Neither did Rodchenko.

Knacker said, 'I like Miami. Sun, sand, nookie.'

Trying to sound as if he were still a partner in good standing, referring to the four other principals in Atropos, Rodchenko said, 'We better warn the guys in Reno, so they can scatter, too.'

Verbotski said, 'Fuck 'em. We only need four to start up again. They were all later add-ons, anyway.'

'You can't launch a new operation,' Speer said, 'if it's top-heavy with profit-sharing talent.'

'Exactly,' Verbotski agreed. 'Initially, we'll be eaten alive by start-up costs, monthly overhead. We need to achieve a reliable cash flow that meets expenses and provides adequate compensation for six before we think about bringing in a fifth partner.'

Speer sighed. 'No rest for the wicked. You realize how much harder it would be to do this if we paid income taxes?'

471

'We'd be working for the man all our lives,' Verbotski said.

At the Oxley house, they parked in the driveway and entered by the front door. On the way through the house, Verbotski made sure each of the thermostats — in the living room, bedroom, kitchen — was on HEAT instead of COOL and that each temperature-control slide was set at forty degrees, to prevent a premature detonation. The current temperature in the house was sixty-eight.

In the kitchen, Verbotski said, 'Rodchenko, you and I will get everyone's gear out of here. Knacker, Speer, go to the cellar and finish setting up the oil furnace to blow like we planned.'

Knacker grimaced. 'Why? The old fart's dead as dead gets, we can't kill him twice. After what's happened, the faster we split, the better.'

'Speer,' Verbotski said, 'Can you explain it to him?'

He worried that Speer would agree with Knacker; but the creepy snake handler came through. 'We may be on the run, Bradley, but we aren't on the run from killing the old man down there. So let's keep it that way, let's not add that to our shit-we're-wanted-for list. We leave here, the furnace blows, the house burns to the ground, there's only bones left of the geezer, and no evidence of nothing.'

'Okay, all right,' Knacker said. 'Let's get it done. But I'm gonna kick that old bastard around some.'

'He's already dead,' Speer said as he opened the door to the cellar. 'What's the point of kicking him now?'

'Because it'll make me feel better.' Knacker followed Speer down the stairs.

Verbotski pointed to a pile of gear — suitcases, duffel bags — and said to Rodchenko, 'Load all that in the Suburban. You and Speer drove it here, you can drive it away. I'll get Knacker's stuff and mine, stow it in the Escalade.'

After Rodchenko snatched up two half-empty duffel bags and a suitcase, and headed along the hall toward the front of the house, Verbotski conducted a quick search of the kitchen drawers until he found interesting cutlery. He selected a meat cleaver.

He hurried along the hallway, intending to stand concealed to one side of the front door and chop the Russian rat as he returned from the Suburban.

Rodchenko, however, had not gone outside. As Verbotski entered the living room from the hallway, the dog-fearing puke lunged at him from the left, wielding a switchblade as he would have a dagger. He plunged the blade into his senior partner's side, burying six inches of razor-edged steel in descending colon and small intestines.

Shock and pain did not prevent Verbotski from swinging the meat cleaver with his right hand. Steel met neck, and steel prevailed. As he collapsed, Rodchenko spouted blood like a fire hose in Hell, but by the time he hit the floor, the stream had already stopped, for he was as dead as he deserved to be.

As Verbotski dropped the cleaver on the corpse and gingerly withdrew the switchblade from his side, his vision darkened at the periphery, though he didn't pass out. The wound was small but deep. A sharp but tolerable pain wrung a light sweat from him. Less blood than he expected. He clamped the puncture closed with one hand. He needed medical attention. In a few hours, acute peritonitis would set in. He was confident he'd be able to drive to Sacramento in the Escalade and get treatment there in a first-class hospital, under the protection of Tio Barbizon.

He returned along the hallway to the kitchen. At the open door to the cellar, he took a deep breath, steadied his voice, and called down to Knacker and Speer. 'Are you about done with that?'

'Finished!' Speer shouted as a hard thud rose from below.

'Just one more kick,' Knacker promised as Speer appeared at the foot of the stairs.

Verbotski closed the cellar door and slid the latch bolt shut. He stepped to the thermostat, which was fixed on HEAT, and adjusted the temperature-setting slide from forty degrees to eighty.

The thermostat was essentially the trigger for the device they had installed in the furnace. A standard HVAC system like this had maybe a five- or six-second delay between the call for heat and the ignition of the electric pilot light. Flame would at once erupt around the oil-fed ring wick, instantly burn away the trigger string, and detonate the explosive.

Speer shouted angrily as he ascended the last

of the cellar stairs, and Verbotski started across the kitchen toward the back door with four or five seconds to go, plenty of time.

Knacker was shouting, too, and Speer pounded on the cellar door. They were never the quality of partners that Verbotski needed to reach the very top of his profession. Knacker was just too thick, and Speer was creepy, with his snake tattoos that, as rumor had it, weren't limited to his arms. There were better associates out there, waiting to be found.

Verbotski was one second away from the exterior door, with at least two or three seconds remaining, an acceptable margin, when something inside him tore. Pain intense beyond his experience robbed his legs of all strength. He collapsed to the floor at the threshold of the back door.

Acid and something worse washed into his throat, and he gagged it down. The furnace blew, the floor leaped under him, the entire house shook, part of the ceiling collapsed. It seemed as though fate — Atropos herself — decided that his paralysis was insufficient to guarantee that he would burn and, to seal the deal, pinned him in place with ceiling joists and other debris.

As he lay there waiting for the flames, he thought of the hard rain drenching the night, but he could take no hope from it. He knew the intensity this engineered fire would quickly achieve; it could not be easily quenched. He heard the flames below, rushing upward, and felt the floor warming under him.

In one of his psychology classes, he'd been

taught that, as a person lay dying, the brain produced hormones intended to induce a sense of well-being. This supposedly explained why some on their deathbeds hallucinated ministering angels and why those who briefly died and came back often spoke of a tunnel leading to a welcoming light and a world of wonder beyond.

He saw no angels, no tunnel leading to a light. But as tendrils of smoke began to slither through the room, a long-repressed memory returned to John, and his heart raced with unexpected delight as images from the past flooded through his mind. He was six years old when his father brought Daisy home, a two-year-old golden retriever that he had rescued from the pound expressly for the boy. Daisy and young John enjoyed many adventures together, and for a while there was a reliable source of joy in a house that otherwise was filled with suspicion, contention, and loud arguments. The marriage didn't last, and one year to the day after Daisy came into the Verbotski home, she died in young John's arms. To his alcoholic mother, Daisy was an avatar of her hated husband, and that was sufficient reason for her to poison the dog. What had been a year of wonder became, with the death of Daisy, too painful for him to recall. Now the fire reached for him, and with the blaze were memories brighter than the flames, memories repressed no longer, recollections of tenderness and laughter and love that he had never experienced before that long-ago year and had never known again in the days that followed.

129

Amory Cromwell, estate manager of the five-acre property in Tiburon, was not a stupid man, quite the opposite, and neither was he a coward.

When he returned to the house on Monday morning, after four nights in a superb resort in Pebble Beach, he arrived at seven o'clock, an hour ahead of the staff, as was his policy. He stopped inside the big roll-up door and got out of the BMW that had been provided with his position, and he disarmed the alarm system with the Crestron panel embedded in the wall. As the door rolled down, he parked in that part of the vast garage reserved for employees, separate from the carousels of collectible cars. When he got out of the BMW this time, he heard the distant yet raucous music of forty-six pinball machines, which were housed in the arcade on the same level of the house as the subterranean garage, the movie theater, and the two-lane bowling alley.

Dorian Purcell's habit, when he spent a weekend here, was to leave Sunday night. On the aboveground floors, when the house was uninhabited, the lights and TVs and music system were programmed to turn off and on in a pattern that suggested to any burglar casing the residence that it was occupied by three or four people. The machines in the arcade were not part of that ruse.

This suggested to Amory Cromwell that Purcell must still be here.

And this deviation from the Great Man's customary practice further suggested that something might be wrong.

Having had martial arts and weapons training as part of his preparation for his profession, and aware that he was being paid not merely for his expertise but also for his discretion, Cromwell did not at once consider calling the police. The überwealthy paid men like Cromwell also to prevent their follies from becoming public knowledge, at least until those follies became felonies. He went to a gun safe concealed in the cabinetry associated with the mechanic's shop that was part of the garage, and he obtained a 12-gauge shotgun that fired slugs. He loaded one shell in the breach, three more in the magazine, and dropped two spares in a coat pocket.

In the arcade, he found Dorian Purcell's body in less than ideal condition. In addition to other evidence of extreme violence and cannibalism, the billionaire's head was missing.

At this point, Cromwell might have called the police if he had not been a man who recognized a golden opportunity when he saw one.

Shotgun at the ready, he followed a trail of bloody footprints and bits of unthinkable debris, which led upstairs to the library on the main floor.

The man, who didn't seem to be strictly a man, who appeared to be something out of an H. P. Lovecraft story by way of a Tim Burton movie, was sitting in an aisle between two rows of bookshelves, his back to one set of stacks, his feet to the other. Purcell's head lay in his lap.

The bizarre intruder had shed his clothes somewhere along the way. Horrid lumps and discolorations covered his pale body. Weeping sores issued gray gossamer filaments that formed webs across parts of him, with radials and spirals sloping up to anchor him to the shelves between which he slumped. These weren't the elegant and precisely geometric webs of a spider, but were without pattern and as ugly as the grotesque individual whom they partly cocooned.

The intruder was perfectly still. Amory Cromwell assumed that this was a corpse before him, but he nevertheless kept his distance and said, 'Sir?'

The man's head, which faced away from Cromwell, slowly turned until the face came into view.

In spite of the distorted features and the dull eyeshine, like that of a cat at night, enough resemblance remained for Cromwell to inquire, 'Mr. Shacket?'

The former CEO of Refine, who was believed to be dead in Utah, formed what perhaps he thought was a smile. He spoke, but his voice was weak, a mutter, and what he said made no sense. The words popped out of him like the numbered balls from an automated bingo hopper. Further diminishing any hope of intelligent communication, Shacket produced, in addition to words, clicks and keenings and chittering noises, like those of insects, and an animal mewling, and a hissing as if a serpent lived in him.

Clearly the man had no remaining strength, no presence of mind, and was dying.

479

Throughout his career, Cromwell had assiduously protected his clients not just from bad publicity but also from rude intrusions into their privacy by media and others of the hoi polloi. Their dignity and the respect they deserved were uppermost in his mind.

Not so much with Dorian Purcell, especially now that the Great Man was dead.

Cromwell laid his shotgun aside and used his smartphone to video Shacket for two minutes as the pathetic creature muttered senselessly, clicked, chittered, and whimpered not like a man but like an animal with its leg caught in a trap. He took a number of pictures, making sure that he got several clear shots of Purcell's severed head.

He retrieved the 12-gauge and returned to the arcade, where he photographed the headless corpse and the carnage around it. Then he went through the mansion, photographing its most fabulous, luxurious features, anything that might thrill readers of the worst tabloids and those who viewed the tackiest cable programs.

While in the employ of a family in Boston, Cromwell had made the acquaintance of Vaughn Larkin, who was an attorney as well as a licensed private investigator. Larkin periodically had done work for that family regarding matters involving a son who had a taste for cocaine, porn stars, petty theft, and revolutionary politics.

He called Larkin now, described what he had found, and asked for an informed estimate of the value of the video and photographs in his possession. The number so impressed Cromwell that he hired Larkin as his agent and sent everything to him before calling 911.

By the time the police arrived, the thing that had been Lee Shacket was as dead as Dorian Purcell.

130

Kipp had his boy, and the boy had his dog.

All was right with the world.

Or as right as things could be in the world's current condition.

Considering how scary things had been for a while, the days after that Thursday in September were remarkably sunny in every sense of the word.

Ben Hawkins sold his house in Southern California.

He rented a place in Pinehaven.

He and Megan began to date.

She finished the painting of Woody and the deer.

The gallery that represented her thought it would bring a record price for her work.

Instead, she hung it in the living room. Behind the piano.

Rosa Leon sold the house in Lake Tahoe.

She moved to Pinehaven to be a part of all that was to come.

In early October, Rita Carrickton and Deputy Andy Argento were indicted for the murder of Sheriff Eckman and held without bail.

Eckman had secreted tiny cameras in his bedroom and bath.

He recorded all his sexual adventures with Rita and every shower she'd taken there.

Including their final, unfinished coupling.

And his murder.

The former sheriff, Lyle Sheldrake, was returned to office in a special election in November.

At the election-night party, Kipp got a good smell of him.

Sheldrake wasn't a Hater.

Or crazy.

In December, Rosa Leon and Carson Conroy began to date.

In January, Tio Barbizon was indicted for covering up events related to the catastrophe in Utah and the crimes of Lee Shacket.

Two days later, he declared his innocence.

And announced that he was running for governor.

Sometimes, Megan and Ben and Woody and Kipp took road trips.

They visited the various communities of Mysterians who, with their human companions, had come to Pinehaven that desperate day.

Which everyone called 'the Day' with an uppercase *D*.

New communities were announcing themselves to Bella.

Some were as far away as Kansas and Alabama.

Then Canada. And Mexico.

In March, Megan married Ben.

Rosa was her bridesmaid.

Kipp was best man.

A court declared that Dorian Purcell's fortune could be used to compensate the families of those murdered in Utah and elsewhere.

Haskell Ludlow was arrested in the South of France.

Living under the name Mary Seldon.

After having undergone gender reassignment.

Cable news would never be done with the genetic-monster-from-Utah story.

They were utterly unaware of the bigger story of the Mysterium and that one day all news would be true.

Then it was May.

Eight months after the Day.

Kipp and family visited a secret Mysterian community in Idaho.

Seventy-five dogs with twenty-six human companions.

Seventy-four of the dogs were paired.

One female golden retriever had no four-legged companion.

Kipp knew her for his destiny.

He worried that she would not feel the same.

But she did.

Her name was Velvet.

She came to Pinehaven.

Another year passed.

It began to be clear that the dogs of the Mysterium were healthier than other dogs.

Some wondered if they might live longer than other dogs.

Woody said he was sure of it.

Kipp's and Velvet's litter numbered eight.

All were healthy.

All remained with Megan and Ben and Woody.

Woody was learning to play the piano. He could rock the keyboard.

Rosa and Carson adopted two dogs.

They were an extended family of five people and twelve dogs, living in perpetual truth, with no moment of deceit, on the Wire with others of their kind, in preparation for the arrival of a new world, a fresh reality, that had been evolving for tens of thousands of years, since men and women and dogs first stood together against saber-toothed tigers and rampaging mastodons. A world impended that had been shaped over perhaps a thousand centuries during which people and dogs had lived together and played together and wondered at the stars together and died and mourned one another and endured in spite of cruel nature and those treacherous humans who were mad for power. This new world would be the world as it should always have been, a world in which troubled waters were as common as ever they were, but where every man and woman and dog would be devoted to one another, would be forever a bridge for one another, from safe shore to safe shore.

Other titles published by Ulverscroft:

BREATHLESS

Dean Koontz

Alienated from the modern world, Grady Adams lives in the wilds of the Colorado mountains. And there, something miraculous comes into his life, and he knows that one of Nature's great mysteries has been revealed to him. He takes his friend, scientist Cammy Rivers, to bear witness to the phenomenal presence. She is stunned and awed, and emails photos to colleagues in far places to try and find a name for the wonderful beings. But soon Homeland Security has the wilderness around them quarantined, with scientists to track down and 'neutralize' the threat to the known world. Grady and Cammy, determined to prevent this atrocity, go on the run, and a pursuit of hair-raising suspense is under way, with no happy ending in prospect . . .

RELENTLESS

Dean Koontz

Being a writer is a dangerous business. Hostile reviews may have hastened the deaths of some authors, and Cubby Greenwich obsesses about the scathing review of his latest bestseller by Shearman Waxx. A feared critic, with an aura of mystery about him, he's deemed an arbiter of taste. An unexpected encounter with Waxx startles Cubby, but what should be a mildly embarrassing incident triggers an inhuman fury in the critic, who becomes bent on destroying Cubby. Waxx is not merely a ferocious literary enemy, but a ruthless sociopath. And for Cubby and his family, forced into hiding, the terror has just begun . . . it will be relentless. Cubby's worst fears seem naive — he has no idea how to save himself or, more importantly, his wife and son . . .

YOUR HEART BELONGS TO ME

Dean Koontz

At 34, Ryan Perry is on a waiting list for a heart transplant, and time's running out. When, miraculously, he receives a new heart and the transplant is a success, he thinks his troubles are over. But a year later, he starts to receive heart-shaped gifts — sent anonymously. $100,000 suddenly vanishes from his bank account and is donated to the cardiology department of the local hospital. And then comes a terrifying threat: everything he has — his money, his freedom, and his new heart — will all be ripped away from him. He is promised a nightmare death. In grave danger, alone with his beating heart and its secrets, can Ryan unlock the mystery of the enemy who threatens his very existence?